# ROME

# NEVER

# FELL

## C.R. FABIS

HUGO HOUSE PUBLISHERS, LTD.

ISBN: 978-1-948261-36-4

Library of Congress Control Number: 2020906880

Cover and Interior Design: Ronda Taylor, HeartworkCreative.com

Hugo House Publishers, Ltd.
Austin, TX • Denver, CO
www.HugoHousePublishers.com

# Dedication

*To David, my son that never got a fair chance at life.*

# Acknowledgments

A SPECIAL THANKS TO MY EDITOR, DR. PATRICIA ROSS. HER PATIENCE and wise guidance turned a pretty good pastry chef into a pretty good writer.

And to British Historian, Tom Holland, whose great history book, *Rubicon* taught me all the real history I needed to write this book.

*"No one is so brave that he is not disturbed by something unexpected."*

—Julius Caesar

# I

# The Arrival

HENRY GARFIELD WAS BUCK-NAKED IN A PLACE HE HAD BEEN BEFORE. It had only been seconds, but now everything was totally different. The air seemed fresher; the light from the setting sun, brighter. He could see the vibrant blue Mediterranean Sea to the west. There was farmland around him growing some kind of grain. A large magnificent wooden villa towered above a small orchard of olive trees. Near as Henry could tell, he was just due east of the sea.

To his left he heard the beautiful sound of a female voice filling the air around him. He thanked the gods above that it was in a language he understood, Latin. It was one of the most beautiful sounds Henry had ever heard, and he forgot for a moment where he was or what had just happened. When he saw the young lady sitting on a large rock, Henry remembered and quickly ran behind a large umbrella pine tree to hide his nudity.

The short skinny Henry listened to the voice and tried to build courage. He needed to speak to her. Would she understand his Latin? Would she summon some men to come and kill him? He had to try to communicate with her otherwise his mission would be a total failure.

He yelled towards her in Latin, *"Girl, Girl! Would you please help me?"* Even his Latin sounded nerdy.

She did understand. Her speaking voice was as soothing as her singing. *"Who is that? Why are you hiding?"*

The young girl was slender with long sandy brown hair, and her eyes matched the vibrant blue of The Mediterranean Sea. The light blue tunic she wore shimmied down her slim body all the way to her ankles, and a white cotton stole was draped across her left shoulder.

She got off the rock and slowly walked to the tree where Henry was hiding.

*"You get off of our property or I will go get my father. Are you one of our slaves?"* she yelled into the clearing where Henry was still hiding.

Henry replied, still in Latin, *"No I am not a slave. I am lost. I am from a place very far away. Please help me."*

She went behind the tree and saw Henry, she laughed, *"What a funny little man you are. Why are you naked? Even slaves have clothes."*

Henry tried to cover his privates with his two hands. *"Can you get me some clothes? I am from a place very far away, and I am lost."*

*"Where did you come from? You had better do as your told, or else. My father is a very powerful man. He owns twenty slaves and has five hundred iugera of land. He could squash you like a bug. It looks like even I could squash you like a bug."*

Henry tried to plead his case, *"In the faraway place I speak of, we know many things. I can help your farm make even more money."*

The young girl asked, *"Where is this faraway place you speak of? I went to school, and I had my own Greek tutor. Are you from India or Egypt? You look like maybe you are from Briton."*

Henry made his first blunder. *"No, this is a place far across the Sea of Atlas, the big ocean."*

*"I don't believe you. My father will either kill you or make you a slave."*

Henry didn't panic. He showed her a small thin box. It was a box of stick matches. He took one out and said, *"These might stink. I had to put it in a very uncomfortable place to get them here."*

He struck the match against the box and a small flamed erupted.

The young girl's eyes got wider. *"How did you do that? You don't have any flint. You made fire with a small stick. Is it a magic stick?"*

*"No, it is a match."*

*"Wait here."* She ran towards the villa.

Henry yelled at the girl, *"What is your name?"*

She turned around. *"My name is Flavia. What is yours? And what is this faraway place you come from?"*

He said to her while still trying to cover his privates, *"My name is Henry, I mean Henrici."* Now Henry made his second mistake. *"I come from a faraway place called America."*

Flavia came back to the tree a few minutes later. She held a light brown, knee length, sleeveless tunic and some brown leather sandals. She threw it down on the ground in front of Henry.

She told him, *"Put those on. They belonged to my brother. I am tired of looking at your little penis."*

*"Thank you for helping me,"* Henry said with embarrassment.

Flavia ordered him sternly, *"Come to the house. My father is home now and don't try anything funny because I have a suitor. He is a member of the Tenth Legion. He rides one of the finest horses in all of Rome and believe me that he has ridden with Caesar himself. If my father doesn't kill you, my suitor surely will."*

The villa seemed like a huge palace to Henry. This was not the house of a poor man. The entryway was decorated with green and blue walls that led to an open atrium filled with plants and flowers with an open ceiling. Flavia guided him through the atrium, past many small bedrooms and a large spa filled with blue water. The floors were white marble with streaks of black. In the back of the villa was what looked like an office. A Roman man sat at a long open desk writing on a piece of papyrus with a metal ink pen. Flavia knocked on the open door. She stuck her head through the doorway, keeping Henry hidden.

*"Can I talk to you father?"*

Valens Antonius was a tall Roman man of forty-eight years. He held his age well. In a time when most Roman men died in their fifties, Valens looked like he could live another twenty years. His hair was brown and lined with grey. He didn't seem too excited to hear his daughter's voice.

He stood up. *"Yes my daughter. I am very busy, Flavia. What can I do for you?"*

Valens spent most of his time in Rome, taking care of his many business dealings. He had managers, servants, and his wife and daughter to run the farm. He would try to come to the countryside villa at least once every two weeks to escape the hustle and bustle of the big city, and to see his beautiful wife and daughter.

Flavia said timidly, *"I found something."*

*"Now you are scaring me, daughter. What have you gotten into now?"*

Flavia smiled, *"I found him behind the big tree. He was hiding naked. He is a man, at least I think he is a man. Please don't kill him father."*

Flavia motioned to the hiding Henry to come forward. He did so slowly making sure not to make eye contact with the aristocrat. He said with a shaky voice, *"My name is Henrici, sir. It is an honor to be here."*

*"Father, he is from a faraway land called America. He knows lots of things. He can be one of our slaves."*

Valens looked him over. *"He looks too scrawny to be a slave. Let me see your hands young man. Where is this America? I never heard of it."*

Henry put out his hands.

Flavia said, *"He comes from a land across the Sea of Atlas. That is where this America is."*

*"That is silly Flavia, nobody has ever been across the ocean."* He looked at Henry's hands. *"Your hands are rough and filled with calluses. Are you a slave? Did you work in the fields?"*

*"No sir, I worked in a factory,"* Henry replied.

*"What did they make at this factory?"*

*"Weapons."*

Valens asked, *"What kind of weapons? Knives? Swords? Spears? Arrows?"*

*"Those and much more. Much, much more."*

*"I don't need any weapons now, and I still don't know why you were running around on my land naked."*

Flavia broke in, *"Don't kill him father. He was lost and he knows things. Henrici, show him the magic sticks."*

Henry took out the box of matches. He struck one, and it ignited with a soft fizzing sound.

Valens smiled. He took the match from Henry. There was an olive oil lamp hanging from the ceiling in the middle of his office. He reached up and lit the wick. *"That was so easy. Can you make more of these boy?"*

*"Yes sir. I can do much more to help you. I can help you with this villa. I can help keep it clean."*

*"That's a job a little man like you should be able to do. I will tell you that I will be going away for two weeks. When I get back, if I find one little mess, I will be forced to kill you."*

Henry muttered in English, "No pressure, no pressure at all."

*"What did you say?"* the Roman Landowner asked.

Flavia said, *"That must be the language of America. Father, I will keep my eye on him. I will make sure he does a good job. I will show him to the servant's quarters."*

*"Yes daughter, go now. I am very busy, and Henrici, make more of those magic sticks. I think I can sell those."*

———◆———

4

The servant's quarters was a small room with six small beds with thin mattresses and torn blankets. The pillows looked more like small cushions.

"*This is your new home. You will have to wear what you have on for now. Our servants wear white tunics, but they are five women. We don't have any for men,*" Flavia said.

Henry asked, "*I have to sleep with five women?*"

"*Yes and no funny stuff, or else...*"

"*I know, I know. Your father will kill me. Flavia, can you tell me something? I have been lost for a long time. What is the date?*"

The only thing on the bare walls of the servant's quarters was a Roman calendar. Flavia looked at it. "*It is January sixth. I love this new calendar that Caesar created.*"

"*What is the year? The Year?*" Henry asked impatiently.

"*710 from the founding of the city.*"

"*That is perfect. This is where I am supposed to be. It is 44 BC.*"

Flavia looked puzzled. "*You say the funniest things, Henrici. What is BC?*"

"*Before Christ.*"

"*Who is Christ?*" Flavia asked.

"*That's not important now. I only have two months. On March fifteenth something terrible is going to happen, and I have to try and stop it. Will you help me Flavia?*"

"*Have I not helped you enough already?*" Then Flavia said sarcastically, "*How do you know what will happen on March fifteenth? What are you supposed to be, a wizard or something? What terrible thing will happen?*"

Henry said with conviction, "*On March fifteenth, the Ides of March, Gaius Julius Caesar will be assassinated.*"

————◆————

Henry spent his first week working with five women and learning his new job. His forewoman was an older, short and stout Roman woman with dark curly hair. Nefeli ran a tight ship by striking the fear of the gods into her subordinates. With one stare, she could make sure her women kept the villa clean and organized. She was not happy having to supervise a man. Along with Flavia, she made sure Henry was doing his job.

Nefeli assigned Henry to the family's personal barn. At first, Henry wasn't sure what to do. The barn was spacious and clean, and his job was to make it even cleaner and more organized. Inside were four young black and brown Maremmano horses. There was a two-wheeled carriage decorated in polished oak with a Roman mosaic of a red and blue half-moon on each side. There were neat piles of hay in one corner. In another was a small wooden table and chair.

Henry had not spoken much to Flavia the first week. If Nefeli constant ordering wasn't enough, Flavia's seemingly constant stare kept Henry on his toes. When she finally walked into the barn to address him, Henry was relieved.

*"Henrici, get the carriage ready. I want to ride to the market."*

Henry struggled to try to get one of the horses near the cart. It was immediately evident to Flavia that he did not know what he was doing. The horse did not seem to want to follow Henry's guidance. The stallion whinnied loudly and reared his front legs high into the air and knocked Henry down on to the ground face first.

He got up and looked at Flavia. *"I have never done this before."*

Flavia laughed and said, *"That is obvious. Let me show you."*

She got near the horse and gently patted his face to calm him down. *"Settle down, Achilles. Henrici will learn to handle you soon enough."*

*"His name is Achilles?"*

*"Yes, after the famous Greek warrior. He is my favorite."*

She put the reins over the horse's head then put a harness around the back. Giving Henry very precise instructions with every step, she moved the horse into position in front of the carriage and connected it to the harness.

*"Now drive the carriage to the front of the villa so I can get on it."*

Henry said again with embarrassment, *"I have never done that either."*

*"Get in. I will show you. You will learn while you drive me to the local forum. I have much shopping to do today."*

Henry got a brief instruction on how to drive, then Flavia handed him the reins. Henry nervously started the horse.

The ride on the paver stone road was surprisingly smooth. They passed acres of farmland and top-heavy umbrella pine trees. Meadows of soft green grass climbed up various hills.

Henry was glad he got the hang of driving quickly. He had much to discuss with Flavia.

*"Flavia, would it be alright if I moved my bed into the barn. Those five always talking ladies gab well into the night. I cannot sleep,"* Henry said.

"*I think that is a good idea and Henrici, now that you are one of our servants, you should call me Lady Antonius and never look me in the eye,*" Flavia ordered.

"*Okay Lady Antonius. I was wondering, am I a slave?*"

"*No, Henrici you are not a slave. You will be paid a very small number of denarius at the end of the month. You can leave anytime you want.*"

"*I do not want to leave. This is the perfect place for me to carry out my mission.*"

"*And what is your mission? That silliness about saving Caesar? Henrici, you cannot predict the future and besides, who is going to kill the most powerful man in the world?*"

"*Some of the Senate; sixty-three Senators to be exact. If I don't do something, they will stab him twenty-three times.*"

"*Even if you are some kind of wizard, I still don't believe you. How are you going to stop sixty-three Senators—you can't just walk into the Senate chambers.*"

"*I cannot. Only Caesar can. We have to get his attention, so we can warn him.*"

"*What do you mean, we?*"

"*You said that you would help.*"

"*I did not. I never said that.*"

"*What, you don't want to save him?*"

"*Of course, I do. I love our great dictator, but that silliness is never going to happen.*"

Henry took that as a yes.

Ahead of them they could see the forum, two long brown concrete buildings with endless tables out in front of them. The street in the middle gave the many vendors and customers just enough room to pass. It looked very crowded.

"*You had better let me park, Henrici. I don't think you can do that yet.*"

Henry handed Flavia the reins. When they got out of the carriage, Flavia made Henry carry two large woven baskets. Once inside the marketplace, Flavia searched the merchandise. There was table after table filled with clothes, vegetables, beans, bread, shoes, and even caged animals.

Flavia quickly had two tunics, a stole, and four pairs of sandals in the baskets. Henry was looking for something else. He found it.

"*I need some of that, Lady Antonius.*" Henry pointed at something that looked like bright yellow soft rocks. "*It is great for cleaning barns.*"

"*No, Henrici. Nefeli has all the cleaning supplies you need. You can buy it if you want. I will take it out of your pay.*"

Henry told the vender, "*Two libras of sulphur please.*"

The vendor had a brass balance with two brass bowls on each side. He put a two libra weight on one side and filled the other with the yellow rocks until it balanced.

*"Buy a small basket for that stuff. Don't put it with my things,"* Flavia ordered.

Henry did that. The three baskets he held started to fill up fast. He soon found the second thing he wanted.

He said to the vendor, *"Two libras of charcoal, please."*

*"What do you need charcoal for, Henrici? You are just buying junk."*

With both of her baskets full of clothes, food, and trinkets, Flavia said, *"I'm done."* Then she sarcastically said to Henry, *"Do you need anything else Henrici?"*

*"No, I need one more ingredient, but we have plenty of that at the farm."*

*"What is that?"*

*"Saltpeter."*

*"That is fertilizer. What are you going to do with this junk?"*

Henry said proudly, *"We have to get his attention."*

⸻◆⸻

Henry took the merchandised-filled baskets into the villa and followed Flavia to her very large bedroom.

Flavia's room was painted with colorful Roman mosaics adorning all four walls with pictures of horses draped in colorful Roman armor. There was one window next to her bed that was topped with a thick feather-filled lavender mattress.

*"Put the baskets on the bed, then leave me, Henrici,"* Flavia ordered.

*"Yes, Lady Antonius."* Henry tried not to look into her eye. *"Can I use that table in the barn as a workshop? Your father did tell me to make more matches."*

*"Yes, make your matches, but not till you finish all of your work. Now leave me."*

Henry retreated back to the carriage. He drove it into the barn and barely managed to unharness Achilles and get him back into his stall. Then he had to feed the four horses and clean up their manure. Once his chores were done, he managed to move his bed out of the villa and into the barn. He was surprised at how heavy it was, but he was determined to drag it near the small work table. He slept, even though it was late afternoon, because he knew that as soon as nightfall came, he would finally be able to start his experiment.

The Roman nights were extremely dark and scary. As Henry went outside to observe the farm, little could be seen at all except for the millions of stars dotting the sky above him. There was only a thin slice of moon overhead making the night even more obscure.

Henry went back inside the barn and found a small olive-oil lantern. Henry lit it with one of his last matches and placed it on his work bench giving him a little bit of light. He had earlier borrowed a few utensils and bowls from the kitchen. The first things he put on the table were four large serving bowls. He filled one of the bowls with some charcoal and a second bowl with sulphur. He also borrowed a finely sanded wooden cylinder that was used for rolling out bread dough. He worked on the charcoal first. Using the flat end of the cylinder he easily managed to grind the charcoal into a very fine powder. Next came the sulphur. This was a much tougher task. He worked well into the night until the hard, yellow rocks turned into sulphur powder.

He took the lantern and one of the bowls out into the night. He slowly walked past an ugly unkept stone structure. A very large man inside saw Henry's flickering light. The man came out to investigate.

"*Who is there?*" Henry heard a low loud voice ask.

As the huge man approached him, Henry thought a giant hideous monster was coming his way. The ogre slowly paced towards Henry, and with each step, the ground seemed to almost shake. When he arrived inside the light of Henry's lantern, he could see that the tunic he wore was faded and torn. His face had a full black beard and his muscular white arms were covered with scars. Both the scars and the muscles were the result of countless years of exhausting bondage.

"*I am Henrici. I am one of the servants that works in the villa,*" Henry said with a shaky voice.

"*Go back to the villa. It is the dead of night,*" the slave told him.

Henry asked, "*I am looking for some fertilizer. Can you help me find it?*"

"*I will help you for a small favor.*"

"*I will do what I can. I need the fertilizer.*"

The slave walked Henry out further into the night until they got to the field of grain. There, on the ground were four large gunnysacks filled with a white powder. Henry was glad to see the saltpeter was already ground into a fine dust. He filled the bowl with the fertilizer.

Henry said to the very large man, "*Thank you, sir.*"

*"Nobody has ever called me sir, little man. You think you can have that for free?"*

*"It does not belong to you. Sir Antonius wants me to have it."*

The slave started to almost whimper, *"This is the favor I require. Please give me something to eat. I am a very big man. The food they give us is often rotten. When they butcher an animal, we get the moldy scraps nobody wants. They give us almost meatless bones to chew on and the fruits and vegetables we have are always half consumed by birds. I work hard for nothing. I will always be in your gratitude if you help me."*

*"Okay, maybe I can share with you some of my rations. Sneak to the barn tomorrow after nightfall. Well after nightfall. Your name is?"* Henry asked.

*"I do not have a name. I am a slave."*

*"You must have a name. What did your mother call you?"*

The big man said, *"My mother was a slave also. I was born a slave and will always be a slave. I think I remember she did call me Cornelius."*

*"Fine, goodnight Cornelius."*

When the big man heard his name for the first time in years, he smiled slightly and walked away with a little spring in his step. Henry then took the lantern and saltpeter back to the barn. He put the lantern back on the bench, then started his work. Using a small cup, he lifted from the villa kitchen, he carefully measured two cups of sulphur into an empty bowl. Next it was charcoal's turn. He measured three cups of it on top of the sulphur. Finally, he took the bowl of fertilizer and measured fourteen cups in total on top of the other ingredients.

Using a bronze metal strainer, he ran the mixture through the small holes four times to make sure it was well combined. The result of all this was a pale black powder.

Henry covered his concoction with a white cloth. It was too late to go any further tonight. He would try his experiment tomorrow night. He had to make sure Flavia was in attendance.

———◆———

*"Get up Henrici! This barn is a mess. Master Antonius will be back soon. Do you want him to kill you?"*

Henry woke up to the sound of the yelling woman. Nefeli was standing above him holding a shovel, *"Clean up the manure, then feed the horses. When that is done, brush them well. After that come to the villa. I need you there. Master Antonius will be home soon."*

Henry could tell by the light outside that it was just after dawn. He quickly got up from a dead sleep and took the shovel from Nefeli. The barn work would not take him that long. He was happy to hear that he was going to work in the villa today.

Nefeli had Henry moving all the furniture in the villa, then sweeping and mopping the marble floors the furniture hid. His back was hurting when he got to Flavia's room. He found her laying on her bed reading a scroll, a long piece of papyrus rolled up between two wooden papyrus spools. She rolled the pages from left to right as she was reading Homer's *The Iliad*.

Henry interrupted her reading. *"Lady Antonius, Nefeli has ordered me to clean under your bed."*

*"Henrici, can't you see I am reading. Come back some other time."*

*"Nefeli says, if I do not clean well, your father will kill me."*

Flavia laughed, *"I know that."* She got off the bed.

As Henry moved the bed she asked, *"Can you read, Henrici?"*

Henry started to sweep as he said, *"Yes, I can read in four different languages."*

Flavia said with mockery, *"Oh sure, I believe you. But I really believe you are lying about that. What languages do you speak?"*

*"The only one you know about is Latin."*

She handed Henry the scroll. *"Read it to me."*

Henry looked at the small hand-written letters. *"This is very small writing. I will have trouble reading this without my glasses."*

*"You say the strangest things Henrici. What are glasses?"*

*"They are lenses that help me see better. I am very farsighted."*

*"I knew you were lying,"* Flavia said with a huff.

Henry focused on the words inked on the scroll. He read out loud, *"Hateful to me as the gates of Hades is that man who hides one thing in his heart and speaks another."*

*"Very good, Henrici. You can read."*

*"I can do more. Can you come out to the barn tonight at hour eight? I have something to show you."*

*"I wanted to finish this scroll tonight. This is the third time I have read it."*

*"I promise that it will only take a few minutes. You will be impressed."*

*"Is it like the match? I have better things to do than spend time with you, Henrici."*

As Flavia started to leave the room Henry said, *"It will very much out-shine the match."*

The small table in the servant's quarters could hardly handle the five women and one man. Henry and three of the women waited patiently as the two girls that worked in the kitchen brought in their food. There were plates filled with wheat bread, a bowl of cured fish and fresh olives. There were dates and grapes galore. Each of their goblets was filled with Falernian wine.

One of the kitchen servants was a dark-skinned African girl who called herself Naima. She was taller than Henry and even younger. She kept her big round pretty eyes focused on their only male co-worker. As the servants all loaded their plates with food, Henry tried to take a little more nourishment than he needed.

While the feast was being consumed, the young African girl kept her eyes fixated on Henry. Naima said to him with a sad face, *"Henrici, I was so sad when you moved into the barn."*

Henry said, *"Lady Antonius thought it would be better if I was near the horses."*

*"Are you like a horse, Henrici?"* One woman asked with a laugh.

Another said, *"I think he is more like a donkey."*

All the ladies erupted in laughter. Henry quietly loaded his plate with more food then covered it with a cloth napkin. He got up and started to leave the room with his plate and goblet in his hands.

Naima said, *"Henrici, why are you leaving so soon? The night is young. We can talk."*

Nefeli said, *"I think Naima wants Henrici for much more than talking."*

All the women erupted in laughter again.

Henry put the plate and goblet on his work bench. He found a large brass bowl in the barn. He filled it with about a Roman pound of his powder, then placed it far away from the horses and the door.

He heard a deep low voice, *"I am here, Henrici. It is well after dark."*

Henry said in English, "Crap! I guess I didn't plan this night too well."

The huge slave Cornelius said, *"What did you say?"* He saw the covered plate on the table. *"Is that for me Henrici? I am very, very hungry."*

*"Yes Cornelius, hurry up. I have things to do tonight."*

Cornelius uncovered the plate and gasped, *"Henrici, I have never seen such a feast."*

The big man used his fingers to start chomping down handfuls of bread, fish, and fresh fruit.

*"Henrici, this is the best food I have ever had."* He saw the goblet. *"Is that wine? Can I try some? The wine they give us tastes like sea water."*

Henry reached into the goblet and pulled out an eight-inch-thick piece of string he had soaking in the wine since his dinner. He took one end of the string and stuck it deep into the powder. The other end dangled over the lip of the brass bowl to about an inch above the ground.

*"Drink up,"* Henry told Cornelius.

As Cornelius guzzled down the wine Henry heard another voice, *"Henrici, why do you have a slave in here?"*

Flavia had her arms crossed around her chest. She stared violently at Henry until he started to shake.

He tried to defend himself. *"Lady Antonius, he helped me find the fertilizer. I promised him a little snack in return. He is my friend. His name is Cornelius."*

Flavia said back, *"He is a slave. He does not have a name. He cannot be your friend. Get him out of here."*

Henry replied, *"Cornelius says the food you give him is mostly rotten and moldy. The bad wine you give him tastes like sea water. He is a big man that works for nothing."*

Flavia watched as Cornelius got up from his feast and walked to the back of the barn. The slave knew when life had defeated him. Cornelius looked straight at the dirt floor and did not say a word.

She said with just a little compassion, *"Okay, he can stay and finish his meal. But only this one time. Now, Henrici, show me what you have, or I am leaving."*

Henry took one of his last matches. He lit the end of the string. The alcohol in the string made it burn brightly as the flame made its way to the powder. Henry asked Flavia to stand by the door.

Flavia said, *"Henrici, the match was a much better trick than a burning string."*

When the flame hit the powder the yellow and orange explosion threw fiery sparks all the way to the roof of the barn. The hissing fire and light turned the dark Roman night into a very brief sunny day. All four horses reared their front legs high into the air and started whinnying loudly. The hissing fire climbed higher into the air and then suddenly started to pop as smaller explosions erupted inside the flames. As the burst of light slowly subsided, the barn was left with a smoking sulphur smell.

Cornelius could not help himself. He laughed loudly, *"Ha! Ha! Little Henrici is like Vulcan, the God of fire!"*

Henry was prepared. The explosion started a few small fires around the barn. He put out a large one with a bucket of water then smothered some smaller ones with a blanket.

Flavia stood by the door with a stunned look on her face. *"Henrici, what in the name of Hades did you just do?"*

Henry looked her in the eye. *"Just a little demonstration. Do you think it will get Caesar's attention?"*

*"Yes, but Henrici, what is it?"*

Henry said, *"It is called gunpowder."*

*"Gunpowder? What the heck is a gun?"*

*"You are going to find out what that is also. Thank you for your time Lady Antonius."*

*"Yes Henrici, and one more thing. You can call me Flavia."*

## II

# The Bad Day

"I DON'T THINK THAT IS SUCH A GOOD IDEA, SHERRIE."

"It is Professor. I know it is."

Sherrie Melbourne sat in front of a big darkly stained oak desk. The office was decorated with trinkets of the ancient Greeks and Romans and colorful jewelry was strewn in glassed displays around the room. The paintings on the wall were colorful mosaics with half-naked Roman women celebrating in the clear outside air. On a small end table was a replica of a Roman sculpture, the head of an unknown Roman noble. It seemed to be staring at Sherrie.

Her Professor and adviser, Doctor Ronald Pillar, was a middle-aged man with greying hair and nicely trimmed beard. He looked and dressed the part of a classic scholar complete with thin-rimmed glasses and tweed jacket. He spoke in a voice that made him sound like a man that knew everything. He indeed did think he knew it all. To Sherrie, he did *not* know everything. He wasn't even close.

"I know you have great passion for your studies, but you should come up with a better subject than that for your senior thesis." the professor looked condescendingly over his glasses at his top student.

Sherrie Melbourne was not going to give up. She said to her mentor, "Professor, I am going to graduate with distinction in Classical Studies. To get that honor, I need to write the thesis. I'm not going to Daytona Beach over spring break. I can start it now."

"Slow down, Sherrie. You still have a semester left in your junior year. Use spring break to think about your subject. Try to come up with something better. Your idea is just a theory. It is practically impossible to research a theory. How are your Latin studies coming?"

She answered him in perfect Latin, *"I already finished the ninth course."*

Professor Pillar followed with his Latin, *"Very good. Let's cut this meeting short. I want to get out of here and start my spring break."* He switched to English, "Use this time off to slow down and relax Sherrie—and come up with a researchable subject for your thesis."

She stayed in Latin, *"I have a subject. I am going with it. I have a whole week to start planning it.* She got up to leave the office, *"Have a nice break, Professor."*

"Remember Sherrie, I am your advisor. I'm sure you realize that I will only accept a thesis proposal that is based in fact." As he said this, his eyes swept down over her torso and across her very firm backside.

Sherrie ignored the gesture at first. She was used to men behaving like this. The ambitious 'A' student was taller than most of the guys she went to school with, but her healthy blond hair and her wholesome good looks trumped any problem her height may have caused.

However, she wanted to make sure that her professor understood that she knew exactly what he was thinking. She suddenly turned around, lowered her reading glasses so he could see her eyes, and bored icy-blue holes through him. "You know I am right. Julius Caesar was a great man. If he lived, our world would be a better place."

———◆———

The campus of Duke University was majestically old and grandiose. Sherrie always loved waking next to the gothic architecture with its dark-colored bricks dotted with bright green North Carolina grass and old thick-trunked oak trees. It was a place for scholars, and Sherrie never forgot the privilege.

As she made her way across campus to the parking lot, she was glad the muggy hot Carolina summer had not yet arrived. This early March day had a chill in the air and the sun was barely peeping through the clouds, but Sherrie was miffed, so she kept her dark glasses on and ignored the crush of students who were all trying desperately hard to get off campus. Most hoped to get south to Florida for a few extra hours of spring break revelry.

This was not for Sherrie. She had turned down an invitation from her live-in boyfriend to go to Daytona Beach. She reluctantly agreed to let him go with his friends. Kern Smith did not take his studies seriously, and this always rankled Sherrie. He was good-looking, but it was his rich parents and political influence that got him through the door.

Sherrie found her little white car and got in for the short drive to her apartment. As she left the school, she couldn't help thinking of how hard she worked to get into Duke. Her parents were well-off and could have easily afforded the tuition, but she wanted to get accepted on her own terms. So, she got all the all the scholarships and financial aid she could and paid most of her own way.

The five-mile drive to the apartment was stop and go, which irritated her even more. Sherrie was trying to keep her eye on the road when her cell phone beeped. She could not resist. She took it out of her bag and looked at it. The text message coming in almost made her cry.

She wrote back a text in all caps, "MOM, YOU CAN'T GET A DIVORCE. YOU AND DAD HAVE BEEN MARRIED FOR 32 YEARS."

She looked at the road and saw that she had veered to the right. Sherrie slammed on her breaks, but it wasn't enough. She hit a stop sign and sent it flying to the ground. She got out of her car to see the damage. Her front bumper was severely smashed in and as luck would have it, soon a black and white car drove in behind hers, red lights flashing.

An older officer got out of his police car and walked up to Sherrie. He asked her, "What happened here young lady?"

She answered with fake tears in her eyes, "I don't know. My car just went right, then I hit the sign."

"You weren't texting and driving, were you?"

"No, I mean maybe. My mom just text me that she is getting a divorce from my dad. I was shocked."

The officer took off his hat and wiped some sweat off his forehead. "That's no excuse. You should have pulled over to text back. I need to see your license and registration."

Sherrie got into the car and got the documents and handed them to the officer. Crying wasn't working, so she tried something else. She gave him a sexy smile and purred, "Officer, I was hoping maybe you would give me a little teensy break today. This is my second offence. They might take away my license. Pretty please?"

The older man laughed, "Sure, and what am I going to tell the super about this sign?"

"Faulty installation? I will pay for the damage."

He walked back near his car and started writing on a clip board. The policeman soon returned and handed her a citation. "Please drive safe Miss Melbourne. We will get a warrant, so we can look at your phone. There may be evidence of texting and driving in there."

Sherrie cried for real, "No, please no. Not my phone."

The officer let Sherrie drive home.

Sherrie drove slow and carefully to her apartment. She parked in her little garage, made her way to the lobby and took the elevator up to the third floor. The one-bedroom one bath was perfect for the two students.

She would say her goodbyes to Kern, send him on his way, then focus on a week of planning her senior thesis.

When she opened the apartment door, she immediately heard the unmistakable sound of a girl moaning. Sherrie went to her bedroom and quickly opened the door. There she saw a naked Kern on top of a young brunette girl. He was moaning as loud as she was.

She yelled, "Kern! What the hell are you doing?"

Kern tried to cover himself and his lover with the blankets. The young girl crawled out of bed, grabbed her clothes off the floor, and scuttled out of the room.

Sherrie yelled again, "Who is that? A freshman?"

Kern said, "It's not what it looks like. You were supposed to be home later."

"This is my place. I can come home any time I want."

"I told you, it is not what it looks like. We are just friends."

Sherrie yelled even louder, "Friends? You were fucking a freshman in my bed!"

Without any further warning, Sherrie opened the bedroom window and started throwing his clothes out until they hit the sidewalk three stories down.

Kern, embarrassed and ashamed, quietly said, "I guess we are breaking up?"

Sherrie walked to the front door and opened it. She calmly said, "The rest of your stuff will be down on the sidewalk shortly."

Sherrie did not cry herself to sleep. It was just a bad day, she thought. She would continue with her plan to start her thesis. Tomorrow will be better, she thought. It would be impossible for it to be any worse.

———◆———

The cafeteria was almost deserted. No wonder, it was first Saturday of spring break.

Sherrie wanted to start the morning right with a good breakfast. She had a fruit salad, an egg white omelet, and a slice of dry whole wheat toast on her tray. She noticed a little guy sitting nearby. She had seen him before. He was always alone.

"What the heck," she said to herself. "The good-looking ones are all jerks. Maybe this little guy will listen to me."

She picked up her tray and walked towards him. She put her tray on his table sat down and stuck out her hand, "Hello, my name is Sherrie Melbourne. I had a really bad day yesterday. Can I sit down here, or is this place taken?"

The little guy did not shake her hand. Instead threw Sherrie a puzzled look out of his coke-bottled glasses and glanced behind him as if she was talking to someone else.

"No, I am talking to you. Do you want to hear about my bad day?" Sherrie asked.

He said with a nasally voice, "Girls like you never talk to guys like me. I am a nerd. To a nerd, every day is a bad day."

"Okay, let's see if you can top this. My professor hates my thesis idea. I caught my boyfriend cheating on me and so I kicked him out. My parents are getting a divorce. I was texting my mom while I was driving and hit a stop sign. It was my second offence. I'm going to lose my license."

"That will be tough to top. At least you had a boyfriend. Most of us nerd guys never get a girlfriend."

"Don't downplay yourself so much. I think you are kind of cute."

He said sarcastically, "Right, I believe you. So, what do you want from me? Do you want me to do your homework for you?"

Sherrie said with a little anger, "I can do my own homework. I have no reason to cheat. Why can't you believe I just want to talk?"

"Because girls like you never talk to guys like me." He stopped talking for a minute then said, "I might be able to help you with that texting situation you have."

Sherrie smiled, "Really? Do you know someone at city hall?"

"No, I will have to show you. You will have to come to my workshop."

"Give me the address. I think they want to take away my phone. What do you do in this workshop? What is your major?"

"Astrophysics. I am in the doctorate program now. In my workshop, I do top secret scientific experiments. Before I let you in, you will have to swear your allegiance to me."

"Okay, I don't know what that means, but if you get me out of this… yes, I swear."

He handed her a business card. Sherrie read it. "Your name is Garfield, like the cartoon cat. Henry Garfield," she said in Latin, "*That is my favorite Latin name, Henrici. You are my little tiny Henrici.*"

Henry said, also in Latin, "*You know I can understand you. I like how you say my name. Come by tonight at seven.*"

When Sherrie entered his workshop, she was surprised at how small it was. There were five plain wooden tables with various sizes of computer screens on each as well as tablets and smart phones scattered about. A bookcase was filled with volumes of physics textbooks and journals. On the walls were hanging digital clocks with the seconds counting wildly to the ten thousandth of a second. Something strange was in the middle of the room. There were two brassy electrical coils wrapped around two iron cylinders. Coming out of the top of one was a silver blue line of lightning hissing its way to the other coil.

Sherrie asked, "What is this stuff Henrici? Looks like something out of a Frankenstein movie."

"Now, what I am going to show you is tip-top secret. You cannot tell anyone."

Sherrie noticed a cot and small dresser in the corner. "Do you live here, Henry?"

"Yes, I cannot afford a workshop and an apartment."

"Where do you go to the bathroom?"

"At school. Sometimes they let me use the one at the gas station down the street. Sometimes I just hold it in till I get to school. I plan on putting one in someday."

"Where? There is no room."

"Anyway, what I will show you I discovered by quite an accident. I was trying to find a way to get power from the earth's electromagnetic fields. I wanted to save money on my electric bill. Then I almost killed myself with a huge electric shock. I was out for hours and blind for over two days."

Sherrie was concerned. "Did you go to the hospital?"

"Why? I just waited it out here until my sight came back."

20

"I won't ask where you went to the bathroom."

"A tin can. After I recovered, I checked all the data over and over. I found that 2.3936 minutes were added. I was shot 2.3936 minutes back in time."

"We all know that is impossible Henrici."

Henry handed her a metal bonded folder, and she opened it. Inside were page after page of numbered and lettered equations and signs.

Henry proudly said, "See, that is proof. It is all there in black and white. It is possible."

"Henrici, I have no idea what all this means."

"I have to show you."

Henry sat down in front of a computer and typed for a while. He got up and took a bathrobe out of his dresser and put it on the floor next to the front door of the shop. He hit a stopwatch.

"I am going to shoot myself back in time precisely for two minutes. I will reappear right here."

He went back to the computer, sat down and typed some more. Then he showed her a shiny black two and a half-inch diameter sphere.

"This is what I call an electromagnetic shocker. It is best if you hold it tightly with both hands."

Sherrie saw big numbers counting down on the computer screen: 10-9-8-7.

"Is it going to shock you?" Sherrie asked with anticipation.

"No, I shock the magnetic field of the earth. I use all the power in the entire electromagnetic field to open a time warp and send myself back in time. That is how I do it. At worst, I might get a little dizzy."

The computer screen continued: 4-3-2.

A fizzing sound filled the shop. Henry glowed with a soft yellow flare that surrounded his entire body. The fizzing and flaring seemed to enter his body and soon, Henry's silhouette turned from a growing bright yellow hot to an even brighter blue hot. The heat forced Sherrie to step back, and she tried to cover her eyes. Suddenly, Henry and all the flames vanished as a pulse of warm air blew through the room. All that was left near his seat was his khaki pants, his short sleeve green shirt, his pen and pencil pack, his glasses, and the electromagnetic shocker.

Sherrie started to panic. "Henry! What happened? Did you finally kill yourself?"

She picked up his empty shirt. She saw on the computer screen that two minutes were counting down.

Henry had never seen this before. He could see Sherrie talking to an empty chair. He wasn't there. He couldn't be because he was two minutes behind her. He counted down the seconds and patiently waited for two minutes to pass. That is when his time would catch up with hers. Henry forgot to put on the bathrobe.

When Sherrie saw the time count down to zero, she heard another fizzing sound. With a big flash, Henry reappeared by the shop door. He was naked.

"Henry, put on the robe. What kind of trick was that? Is this your nerdy way to try to get me into bed?" Sherrie asked.

"No, I am sorry. I forgot to put on the robe. I told you. I went back in time. Precisely two minutes back."

"Slow down cowboy." Sherrie was breathing hard. "Why were you naked?"

"It only works on living organic material. I have not figured out how to send clothes back in time."

"Okay, let me catch my breath. How is this light show going to help me with my problem?"

"I have never tried this on another person, but I know it will work. I can send you back to the time right before your stop-sign accident."

Sherrie's eyes got wider. "What! You want to pull that trick on me?"

"Do you remember the time of the accident?"

"I do. When I picked up my phone, it read 12:36 p.m."

Henry hooked the black-sphered shocker up to his computer with a USB cable. He began typing again.

"This electromagnetic shocker is also a very powerful computer. The first thing you have to do is take off all your clothes and move the shocker around your body. It will scan you."

"Wait a minute. I knew it. You just want to see me naked. Do you have cameras in here?"

"No. No I will not use them. I will wait outside. The computer screen will tell you when the scan is complete. Then we have to go near to where the accident happened. If not, you might end up somewhere in-between here and your car. Nobody would be driving it."

"Henry are you sure this is safe? I don't want my molecules scattered all over town."

He reassured her, "It is. I have done it myself fifty-six times. Once in a while I get a little dizzy."

"When do you want to do this?"

"Right now. When you go back in time, here are the things you have to remember: do not look at your phone. Drive carefully to wherever you were going. Try do everything the same way until you meet me again. Oh, and one other thing, you will be naked."

"There you go with the naked again. How am I supposed to get to my apartment naked? The lobby is always very crowded. Wait a minute," Sherrie's smile brightened up. "I always have a blanket in the back seat of my car. I can wrap myself up in that. It might look a little weird, but whatever. Go outside little Henrici."

Sherrie felt strange moving the little ball around her body. After a few minutes the computer screen read SCAN COMPLETE. She put her clothes back on and called for Henry to return.

Henry typed into his computer some more, then he said, "Everything is ready. Let's go."

"Your car or mine?"

"I do not have a car. I do not know how to drive."

"I guess it's mine. You invented time travel, and you can't even drive. You know Henry, if this works, I am going to give you a big kiss."

They arrived a little after 8:30 pm. Henry had her park on the side of the road. They were about two hundred yards from the fallen stop sign.

"How fast were you going?" Henry asked Sherrie.

"Forty, maybe forty-five."

"You had better back up a bit."

She did, then they got out of the car. Henry guided her to behind a large oak tree. He handed her the electromagnetic shocker. He had his laptop and started typing again.

"I am hooked up to the shocker. When I hit enter, you will have ten seconds. Remember, do not pick up your phone when you arrive in the past. Now, hold the shocker tightly with both hands."

Henry hit the enter key. Sherrie could see on the laptop screen large numbers counting down: 10-9-8-7.

Sherrie was shaking with nervousness. "I'm scared. Henry."

"Do not be scared. It will be fine."

Henry continued counting: 3-2-1. The fizzing sound returned. Sherrie glowed with a yellow blaze that surrounded her. The heated light turned from a fiery yellow to scorching violent blue, then she was gone with a large flash of light and heat. All that was left was her clothes on the ground and the shocker on top of them.

Henry picked up the clothes and wanted to put them in her car when he noticed that the car had vanished with her. He put the electromagnetic sphere in his pocket and hid the clothes behind the oak tree. Henry started on his long walk home. All he could do now was wait for the cycle to be complete.

———◆———

Sherrie did not hear the fizzing sound. In an instant all she saw was her shaking hands holding the steering wheel.

"I'm driving. It's daytime and I'm driving. Slow down Sherrie."

Sherry heard her smartphone beep, "Do not pick it up and do not text. Slow down and stop at the stop sign, just like you've done a thousand times," she kept telling herself over and over.

It worked. She slowed down and made a complete stop at the sign. Because she still wasn't sure if this was real, she told herself, "Look both ways and slowly proceed."

She noticed an old man in the left lane in a car parallel to her. He was staring at her with a big smile on his face.

She looked down at herself, "Oh my god! I'm naked." She reached into the back seat and pulled out a red blanket and did her best to cover herself. Sherrie slowly and carefully drove to her apartment.

She did get a few stares from tenants in the lobby, and she was prepared for them. When she got in the elevator, an even younger girl student got in with her.

She said to Sherrie, "That's a strange look you have there."

Sherrie quickly said, "I'm cold."

"If you're so cold, then why don't you have any shoes?"

She whispered to the young girl, "Listen sister. I am going to let you in on a big secret. This is the latest new look from Hollywood. Soon, everyone will be wearing it."

"Thanks for the info," the young girl said as Sherrie got off on the third floor.

Sherrie walked into her apartment She went right to her bedroom and barged in, just like the first time.

Kern stopped moaning and said, "It's not what it looks like. You were supposed to be home later."

Sherrie did not say a word. She went to the closet and opened it. She let the blanket fall to the floor.

Kern saw his bare girlfriend. "What's going on Sherrie? Are you going to join us?"

Sherrie put on her bathrobe and then grabbed a pile of Kern's clothes. She went to the window, opened it, and threw them down to the sidewalk below.

Then she said, "You know what's great about this Kern? I get to throw you out twice. Get out! All your stuff will be down on the sidewalk shortly."

With Kern gone she sat down on her couch and tried to fathom what just happened. Henry told her to do everything the same as she did the first time. She called her mother. She called her father. She read a history book about Julius Caesar, then she went to sleep. She got up early and drove to school to have her breakfast and meet Henry.

——◆——

Just like the last time, the cafeteria was almost deserted. It was the first Saturday of spring break after all. Sherrie remembered what she had for breakfast. She got a fruit salad, an egg white omelet, and some dry whole wheat toast. She got excited when she saw Henry sitting alone at his table. She rushed to him.

With a big smile on her face she said when she got close, "My little Henrici, it worked! I didn't hit the sign. It worked."

Henry stood up with a startled look on his face. Sherrie took his face in her hands and gave him a big kiss on the mouth.

Henry looked scared. "Are you making fun of me? Are you making fun of me because I am a nerd? Shame on you, whoever you are."

"No, Henry it's me. I'm Sherrie. Oh my god! I am such an idiot. Oh my god. You haven't met me yet. Henry I'm so sorry."

"You should be."

"No, you don't understand. I was telling you about my bad day. I told you I caught my boyfriend cheating on me and that my parents are getting a divorce. I hit a stop sign while texting and driving, and my Professor hates my thesis idea."

"I do not remember this."

"Henry, I was at your workshop. You put me back in time, and I didn't hit the stop sign. You helped me."

"You were at my workshop? When?"

25

"Last night. No, I mean tonight."

"And what time did you go back in time?"

"I think it was between 8:30 and 9:00."

"We have to wait until then. That's when the cycle will be complete. I should remember then."

Sherrie smiled at him. "I promised you a big kiss if it worked, and it worked."

"I never kissed a girl before like that."

"We have time. Let's talk awhile."

Henry asked, "What do you want to talk about?"

"Professor Pillar is such an asshole sometimes. He thinks he knows everything about everything, but all he wants to do is stare at my ass. And now he says he will not support my thesis subject."

"I would call him what you called him, but I do not like to say swear words."

"You hang around with me long enough and you'll be swearing like a sailor. I don't care what he says. It's my thesis, and I will choose the subject."

"What is the subject?"

"I am passionate about the history of Julius Caesar. I am convinced if he would have survived his assassination, the world would be a better place, even today. In my thesis, I want to create this world."

"That sounds good to me, very creative. What are you going to call it?"

"Many Italians really believe this. Rome is a thriving metropolis today and since ancient times it always has been a thriving metropolis."

"True, but what are you calling the thesis?" Henry asked again.

Sherrie firmly said, "Rome Never Fell."

# III

# The Roman Bath

I T WAS A COLD MORNING IN THE SUBURBS OUTSIDE OF ROME. THERE was a thick misty fog in the air, not quite a rain but just enough to keep their skin moist. Henry was driving Flavia on another shopping trip, and she was constantly complaining about her tunic getting wet and wrinkled. Henry wondered what she would do if he told her about cars. Instead, he decided to stick with what would be real to her and told her about how he managed to get Achilles the horse hooked up to the carriage all by himself.

*"I got the large horse's trust by feeding him a fresh apple twice a day,"* he told his mentor proudly.

But then he got serious. *"I am running out of time,"* Henry said to Flavia, his Latin having improved immensely since he arrived, *"We only have forty-one days left until the Ides of March. We have to warn Caesar."*

Flavia said, *"No us Henrici. I never said I would help you."*

Henry tried to ignore that. *"Here is my plan. We go to the Temple of Jupiter. I will set off some special gunpowder near the entrance. The soldiers will be amazed and take us to show Caesar the gunpowder. Then we can warn him of his upcoming death."*

*"Maybe the soldiers will think you are some kind of a wizard and kill you."*

*"I know. It is a chance I must take. I wish the Temple had the original Scrolls of Sibylline, written by a great prophet, the Sibyl."*

*"I know the story, Henrici. An old woman came to our last king hundreds of years ago. She tried to sell King Tarquin nine scrolls. The old one wanted an extraordinary amount of money for them. The King refused to pay. She left and burned three of the scrolls. When she returned, she offered the King the remaining six books for the same outrageous price. He refused again. The lady returned again one last time. This time with only three scrolls. King Tarquin caved. He bought the three scrolls for the same big price. He could have had all nine for the same money."*

Henry added, *"We…I mean I, believe the original scrolls had a prophesy of the murder of a great leader on the Ides of March. If Caesar saw that he would know what to do to protect himself."*

*"I think the scrolls are still in the temple, Henrici."*

*"No, the temple burned down over twenty years ago. It was struck by lightning. The scrolls were a total loss. They got some new ones, but they are not authentic."*

Flavia questioned Henry, *"Who is this we? And why do you know so much about Rome. Do they like us in this America place?"*

*"It is not me. I know a girl that is studying Ancient Rome."*

*"What is Ancient Rome? Is there another Rome somewhere?"*

*"No, only one Rome. She is studying your Rome. She is almost my female suitor."*

*"You have a girlfriend, little Henrici? I do not believe it,"* Flavia asked with a little jealousy in her voice. *"Is she pretty?"*

Henry's voice got delightful, *"Yes, she is the most beautiful girl in the world. She is tall with blond hair. She has wonderful blue eyes."*

*"I would love to meet her."*

Henry suddenly said, *"No! No, you cannot meet her. She is too far away, way across the Sea of Atlas. She does not love me yet. She told me if I do well on my mission, when I get back, she will let me have sex with her."*

*"Sex Henrici? That sounds like a prostitute to me."*

*"No, she is a very good girl."*

*"So, what is this girl's name?"*

*"Her name is Sherrie,"* Henry said proudly.

Flavia said with sarcasm, *"Sherrie? What kind of name is Sherrie? That sounds like a glass of some kind of Spanish wine."*

Flavia let Henry buy five Roman pounds of sulphur and charcoal, but this time she paid for it. She bought herself the usual clothes, sandals, and fruits and finally stopped complaining about the weather. Henry was relieved.

When they returned to the villa, Henry did his chores as fast as he could. He got Achilles into his stall, then fed the four horses and cleaned up their mess in record time. He needed as much time as possible for his "real" job.

When his work was done, he went inside the villa to get his rations and some extra which he carried towards the old stone slave quarters. With the evening sun disappearing behind a grassy hill, he whispered loudly towards the dirty unkept den, *"Cornelius. Come to the barn at once."*

He did hear him, *"Who is that? Is that you Henrici?"*

*"Yes, I have a snack for you and some work for you also."*

The very tall and muscular slave entered Henry's living space. His bearded face looked tired, almost to the point of exhaustion.

He quietly said to Henry, *"I should not be here. If Lady Antonius finds me here, she might have me killed."*

*"I will worry about Flavia, and besides I need you to do some work. You are a slave. That is your job."*

*"I am owed by Valens Antonius. I only answer to him, the farm foreman, and Lady Antonius."*

Henry tried to sound like he had authority, *"Eat your meal, then I will show you what to do."*

Cornelius went to the work table and took the cloth off the plate that was there. It was loaded with fresh dates, some cooked beans, and plenty of freshly grilled meat.

*"Henrici, is this fresh meat? I have never tasted fresh meat before."*

*"Enjoy Cornelius."*

It didn't take long for Cornelius to wolf down the food. He ate everything and looked like he could eat three more full plates. Once he finished eating, the slave got to work. He made it look easy, sitting at the worktable with Henry's makeshift mortar and pestle, grinding the hard sulphur into a fine powder.

Henry was sitting on his bed trying to come up with a plan on how to meet Caesar. Maybe he and Cornelius could borrow a horse and the carriage to get to Rome. Henry was sure he could find the Temple of Jupiter.

He heard a familiar voice at the door of the barn, *"Henrici, I have been thinking about what you said."* Flavia's voice suddenly got angry, *"Henrici! What did I tell you about having slaves in here?"*

Henry quickly got up from his bed. *"I know Flavia, but he is working like a slave. It is very hard for me to grind the sulphur. Cornelius does it with ease."*

Cornelius once again got up from the table. He looked down at the ground and slowly walked to the back of the barn not saying a word.

*"I told you. He does not have a name. He cannot be your friend."* Flavia looked at the huge man as he slowly walked away. She said to him, *"Slave, why do you have all those scars all over your arms?"*

Cornelius continued to look at the ground making sure not to make eye contact with the Lady. *"I work very hard for Master Antonius. Sometimes the farm foreman thinks I am not working hard enough. He uses a horse whip to slash my arms."*

Henry said, *"Cornelius works very hard in the fields for nothing. I see him every day."*

Flavia seemed undecided. *"That is not just. He works so hard and gets whipped like an animal? Okay, I guess it is okay he is here, as long as he is working. I came here for another reason. I was with some of my friends today, and they say there is a rumor passing through Rome as fast as lightning. The rumor is that Julius Caesar will soon be named King of all of Rome. I would like to meet our future King."*

Henry said, *"Yes, the Senate will not like that at all. They think he is a tyrant. That is why they want to kill him."*

*"Right Henrici. I am going to Rome in one month. We can try your plan then. If the soldiers kill you, I might even be a little sad."*

*"If we leave in one month, that only leaves us two weeks until March fifteenth. Maybe that is not enough time to warn him."*

*"I am leaving in one month."*

Henry tried to ask with authority, but it came out more or less wimpy, *"I think we should bring Cornelius, no I mean this slave. He is very big. We might need some muscle riding through some of the tough streets of Rome. He won't escape."*

*"Bring him if you want. And Henrici, tomorrow is the day the servants get to use the main bath. You are starting to stink. You had better join them."*

◆

Henry had learned that the servants were only allowed to use the Roman bath on the night of the moon between hour eight and hour ten. Henry knew he needed a bath, so he got there a little early.

The bath was a large perfect circle about twenty feet in diameter. Inside the clean blue water was a stone bench that spanned the circumference. The walls were made of multi-colored shaded stone, polished to a bright brilliant shine. Henry had read about the Roman baths, but that didn't prepare him for their opulence. He was impressed. Not only did they look inviting, but they smelled fresh and clean. He remembered that they were fed by aqueducts, and now he knew why that was important.

Henry did not know what to do, so he just waited. Soon all five of the female servants rushed through the open arched entrance. One by one they started taking off their white tunics and entering the warm water. Henry took this as his cue to leave.

He started for the exit when their leader and forewoman, Nefeli yelled at Henry, *"Henrici! Where are you going? Block his way, Julia."*

Julia was the oldest and the biggest of the five female servants. She got ahead of Henry and blocked the archway with her heavy-set body. Her brown-eyed stare told Henry that he wasn't going anywhere.

Nefeli said, *"Henrici, you have to get in. You smell like the stink."*

*"That is fine. I will come back later,"* Henry said.

He looked and Julia's firm glare as she said, *"Get in!"*

Henry slowly walked toward the bath. He took off his sandals and stepped in the water.

*"Not like that,"* another servant said. She stood up grabbed Henry's tunic and pulled it off over his head. Soon another one took the loin cloth from around his waist and pulled it down to his knees. Henry dunked his body under the water to hide his nakedness.

Four of the females started to massage and caress Henry's body, their hands spreading exotic oils all over him. He noticed the dark young Naima with her body completely submerged in the water. All he could see was her pretty face.

She looked at him with her big opulent eyes and smiled, *"I get to wash Henrici first. He is mine."*

An argument erupted between all the women.

*"No, I am first!"*

*"I saw Henrici first. I want to wash him."*

*"I will fight you all. I am first!"*

Nefeli tried to calm down her troops. *"Stop arguing everyone. We will all get a chance to wash Henrici. Naima is the youngest, so she goes first."*

The young African girl moved closer to Henry. She tried to kiss his cheek. Henry made one last ditch effort to escape the pool and he almost made it. He got his body out of the tub, but the big servant, Julia, managed to grab him by his ankle. With the help of two others they dragged Henry back into the center of the large bath.

With all the women sitting around him giggling and laughing, Naima approached Henry again.

Henry put his arms high in the air and said in English, "This is not the way I am supposed to lose my virginity."

——◆——

Cornelius sat in the back of the carriage. The big man assumed he had lived for twenty-eight years. He was never really sure. He spent all of those years on farms, working for nothing and unable to ever leave. He went to sleep each night knowing the following day would bring countless hours of back-breaking bondage and a possible whipping. This was his life, so that's what made this day so special to him, riding in the horse driven carriage watching the green Roman countryside go by. He was going to Rome. He was going to actually get to see Rome. In the back of the carriage were two large woven baskets. One was empty. The other was filled with food. Flavia Antonius had the servants pack a lunch, and Cornelius hoped he would get just a little taste of the feast. He listened to the two in the front talking.

"*I am feeling very confident that my plan is going to work, Flavia,*" Henry said as he guided Achilles with the reins.

"*For your sake it better. Let's go to the Temple first. After that, I will be staying with friends for a few days. You and the slave will have to sleep outside.*"

"*Nice. What are we going to do for food?*"

"*I will give you a few denarii for food.*"

"*Thank you, Flavia.*"

"*Do not thank me. I am going to take it out of your pay.*"

The Roman countryside had abruptly given way to a dense forest. In order to get to Rome, Flavia knew they had to pass through five miles of this densely wooded area that was infested with highwaymen, ruthless bandits of the worst kind. When Flavia would pass this land with her father, the criminals would never attack the former Roman officer. Now Flavia was glad they brought Cornelius along.

The brothers Marcellus were hiding in the thick layers of trees. The sunny day was completely gone here, and it made this dark and dingy forest the perfect place to hide. The older brother Titus was much larger than his younger sibling Lucius. Titus had big muscles while Lucius looked like skin and bones. They both had on black tunics that matched their black hair and beards. Attached to their belts were identical long sharp iron swords and numerous sized knives.

Lucius whispered to Titus, "*Look at what is coming. This is our lucky day.*"

The older highwayman said to his brother, "*Yes, I see. That carriage alone could be worth four or five aureus. I will stop the horse then you pull your sword on the two in front. Don't worry too much about that slave in the back.*"

32

When the carriage got close, Titus jumped out of hiding and grabbed Achilles by the reins slowing the horse to a stop. He let out a bloodcurdling scream as his brother Lucius ran to the cart and pulled his sword on the two riders up front. The bandit saw a ruby red stone hanging from a chain around Flavia's neck. He reached up and yanked it hard, breaking the chain. He showed it to his brother. *"Look at this, at least another aureus."*

The younger brother nodded then turned to his new captives. *"This is what we will do. If you give us all your belongings, and if you do not yell and scream, we will kill you quickly. If not, we will kill you very slowly."*

Flavia yelled at the two, *"Be gone latrones. I am the daughter of Valens Antonius. If you harm us, he will find you and kill you along with all of your families."*

Cornelius got out of the cart and stood next to the much smaller robber. When Lucius saw him, he said, *"Get back slave, or I will slice you into two."*

In a flash, Cornelius grabbed the right wrist of the robber. He twisted it counterclockwise breaking it with a snapping sound. The sword fell to the ground as Cornelius then picked up the little man and held him high above his head. He threw the screaming little man seven feet through the air towards a pile of rocks. The smaller robber's head landed on a sharp rock, ripping it open as blood escaped in huge gushes.

Flavia and Henry jumped out of the carriage. Flavia tried to get the sword on the ground. When she held it in her hand, she saw the other highwayman had a firm grip on Henry and held a knife at his throat.

As he saw his brother's blood stain the rocks red, he demanded, *"Give me all your money or I will kill him."*

Cornelius was still nearby. He quickly grabbed the right wrist of Titus and pulled the knife away from Henry's throat. The two large men struggled for control of the knife as Henry escaped and ran towards Flavia. Time seemed to stand still as the knife moved first toward Titus, then towards Cornelius.

Flavia saw a good-sized stone on the ground. She picked it up and yelled, *"Cornelius, Look out!"* She threw the stone at them.

Cornelius pulled his head back. He saw the stone go past his face and strike Titus right between the eyes. Then he felt a break in Titus's grip on the knife. That was all he needed to take control. He plunged the knife deep into the bandit's gut. Using all of his strength, he pulled the knife up through the bandit's abdomen. The sharp blade easily cut through Titus's ribs until it sliced his heart in two.

Cornelius dropped the gagging, soon-to-be-dead man to the ground. With his hands covered in blood, he noticed Flavia staring at him. He lowered his eyes to the ground and walked to the back of the carriage not saying a word.

"*He saved us Henrici,*" Flavia said, then repeated as if it didn't quite make sense to her. "*He saved us. If you did not bring him, we would be dead.*"

A badly shaken Henry said, "*I thought it would be a good idea. He is very big.*"

Flavia picked up her ruby necklace off the ground. "*Let's get out of here. We will arrive at the gates of Rome soon.*"

Henry was a little amazed at how quickly he got Achilles back on the road and out of the forest When the bright Roman sunshine appeared again, Flavia turned around and said to her slave, "*Cornelius, use the cloth that is over the food to clean your hands and thank you.*"

Henry said to her, "*You called him Cornelius, I thought slaves did not have names.*"

"*I know what I said Henrici. Slavery is a part of our Roman culture. It is a part of Roman life and I have to live with it. That does not mean I have to agree with it. Cornelius has taught me something.*"

"*You are a Roman and you do not like slavery? What did he teach you?*"

"*He taught me that slaves are human beings—just like you and like me. I now firmly believe that we would get a much better quality of work if we paid them a little.*"

Henry said, "*You are a progressive thinker.*"

"*What is this progressive thinker?*"

"*You are open to change. You think about the future and better ways to do things.*" Henry explained.

"*I don't know where that comes from. Last week I told my father this idea and all he did was laugh at me.*"

Henry didn't know how to respond to that, so all he did was stare straight ahead and keep Achilles moving on the road. Outside the gates of Rome, the three stopped near a large shady umbrella pine tree. Flavia spread out a large blanket in the shade, and the three sat down for lunch. Cornelius got an extra-large helping of the Roman feast.

——◆——

The old and unkempt Servian Wall that surrounded Rome was starting to crumble but it was still impressive. The brown stones rose thirty-one feet and were twelve inches thick, but there were large gaps where stones had broken off, creating holes in the barrier. The guard at the large iron gate checked Flavia's Roman citizenship then let the three travelers through. The gate they entered was to the southwest of Rome. Called the Porta Lavernalis, it took them into the Roman district of Aventinus.

*"We should have come in further to the north,"* Flavia told Henry. *"This district is really turning into slums."*

The rickety street was crowded. Merchants peddled their wares from person-to-person, while prostitutes openly walked in groups of two, trying to find a cheap score. The wood and stone apartments they drove by were starting to fall apart. There was a strong stench coming from the four-story dwellings, filling the streets with even more despair.

*"I know about this district, Flavia. I know in the future it will become better,"* Henry said.

*"I do not see how,"* Flavia looked around with disgust. *"This is not the Rome I want to be a part of."*

As they travelled downwind of Aventinus Hill, things started to look better. As they neared the center of the city, they could not miss the gigantic Circus Maximus on their right, the largest chariot arena in Rome. Here professional racers rode around the track with the best chariots guided by two to ten of the best horses. These professionals would do their best to cause their competitors to crash, oftentimes resulting in spectacularly gruesome death. The long brown-stoned structure was bustling with people of all types. A race was just about to start.

When Cornelius saw the spectacle he said with glee, *"I have never seen anything so wonderful."*

Flavia turned around and said to her slave, *"Yes Cornelius, it is. Caesar rebuilt it a few years ago. It can now hold 250, 000 people."*

Henry said, *"That is way too big. We do not have anything that big where I come from."*

They rode straight north past Palatium Hill and towards Capitoline Hill, the home of the Temple of Jupiter Optimus Maximus.

Flavia took a bag that Henry had brought and asked, *"What is in this bag Henrici? Is it more of that black powder?"*

"*Yes it is, and I made something with it. I only had time to make six of them, and I made three different kinds. I did not want to burn the barn down, so I made them by the sea.*"

Flavia reached in the bag and pulled out one of the odd packages Henry had made. The first one she had in her hand was a foot-long cone of tightly wrapped papyrus. At the top point of the cone was a small string. The next one she pulled out had an eight-inch wooden base. Out of the base was a four-inch tube of papyrus eighteen inches high. It had a closed top, and it also had a string. Then she pulled out the last one. It was a two-foot-tall tube made of wood. The hole in the middle that went down to the base was eight inches. It almost looked like a large mug. Inside the mug was a sphere made of papyrus. It fit perfectly into the mug. It also had a string.

"*Henrici, what is this stuff?*" Flavia asked with a smile.

"*We need them to get Caesar's attention.*"

"*But what are they?*"

"*They are called fireworks.*"

The temple felt new and was filled with life all around it. Worshipers and tourists alike were gathering to get a glimpse of the beautifully built temple. Henry couldn't help thinking that the four large columns that adorned the entrance seemed a little out of place, just like in the pictures Sherrie had showed him.

Henry found a yard nearby where they parked Achilles and the carriage. They had to walk about a half mile, and as they approached the Temple, the evening sun started to set. It was the second day of March, 710 years after the founding of the city, or 44 BC.

When they got to the white and light brown temple Flavia explained, "*We had a great general and brief dictator named Lucius Cornelius Sulla. He conquered Athens in Greece and looted the city. He destroyed their temple of Zeus and had those four columns sent back to Rome for our Temple of Jupiter Optimus Maximus.*"

"*This is great. It is very crowded here. We will get much attention,*" Henry said.

"*Let us do this, Henrici. I want to get to my friend's house.*"

"*Just a few more minutes, Flavia. It will be much more effective if it is dark.*"

When Henry felt it was dark enough, he took three of the fireworks out of the bag and placed them on a walkway near the temple. He tried to get everyone's attention with his nasally English-accented Latin, "*Listen one and all. I pay homage and sacrifice to the great Jupiter Optimus Maximus.*"

Nobody seemed to understand or at least pay attention.

Cornelius understood Henry's predicament. He stood beside him and said with his loud deep Latin voice, *"Listen one and all. I pay homage and sacrifice to the great Jupiter Optimus Maximus!"*

Henry had long before run out of matches. He warned, *"Stand back everyone, please stand back."*

As more people started to gather, he used one of his homemade matches and struck it against the stone walkway. The small instant flame had already amazed many of the onlookers. He lit the fuse of the cone-shaped pyrotechnic first. When the fire hit the powder, the sparkly flame started off slowly, but soon it filled the night with red, orange, and yellow fire climbing to fifteen feet above the cone.

People gasped. Some had looks of fright on their faces while others looked fascinated. Henry knelt over the second one. He lit it and moved away. The fire immediately flew out of the top of the papyrus tube. This time the flames were a beautiful red, turning to green and then to blue. At the same time, there was a loud, almost deafening whistle coming from the cone.

People covered their ears. Some started to panic and run. An old woman yelled, *"This is not a homage to Jupiter!"*

As Flavia looked on with amazement, Henry got to the third firework. He lit the fuse on the sphere inside the wooden mug like mortar. When the fuse finished its job, there was a loud pop. The ball shot straight up thirty feet into the air. When it reached its peak, it exploded into a brilliant red pinwheel, circling in the sky with red fire.

The same old woman yelled again, *"This is not a homage to Jupiter. This is a homage to Hades, the god of the underworld!"*

Some started to scream. People ran in every which direction. A full panic of terrified Romans were running everywhere.

Soon Henry was confronted. He was facing two Roman soldiers. The head soldier said, *"How can you disrespect the gods like that? Are you a servant of Hades?"* He raised his sword. *"I shall strike you down right now."*

Cornelius moved in front of Henry. *"Strike me down."* Cornelius crossed his arms and waited his for his bloody fate.

Flavia tried desperately to get past the almost stampeding crowd. She pushed and shoved and got in front of Cornelius just in time. She put her hand up to the Roman and stared at him right in the eye. *"Stop! I am the daughter of Vales Antonius. I am the suitor of Victor Rallis. Both men have fought battles with the great one. If you harm us, you will have to answer to Caesar himself!"*

The soldier looked at Flavia's fiery eyes. He lowered his sword and said, *"Come with me."*

He led them to a horse-driven cage on wheels. He opened the cage and motioned them to get inside. He locked it and led the horse and cage away.

As the three sat on the floor of their enclosure, Flavia said to Henry, *"Henrici, I really wanted to see my friend tonight. I am not pleased."*

*"Do you think we got his attention?"* Henry asked.

*"I do not know if we got Caesar's attention. I know we got somebody's."*

# IV

# The Summer Job

S HERRIE MELBOURNE WAS NOT A HAPPY YOUNG LADY AS SHE HURRIED across the university. She was so angry, in fact, she didn't even see the humor in the fashion statement a few of the young women students were trying to make. They were walking around campus with a colorful blanket wrapped around them, obviously naked underneath.

She was screaming to herself as she drove to her apartment on this Friday afternoon just outside of Duke University. She saw the infamous stop sign up ahead. Sherrie was so angry she wanted to hit the sign again or hit it the first time. She wasn't sure. She just wanted to hit it.

Sherrie resisted the temptation to take out the sign and made it to her third-floor apartment. Once inside she threw her backpack on the floor and then threw herself on her bed.

She yelled at the ceiling, "He cannot do that!"

Her smartphone beeped. It was a message from her friend Linda.

"Oh shit, I don't want to talk to her. I don't want to talk to anyone," she said as looked through her contacts. When she got to Henry's name, she thought, "What the hell, he listens to me."

The phone rang once, then she heard, "This is Henry Garfield, soon to be Doctor Garfield, at your service."

"Hello Henry, It's Sherrie. I am so angry."

"I am so sorry I made you so angry. All I did was send you back in time, so you would not hit the stop sign."

"No Henry, I'm not angry with you. I just need someone to vent to. Can I come over?"

The surprised Henry said, "I am very busy doing top-secret science experiments, but I always have time for you, Sherrie."

When she knocked on the door, Henry opened it, let her in, didn't say anything, and went back to his computer and started typing frantically. Sherrie entered the small workshop for the second time. There seemed to be even more computers, tablets, and phones this time. The coiled blue lightning was still hissing across the rods. She noticed that there were two black-sphered electromagnetic shockers connected to his computer.

Sherrie's eyes were still red from crying. "Thanks for seeing me Henry. I actually started to cry on the way over here, and I never cry. I'm having another bad day."

Henry spun in his chair to face her. "Oh, do you want to go back in time again?"

"No, I just need to talk. It is my damn, soon-to-be-senior advisor Doctor Pillar. He refuses to support my thesis idea. He suggested my thesis should be 'The agricultural challenges of the last years of the Roman Republic.'"

"That sounds boring, even to me. Caesar surviving the assassination attempt is much more interesting."

Sherrie eyes lit up, "Right? But here is the worst part, he said if I could spend a little of my spare time with him, he might, he said he *might* support my idea. Then he invited me to his place for a drink. I think he will support me if I sleep with him."

Henry looked a little mad, "That is very unethical and not right. You should report him."

"To who? Can we send him back in time? I know, we can send him to the Civil War era, the battle at Gettysburg. We can put him on the Confederate side."

"That would be unethical also. He would most probably be killed, and then you may not be here. You know, when you start messing with what happened in the past, the future is always affected."

Sherrie tried to laugh, "I'm just kidding Henry. I will think of something. How far can you go back in time with those shocker things?"

"The furthest back I've been is about two days. I wait until the cycle is complete. I make sure I don't change anything, and once I return to the present, everything is normal."

Sherrie looked deep in thought, "Hmm, could you go back 2,064 years?"

"I suppose so, but I would have no way to get back. The electromagnetic shocker stays in the present time."

Sherrie saw the two spheres on Henry's desk, "Hmm, you have two there. They are pretty small. Why don't you put one in your mouth? Then you would have it when you arrive in the past."

Henry looked intrigued, "I have never tried that experiment before. I know it takes back food in your stomach. One time, when I arrived in the past, I threw up."

Sherrie's eyes again lit up, "Let's try it Henry. We can try it now."

The blue lightning between the two coils suddenly stopped. A red light on the wall that looked like the light on top of a police car started blinking in unison with a loud honk. Henry got up from his computer and quickly opened a small closet. Inside were fourteen two-feet by one-foot battery cells all connected and surrounded by an aluminum bar. There were violent surges of blue lightning coming off the batteries, filling the closet with electricity and a hissing that sounded like a million snakes. Henry hit a switch off to the side and everything went dark, including every light in the workshop.

Sherrie said to the now invisible Henry, "What the hell happened? What is that?"

"These are my Tesla batteries. I use them to store my electricity. I get all my power from the earth's electromagnetic fields. Sometimes the earth gives me more power than I need, and it overloads."

"Can you fix it?"

"Yes, it will take me awhile. Come back tomorrow evening. I should have all repairs completed by that time. We can try the experiment then."

———◆———

On the short drive to her apartment, Sherrie's phone rang a tune. She wisely pulled over to the side of the road this time. It was her father.

"Hello Dad. I hope that marriage counseling is going well for you and Mom. Thirty-two years of marriage should not be flushed down the toilet."

"We are trying, Sherrie. I don't know if it's doing any good. It is costing me a fortune. Anyway, I called to invite you to a retirement party."

"Who's retiring?"

"It's your Uncle Willis. You know he spent forty years at that factory. He's now running the whole place. A lot of our extended family will be coming to the party."

"Hmm, Uncle Willis. Yes Dad. I'll be there. Do you think Uncle Willis would do me a favor? He always said I was his favorite niece."

"I'm sure he would. What's the favor?"

"Oh, I have this little friend that needs a summer job. He is a little financially strapped. You know how expensive it is to go to Duke."

"If anyone knows that, it's me. What can he do?"

"He can do a lot. I want him to learn everything about the production of their product."

"Okay, sweetheart. I will talk to Willis."

On the rest of the drive Sherrie felt much better. It was good therapy to talk to Henry and see his workshop almost explode. There was a chance her parents were going to work out whatever was wrong with their marriage, and as far as Doctor Ronald Pillar went, she had a plan. With the help of Uncle Willis, she could even stack the deck.

———◆———

Henry started his stopwatch. The two students stood in front of a gas station in Durham, North Carolina near Henry's workshop.

Henry told Sherrie, "I will come back to this time. When we get back to the workshop three or four minutes will have passed. I will come back to this moment in time."

"Shit Henry you are forgetting something," Sherrie said. "You will be naked. There are a lot of people here. Maybe we should go in the back."

When they convened at the deserted back of the gas station, Henry started the stopwatch again. He continued, "I will be transported to this point in time. If I have the other shocker, it will be already set."

Sherrie put a pair of Henry's shorts on the ground next to him, "That's just in case this doesn't work. Little Henrici, let's get back to the shop and do this."

They hurried back in the shop Henry said, "We are actually performing three experiments at once. I had a breakthrough last week."

He started to put the second shocker in his mouth when Sherrie stopped him. "Wait a minute Henry. Shouldn't you wrap it in plastic or something? You don't know where that shocker has been."

"I know exactly where it has been because I invented it."

Sherrie looked around the shop and saw a Ziplock bag full of yellow grapes. "You eat grapes, Henry?"

"Yes, they are very good for you, chock full of antioxidants and nutrients."

"I think they are good for making wine."

Sherrie dumped the grapes out of the bag and took the black shocker from Henry. She placed it in the bag and wrapped it tightly. She handed it back to Henry and said, "I don't want you to electrocute yourself."

"Very thoughtful, Sherrie." He put the electromagnetic shocker in his mouth.

Sherrie laughed at Henry who looked like a chipmunk and said loudly, "Let's go Henrici. It's showtime!"

Henry typed briefly into his computer then he held the first shocker tightly with both hands. Sherrie saw the screen count down, 4-3-2. The fizzing sound returned as Henry again glowed with a soft yellow flare that surrounded his entire person. The yellow flare soon changed into a brilliant glowing blue. In a gigantic flash he was gone.

Sherrie looked at his pile of clothes. She reached into it and found only one shocker.

Another hissing sound returned, then another huge burst. Henry reappeared in his birthday suit with a big smile on his face. "All three scientific experiments were 100 percent successful. My calculations were 100 percent correct. Sherrie, we have to return to the gas station now to retrieve the other electromagnetic shocker."

Sherrie grabbed Henry's clothes and hurled them at him, "You'd better put those on first. What are the other experiments Henry?"

"The second experiment was to use a GPS to program the second shocker to take me precisely one meter from the first shocker."

"That seemed to work, and the third?"

The young scientist gloated, "I knew the electromagnetic shocker could take me into the past. Now, it can also take me into the future. Sherrie, now I can successfully complete my master plan. All my top-secret work will have a purpose."

Sherry looked concerned that Henry would have a larger plan for his work. "You have made this amazing discovery Henry. You can travel through time. As a historian, it is my responsibility to make sure you don't fuck this up."

"How will I mess this up? I am a very capable astrophysicist."

"That's just it. An astrophysicist needs the advice of a capable historian like me. What is your master plan?"

"You have heard the theory that if you want to eliminate somebody, go back in time and kill their grandfather."

"Yes, I have heard that. With no grandfather the person you want to eliminate would never have been born."

"Precisely, I plan to go back in time and exterminate Adolf Hitler's grandfather. With no Hitler existing, this would stop World War II and the Holocaust from ever happening. Millions of lives would be saved.

Sherrie smiled, "That is an okay idea, Henry. But as a historian, I know if you really want to save lives, you have to go back much further than that."

Henry looked at her puzzled.

———◆———

Sherrie waited a week for the response from the factory. She knew her Uncle Willis would grant her request. With the college semester coming to an end shortly, it was time for her to put the next phase of *her* plan to work. Henry needed a summer job, and she knew just what he needed to do.

With Henry sitting on his cot, Sherrie sat at the desk in his workshop with a pen and paper and started asking Henry questions, "Henry, when is your birthday?"

"July twelfth, 2001," he answered.

"Okay, I have your address, this place. What work experience do you have?"

"Sherrie, you know the only work I do is top-secret scientific experiments."

"Yes, I know. I will put down free-lance entrepreneur."

Henry looked puzzled and adjusted his glasses. "Why are you asking me all these questions?"

"Didn't I tell you? You need to get a summer job. I am helping you fill out the job application. Now, do you have any references? Never mind, I'll be your reference."

"I do not want a summer job. That would be very disruptive to my work here."

"I am going to work there also for the summer." Sherrie gave Henry a sexy smile, "We could see each other every day."

The smile got to Henry. "So, what is this job and where?"

"My Uncle Willis runs the whole place. I want you to learn everything about the production of their products. We will have to move to Massachusetts for the summer and I already found us a place to stay. You can bring all the essentials for you to continue your experiments."

Henry almost fainted. "You mean we are going to live together?"

"I am sleeping in the bedroom, and Henry, you are sleeping on the couch."

"Okay, understood, but what am I going to do there?"

Sherrie reached for her backpack. "I almost forgot. I brought you some presents."

She pulled three large colorful books out of the pink backpack. They were titled, *Gunsmithing Rifles*, *Advanced Gunsmithing*, and *Gunsmithing Made Easy*. "I want you to study up for your new job."

Henry looked at the books. "I do not like guns very much. They make too much noise."

"Get used to it. Suppose the astrophysics job market dries up? You need a trade to fall back on."

Henry didn't look happy, but he didn't want to hurt Sherrie's feelings. "So, where are we going, and what is my job?"

Sherrie got up from the desk and took Henry's hand. She looked deep into his eyes, making sure her own blue ones sparkled. "You are going to work at the Smith and Wesson gun factory in Springfield, Massachusetts."

———◆———

Sherry went behind the large desk and gave her Uncle Willis a kiss on the cheek. "Hello Uncle. Thank you so much for giving us jobs for the summer. College is so expensive." She went in front of the desk and sat down next to Henry.

Willis was a tall six-foot-four. His slender build and trim gray hair made him look much younger than his sixty-five years.

"I usually do not do interviews. But since you are my favorite niece, I thought I would meet your friend."

"Thank you, Uncle. This is Henry Garfield."

Henry stood up and shook the much taller man's hand. "Hello sir," Henry sounded nervous, "I have never had a job before. I just do scientific experiments in my workshop."

Willis laughed as he looked at Henry's job application, "It says here that you are an astrophysicist? What is that?"

Henry explained, "Astrophysics is the branch of astronomy that employs the principles of physics and chemistry to ascertain the nature of the astronomical objects rather than their positions or motions in space."

"Okay, that was a mouthful. I'm not sure we need one of those here. Can you sweep the floors?"

Henry quickly answered, "Yes sir. You can ask Sherrie. I always keep my workshop neat and well-swept."

Sherrie intervened, "That is true Uncle, but Henry is super smart. He wants to learn how to make guns. He needs to learn rifling."

"That is very advanced for a beginner," Willis said. "Let's start him off in the testing department. He will have to take all our safety courses and learn how to properly discharge a weapon. Have you ever shot a gun before, Henry?"

"No sir, but I see them on TV sometimes. I like to watch *Law and Order*."

"This is not TV. We make real guns here. Safety and quality are our biggest priorities and responsibilities in my plant. Why do you have such a passion about making guns Henry?"

Henry replied, "I do not know. You will have to ask Sherrie that question."

Henry learned the trade fast. He had an amazing memory and could remember even the most complex and trite specifications of every weapon he worked with. Sherrie wanted Henry to learn something much simpler than the complex modern weapons the factory was now making. She got her uncle to let her borrow "the gun that won the west," a Model 73 Winchester repeating rifle from the Smith and Wesson Museum. The original prototype was designed by Smith and Wesson but was perfected by Oliver Winchester in 1873. Between the years of 1873 and 1919 the Winchester company manufactured 720,000 of the rifles.

Sherrie also had the specifications. "Can you make one of these, Henry?"

Their apartment in Springfield was a small one bedroom with a kitchenette and a living area. There were a few tables with computers, tablets, and phones scattered around them. The main computer had four electromagnetic shockers connected to it. The lumpy couch in the living area served as Henry's bed, which was fine with him. He could work late into the evening, uninterrupted.

Henry sat on the couch and looked at the old classic rifle. "I think so. This is an old Model 1873. Do you have the specifications?"

Sherrie handed him a stack of papers. "Why don't you memorize the specs." Sherrie smiled, "You never know you might need one and one more thing."

Henry was trying to understand what she was up to. "Okay, one more thing?"

Sherrie switched to the classic Latin language. *"I think we should speak more Latin to each other from now on."*

Henry said in the same Latin, *"Why? What is the point?"*

*"I will have to pass my Latin final next semester. Don't you want to help me? And your Latin is a little rough. You need to get better. You never know when you might need it."*

—◆—

They were now two months into their internships at the munitions factory. Sherrie worked in the accounting department while Henry held the job of plant rover. Whenever a part of the factory was running behind, they sent Henry to help out. This way he quickly learned almost every part of the manufacturing process. He even got to work in the ammunitions department.

Henry was pounding on his computer keyboard when Sherrie entered the apartment.

*"I gave my Uncle our two weeks' notice. We don't need to work here anymore."*

Henry seemed happy; he answered also in Latin, *"That is very good Sherrie. I am so anxious to get back to my studies and my secret workshop."*

*"We are not going back to Duke just yet."*

Sherrie put a printed itinerary in front of Henry. It was for two passengers, Sherrie Melbourne and Henry Garfield. The flight was from Logan International to Leonardo da Vinci Airport.

*"We are going to Rome?"* Henry tried his luck. *"Is this a romantic getaway?"*

*"No, Henry. I have some work to do, and so do you."*

*"My work is in my workshop."* Henry tried his luck again, *"I know you do not love me, but I have been helping you so much lately. Do you think we could have sex together?"*

Sherrie went up to Henry and lightly kissed him on the cheek. She said in English, "You are wrong, Henrici. I do love you a little. I am just not ready for that yet."

"Then why can't we have sex?"

"I'll tell you what, if you do well on this mission, we will have sex when you get back."

"This mission? You mean to kill Hitler's grandfather?"

47

"No Henry. I have a much better plan. I told you I am a historian Henrici. I know what I am doing here. My plan is far superior to this grandfather-killing shit."

Henry looked a little uneasy. "So what is your plan Sherrie?"

"I will brief you on the plane to Rome. Remember Henry, if you do well with my plan, I promise you that we will make love all night long."

# V

# The Departure

THE LONG FLIGHT FROM BOSTON WAS BEGINNING ITS INITIAL DESCENT into Leonardo Da Vinci International in Rome. Sherry had booked a red-eye with Alitalia Airlines and splurged on wide, business-class seats so they could get some sleep. The luxurious service on the Italian Airline made the over eight-hour flight go quickly.

But as the plane descended closer to the earth the flight got bumpy. This made Henry get very nervous and very tense. He was holding both arm rests with all his might and sounded like something out of a Dr. Seuss book: "I do not like this. I do not like this at all, Sherrie."

"Holy shit Henry, you can travel through time, but you're scared of a little turbulence?"

"This is not a little turbulence," Henry looked out of the window. "It looks like we are going through a thunderstorm." The plane made two quick violent dips downward then slowly came back up.

Sherrie laughed out loud and threw her arms up, like she was on a roller coaster, "Why are you so scared Henrici? This is fun."

Henry's eyes looked even wider through his thick lensed glasses. "No, not fun. Not fun."

Soon, the plane dipped below the storm, the turbulence calmed down, and Henry finally let go of the armrest. He looked at Sherrie and asked, a little sheepishly, "Okay, why am I going to Italy?"

"Well, I suppose now that you are wide awake and we're almost there, I should tell you about your top-secret mission. Did you bring the shockers? How many do you have now?"

"Yes, they are in my suitcase. I have six total and they are all fully charged."

"Do you have all the computer stuff you need?"

"I do."

The binging sound of a text went off on Sherrie's phone. She looked at it, then got disgusted. With a shocked angry expression, she said, "Look at this Henry."

There was a picture of a man with no shirt and a revealing black thong was barely covering his privates. Below a caption read "I showed you mine, now you show me yours".

"That is my so-called senior adviser Doctor Pillar. What a creep."

"Save it Sherrie, save it." Henry told her.

She looked at her phone again, "The text is gone now."

Henry explained, "He has an app that lets the text last just a few seconds. If you don't save it or respond, it deletes. It is called the Anthony Wiener app. Sick people can send inappropriate texts with less chance of getting caught. Now you have no proof."

"I don't need proof. That creep gives me more resolve to prove that I am right. Henry, you have to do this favor for me."

Henry looked a little nervous, "Okay, what do I have to do?"

"Henry, do you really think you have what it takes to kill Hitler's grandfather? You are scared of a little turbulence. You can't even drive a car and you are going to kill a man?"

"I will do it for the good of mankind and for the good of science," Henry said

"With my plan, you don't have to kill anybody. I want you to go back in time to the year 44 BC a couple of months before the Ides of March. I want you to stop the assassination of Gaius Julius Caesar. That is stage one of two stages of my plan."

Henry got serious. "I greatly advise we not to do this. This will change history in ways that I cannot control. The results of this could be a disaster."

"You're full of shit Henry. It is same thing as going back to kill Hitler's god-damn grandfather."

"That is not true. I only want to go back under two hundred years. You want me to go back over two thousand."

"Henrici, you know I am a historian, and it doesn't matter if you go back two hundred or two thousand years. Once you change the timeline of history, the present as we know it will cease. So why not go back two thousand and handle the Hitler issue non-violently? You know how strongly I believe if Caesar survived the assassination, the world would be a better place."

"I know you believe that Sherrie, but changing history that far back could result in a cataclysmic catastrophe. I will not do it."

"It's the same difference. Why don't you see that Henrici? If you go back to kill Hitler's grandfather, the same catastrophe could happen. In both cases it won't."

Sherrie felt she was getting nowhere with Henry. She tried a different approach. With a fake tear falling down her cheek, she said with a sad voice, "I know why you don't want to do this. You don't want to have sex with me because I am so ugly."

"No Sherrie, you are the most beautiful girl I have ever known."

She smiled a little. "You really think so?" Sherrie slowly rubbed her legs, "So you will consider it?"

Henry looked at her long slender legs. "Okay, I will consider it."

"You don't have much time to consider this. I just rented us the seaside villa for three days."

The Italian pilot made a smooth, near-perfect landing. As the plane rapidly slowed to a stop, Henry asked, "So, what is stage two of this plan?"

Sherrie turned to him and sternly said in Latin, "*I want you to show Caesar how to make a Model 1873 Winchester repeating rifle.*"

———◆———

The large villa Sherrie rented was a fifteen-minute walk from the Beach of the Pines. About forty miles south of Rome, the Lido Dei Pini was a Mediterranean beach near the coastal town of Anzio, Italy. The beautiful villa was more than adequate: three bedrooms, two baths, a full kitchen and an office where Henry could do his computer work. There was a huge front yard filled with lush green grass and pine trees surrounding the luxurious property.

The two Americans arrived in the morning, and they both needed a nap after the all-night long flight. Sherrie woke up around two in the afternoon. She went into the office to find Henry banging away at his laptop computer. One of the shockers was connected to it.

"Good afternoon Henry; did you sleep well?"

"Yes, I napped for eighteen minutes. Very refreshing."

"I know you don't sleep much. Let's walk to the beach. It is beautiful outside."

Sherrie was wearing a red and yellow flowered bikini over which she wore a see-through beach cover up. Her red flip flops and full dark glasses made her look exotic.

Henry looked at her and tried to stay calm. "Ah, um, so, so, um, that is very good. I have to do one more top-secret experiment before the big one. We can do it there."

"I hope you brought a bathing suit."

"I did not. I brought some shorts. I will go change."

The short walk was accompanied by a perfect seventy-two-degree afternoon. The sidewalk they followed was adorned by thick trunked pine trees and light green grass. They could see the dark blue Mediterranean Sea in the view ahead.

Henry looked out of place in this quaint Italian town, even more so walking next to the tall, blond, and gorgeous Sherrie. It didn't help that Henry's shirt pockets were jammed full of pencils, pens, and various small scientific instruments. He was carrying his laptop and one of the black sphered shockers.

Sherrie asked, "What do you have to try? Haven't you tried this enough already?"

"I have never gone back this far before. I need more data. Also, I have made a few modifications to the shockers. I need to test them out before we try the big one."

Henry showed Sherrie the shocker. It now had a small blinking red light. "When the light blinks red that means it is activated. When the blinking light turns green, that means it will go off in twenty seconds."

"Cool, when do we try the big one?"

"By my best estimations, I should have all the data I need by 9:01 PM tomorrow."

Sherrie saw a dumpster behind a seafood restaurant. "Let's go behind that and do your experiment."

When behind the barrier, Henry sat on the ground and started typing into his computer. "In two minutes, the light should turn green. I will go back in time six minutes."

They were soon surprised by a short Italian man with a black unkept beard. His black curly hair looked even more disheveled. He pointed a large hunting knife at the couple.

He spoke broken English with a thick Italian accent, "Give me alla you money. Give me thata computer or I cutta you good."

He took Sherrie's beach bag, then he grabbed the computer away from Henry.

Sherrie looked down at the little Italian. "Take our money if to have to, but please don't take the computer."

The electromagnetic shocker was dangling from a USB cord. He took it in his hand. "What this thing? New tech toy? What it does?"

The shocker was now blinking green. A hissing sound surrounded him as he lit up like a first yellow then blue Christmas tree. The hairy bandit's eyes got wider than two quarters, and then in a loud flash he was gone. All that was left was his clothes, the knife, the computer, and the shocker.

"Where did he go, Henry?" Sherrie asked.

"He went to wherever he was six minutes ago."

"Henry why did he go back in time without being scanned?"

"That is one of the new modifications. Scanning is no longer necessary."

"Bullshit. You just wanted to see me naked that night."

Henry didn't answer. He just plopped down in front of his computer and started typing frantically.

Sherrie told him, "Not now Henry, Let's get out of here; let's get to the beach. He might come back. There should be lots of people at the beach."

When they got to the beautiful shore, Sherrie took two large beach towels out of her bag and laid them out in the sand. She took off her cover up and laid on her back to worship the bright Italian sun. Henry tried his best not to stare at his beautiful friend.

Soon she pointed and barked, "Holy crap Henry. Look at that!"

Even Henry laughed as they saw two Italian police officers escorting the hairy, naked Italian man off the Beach of the Pines.

"That is a great way to get a rid of bandits; send them into the past. I would still like to try it on creepy Doctor Pillar." Then Sherrie said, "Take your shirt off, Henry. Get some sun, you always look so pale."

"I cannot do that. I burn exceedingly easy. I have to be in good shape when I go back to ancient Rome. I must go now; I have too much to prepare."

"Okay Henry. I will see you in a couple of hours. I'll pick up something at that seafood place on the way back. What do you want to eat?"

Henry answered, "Just get me any kind of basic nutrition. Oh yes, and I am going to need a sample of your blood."

Sherrie put down a large order of Italian fish and chips in front of Henry.

He told her, "I do prefer grilled fish over the deep-fried variety. I do not want to be fat for my long journey."

Sherrie laughed, "Henry, you are so petite, you could eat ten orders of that and not put on a pound."

Sherry had some grilled swordfish de Sicily and a side of raw broccoli. While they ate, she saw a syringe wrapped in plastic next to Henry's computer. "What is that for? Are you going to give yourself a vaccination or something?"

"No that is for you. I told you I need a few drops of your blood."

"My blood Henry? What the hell for?"

Henry explained, "It is a backup plan. If something is a little different..."

"Wait a minute Henry, I thought you were going to set the return shocker to come back one hour after you leave. I will be here waiting for you."

"The blood is for a backup. Once I have your DNA in the computer, the return shocker can use the internet to find you if you are in a different location than the departure point. If the shocker cannot find you, I will return to the departure point."

"Okay Henry," Sherrie looked away as Henry stuck the needle into a vein in her wrist. "Ouch Henry! That hurt. You have a terrible bedside manner. Now, let's go over the plan once again."

Henry recited, "According to my new calculations, I will need two shockers to generate the power to get me to 44 BC. Once I arrive at my destination, I will need eight months twenty-six days and five hours to complete the two stages of my mission. I will program the return shocker to go dormant for this duration. Once the time has passed, I will have five minutes and twenty seconds to get a hold of the return shocker. I will then arrive one hour after my departure from this time."

"Yes, you said you would be ready at 9:01 tomorrow night."

"I believe my estimation was correct."

Sherrie smiled and gave Henry a little hug. "Okay little Henrici, tomorrow at 9:01, it's showtime!"

———◆———

It was past twelve midnight and Sherrie could not sleep. She got up and put on a bathrobe over her nightie. She went towards the office and could hear Henry busily typing data into his computer.

She whispered, "Henry, shouldn't you try to get some sleep?"

He turned around. "I never sleep much, and I am very nervous about our big day tomorrow."

"Yes, me too. I really thank you for helping me with this."

"It is for the good of science." Henry tried his luck again. "I know you said when I get back, but I thought maybe we could have sex now, before I go."

"No, Henry. I will keep my promise and I need you strong for tomorrow. I can be very exhausting in bed."

Henry looked disappointed. "For just once in my life, I want to be exhausted like that someday."

———◆———

Sherrie felt the green grass in the large backyard behind the villa was the perfect place to launch Henry into the past. "Henry, two thousand years ago, this area was a place the rich aristocratic Ancient Romans would build very elaborate villas. They used them to get away from the clutter and nonstop hustle and bustle of Rome."

"So, I should look for a villa?"

"Yes, and remember, the first thing you need to do is find some clothes. I'm not sure how they will react to a naked little guy running around."

Henry sat on the grass and typed for a while. Then he abruptly stood up and showed Sherrie a thin pack of stick matches wrapped in plastic. "These might come in handy. The first self-striking match was not invented until 1805 AD. The Ancient Romans will be fascinated by them." He took them and put them down the back of his pants. Then he made a long grimacing sound.

Sherrie looked a little shocked. "Henry, did you just cram those matches up your ass?"

"Yes, there is no room in my mouth with the shocker in there. It is time to start the shocker. It is 9:00 PM."

Henry typed a little more, then he put the plastic-wrapped shocker in his mouth.

Sherrie kissed him on the forehead and said, "I will see you in one hour, Henrici. Good luck."

Henry tried to say, "I will see you in eight months twenty-six days and five hours."

Suddenly Sherrie started waving her arms. "Wait Henry. Stop! Stop! Abort the mission."

Henry quickly typed some more shutting down the shockers. He took the return shocker out of his mouth. "What is the matter? I thought you wanted to do this?"

Sherrie let out a large sigh. "Henry don't you think that if you need two shockers to get there, you will need two shockers to get back?"

"I think I overlooked that data."

Henry awkwardly ran back to the villa to retrieve another electromagnetic sphere. When he returned, he briefly programed it then said, "If you had not stopped me, I would be stuck in the past forever."

"That shows I do have feelings for you."

"Yes, I do believe you. Where are we going to put the other one?"

"We can't put it up your ass with those matches in there. Let me help you."

Sherrie took a shocker and put it over the left side of his mouth, stretching out his cheek as far as it would go. She repeated this on the right side. She laughed when she saw him. With the puffy cheeks he looked like a nerdy blowfish with glasses.

Sherrie said loudly, "Come on Henry. It's showtime!"

Henry typed, then tried his best to muffle out "It's showtime," in response.

The hissing sound was twice as loud. The glowing light around Henry grew twice as bright. When the brilliant yellow flame surrounding Henry turned to a vibrant blue, Sherrie had no choice but to stand back. The flash and warm pulse of air that accompanied Henry's disappearance was so strong it knocked Sherrie to the ground.

Henry was gone and in less than a split second everything around her changed. This was not good news for Sherrie. She would have to stay in Rome for much longer than she anticipated.

# The Master of the Horse

T HEY RODE SLOWLY THROUGH THE DARKNESS OF ROME. THE BUMPY horse driven cage felt like it had one of its wheels shaped like a square, knocking Henry, Flavia, and Cornelius back and forth and up and down like they were in a popcorn machine.

This aggravated Flavia even more. Again, she said to Henry, *"This is not good Henrici. I wanted to see my friend tonight."*

Henry didn't know what to say so he didn't answer her. Instead, to take his mind off of how uncomfortable he was, he thought of Sherrie and one of the more memorable history lessons a person could ever receive.

———◆———

It was a Friday night in Springfield, Massachusetts. Sherrie and Henry had just finished their second week of work at the Smith and Wesson gun factory. Henry remained busy typing away at his laptop, when Sherrie sat down on his couch/bed in their little apartment. She was holding a glass of red wine.

"Do you want some wine Henry? It is Friday night," Sherrie asked.

"I am not old enough to drink wine, and neither are you Sherrie," he said.

"Do you think I give a shit about that? If I want a glass of wine on a Friday, then I am having a glass of wine on a Friday."

"You should try to obey the laws of our society, Sherrie."

"Shut the fuck up Henry. This wine is making me want to talk. Stop typing and listen to me. You know I am passionate about the life of Julius Caesar."

"I know that. You have told me many times."

She asked Henry, "Did you take much history at Duke?"

"Very little. Not much was required to become an astrophysicist."

"Then as a historian, it is my responsibility to teach you. You never know when you might need it."

Henry stopped typing and listened. He looked at his beautiful friend and tried to pay attention to what she said, and not what she looked like.

Sherrie put on her reading glasses, to make her look more professor-like, and said, "I am going to tell you some wonderful history. I am going to tell you how Julius Caesar crossed the Rubicon River."

Sherrie stood up in front of Henry, like she was teaching a class. "Listen and learn, Henry. On January 10, 49 BC (705 AUC since the founding of Rome), Julius Caesar had his Thirteenth Legion assembled just north of the banks of the Rubicon River. The shallow river was the boundary that separated the northern province of Cisalpine Gaul to the north-east and Italy Proper (controlled by Rome) to the south. Caesar had ruled Gaul (which is current-day France) as Governor and as General of the province's army. Earlier on January first of that same year, his term of Governorship expired, and he was ordered by the worthless Roman Senate to disband his army and return to Rome."

"Did he do that?" Henry asked.

"Shit no just listen to me Henry. Outside of Italy, a Roman General had the right of imperium, or the right to lead. Caesar had this right over the province of Gaul and his powerful Thirteenth Legion. If the head of an army came into Italy with their army intact, his power of imperium was revoked by law. If Caesar crossed the Rubicon River still ruling his army, this was a most serious capital crime. The Senate would consider not only Caesar but his entire Legion as traitors and outlaws. In fact, they would consider this a declaration of war on the Roman Senate. The punishment for this was certain death, or in this case, civil war. Caesar had communicated to the Senate that his army, and the Army of General Pompey the Great should be disbanded at the same time. The great General Pompey was now a serious rival to Caesar, and he had most of the conservative Senators safely packed in his back pocket. The Senate again disagreed and ordered Caesar to immediately disband his army and return to Rome."

"Caesar should do what the Senate demands. That would stop any unnecessary wars and unnecessary deaths." Henry commented.

"Caesar was not as gutless as you Henry. As he paused at the bank of the Rubicon, Caesar did have an agonizing decision to make. Crossing the river would no doubt start a vicious civil war.

"Now, listen to this Henry." She pointed her finger at him as if to make a bold statement, "A fable suggests that a young male god came down from the heavens playing a lute. He then grabbed one of the soldier's trumpets and played it loudly as he slowly crossed the river. Caesar ordered his legion to advance, yelling the Latin phrase ālea iacta est (the die has been thrown). Caesar broke the Senate's precious law and crossed into northern Italy, basically ending the four-hundred and sixty-year-old Roman Republic forever. Caesar steered his Legion towards the city of Rome."

---

When Flavia, Cornelius, and Henry were arrested the Roman soldiers had confiscated all their belongings including the fireworks and Henry's homemade matches. After the bumpy ride outside the gates of Rome in the horse-driven cage, the Roman guard opened it and let the three out. He guided them to another cage, a small jail cell with thick iron bars as a door. The three entered and sat down on a wooden bench as he closed the bars.

Henry spoke first in his English-accented Latin, *"Do you think they are going to kill us, Flavia?"*

*"No, Henrici. If they wanted to kill us, we would be dead already."*

They did not have to wait in the jail for long. They heard a low strong voice say, *"Let them out of there. She is the daughter of Valens Antonius. I fought under him during the first Gallic war back in 696. A fine man and commander he is."*

Centurion Maximus now commanded over two-hundred legionaries. He wore shiny iron amour and a helmet made of a half circle of six-inch spiny red hairs set in a half circle silver base. The proud Roman Centurion was just as tall as Cornelius. He held the tube-shaped firework in his hand.

Flavia was the first of the newly freed prisoners to speak, *"Thank you sir Centurion. My father will learn of your chivalry."*

The bold commander said, *"Yes, you are Flavia Antonius. You know your little friend caused quite a commotion with these things. What are they?"*

*"They are fireworks,"* Henry said in his nasally voice. *"I made them to get Julius Caesar's attention. We have to warn him about his imminent assassination."*

Flavia tried to defend Henry. *"I am so sorry Centurion. Little Henrici has such a wild imagination sometimes."*

*"And who is the big guy? He doesn't say much."*

Henry spoke up again, *"He doesn't say much because he is a slave. He is trained to be silent. His name is Cornelius."*

The Centurion laughed a little, "*So, we have the beautiful Flavia Antonius, the little man-child Henrici, and Cornelius the slave. Do I have that right?*"

"*Yes sir. That is very correct,*" Henry said.

"*Okay, little man-boy, you seem to be the talkative one. What does this firework do?*"

"*I must show you. Do you have my matches?*"

"*Matches?*" Maximus asked

Flavia interrupted, "*They are little sticks. I call them magic sticks.*"

A soldier brought over a handful of Henrys' crude-looking homemade matches. Henry took one then he took the tube from the Centurion. He knelt down and put the firework on the cobblestone floor. He struck the match then lit the fuse of the pyrotechnic.

Henry warned, "*Stand back. It will not hurt you unless you touch it. Then you will be burned.*"

The fire again flew out of the top of the papyrus tube. The flames were a beautiful red, turning to green, then turning to blue. The deafening loud whistling sound did not faze the Centurion at all. He just showed a wide smile as he watched the show.

When the firework phased out, he said, "*Little Henrici, that was quite a spectacle.*"

"*Thank you, Sir Centurion. I want to show it to Caesar. Then I can warn him.*"

The Centurion said, "*I want you all to sleep in the barracks here tonight. I cannot get you an audience with the great one, but I am very close to someone who might be able to help. Be gone now.*"

As the three took the short walk to the barracks, Flavia said to Henry, "*I don't believe this Henrici. You just might pull this crazy scheme off.*"

"*Yes, this is my mission. This is why I am here. Saving Caesar is stage one of my mission.*"

"*What is stage two Henrici?*"

The Centurion gave the three a private room with a few cots and a guard outside, mostly to protect Flavia from the hundreds of sex-starved soldiers stationed at the barracks.

Henry lay down on his cot to sleep and he heard Flavia say, "*This is much more exciting than visiting my friend. Like I said, you might pull this crazy scheme off. Goodnight Henrici.*"

As he listened to the voice of an angel, he thought of the voice of another angel, and Henry couldn't help but long for her.

———◆———

Sherrie got up from the couch and went into the kitchenette to pour herself another glass of wine.

When she returned to the couch, Henry was staring at her through his thick lensed glasses, he said, "That was a very good history lesson. I loved the way you told it."

Sherrie took a sip of her wine and said, "There is more. Did you ever see that movie called *Cleopatra*, Henry?"

"No."

She went on, "Elizabeth Taylor was beautiful in the role, but the movie itself is an over five-hour shit-filled train wreck. They even got some of the facts wrong. Let me tell you how some of this really happened."

Henry could not wait for the story to come off of Sherrie's tongue.

This time Sherrie sat next to Henry to continue her lesson, "After he crossed the river, Julius Caesar had little trouble conquering village after village on his way to Rome. Most of these victories were without a fight. The villages voluntarily gave up, and their soldiers were more than happy to join Caesar's Legion."

"I bet you they were scared of him."

"No Henry, they loved and admired him. They were happy to support him. Now, down south in Rome, Pompey the Great and the conservative members of the Senate were surprised and astonished by the rapid advancement of Caesar's Thirteenth Legion. They hastily tried to put together two legions and even though they had twice as many men than Caesar had, they had little confidence that these new troops would have a chance against the battle-tested mighty Thirteenth Legion. Pompey, with his loyal troops, and the conservative Senators turned into gutless cowards. They turned yellow and fled southeast to the Port of Brindisi, where they used every available ship to escape to Greece. Pompey's plan was to reinforce his troops in Greece with the hope of defeating Caesar in the near future.

When Caesar got to Rome, he was designated as Dictator, he named Marcus Aemilius Lepidus as Prefect of Rome, and he left the rest of Italy under the General Mark Antony as a tribune. He quickly left Rome and headed south in his pursuit of Pompey. When he broke through a small force trying to block his entrance into the harbor, Pompey had already escaped."

"With winter approaching and with no ships to chase his rival, Caesar then went on a campaign west into Spain. He defeated two of Pompey's lieutenants in a massacre that only lasted an astonishing twenty-seven days."

"This Thirteenth Legion must have been very powerful," Henry said.

"No shit Sherlock. Now, Caesar spent the next year chasing Pompey around the Mediterranean Sea with victory after victory. During the battle of Pharsalus in central Greece, Caesar was greatly outnumbered. He outsmarted Pompey and easily defeated the Roman Republic's army. Caesar lost only two-hundred-seventy men while Pompey lost over six thousand. Pompey was forced to flee in one ship. He left for Mytilene to reunite with his wife Cornelia and his children along with some of his top men and servants that he had left on the island some months before. From there he headed for Alexandria, Egypt.

When the advisers of the Egyptian boy king, Ptolemy XIII, heard of Pompey's soon-to-be arrival in Alexandria, they were really pissed off. The Egyptians were heavily indebted to Rome. Pompey would expect favors, but Pompey was now defeated. They wanted to impress the new leader of Rome, Julius Caesar. They advised the boy king to okay a dastardly plan."

"What was this plan?"

"The Egyptians lied like a bunch of pathological scumbags. When Pompey's ship arrived, the visitors were told the water was too shallow to come close to shore. The Egyptians would bring a small fishing boat to bring Pompey to land. Something did not feel right to Pompey's wife, Cornelia, and to his entire entourage. They advised him not to enter. Pompey did not listen. He got in the small boat with just a couple of servants.

The Egyptians had three men in the boat. One of them was the head of the Egyptian Army, Septimius. He was a man that had actually served under Pompey at one time. On the short ride to Egypt, Pompey was said to have asked, "Am I mistaken, or were you not once my fellow soldier?" His question was met by a somber silence.

When the boat got close to land, Septimius got Pompey to stand up. He looked him in the eye, then he stuck his sharp dagger deep into Pompey's stomach, twisting it as hard as he could the deeper it went. The two other assassins attacked Pompey from behind using their daggers to help finish the job. Pompey tried to cover his face with his toga to try cover his humiliation.

Septimius then took his sword and with one mighty swing he sliced off Pompey's head. They threw his body into the ocean and they took the severed head and wrapped it in a tunic. All this was done in full view of Pompey's poor wife, children, and his entourage. There was nothing they could do, except watch in horror."

"This is the very most unfortunate situation for Pompey's family," Henry said.

"Just listen to me Henry, or I'm going to flunk your ass. Caesar arrived in Alexandria a few days later hoping to end the civil war once and for all. Pompey had married Caesar's first daughter Julia (who later died during childbirth), so he was his former son in law, he was his respected political rival, and his almost equal on the battlefield. Caesar knew why they called him Pompey the Great.

When Caesar met with the Egyptian welcoming committee, they hoped to gain favor with the new Dictator of Rome. They showed him the severed head and gave him Pompey's signet ring. Caesar was appalled by this. He wept loudly at the sight of his fellow Roman murdered so barbarically. The Egyptians were expecting to gain favor with Caesar, but those dumb fucks got the exact opposite effect. He started his revenge by having all the assassins and conspirators executed.

There was also a civil war going on in Egypt. The army of the boy king, Ptolemy XIII, was going against the forces of Ptolemy's sister Cleopatra VII. Caesar took up residence in the very large royal palace in Alexandria as he tried to create a truce between the two warring siblings. The boy Ptolemy was playing with half a deck. He had a room temperature type IQ and felt that Caesar's plan was favoring his sister. He furiously went to the streets and incited a riot to get these Roman foreigners out of Egypt. His mob and soldiers trapped Caesar inside the palace for weeks. He was totally cut off from the outside world."

"So. what did he do?" Henry asked with anticipation.

"You are not going to believe this shit, Henry. One night a very small boat showed up at a dock near the palace. A Persian merchant got out, carrying a carpet bag full of carpets. He entered the palace and found Caesar and presented him with the contents of the bag. He unrolled the carpet out in front of him. Inside, rolling out of the carpet on the floor in front of him was the beautiful Queen of Egypt, Cleopatra. Loving the theatrics of her entrance, Caesar immediately took to the side of Cleopatra. When reinforcements finally did arrive from Rome, Caesar stayed in Egypt and helped her defeat Cleopatra's brother. He then endorsed her as the new Pharaoh of all of Egypt.

To solidify the relationship, Caesar had a love affair with the beautiful Queen. That must have been so hot, Henry. It was a relationship that would last for five years. He never admitted it, but she said that she gave him a son. She named their son Caesarion (which literally means, little Caesar). Rumor has it that Cleopatra visited Rome often. Rumor also has it that she was staying at Caesar's villa just outside of Rome on March 15, 44 BC, on the Ides of March."

---

Flavia, Henry, and Cornelius were in a large dining room filled with hungry soldiers. The Centurion had agreed to give them a meal while they waited. They were breakfasting on dry rye bread with a little roasted ox on the side.

Flavia asked her slave, *"Do you have a mother, Cornelius?"*

*"I must have a mother because I am here,"* Cornelius answered.

*"I know you have a mother. I did not think you got here by coming down from the heavens. Do you know where your mother is?"*

*"I do not know. I think my mother's name was Albina, but I am not sure. She was a slave, so I am a slave."*

Henry said, *"I do not have a mother either. She died when I was six years old. She had brain cancer."*

Flavia sounded sympathetic, *"I am so sorry to hear that Henrici. But at least you had a mother for a few years. Cornelius barely remembers his mother. I am starting to hate slavery more and more."*

The big bearded slave spoke up, *"I do not like slavery either."*

*"Cornelius what would you do if you were free?"* Flavia asked.

The big man let out a rare smile, *"I would love to get a little piece of land and start my own farm. Then I would find a good wife and start a family."*

Flavia smiled back, *"Do you see that Henrici? Cornelius has the same wants and desires as any other Roman. I know I should be quiet when I say this around here, but slavery is wrong."*

Henry said, *"Then you should ask your father to let him go free."*

*"He would never do that. He would rather kill him then let him go free."*

Henry tried to convince her, *"You can tell him how Cornelius saved your life. That might soften his heart."*

*"Henrici, Cornelius, I will try this when we get back. I will tell my father how Cornelius bravely saved us from evil bandits."*

Soon the Centurion was by their side in his full armored and cloth uniform. He said to the trio, *"Come with me quickly. He agreed to see you for five minutes only."*

They quickly walked down a long white corridor swarming with men all trying to get to some important place fast. Some were dressed in military uniforms, some had on colorful togas and tunics. Flavia was the only woman they saw in the building. They entered a huge office. In the white-draped room there were three small desks. Each desk had a man in a white tunic writing on papyrus sheets. In the back was a much larger desk that was elevated three feet off the floor. Whoever sat at that desk was in charge.

Soon a man entered from a side door. He wore a white toga with a purple cloak over his left shoulder. He looked to be in his thirties, he had brown curly hair. His skin was healthily tanned, and his muscles were well developed. Flavia gasped when she saw him.

He said to them, *"Okay quickly. My Centurion says you are the beautiful Flavia Antonius, the little man child Henrici, and Cornelius the slave. I did battle with your father Lady Antonius. That is why I let you in. Show me what you have."*

Henry got down on one knee, placed the cone shaped firework on the floor away from the desks, then he found a rough spot on the marble floor and ignited a match.

*"Wait a minute,"* the leader said. He walked down the three marbled steps toward Henry. *"How did you make fire so easily? Give me one of those, let me try it."*

The tall Roman struck another match at the same spot. It ignited again. He smiled at the little inferno. *"Can you make more of these?"*

Henry said, *"Yes, but first light the fuse, I mean light the wick and then stand back."*

The distinguished Roman did that. When the fire hit the cone, the sparkly flame started off slowly but soon it filled the office with red, orange, and yellow fire climbing to fifteen feet above the cone.

Their host was standing a little too close. He quickly backed away from the show and enjoyed it with a glow in his eye. *"Okay you have my attention. What do you want from me?"*

Henry said with a little arrogance in his voice, *"I have an important warning for Julius Caesar. I need to know who you are before I say anymore."*

Flavia started poking Henry in the side with her elbow. *"Hen–ri–ci!"* Then she tried to apologize, *"I am so sorry sir, little Henrici is from a land far away. He has not been in Rome for very long. He is from a place called America."*

Their host laughed at the little man, *"I have been all over the world. I have never heard of a place called America."*

*"It is across the sea of Atlas,"* Henry said.

*"Nobody has ever been across the Sea of Atlas. Okay little man, I will tell you who I am. I am second in command around here. I am the Master of the Horse. My name is Mark Antony."*

# VII

# The Prophecy

"*I HAD THAT DREAM AGAIN LAST NIGHT, JULIUS,*" CALPURNIA SAID.
She was twenty-five years younger than her husband, but she was almost the same height. She was soft spoken but strong willed, and her hair was a long golden brown. Her soft eyes welled with tears. "*Please do not leave the villa. The dream is so real. Your statue is soaking the floor with your flowing blood.*"

The fifty-five-year-old Dictator looked tired and stressed. His once full head of hair was now half gone. He hugged Calpurnia and said, "*What kind of man would I be perceived to my public if I listened to the dreams of women?*"

She warned him again, "*The dreams are so real. Besides Mark Antony and your doctors all agree with me. There is a foul smell stinking the entire heart of Rome.*"

Caesar looked out a window at the morning sun shimmering off the water of the Tiber. His mansion was located outside the gates of Rome on the banks of the river. New, modern, and spacious, the villa was made exactly to Caesar's specifications.

He told her, "*You know, Antony tried to put a crown on my head. People started chanting, King! King! King! I told them I am not a king, I am Caesar. Tomorrow on the Ides of March, the Senate wants to bestow on me more honors. I should oblige them.*"

A female servant entered and said, "*Mark Antony requests a word with you, sir.*"

"*Show him in.*"

The handsome Mark Antony entered the parlor and greeted the married couple.

Calpurnia said to him, "*He is not listening to me, Antony. He insists on meeting with the Senate tomorrow.*"

*"He is stubborn and proud, but Caesar I met someone last week that might change your mind. A strange little man that we could squash like a bug in a second. He knows things that seem to be unknown."*

The Dictator said to his fellow consul, *"What does this little man know? Is he having dreams like Calpurnia?"*

*"He is not having dreams. He claims to know precisely what will happen tomorrow. You have to hear it for yourself, and by the way his companion is the daughter of Valens Antonius."*

Caesar looked sternly at Mark Antony. *"Valens Antonius? Yes, a fine fellow and soldier. He retired into private life."*

Antony said, *"You may remember he had a daughter, an intelligent, vibrant young woman of twenty-one years."*

Caesar remained stone-faced for a moment, then relented. *"Okay Antony, I will meet your little man briefly. Bring him by tonight and bring the daughter of Antonius also. I would like to meet her. What is her name? Flavia no?"*

*"Yes, she is Lady Flavia Antonius."*

As Antony left them, Calpurnia asked Caesar, *"Can you answer me one more thing? Why does that woman have to stay here? There must be thousands of places in Rome that can accommodate her."*

*"Ah, Calpurnia, we must give her all our respect. Not only is she queen of Macedonia, but she is Pharaoh of all of Egypt."*

Calpurnia looked away. *"I may speak softly of mouth, but I am not naive."*

———◆———

Henry was working with papyrus at his workbench in the Antonius barn. He had made a tight tube about three inches tall and one-half inch in diameter. He put it on a flat circle of papyrus that was an inch in diameter. He had spent the previous day looking for small rocks that were the perfect size and cone shape. Cornelius was then in charge of sanding the rocks down, so the bottom of the cone was flat. Henry filled the tubes with black powder and inserted a thin string for a fuse. The shaved rock fit perfectly on top of the thin tube. He had made four of these so far.

His work was interrupted by the sound of galloping horses. Henry looked outside. There were five horses that stopped at the front door of the villa. Four of them carried Roman soldiers, the fifth carried the same Centurion Maximus that they had met before. With Valens Antonius away in Rome, Flavia was there to greet them. They talked briefly, then Flavia pointed towards the barn. She ran towards Henry. *"Henrici! Hook up Achilles to the carriage. We have to go right away."*

Henry ran to the horse. *"Why? What do those soldiers want?"*

*"I will tell you on the way. Bring the latest fireworks and some matches."*

Henry got a small basket and put the fireworks and matches inside. He also put the four raw prototypes he was working on along with a rolled-up sheet of papyrus.

Achilles was running at a slow gallop on the way to Rome, but he was still barely keeping up with their five-horse escort. Flavia was holding the reins, trying to keep up. Henry was sitting to her right. They even brought Cornelius along in the back.

She told Henry, *"I don't know how you did this, but we pulled it off."*

*"Where are we going?"*

Flavia yelled, *"We pulled it off! We have an appointment tonight with Caesar himself!"*

*"I knew Mark Antony would not let us down and it is just in time. Tomorrow is March fifteenth, the Ides of March,"* Henry said with a gleam in his eye.

They arrived at a six-foot stone wall surrounding a large villa. They approached a wooden gate, which one of six soldier guards out front opened for them. The carriage and the Centurion entered the complex. A tall, wide, arched and darkly stained oak double door seemed to be the entrance to the palace. There were two more solders on each side of the archway. Flavia guided the carriage near the door.

The Centurion got off his horse and told them, *"Come with haste. We are right on time. Your slave will have to wait here."*

Once inside, they were greeted by a servant who motioned them to follow him through a large parlor. There were marble floors, marble columns, marble everywhere. The bright polished marble furniture was covered with soft and colorful cushions. To the left was a ten-foot-tall waterfall. The water spilled down large brown volcanic rocks until it met a small creek that ran through the middle of the enormous room. They walked over it on an arched wooden bridge. On the other side were smoothly polished statues of famous Romans from days gone by. The walls were covered with beautiful mosaics of red, blue and brown all depicting Roman armies victorious in battle.

*"Do you see this, Henrici? Do they have anything this magnificent in America?"* Flavia asked.

Henry replied, *"Only at Caesar's Palace in Las Vegas."*

*"Henrici, don't say anything odd like that in Caesar's presence,"* Flavia warned him.

Soon they came to a door that led to a square outdoor patio all surrounded by more palace. There were exotic flowers and plants of every shape and color all about the open-air atrium. They could see two men in the distance enjoying the cool March evening. Julius Caesar was sitting on what looked like a throne. Mark Antony was sitting to his right in a similar chair.

Flavia gasped and almost cried when she saw them. She approached them slowly got down on one knee and said, *"Hail Caesar. Hail Antony."*

Henry knelt and nasally said the same thing.

*"Get up children. I am not a god. I am not a king. I am Caesar."*

Mark Antony saw the firework and matches in Henry's basket. He got up and said, *"Watch this, Caesar. You will not believe it. Henrici, let me light it."*

Henry said, *"It is a good thing we are in the open air. This one will go high into the sky. After you light it, put it into this mortar, and stand back."*

Mark Antony took the firework and a match out of the basket. He showed the match to Caesar. *"Look at this Consular, instant fire."*

He struck the match against the red and white brick paver floor. He showed him the igniting flame.

*"Impressive,"* Caesar said.

Antony lit the fuse on the pyrotechnic sphere and put it in the mortar and stood slightly back. There was a glow of anticipation in his eyes. Soon, there was another loud pop. The ball again went straight up thirty feet into the air. When it reached its peak, it exploded this time to a brilliant yellow and orange pinwheel, circling the sky and turning the dimly lit patio into sudden daylight.

Caesar stood up and smiled wide. He applauded the show and said, *"Amazing little man. Can you make more? Antony, can we use this as a weapon?"*

Outside in front of the mansion, one of the guards moved near Cornelius to try to taunt the big slave. He saw the fiery light coming out of the center of the complex. He got scared and alarmed when he saw the show. He said to his partner, *"Come and see this. It looks like a message from Hades himself."*

The other guard said, *"What should we do? Should we go in there? Are Caesar and Antony in danger?"*

*"In danger by that little man and a woman?"*

Cornelius laughed loudly. In his deep ultra-bass voice, he said, *"There is no danger. That is just my little friend Henrici, pretending to be Vulcan, the god of fire."*

Henry turned to Caesar, *"Sir Caesar, I can make this into a weapon, but I can also make you a weapon that will make you invincible on the battlefield. Your enemies will tremble in fear and run and try to hide, but they will not be able to. They will give up at the sight of one of your Legions. I can make you this weapon."*

Henry pulled out the sheet of papyrus unrolled it and gave it to Caesar. On it was a crude drawing of a bullet with the word *"LEAD"* pointing at the bullet and the word *"BRASS"* pointing at the cartridge case. There was also a crude drawing of a rifle. It was a Model 1873 Winchester repeating rife.

Caesar looked at the papyrus, *"What do you make of this, Antony? It looks like some kind of fancy club."*

Antony looked and asked, *"How is this club going to make our enemies succumb with such fear?"*

*"It is not a club."* Henry tried to explain, *"It is called a gun or a rifle. That small drawing is called a bullet. Inside the brass section is some of the black powder, the same powder I used to make the fire show. When the bullet is placed inside the rifle, a trigger is pushed causing a small hammer to strike the flat end of the bullet. This will cause the black powder to explode sending the lead projectile out through this tube or barrel. It will be going so fast you cannot even see it. It will easily go through a man, killing him at once. Let me give you a rather simple demonstration. I did not have access to any brass or lead."*

Henry took his papyrus bullets out of the basket. He placed it on a marble table and lit the fuse with one of his matches. The fizzing explosion tore the papyrus cartridge case to pieces. It still sent the cone-shaped rock towards the sky until it disappeared into the darkness.

Both Romans looked very impressed. Antony asked, *"How far will it go? How far away can it kill?"*

Henry answered, *"I believe a well-trained soldier could kill his target from one and a half stades (300 yards)."*

Caesar asked, *"If I give you my blessing, how long will it take to make this rifle?"*

*"According to my best estimations, it will take twelve weeks to create a prototype. I will need one of your best iron carbon steel blacksmiths, another one that is skilled in brass, and one that is skilled in lead. I will also need your most skilled wood worker."*

"*Lady Antonius, you have been very quiet, what do you make of all this? Where did you find this little man?*" Caesar asked.

Flavia answered firmly, "*I found him behind a big tree. He was naked and I had to give him my brother's tunic.*" Both men lightly laughed and she continued, "*I can tell you this, Henrici knows things nobody else knows. Ever since I met him, he says his mission here in Rome is to warn you, to save you from an assassination attempt on the Ides of March.*"

Antony said, "*Yes little man, tell Caesar the story you told me last week. Tell it in the same precise detail.*"

Henry stood before Rome's Dictator for Life. He tried to keep his voice steady and not shaky, "*What will happen is led by three traitorous Senate conspirators and with the help of over sixty other Senators of the Roman Republic.*

"*Tomorrow, on the Ides of March, you have an appointment to meet with the Senate at Pompey's Great Assembly Hall at the hour of eight in the morning. You will be undecided about keeping this appointment, and you will be late. Decimus Brutus, your friend and apprentice will be sent to retrieve you. He will tell you the Senate has been waiting for hours and convinces you to attend.*

"*When you arrive at the Assembly Hall, Senator Lucius Tillius Cimber presents you with a petition to recall his exiled brother. More Senators will crowd around you, faking support for the petition. Cimber will savagely pull down your toga as you say, 'What is this violence?' Then, you will see that sixty-three Senators all have daggers hidden under their togas.*

"*They pull the knives out, and the stabbing begins. You fight the first stabbing dagger off but soon you are hit in the shoulder. You try to fight them off, but there are too many. You give up when you see one of the assassins is your beloved almost son and protege. You will then try to pull your toga over your head to hide your humiliation and pain. You will be stabbed twenty-three times, finally dying under the statue of Pompey the Great. You die of massive blood loss.*"

Caesar sat there in total silence. The look on his face was one of disbelief and shock. He said to the two young informers, "*Be gone you two. Centurion take them away. I have much to discuss with Mark Antony.*"

When they were gone, Caesar said to Antony, "*Keep them in a very comfortable custody. What do you make of all that? Is the Senate capable of such treachery?*"

"*It can't be ignored, and Caesar, I do have a plan.*"

"*Tell me.*"

VII • The Prophecy

*"Be late for the assembly. If Decimus Brutus arrives at your villa to convince you to attend, there is a good chance this is a coup and an assassination attempt. Come with Brutus to the hall. I will be waiting there with fifty good men. We will enter first and search the Senators."*

*"You know we cannot do that. In the history of the Republic, there has never been a soldier allowed anywhere near a session of the Senate."*

Antony said, *"So we break a little rule. If there are no daggers, we apologize to cover our misdeed. If there are daggers, we have some big decisions to make."*

Caesar stood up and slowly paced to the other side of the yard. When he got back to Antony, with his hand on his chin he said, *"Very well. Let it be so. I have grown very impatient with this Senate."*

Antony agreed, *"This is good. You will sleep well tonight Julius. What about that other thing, the weapon, the rifle?"*

*"We let him try to construct it. What have we got to lose, a few blacksmiths and a wood worker? But first we have to survive. I have to survive the Ides of March."*

# VIII

# The Ides of March

THE SENATE WAS GROWING INCREASINGLY IMPATIENT WITH EVERY minute that passed. Where was Caesar? Most of the over-four-hundred Senators in the Assembly Hall were not aware of the conspiracy. Only sixty-three were, and they were the most aggravated and tense. They were getting more irked with each minute that Caesar was tardy.

The Theater of Pompey was constructed in 55 BC by Pompey Magnus the Great. Long before his murder in Alexandria Egypt, he used the spoils of war from his many very profitable conquests and the looting of his enemies to finance the three-plus-story structure. The stage was lined with large columned porticos in front of the bench-like seats that could accommodate thousands of Roman citizens. Behind the theater was a huge garden with polished statues, magnificent waterfalls, and flowing brooks. Out front of the complex was the Assembly Hall with an enclosed meeting place where civic leaders could practice their politics. This is where the Senate would convene on that fateful day to bestow their "honors" on Julius Caesar.

The Senators Cassius Longinus, his brother-in-law Marcus Brutus, and Decimus Brutus were the most impatient of all. This operation was these three Senators' master plan. They were trying to protect Rome from the tyranny of kings, and they knew that Caesar grew more powerful by the day. They had to stop this for the all the people of Rome, and more importantly to save their precious Roman Republic. Caesar *had* to attend the session.

The three met in a corner of the hall and whispered quietly.

*"It has been over two hours and no Caesar,"* Cassius Longinus said.

Marcus Brutus whispered, *"It is said he will not attend. His wife has dreams of his death. His doctors warn him about his health. Even Mark Antony advises him not to attend."*

Cassius turned to the other Brutus, *"He trusts you, Decimus. Take your lictors and ride to his residence. Use all the power you have to convince him to attend."*

Julius Caesar met his friend Decimus at the front door of his villa. The dictator did not invite the senator in. Decimus Brutus and his two guards got off their horse, and the senator greeted the dictator with a pound on his chest and a vibrant "Hail Caesar."

Caesar did all he could to stop the tear that was threatening to leave his eye. He said to him, *"Decimus, I will not be able to attend the Senate's session. My wife prophesizes a bad scene for me, and my doctors advise against it."*

Decimus tried to change his mind, *"Great Caesar, are you going to listen to the emotions of women and the advice from the mouths of fools? The Senate waits for hours. They wait to give you all you deserve."*

As the tear dropped from his right eye, Caesar said, *"Go now Decimus. I will attend shortly, please let the Senate know I will receive their gifts."*

When they left Caesar went back inside his home. The now weeping man was distraught by the betrayal of his confidant and friend, Decimus. The little man child Henrici had to be right in his prediction. If he was right about Decimus' visit to convince him to attend, he had to be right about the daggers. Caesar quickly wrote a message. He summoned his youngest and fastest courier and he told him to deliver this message with all the utmost urgency to Mark Antony.

The night before Henry and Cornelius had to sleep inside the back of the carriage. Flavia slept inside a nice Roman apartment in the Palatium District of Rome while visiting her friend Cassia. Henry was fidgety and nervous all night. He didn't even get his usual four hours of sleep. Now, it was after one in the afternoon when Flavia came out of the apartment complex with a basket of fruit and nuts.

She asked Henry, *"So Henrici, what time is this murder attempt supposed to happen today?"*

*"No one really knows the exact time. Most historians, I mean most sorceresses, believe it happens a little after noon."*

Cornelius took a bite out of a fresh apple and said, *"Maybe we should go to the Theater of Pompey to help Caesar. It would be an honor to fight to my death to defend such a great man."*

*"I do not think so Cornelius. How can we help against sixty-three armed Senators? Only Mark Antony and his best soldiers can save him,"* Henry said.

Flavia broke in, *"I think Cornelius is right. We are just sitting here, and I have already seen enough of Cassia. If nothing happens, nothing happens. If it does, at least we will be there to show support for Caesar and Antony. I will be right back; I need to get my things."*

As she left, Cornelius said to Henry, *"Lady Antonius is a very brave young girl."*

Henry said in his nerdy Latin, *"Yes Cornelius, she certainly is. She certainly is."*

---

Mark Antony was in his full General's armor and weaponry. When he saw Caesar's courier approaching, he ordered one of his legionaries to retrieve the message. The Master of the Horse had already stationed twenty of his best Legionnaires and Centurions at the front of the Assembly Hall entrance and twenty more in the back. Ten of his men stayed with him. Antony read the note and as he looked up, he saw Decimus Brutus and his two lictors approaching the blocked front entrance on horseback. Like Caesar, he also realized that the little Henrici man was right, just as the note said. He motioned Decimus to come near.

When the lictor guards saw Antony and his men, they turned and quickly rode away. Decimus did not. He trotted towards the Consul of Rome.

Antony looked up at him and yelled, *"Decimus Brutus, what treachery have you brought to Rome today?"*

Decimus got off his horse and looked at Antony. *"Treachery? There is no treachery. I am here for the assembly of the Senate. I am slightly late, Antony. A little too much wine last night, I am afraid."*

Antony ordered his men, *"Hold him here."* He marched to the front entrance of the Assembly Hall. By now his reinforcements had arrived. Mark Antony ordered his men to completely surround the entire theater. They were to evacuate all the civilians while no Senators were allowed to leave.

The conspiring Senators had a backup plan. If their plot was discovered, they were to turn their razor-sharp daggers on themselves. Mark Antony was about to do something never imagined in the four-hundred-and-sixty-year history of the Roman Republic. He was going to enter a session of the Senate with one hundred of his best Centurions and Legionaries. Mark Antony entered first.

When the army entered the marble and white stoned hall, they were first met with gasps and groans. This soon turned into deafening howls of boos and screeches. Over four hundred Senators stood up shaking their fists at the entourage of marching soldiers, most of them shouting obscenities and accusations of treason. Antony marched on. He saw Cassius Longinus and Marcus Brutus near Caesar's throne-like chair, right below a large statue of Pompey the Great. They were pointing and yelling at him. He pulled his sword.

As he got closer to the statue, several senators near the front of the hall pulled daggers from under their togas. They plunged the knives into their bellies, gagging in pain and painting the new, clean hall with pints of their splattered blood. A few more Senators tried to attack the heavily armored soldiers. The soldiers quickly struck down their adversaries. Some were easily beheaded leaving more blood gushing out of their necks.

Antony stood in front of Cassius and Brutus, he yelled as loud as he could, *"What foul deceit have you bestowed on the people of Rome?"*

Marcus Brutus yelled back, *"He is a tyrant! For the good of all of Rome he must be killed!"*

Marcus pulled his dagger. He pointed it towards his stomach and prepared himself for suicide. Antony swung his long sword knocking the dagger out of his hand. He told him firmly, *"You, Brutus will answer to Caesar!"*

The commander ordered every Senator searched. The unarmed dignitaries were placed on the right side of Hall. The disarmed Senators were segregated on the left side near the statue of Pompey. So far, they counted twenty-one dead by suicide, sixteen dead by soldier. That left twenty-five conspirators still alive. Antony had them sit near Caesar's throne.

The tall Centurion Maximus came through the entrance. He marched to Mark Antony and pounded his chest then said, *"Sir Antony, he is here."*

---

Flavia returned to the carriage with her bag. She got in and took the reins. She lightly tugged them and slowly started Achilleas on a slow trot. Soon a woman with a small child in hand and a baby in arms came running past them. Her face was panicked.

*"What is wrong, lady? Why such haste?"* Flavia inquired.

She stopped and said, *"Run and lock yourselves in your houses. Something terrible has happened at the theater. The Theater of Pompey is totally surrounded by hundreds of soldiers. There was an important session of the Senate going on inside. People are fleeing by the thousands. I heard there was an entire Legion within view."*

Flavia stood up. She took her whip and cracked it onto the back of Achilles sending him into a fast gallop. She cracked it again and again until the healthy horse was running at full speed. The carriage bounced wildly up and down making Henry and Cornelius hang on for dear life.

Henry yelled at her, *"She said we should lock ourselves in our houses."*

*"No Henrici, we are not going to hide in houses. We are going to do what Cornelius suggested. We are going to help Sir Caesar and Sir Antony."*

Flavia kept cracking the whip. She guided the speeding carriage towards the Theater of Pompey.

---

Antony met Caesar near the front entrance of the theater. They greeted, then the Master of the Horse told the Dictator of Rome, *"It looks like that little Henrici is some kind of a wizard. Not only was he right about Decimus, but the daggers also. We have twenty-one conspirators killed by suicide, sixteen dead when they attacked my soldiers. That leaves twenty-five still alive. A total of sixty-two. The little man was only off by one."*

The two friends looked at each other, then they looked at Decimus about one hundred yards away. Antony waved at his men to bring him to them.

When he arrived, Caesar told Decimus, *"I have shed enough tears over your treasonous betrayal."*

Decimus looked at him coldly, *"You are the traitor and tyrant. You must die."*

He took his dagger from under his toga and tried to stab it at Caesar. Antony and the soldiers had little time to react. Mark Antony drew his sword and swung it wildly at the Senator, cutting off his right arm just above his bicep. Decimus screamed in pain as he looked down on the ground at his severed arm still holding its dagger. A soldier gave him a cloth to cover the bleeding wound.

Caesar said, *"Take him inside with the others."* He gave Antony his orders then said, *"I will be inside in fifteen minutes."*

---

It tookPut Flavia quite a while to convince the guard at the Gate of Sanqualis to let them through. There was a huge crowd of people trying to get into the city. They were the only ones trying to get out. Flavia's arguing with the guard was good for Achilles. The exhausted horse needed a rest.

Once outside the walls of Rome, Flavia again stood tall in the carriage. She cracked her whip again to get Achilles going at full speed. They passed mobs of frightened Romans trying to get back into the city. There was a feeling of repugnance in the air as panicked people were fleeing as fast as they could go. Mobs of villains were growing around them, hoping for a good day of looting and pillaging. All of them were heading for the anarchy of the city of Rome.

The galloping horse brought them to about one-hundred meters from the complex. There they were stopped by a soldier.

Henry pointed, *"Look! It is Caesar."*

They arrived just in time to see Caesar walk into the Assembly hall.

*"He is taking soldiers into the Assembly Hall where the Senate convenes. That has never been done before,"* Flavia told them.

Henry said with excitement, *"He is alive. By all my best estimations, he should have been killed by now."*

As Caesar entered the hall there were a few gasps and cries but soon his supporters rose and yelled "Hail Caesar," giving him a high-hand salute. As he slowly walked towards the statue of Pompey, more and more of the innocent Senators rose. The sound of a loud "Hail Caesar!" Echoed through the Hall.

Antony had followed Caesar's orders to near perfection. The remaining twenty-six treasonous senators—six rows in all—were kneeling in front of Caesar's throne. To the right of each kneeling man was either a Centurion or a high-ranking soldier. On the floor to their left were their daggers, the daggers that were meant for Caesar.

The three main conspirators knelt in the front row. When he saw his revered son, Marcus Brutus, as a main planner of this treachery, Caesar briefly fought a tear. His heart then hardened quickly when he looked at all the men. Some were his rivals, but many were his dear friends.

He said to Marcus Brutus in Latin, *"Et tu, Brute?"* (Also, you Brutus?) Brutus looked away.

Caesar went on, *"I will give you traitors a chance to die with dignity. You can die like a Roman. Soon your foul treason will be known throughout all the provinces of Rome. Use your most obscene knives to finish the day."*

Several Senators took the daggers and plunged them into their bellies. They were screaming boisterously has they watched their life-giving liquid spill out of them onto the floor of the hall.

Cassius Longinus tried to talk above the screams, *"Great Caesar, I grow old for my age. I was not a man of this bad deed. I ask you spare to me for I am innocent."*

Caesar waved his hand at the Centurion that was guarding him. The Centurion drew his sword and promptly sliced the head of Cassius off his body. His body stayed upright for a few seconds with blood popping out of his neck like a red fountain before it fell to the ground.

Decimus Brutus did not have the strength to take the knife. The one-armed Senator did not have to. It wasn't long before he fell to the floor, dying of massive blood loss.

Marcus Brutus took his dagger, and as he looked up at Caesar, he said, *"You are a tyrant! But a noble tyrant indeed."* He stuck the blade into his belly twisting it in a circular motion as he dug it deeper. The blood shot far out of his abdomen until the splatter almost hit Caesar.

As he fell to the ground, he looked at Caesar in the eye. His dying words came out, *"Forgive me father. Please forgive me for this treachery."* He closed his eyes and waited for his journey to the afterlife.

Three Senators tried to attack the guards with their knives. Their heads were quickly removed from their bodies. Of all the now dead twenty-six, most died with the dignity of a Roman that Caesar gave them.

Julius Caesar with his white toga with a bright blue cape left the death scene and marched toward the exit. With Mark Antony to his right the two consuls marched in step past the surviving Senators. This time they all stood up. The screams and cries of death were replaced by loud chants of "Hail Caesar!"

———◆———

The Roman Forum was packed with tens of thousands of people. Romans, slaves, tourists, dignitaries, all were all trying to get a glimpse of what was the biggest spectacle in Roman history. The crowd was already in a hysterical frenzy. Flavia and Henry used the large Cornelius to squeeze them through the manic crowd. As they got closer, they could see a magnificent white stage twelve feet above ground. There were twelve columns holding up a polished wooden patio ceiling. In the center was a throne, made of marble and gold; the tall back was laced with gigantic stones of ruby, emerald, and amethyst.

As they squeezed closer, Henry had to yell his loudest to get Flavia to hear him, *"Flavia! What day is it?"*

Flavia yelled back, *"Henrici, you already asked me that!"*

Soon, they were close enough to see him. Caesar wore a white toga laced with solid golden trim and gemstones of every color. He had on a purple cape with symbols of Rome embroidered into it with golden lace. On his head was a golden wreath shaped like leaves of many different trees.

The hordes of people gasped and moaned as he told them of the murderous plot of the dead sixty-three Senators. Soon, they could see Mark Antony dressed just as gloriously, in white, red, and gold.

They started to cheer when Caesar promised all retired legionaries a large plot of land and a generous pension plan. They cheered louder when he told them he would give all of the mass fortunes of the treasonous Senators back to the citizens of Rome.

The three were now only a few rows of people back. They could feel tons of energy coming from the crowd and the charismatic man on stage. The adrenalin was rushing through their bodies.

Henry yelled again, *"What day is it?"*

Now Caesar stood in front of his people. He raised his arms into the air and said, *"I am Guise Julies Caesar."* He sat down on the throne.

The people got even more hysterical. The yelling and chanting was so loud eardrums were being pierced. Solders had to be brought out on stage to keep the frenzied crowd from rushing the stage. Mark Antony, standing to Caesar's right, took the golden wreath off of his head. He replaced it with a silver crown. This time Caesar did not remove it.

The almost mobbing crowd started to chant King in Latin. *Rey! Rey! Rey!* Rang out in glorious unison.

Through the chants of King! Henry asked Flavia again.

Caesar stood up from the throne. He said as loud as he could, *"I am Augustus Caesar! I am Augustus, the first Emperor of all of Rome."*

People were jumping up and down while yelling and screaming, including Henry, Flavia, and Cornelius. Flavia cupped her hands around Henry's ear and yelled the answer to his question.

Henry got even more excited. He yelled at her, *"We did it, Flavia! We did it!"* He raised his hands high in the air. *"The Ides of March has passed! Caesar is alive!"*

Henry looked at the frenzied crowd, every person going crazy with a passion never seen before in Roman history. He saw the proud group of Roman royalty embracing each other on stage.

Henry had a sudden realization. With a concerned look, he borrowed a word from Sherrie Melbourne's vocabulary and said loudly in English, "What the fuck did I just do?"

The date was March sixteenth, 710 years after the founding of the city (44 BC). Henry had successfully completed stage one of his mission. Now he had to begin working on stage two.

# IX

# The Weapon Most Foul

Again, Henry heard the thunderous sound of charging horses. And again, the high-riding Centurion Maximus sent Flavia running towards the family barn. Henry was in there working on the papyrus specifications of his theoretical contraption.

Flavia told him, *"Help me get Achilles hooked up to the carriage. They are taking us to the Aventinus District. That is where we went through the first time, I took you to Rome."*

*"I remember it well,"* Henry said. *"Not the cleanest place. It was kind of slummy."*

*"Is slummy a word, Henrici? They are taking us there because that is where the shop is. Bring Cornelius also."*

*"What shop?"*

*"The blacksmith's shop. That is where you are going to make your invincible weapon."*

Henry brought all his papyrus specifications along with a ten-pound bag of gunpowder. As he got into the carriage, Henry thought about giving Flavia a clue as to how he could predict the future because he had so much doubt on whether or not he could succeed with this task of building this weapon. When he thought about his would-be girlfriend, he decided against this. He would create this weapon for Sherrie Melbourne.

The shop was located on the west side of Aventine Hill. Behind the broken-down brown- stoned building was a large yard that was stopped by a wall in the back. The wall in the back was the unkept and crumbling Servian Wall that surrounded Rome. The four walked in the front door of the dark building with the Centurion leading the way. There were three men standing inside waiting for them.

Maximus told the three men in his proud Roman voice, *"Blacksmiths, this is Henrici."* The tall man looked at little Henry, *"Do you have family name, or is it just Henrici?"*

Henry replied, *"My last name is Garfield."*

Flavia looked puzzled, *"Garfield? What kind of name is Garfield?"*

*"Sherrie says I am named after a cartoon cat."*

The Centurion asked, *"What's a cartoon cat? You are a cat? Never mind. Blacksmiths, this is Henrici Garfield. By the orders of the great Caesar and the great Mark Antony, you are to follow his orders and guidance precisely."*

Henry looked through the dimly lit shop. There were three red brick forges filled with charcoal. Each one had a red brick chimney that went up through the ceiling. There were sturdy benches with black iron anvils about the shop along with the tools a blacksmith would need. Hammers, chisels, metal tongs of many shapes and sizes were scattered about. It was cool in the shop now. The hot charcoal forges had not yet been ignited.

The Centurion saw the drawings of the weapon that were on Henry's papyrus sheets. *"Let me see that Henrici. Let me see this weapon most foul."*

Henry handed Maximus the diagram of the finished product. *"These drawings are not to scale. It will be about this big."* Henry stuck out his hands till they were about forty-nine inches apart.

The Centurion looked at the drawing, *"What is this? It looks like some kind of fancy club."*

Flavia said, *"It is not a club. It is called a gunclub or a rifleclub. It will be very powerful, when Henrici makes it."*

*"Very well, the great Caesar is on a military campaign to the east to conquer the Parthenian Empire. He wishes to return early to see this club. He will return briefly in 197 days for a demonstration."*

Henry said in English, "No pressure. No pressure at all."

*"What is that gibberish you speak, Henrici?"* Maximus said.

Flavia said with confidence, *"That gibberish is the language of America, and I promise you, Henrici will have it finished in 196 days."*

The Centurion left them, and Henry, Flavia, and Cornelius met the team of workers.

The leader was Tiberius, a man that had spent more than half a lifetime in front of one thousand-degree forges. His hair and eyebrows were gone, and his hands were permanently black from the iron ore, which had also branded his broken fingernails. He looked like a body builder, with a huge chest and enormous arms, built over many years of constantly hammering and molding his specialty, carbon steel.

Next, they met Lucius and his is specialty was brass and lead. The much smaller man still had his hair, and he didn't need the muscles of Tiberius. The Roman forges could not get hot enough to melt Tiberius' iron, but it was sufficient for lead and brass (copper combined with tin). Lucius could melt his metals and pour them into molds to create pots, pans, tools, or whatever was required.

The last man looked out of place in the blacksmith shop. He was young and looked more refined. His clothes were clean, and he had the appearance of an artist. Atticus was the woodworker Henry had requested. The handsome blond man seemed bored, that is until he saw Flavia.

Atticus hurried to his work bench and returned with a wooden figurine. It was beautiful, a darkly stained and shiny lion. The legs, the face, the mane—each part showed exceptional detail. The eyes looked like small red rubies.

He said to Flavia, *"Please accept this little gift my lady, for I have never seen one as beautiful as you."*

Flavia barked at him, *"Stop this talk. I have a suitor that rides with Caesar himself. If he learns of this, he will surely kill you."*

Young Atticus backed off. Flavia grabbed the wonderful wooden statue and said, *"I will take this though."*

She took Henry's hand and led him outside the shop, *"Okay Henrici, it is time for me to go. Father has agreed to let Cornelius help you on this project."*

*"You mean I have to live here?"*

*"Did you see the cots in the back yard? I believe there is a facility out in the back also."*

*"Will you come and visit me?"*

*"Yes, Henrici, I will come once a week or so to see how you are doing. I want to see this gunclub. I will be staying in Rome with Cassia until father can escort me home."*

Flavia kissed Henry on the cheek, then got in the carriage. She waved goodbye and let Achilles take her to her friend's apartment.

They started the project early the next morning. Henry tried to tell his team how important precise measurements were. He had translated all his length measurement from the metric system's centimeters and millimeters into Ancient Roman system of digitus and uncias. He was surprised that they already seemed to understand that. They had rulers that went down to the sixteenth of a uncia.

Henry had a papyrus spec sheet for every component that went into his custom Model 1873 Winchester. In his design, he tried to use as much brass as possible. Since it could be melted, they could use molds to create the parts needed. He also knew the biggest challenge was going to be the construction of the barrel. Carbon steel was the only metal strong enough to work. Since they could not melt the iron, they would have to use all the heat the forges could muster to soften it as much as possible, folding and banging it with a hammer, flattening it out over and over again. The iron would absorb some of the carbon coming from the blistering hot charcoal. This would create the carbon steel they needed. Molding it into the exact measurements and rifling the inside of the barrel gave Henry nightmares.

Henry gave every man their assignments. He gave the lead man Tiberius only one: making the barrel. There were other carbon steel parts needed, but Henry would help with that. He assigned Lucius with making the .44-.40 cartridges, both the brass castings and the lead bullets. Lucius was given the specs for every other brass component required. Henry would make the laced gunpowder and fill the castings when completed. Atticus would work on the wooden back stock and the wooden fore stock. The wood had to be strong and sturdy, and with Atticus's skill, Henry knew they would be beautiful. Finally, Cornelius was assigned to help wherever needed. He would cleanup and try to help keep the shop as cool as possible. During the hot summer months with three forges baking and melting, the shop would be an inferno.

The first day they worked for fourteen hours. All of the metal work on the first day was rejected by Henry. The molds for the bullet castings were all just a little off. At the end of the day, Tiberius brought Henry his first attempt at a barrel.

Henry looked it over, *"This is good for your first attempt, but it is all wrong."* The barrel had an arching bend. *"It needs to be perfectly straight. It has dents and dings all over it. This would surely cause a backfire of the weapon."*

A frustrated Tiberius took the barrel and threw it in his scrap pile.

Atticus had moved his woodworking bench outside into the back to avoid the unrelenting heat of the forges. Henry was amazed at the progress he made in one day. He already had the rear stock roughly carved close to

Henry's specifications. It was made from a strong maple wood. Henry told him it would be quite suitable.

Atticus asked Henry, *"I am so happy you like it. Is that girl that was here coming back soon? I made her a special gift."*

Henry said with a little jealousy, *"You should be careful. She has a suitor that will want to kill you. And besides, you should be working on this project, not making gifts for Flavia."*

*"Her name is Flavia? Such a wonderful name. Very well. I will only work on your project. But all the work I do here is only for Flavia, the most beautiful girl in all of Rome."*

When Flavia arrived on day seven, she met Henry in the front of the shop. All Henry had to show her was the rifle stock that Atticus had made. It was smoothly sanded and stained an almost golden color with dark grains of the wood spiraling around it. He had carved in and painted a Pegasus, the winged horse on one side of the stock. On the other was a hydra, a three-headed snake.

*"This is so beautiful Henrici, Atticus is so talented. I put the lion that he made me by my bed."*

Henry said abruptly, *"Yes he is very talented. But he knows nothing of astrophysics, nothing of chemistry, and nothing about the earth's electromagnetic field, and he cannot build a Winchester Model 1873 repeating rifle."*

*"What are you talking about Henrici? Do I detect a little jealousy?"* Flavia played it up. *"I think he is kind of handsome."*

*"Not handsome. No jealousy. And besides, I am saving my heart for my beautiful Sherrie back in America."*

*"Yes, the beautiful Sherrie. I hope to meet her someday."*

*"No, you cannot meet her. She is too far away."*

Flavia said with a big smile, *"I can travel far away, Henrici. My father took me to Egypt once when I was a little girl."*

When Flavia made her fourth visit on day thirty, Henry finally had something to show her.

He showed her a small brass tube. *"This is perfect. Lucius did it. The diameter of the rim, the diameter of the base and the length of the canister are precisely to spec. We only have one mold, but we can make more now. Now, I am going to have him start making the lead bullets."*

Henry took Flavia to the front of the shop. There was a bench where Henry put the approved parts of the rifle. He showed her the brass trigger, the brass lever, and a carbon steel plate with an oval hole in it.

"*I made this plate. The hole is where you load the bullets.*" Henry put the canister through the hole. "*The tubular magazine will hold fifteen of them.*"

On the table was also Atticus's back rifle stock. This time he had completed the fore stock also. It had the same golden stain. This time he carved in different symbols of Ancient Rome on both sides.

When Atticus saw them by the table he came over. He got on one knee in front of Flavia, "*Lady Flavia, I know your suitor will surely kill me, but I would rather die than live without you. I ask you for your hand.*" He gave her another wooden figurine. This time it was a muscular horse, all carved in the same stunning detail as his previous lion.

"*The artist is always too passionate, Henrici.*" Flavia looked down at Atticus. "*I will not tell my suitor of this inappropriate behavior because of your skill and passion. I will not tell him yet. Keep this up and it won't be my suitor that kills you it will be me. Be gone!*"

Cornelius stood in front of Flavia. In his deep base voice, he said, "*I believe Lady Antonius wants you to get back to work.*"

Atticus did exactly as he was told. He ran out the back door of the shop.

Flavia gave Cornelius a smile and said, "*Thank you Cornelius.*"

Once outside, Flavia again gave Henry a kiss on the cheek. She got in her carriage, "*You have made some progress, Henrici. Do you think it will be finished by day 196?*"

"*If we can construct a proper barrel, I am sure we will have a more than acceptable prototype to show Caesar and Antony.*"

———◆———

It was now day one-hundred and two. The team had only sixty days left to complete the project on time. Atticus had completed his work so early that Henry had him make five more rifle stocks. He soon realized that he would be much more helpful if he were making bullets. So far, they had 256 completed. Henry had the gun almost all put together. All he needed was the barrel.

He went out back with his barrel-less weapon. With his team watching, he loaded the magazine with fifteen bullets that had no gunpowder in them. He pulled back the hammer of the rifle, then put the stock against his shoulder. He pulled the trigger. Then, he pulled down the oval shaped lever. This sent the blank canister popping out of the ejection point. He pulled the lever back into place. This put the next bullet into position in front of the hammer. This also pulled the hammer back into firing position. Henry did this fourteen more times and it worked to perfection every time. Everyone on the team, including Henry, yelled and applauded with delight at the successful test.

It was late that evening and the summer sun helped bake the forge-heated shop until the men's sweat was flowing down their bodies, coating the stone floor with fluid. All they now needed was the barrel. Tiberius brought Henry his latest attempt. Henry measured the length, the diameter of the tube, and the diameter of the inner bore.

"*It is precisely 30.87 uncia long. The diameter measurements are as equally precise.* Henry lit a match and looked inside at the rifling. He said in his annoying Latin, "*No, this will not work. If the rifling grooves inside are not perfect the bullet will not spin properly as it leaves the barrel, the weapon will not be accurate. Try it again*"

The sweaty Tiberius looked at Henry. His eyes started turning red as if smoke was coming out of them. He grabbed Henry by the neck and lifted him into the air. "*You little mouse! The barrel is perfect! I cannot do any better.*"

Cornelius quickly tackled Tiberius to the ground making him drop the choking Henry. This started a wrestling match between the two big men. They punched and choked each other as they rolled around the sweat laden floor. After ten minutes of trying, the other three managed to separate them.

Lucius tried to be the peacemaker. "*Everyone calm down. We are almost done with this. We will surely please Caesar with this effort of ours.*"

An ashamed Tiberius said, "*I am so sorry Henrici. It is so hot, and all my best efforts fail. I am nothing but a failure.*"

Henry told him, "*No Tiberius, you are almost there. The measurements were perfect. We have many more days until Caesar arrives. Be patient because rifling is an art form. It will take time. Wait a minute,*" Henry looked deep in thought. "*Rifling is an art form and we have an artist here. Atticus, your new assignment is to assist Tiberius with the rifling of the barrel.*"

Tiberius made Atticus work well into the night. They worked until just after dawn. Henry slept an unusually long five hours that night. When he was awoken by Tiberius and Atticus as the Roman sun started to rise, they handed him a new barrel.

He took it into the shop and repeated all his measurements. Then he inspected the rifling. *"I think this will work. It is precisely made to my specifications."*

He took the barrel to his bench to attach it to the rifle. As he worked, he told his brass man, *"Lucius, ride to the apartment and summon Flavia."*

*"No, Henrici. Let me go and summon Flavia. I am a fast rider. Please let me go."* Atticus pleaded.

Henry repeated in stern nerdy Latin, *"Lucius, go quickly and summon Flavia at once."* He held the completed firearm high in the air. *"When Flavia arrives, we will perform our first test with live ammunition."*

Flavia arrived around noontime. It was a near perfect day. Morning clouds had spared the Romans from some of the intense summer heat. Lucius took Flavia to the backyard where all his men waited. Henry took Flavia to an outdoor bench. It was there he had the rifle displayed.

The weapon was truly a work of art. With the combination of golden brass and polished carbon steel it sparkled in the afternoon sun. The stunning artwork on the wooden stocks truly made the weapon a masterpiece.

When Flavia saw it, her eyes got bigger. She was excited and intimidated just by the sight. *"It is so beautiful, Henrici. How can something so fine cause such damage?"*

Henry picked it up off the bench. *"Let me show you."*

Henry had the Romans bring three bullseye type targets that they used to train archers. They were about one hundred yards away. He wanted his weapon to be loud. Henry loaded the magazine with fifteen of the brass and lead bullets. He put on some safety earmuffs he made to protect him from the noise. Henry had tested many guns at the Winchester factory and had become a pretty good shot. He put the butt of the rifle stock against his right shoulder and he lined up the sights till he pointed the weapon at the center of the target. He pulled back the hammer and gently pulled the trigger. A huge explosion filled the west of Rome with a deafening sound.

Flavia covered her ears. *"Henrici, what just happened?"*

All the men applauded. They could see a hole ten inches away from the center of the target.

Henry pulled down the brass lever sending the spent bullet flying out of the rifle. He put the lever back into place, making the next shot ready to go. He adjusted his aim and fired again. This time the hole was only six inches from center.

Henry pulled the lever up and down quickly. Under the applause of his men, he fired for a third time. This time there was no loud noise. Just a fizzing sound of flaming black powder coming out of the top of the gun, filling Henry's right eye with a fiery hell. Henry fell to the ground. He laid on his back as the fizzing powder burned deeper into the wound.

Flavia rushed to his side along with the other men. She yelled, *"Henrici! Are you alright?"*

*"I shot my eye out! I shot my eye out!"* Henry yelled. *"Get some water! Get some fresh water!"*

Cornelius came back with a bucket of water. Henry ordered, *"Pour it over my eye; slowly wash it out."*

Flavia did that and said to Cornelius, *"Bring some clean cloths, hurry."*

After they flushed his eye out with the water, Flavia gently covered it with a cloth. She could clearly see there wasn't much left of Henry's eye.

She took control, *"Cornelius, pick Henrici up and put him in the back of the carriage. I am taking him to the villa. We have a doctor that lives nearby."*

Before Flavia left, Henry gave his orders. He could barely speak, *"There is a flaw in the weapon but do not give up. Make all the parts again. Look for the flaw. We have plenty of time until Caesar arrives. I will require a short amount of time to recover from my unfortunate injury."*

Flavia took Achilles to a full gallop towards the Antonius villa.

◆

Flavia called out to the villa's front door, *"Nefeli! Naima! Come out and help! Come out and help at once!"*

The two servants came running out of the villa. When Naima saw Henry with a bloody cloth over his eye, the alarmed young African said, *"Henrici! What happened to my little Henrici?"*

Flavia ordered, *"Help me get him into the villa. Take him to my bedroom."*

The three managed to get Henry into Flavia's bed. A short Roman doctor entered with his ancient doctor bag. He told Flavia, *"This is a very serious eye injury. He will not see out of it again. This is the best treatment for this type of injury."*

The doctor took a small piece of boiled ox liver and placed it over his wound.

Henry smelled the foul organ. He managed to say, *"That will not help. Bring me some wine. Some of your strongest wine."*

Soon, Flavia had a goblet of wine. She said softly to Henry, *"Drink this, Henrici. It will help with the pain."*

Henry threw the piece of liver onto the floor. He took the goblet and poured the wine into his wounded eye. He screamed loudly in pain.

The doctor protested, *"That will not do any good son."*

Henry said, *"It is for the infection. The alcohol in the wine will kill the bacteria."*

The doctor took Flavia aside. He told her that he thought Henry was delirious from the pain and that he did not know what he was talking about. He gave her more ox liver with some more instructions, then left the villa.

Soon, there was another man at Henry's bedside.

*"What happened to Henrici? That does not look good,"* Valens Antonius asked.

*"Yes Father. There was an accident at the project. Henry shot his eye out. I am going to nurse him back to health."*

Valens took Flavia away from Henry just outside the room. *"Yes the project. Flavia, I am a little concerned about the attention you are giving this boy. Do not forget that you have a suitor."*

*"Yes Father. I have a suitor, the great Victor Rallis. He has ridden into battle with Caesar himself. You know I have only met him once Father,"* Flavia said sternly. *"Here is what I am going to do. I am going to nurse Henrici back to heath; then we will return to Rome and finish the project. I have seen this weapon work. It is utterly amazing. It will amaze Caesar. It will amaze Antony. It will amaze you. This weapon will amaze all of Rome!"*

Valens Antonius did not try to argue with his strong-willed daughter. He simply said, *"Do as you wish, Flavia."*

Flavia returned to Henry. She covered him with a blanket and gave him another goblet of wine. This time Henry guzzled it down fast. She lifted the blanket and got into bed besides Henry.

Henry was almost unconscious, but he managed to say, *"Flavia, maybe the Centurion was right when he called the rifle a weapon most foul. We should stop this."*

*"No Henrici, you were right when you told the team not to give up. We will finish this. We will finish this for Caesar."*

Flavia put her head on Henry's shoulder. He could feel her warmth running throughout his body. Before he passed out to sleep, he only had one thought, *"Why do I need Sherrie Melbourne?"*

# X

# The Demonstration

THE STRONG WINE DID NOT WORK. HENRY CAUGHT A FEVER. HE STAYED in bed for over three weeks. The fever kept him in an unconscious sleep most of the time. Flavia and the servants did their best to keep him as comfortable as possible. They took shifts sitting at his bedside, keeping him clean and dressing the wound when needed.

Occasionally Henry would briefly wake up in an almost oblivious state of mind. This is when the servants would make sure he got all the food and water he needed to survive. There was always someone by his bedside twenty-four hours a day.

Henry had powerfully real dreams. He dreamt of his world in 2020—his workshop, his secrete scientific experiments, and of course he dreamed about Sherrie Melbourne. He had nebulous visions of Ancient Rome, of Caesar, Antony, and Flavia, all surrounded by colorful fireworks of brilliant red, yellow, blue, and orange. Then he dreamt of another place. It was a night-marish place that was all wrong. Everything was out of place and nothing made any sense at all—slaves were everywhere, and the good people he knew, now seemed bad. It was like big brother was watching everyone all the time. Henry wanted to get out of this place at once. He did all he could to awaken his mind. He had to get out.

On the twenty-fourth day after the accident, Henry's fever broke. Henry suddenly popped upright in his bed in a self-aware state of mind. It was dark out, but an oil burning lamp dimly lit the room. He saw young Naima sitting by him. She took a damp cloth and wiped the sweat of off Henry's face. She yelled, *"Lady Flavia! Lady Flavia! He is awake. Henrici is really awake this time!"*

Flavia woke up from her slumber in a nearby room and rushed to her bedroom. She smiled when she saw Henry sitting up. He was even more pale than usual. He had musty unkept hair and a coating of peach fuzz across his face.

*"Do you usually sleep that much, Henrici?"* Flavia asked.

With a daze in his eye, Henry said, *"I do not know. I only require four or five hours of sleep a day."*

*"Henrici, you have been out of it for over three weeks."*

Flavia looked at the wound. She cleaned it and replaced the soft cloth bandage.

*"It is healing well. Can you see alright Henrici?"* Flavia asked.

*"I can see only half as well as before because I used to have two eyes. Now I only have one."*

Flavia and Naima got Henry up on his feet. The two escorted him to the other side of the room. Henry asked them to let him try it by himself. He stumbled and staggered his way back to the bed by himself, then he sat down with a plop.

*"I am so glad that Henrici is better, Lady Flavia,"* Naima said.

*"He is going to be fine."* Flavia looked at Henry. *"I almost forgot. I made you something, Henrici."*

Flavia left the room and abruptly returned. The patch she held was a perfect black three-inch circle. There were two strings attached to each side. She placed the patch over his bandaged right eye and gently tied the strings behind his head.

She told him, *"You will need the bandages for a few more weeks, but when they are gone, nobody is going to want to look at that hole in your head."*

Naima looked at the eye-patched Henry. She laughed, *"Henrici looks so handsome, so mysterious."*

Flavia laughed also, *"He does Naima. It makes him look ten years older."*

Henry was alarmed. *"Why are you laughing at me. Do I look like a pirate? I do not want to look like a pirate."*

Flavia asked, *"Do pirates wear eye patches Henrici?"*

*"They do where I come from."*

*"Did you know that Caesar was once kidnapped by pirates?"* Flavia asked playfully.

Henry, in his usual seriousness, told the story, *"Yes I know. In 679 AUC the twenty-five-year-old Julius Caesar was sailing the Aegean Sea when his ship was confiscated by Cilician pirates. They held him for ransom. When they told him, his ransom would be twenty talents of silver. Caesar laughed at the stupid pirates and told them he was worth much more than that. He told them he was easily worth fifty talents. When Caesar's friends paid the ransom, he swore to his capturers that they would be killed for their crime. He then raised a small army, hunted down and captured all the pirates. Then he had them all crucified."*

*"Why do you know so much about Rome, Henrici?"*

*"Sherrie told me many stories and made me study about Roman history before I came here. She is the real expert."*

Flavia said with a little envy in her voice, *"Oh no, not the beautiful Sherrie again. I have to meet this girl. Rest for a few days and you should be ready to return to the blacksmith shop. The team is making good progress without you. Naima bring Henrici some food and wine."*

Henry told her, *"I do not need wine. I need lots of water because I am very dehydrated. And you cannot meet Sherrie. It is not allowed."*

*"Do not tell me what to do Henrici. I promise you; I will meet her someday."*

———◆———

The gunclub team took apart the failed weapon and tried to find out what caused the backfire into Henry's eye. Tiberius felt there was too much brass contained in the bolt and the ejection port. With Atticus' help they managed to replace some of the brass pieces with the same specifications, only using carbon steel.

Tiberius and Atticus had designed a tripod out of steel and wood that held the weapon firmly. They attached the tripoded weapon to a bench outside and pointed it at one of the targets. Cornelius used a six-foot metal rod to maneuver the hammer, lever, and trigger of the gun from a fairly safe distance away.

The unloaded gun was ready for test number two. Flavia and Henry would arrive shortly.

When they did, the team was happy to see Henry up and about. Each one made a comment about the black eyepatch.

*"The tripod is ingenious,"* Henry said when he saw it. *"It will work well for future tests. But when the time comes for the demonstration to Caesar and Antony, I will have to fire it."*

Tiberius took the rifle off the tripod and took it into the shop. He and Henry took it apart as Tiberius showed him the modifications. Henry was very pleased. He felt it was ready to go.

Outside, Cornelius loaded the weapon with fifteen shells and placed it securely on the tripod. The large slave pulled the hammer back and used the same rod to activate the trigger.

A loud explosion was followed by a tearing of the target. He pulled down and then up on the lever and then pulled the trigger, all using the same rod. Again, an explosion, a slash in the target, and no backfire. Thirteen more shots were filling the western Roman air with loud explosions, a new sound never heard before in Rome. Soon the battered and torn target fell to the ground.

People started arriving in the back of the shop. Some in fear but most in curiosity. Some started asking questions about the strange popping weapon, and soon the crowd grew to over one hundred people.

Cornelius and Tiberius tried to get them out of the compound but to no avail. More and more arrived to witness the spectacle.

Henry said, *"We must stop the tests. This has to remain top-secret. No one should learn about our mission. Atticus, ride to the barracks. Try to find the Centurion Maximus. Have him bring guards and soldiers."*

Henry took the rifle into the shop and hid it out of the view of the curious crowd. He waited for reinforcements. In less than an hour he heard the sound of the thundering horses. Centurion Maximus had arrived with fifteen soldiers. He ordered them to dismount and get the horde of people out of the compound, then he ordered them to surround the blacksmith shop and let no one enter.

When Maximus saw Henry and Flavia he said, *"Oh yes. It is the beautiful Flavia Antonius, the man-child Henrici, and Cornelius the slave. Why the eyepatch Henrici?"*

*"I shot my eye out when there was a malfunction with the new weapon. We are working on a solution."*

*"Let me see this solution you are working on,"* Maximus demanded.

*"I guess it is okay if a Centurion sees it,"* Henry said to no-one in particular. Henry went inside and brought out his version of the 1873 Winchester repeating rifle. He loaded it and placed it in the tripod.

When the Centurion saw it, he said, *"That fancy club is a weapon that will make Caesar invincible? You must be crazy, Henrici."*

Henry had Lucius put another target about one hundred yards in front of the rifle. This time Henry used the rod to fire the weapon. With his make-shift earmuffs and black eyepatch on, he was quite a sight as he fired the repeater quickly, filling the yard with a sulfurous smell and the sound of glorious power. After seven shots the tattered target again fell to the floor. Henry kept firing the remaining rounds hitting the crumbling Servian Wall two hundred yards away, creating puffs of dust and sand with every shot's penetration.

Centurion Maximus stood wide-eyed with his mouth open. *"What did I just see? Will this exploding club kill a man?"*

*"Yes,"* Henry said. *"If you hit him in a vital organ, one shot will kill him."*

Flavia said, *"That is thirty shots without a backfire, Henrici. I want to try it. I want to hold it and try it."*

*"Not yet, Flavia. We have to take it apart now and inspect for any damage. Then many more rounds of tests will be necessary."*

Maximus got on his horse. He said to them, *"I must leave you now. My men will remain on guard until completion of the weapon. Flavia, Henrici, if you need further assistance send your man to me at once. I look forward to using the gunclub on the battlefield someday."*

It was now day 127. Thirty-nine days until the completion date of the rifle and forty days until the return of Julius Caesar.

Henry used this time for testing and more testing. The rifle had to perform to perfection. He also gave his team another task. While he was testing, they could build two more rifles along with more ammunition to go along with them. Henry had one more thing to do. He was right eye dominate but he no longer had a right eye. He had to learn how to shoot from the left side.

On day 160, and after shooting hundreds of rounds and inspecting the rifle ten times, Henry felt it was safe to hold the rifle again and shoot. He summoned Flavia to accompany him for the test. Cornelius came out of the shop also. They had obliterated twenty-six targets so far. The Centurion's men kept bringing them more.

Henry said to them, *"I very, very nervous about this, but I have to do it."* He put the butt of the rifle against his left shoulder.

Cornelius said, *"Let me do it, Henrici. I don't need two eyes. I am only a slave."*

*"Thank you, Cornelius. But I must do this."*

Henry aimed at the target with his left eye. He pulled back the hammer and gently pulled the trigger. His loud shot missed the target completely. He cocked the weapon with the lever and tried again. Another loud miss resulted.

Henry turned to Flavia, *"It seems I need lots of practice with my left eye."*

*"Practice you need Henrici, but the weapon is safe now. I want to try it."*

*"No Flavia. This is too dangerous for a girl."*

She looked at him angerly. *"Do not tell me that. I said you cannot tell me what to do. Let me try it."*

Henry reluctantly handed her the gun. *"Are you right or left-eye dominate?"*

*"I don't know what that means Henrici."*

Henry gave her an eye test and determined she was left-eye dominate. He showed her how to line up the two sights and told her to hold it tightly against her left shoulder. He told her about the hard kick. He put his arms around her and helped her secure the rifle. She pulled back the hammer and fired. Her shot hit ten inches to the right of the bullseye.

She was thrilled. *"Wow Henrici! This is fun. Back off and let me try it by myself."*

Flavia continued to hit the target until it fell apart. Out of ten shots she got four bullseyes.

*"Looks like I am doing better than you,"* Flavia boasted.

*"That is because you have two eyes. I have one only. I need much more practice."*

Henry would use the remaining seven days to fine tune his left-handed shooting and to plan for Caesar's arrival. He would also work with Flavia on planning The Demonstration.

———◆———

It was now day 194, three days before Caesar's return. There was a big Roman banquet planned for his return at the Theater of Pompey. Over two-hundred guests were going to attend. Only the richest and most culturally influential would be invited to this social event of the year.

Henry was in the yard behind the shop early in the morning practicing his marksmanship skills.

Flavia showed up with Cornelius. He was holding a large four-foot-tall glass vase painted in blue, green, and violet. He put the heavy vase down next to Henry.

*"Will this do Henrici?"* Flavia asked.

*"Yes, that will be quite adequate."*

*"Why do you need thirteen of them? I could barely fit them in the carriage."*

*"I told you it is for the demonstration. We will be the last of the so-called entertainment."*

Flavia heard an oinking sound coming from near the shop. She followed the sound to investigate, *"Henrici, why do you have a huge boar back here?"*

*"I requested one from the Centurion. Two hours later he was here."*

The pig was pink skinned with white scattered hair. He looked like he weighed in at over four-hundred pounds. He oinked happily as Flavia approached him.

Flavia petted the big swine's head. *"I love animals so much, Henrici. Why do we have to eat them?"*

*"They are an important source of protein, an essential nutrient for human survival."*

*"Again, I do not know what you are talking about. Maybe we should name him. Like I named Achilles the horse. How about Felix?"*

Henry tried to discourage her, *"Do not name him. Do not become too attached to him."*

Flavia protested, *"Henrici! Tell me no! You are not going to eat him!"*

*"No, I am not. But somebody will most certainly eat him."*

———◆———

The banquet was to start at five at night and the guests would not be late for this one. This was the biggest celebration of the year in Rome. The party was arranged by Mark Antony to celebrate the return of Julius Caesar. His successful campaign to the east to conquer the Parthian Empire was going very well. At least that is what the citizens of Rome were led to believe.

Flavia, Henry and Cornelius arrived early to set up their portion of the entertainment. The large dining hall was filled over sixty large double king-sized beds topped with white blankets, each one containing fluffy pillows of many different sizes and colors. Around each side of the beds were green and white marble tables, well within reaching distance of the diners. The Romans preferred to enjoy their feasts from a mostly inclined position. There was a large open space in front of the dining area, a huge stage, where all the entertainers would perform. In front of the stage were the largest three beds of them all. They were raised four feet into the air with an intricate white staircase with four steps that led the guests of honor to their comfortable eating and drinking domain.

Flavia and Cornelius set up the thirteen colorful glass vases on the back of the stage. They put seven of the four-foot multicolored urns in a half circle on the right side, then six of them in a half circle on the left. There was a ten-foot space in-between the vases. Flavia had the banquet's master florist fill the vases with water. The florist then created bouquets of every color and shape of flowers and plants imaginable. Each one was a floral masterpiece that was truly a treat for the eye to behold.

Flavia said to Henry, *"I think there is a better way we could do this. Felix is so cute."*

*"No, Flavia, this is best. We have to impress them with everything we have. It is going to happen to him anyway."*

At five in the evening, over two hundred Roman elite had already arrived. The men were dressed in mostly white togas with gold and silver trim along with colorful capes, some with their family emblems embroidered on them. The women were in long elegant tunics that shimmied across their slender bodies, each girl trying to outshine the next.

The festivities began as trumpets blared out a marching cadence, loudly announcing the arrival of the first Emperor of Rome. He walked slowly to the rhythm of the trumpets watching all the guests rise with the constant shout of "Hail Caesar" filling the banquet hall with cheer. His toga looked like it had been woven with solid gold, and only Caesar could wear a cape of purple and gold. His head was adorned with a gold and silver wreath of leaves. With his wife Calpurnia at his right he waved to his guests as he passed them. Some of the women gasped and some cried just at the sight of him.

Behind Caesar was his Master of the Horse, Mark Antony. The handsome man had a toga of white and gold with a blue cape and a solid silver wreath around his head. He was escorting a woman that everyone knew—a woman that Calpurnia did not want to see at this celebration.

Following them was Caesar's newly adopted son. Gaius Octavian had now taken his father's name. The young man's head was filled with blond curly hair and wreath of green emeralds. His silver toga covered by a cape of red and blue couldn't hide his unattractive, skinny body. But that didn't matter as he followed Mark Anthony, then his father, as the three slowly walked up the small staircase and took their places on the plush dining sofa. The Emperor wanted Mark Antony at whispering distance but had given orders to keep Antony's companion and Calpurnia as far apart as possible.

Soon servants started to arrive with the food and drink. The soft music of hundreds of lutes and harps decorated the air as the servants brought in large bowls of dates and green, purple and blue grapes. As soon as they placed one bowl of food on the sofa side table another bowl would appear. Now they had roasted ostrich, roasted peacock, and an unlimited variety of oysters, green and red tomatoes, and peppers of every color. The main course of the banquet was being run around the hall by two muscular shirtless slaves, each slave holding the front and the back handles of a gurney. The pig they carried around the diners was roasted to a crispy golden brown. The slaves ran from bed to bed with a servant who sliced off a piece of the sweet juicy meat to anyone who wanted some. Then came the wine. Dark green flowered jugs of Falernian, Alban, and Caecuban wines were being poured into matching goblets.

Caesar was enjoying his pork when he whispered to Antony, *"I told you I had to stop the assault in Parthia. The resistance was greater than expected. I think I need two more, maybe three more legions to finish this."*

*"Yes, that can be done. Maybe this new magic weapon will help. We are going to see it tonight."*

Caesar laughed, *"Oh yes, The magic weapon of the little man child Henrici."* He said sarcastically, *"The little man child is going to save the day."*

Henry was seated on a sofa in the far back corner of the hall. Cornelius had to wait outside with his new-found friend Felix the pig. Henry did not eat the feast on the table next to him. He was too nervous, and Flavia had not arrived.

When Henry saw her approach, he stood up. Flavia's tunic was a silver and blue silk that flowed to her ankles. She wore a shawl of gold and around her head was a crown of bright blue sapphires bringing out the color of her bright blue eyes.

Henry tried to speak, "uh, uh, ma, uh." He finally blurted out in English, "You are so, so. You are so, so, beautiful."

Flavia reached down to the table and picked a red grape. She plopped it into his mouth and said, *"What is that gibberish, Henrici? Did you forget how to speak Latin?"*

At hour eight the entertainment started. Henry was amazed that the MC's voice carried through the large hall as he announced the first act. She was a wonderful young Roman with a voice of gold. Accompanied by a harp, she sang a musical version of some of the poetry of Virgil. More acts of singing and dancing followed. As the wine filled the guests, they got louder and more rambunctious.

The next-to-last act was a group of African drummers. They pounded their drums in a wild steady rhythm as exotic African dancers paraded across the stage in perfect harmony. This got the drunken crowd worked up into a frenzy. Some stood up dancing and yelling to the rhythmic drums.

When they finished the MC yelled, *"Now, finally our last performance of the evening. I bring you Henrici and his invincible weapon."*

When Henry entered the stage with his rifle, many in the drunken crowed jeered and taunted him. Some shouted out drunken obscenities at the little eye-patched man. He stood in front of Caesar and Antony, just to their left. The heckling got louder when they saw what came next. Cornelius had the large swine on a leash. He led the pig in between the two circles of flower-filled vases. Flavia brought a large bowl of some of the night's feast and put it in front of the animal.

As Felix the pig started to scarf down his meal, he had no idea this would be his last.

Henry put the butt of the rifle against his left shoulder. He aimed it carefully and pulled back the hammer. He fired. Quickly reloading it with the lever he fired again. The ear deafening explosions echoed through the hall. That was followed by another ear deafening squeal from the dying pig. The animal fell to the ground.

The rumbustious crowd was now totally silent. Most covered their ears and a few women ran away in panic. Caesar and Antony both stood up. They looked at each other with amazement.

Henry's confidence grew as he said as loud as he could, *"Doctor please."*

On older man in a white toga went to the animal and briefly examined it. He said loudly, *"This swine is dead. It looks like something went right through it, twice."*

Henry ordered the doctor, *"Stand back please. This is very dangerous."*

Henry aimed the rifle at one of the flower filled urns. He fired, sending the bullet towards the target. Shattered glass and flowers went flying through the air as water poured to the floor. He quickly levered the gun and fired at another vase. In less than thirty seconds he had hit all thirteen urns. All that was left was shattered glass and scattered flowers on a water-soaked floor.

As the sound still echoed, Henry turned to the standing Caesar. He put the butt of the rifle on the floor and held it up by the barrel. The now silent hall was broken by a slow clapping. It was only one person, the Emperor of Rome. Antony joined in as did all of the guests. Soon they were all standing yelling and applauding. Flavia joined Henry and gave him a quick hug. They both faced Caesar and gave him a long bow.

As the noise started to die down, Mark Antony said, *"Little Henrici, I like the eye patch. Your weapon can kill a pig, but can it kill a man? Shoot it at your slave."*

Henry thought fast, *"It would not be wise to shoot Cornelius. It would surely kill him, and he is one of the only people that can construct this weapon. He is quite a gunsmith."*

*"Okay then bring another slave,"* Antony ordered.

A soldier brought one of the bare-chested slaves that carried the roasted pig. He made him stand behind the dead boar.

Henry reloaded. He stood and aimed at the man. He turned around and said, *"I can kill a pig we will eat anyway. I cannot kill an innocent man."* Then he said in English, "Sherrie was right. I cannot do this. I could never have killed Hitler's grandfather."

Caesar said, *"He is not innocent. He is a convicted slave. Do as you are told son."*

Antony interrupted, *"Wait a minute Caesar, I want to try it."*

Antony came down the stairs and Henry gladly handed him the rifle. He asked Antony, *"Show me how you shoot an arrow."* He did that, then Henry said, *"You are right-eye dominate."*

Henry taught him how to work the weapon. He told him how to line up the sights. He told him about the hard kick after firing.

Antony pointed the weapon at the slave. He held it firmly and fired. After the loud pop, blood appeared in the middle of the man's chest. He grasped it and howled in pain as he looked at his blood drenched hands. He fell to the ground. The Doctor returned and examined the fallen man, He simply said, *"This slave is dead."*

Again, the crowd erupted into even louder cheers. Mark Antony levered the gun and fired at the dead corpse. He fired again, like he had done this a million times before, again and again, until the gun was empty.

He turned to Caesar. *"Julius, you have to try this. It is a feeling of ultimate power."*

Caesar said to Henry and Flavia, *"We have a meeting tomorrow at one."*

Flavia and Henry returned to their sofa bed in the back running through the cheering crowd. Henry put the rifle down on the bed as Flavia filled two goblets with wine.

They touched goblets and Flavia said, *"To the gunclub."*

Henry replied, *"Not gunclub. To the rifle."*

As Henry took his first sip of wine, he told her, *"Sherrie was right. I could have never gone back in time to kill Hitler's grandfather. I could not kill the slave."*

Flavia looked confused. *"What are you talking about Henrici? Who is this Hitler's grandfather? No one can go back in time to kill anyone. Are you okay? Why can't you just enjoy our glorious moment?"*

Henry was distraught. *"I know you do not know who Hitler is, but don't you see, Flavia? Hitler's grandfather did not commit any crimes, Hitler murdered millions and his grandfather did nothing. He would not have deserved to die. The slave was also innocent of any capital crimes and he was shot dead. Mark Antony pulled the trigger, but I killed an innocent man."*

Flavia tried to console him. *"You are a hero, Henrici. What you did was for the good of all of Rome. Have some more wine. That will make you feel better."*

Henry again had one thought, one horrendous thought. He repeated it in English, "What the fuck did I just do?"

# XI

# The Exodus

SHE LIVED AT ONE OF JULIUS CAESAR'S VILLAS JUST OUTSIDE THE SERvian wall of Rome. The majestic palace on the banks of the Tiber River had been her residence for months now.

"*Octavian is not your son.*" Her violet eyes were almost red with anger, "*I have given you a son. Caesarian is your son. He is your blood. He should be the next Emperor of Rome.*"

Her skin was a soft and shiny amber, the perfect blend of a Greek and an Egyptian. Her straight long black hair had an occasional braid of gold. The silky green tunic she wore barely covered her thighs. One of her legs was covered with rings of silver. The other was completely bare. She only wore one golden sandal. This magnificent lady was adorned with bright purple gems of amethyst around her neck, arms, and wrists, all matching her glistening eyes. The air around her was scented with sweet peach and a hint of clove, the best Egyptian perfume money could buy.

Caesar said to her, "*Octavian is my adopted son. He has passionately studied commerce, business, and soldiering. He is also passionate about helping the people of Rome. Octavian will be the next Emperor of the Roman Empire.*"

"*But Caesar, he does not have your blood. A distant cousin should not come before your own son.*"

"*I do not take that he is my son.*"

She screamed, "*Bullshit Caesar! Look at him! He is only three years old and he already looks just like you.*"

"*Nonetheless, you will do as I say.*" He tried to be stern to her, "*You will return to Egypt. Once I march through Parthia, my legions will enter Egypt. You will surrender to me without a fight.*"

The beautiful woman was almost as tall as Caesar. She looked him in the eye and hit him with both hands on his chest. *"No, Caesar. We will fight you. We will fight you until every legionnaire is dead."*

*"Do you think your puny army will have a chance—a chance against one legion armed with the weapon you saw last night?"*

She looked a little concerned. *"That was no weapon. That was just trickery, the trickery of wizards and magicians. That was an embarrassment to me and all of Egypt last night. You put me with Mark Antony. I should have been by your side. Where is the son this so-called wife, Calpurnia, has given you? Nowhere!"*

Caesar continued, *"You will return to Egypt immediately. Once I arrive, I will annex Egypt as a province of the Roman Empire. You will keep your throne and remain queen, but a queen as a symbol only. You will be a symbol of all that is good in Egypt. You will have no authority. You will answer to the Roman Empire."*

She screamed at him again, *"No authority?! No authority?!"*

She went to Caesar and started hitting his chest. She cried as she screamed. Caesar put his arms around her then she did the same. He kissed her lips long and hard. She used all her sexuality, all her passion, all her beauty to try to suck the will out of him. Caesar picked her up and carried her to the bedroom.

It was impossible for a heathy man to resist her. At fifty-seven, Caesar was still a fairly heathy man. He could not resist the young queen. It was impossible to resist Cleopatra.

———◆———

*"Wake up, Henrici. We have the meeting with Caesar, soon."*

Flavia and Henry were sleeping in the same bed. It was a lost night for Henry. He had never consumed that much wine. He had guzzled two full goblets of the wickedly sweet liquor the night before. He was soon singing and dancing with a large Roman woman, to the delight of the crowd.

Henry woke up. *"Ow! My head. My brain seems to be extremely damaged. What happened after the demonstration last night?"*

*"It was so funny, Henrici."*

Henry sat up. He was holding his head with both hands. *"What was so funny? I do not remember anything."*

Flavia was smiling. *"The African drummers started pounding a fast-erotic rhythm. You were singing a strange song in the language of America to the drumbeat. Then you started dancing crazy with a very large socialite that was as drunk as you were. She was maybe three times bigger than you. Then she started giving you a Roman strip tease."*

*"I do not remember this. This did not happen."*

*"Everyone formed a circle around you two. They were yelling you on and clapping. Everyone was laughing, even Caesar and Antony. Then you suddenly went to a bed and passed out. Cornelius had to carry you out of there. Get up Henrici. We have to get ready for our meeting."*

*"We have to postpone the meeting. I cannot go with my head like this. It is enormously damaged with pain."*

*"No, we cannot. We cannot postpone a meeting with Julius Caesar. Give it to Hades, Henrici. You only had two goblets of wine. Get up now,"* Flavia ordered.

*"May I first ask, where are we?"*

*"We are in my friend, Cassia's apartment."*

Henry inquired, *"We slept in the same bed? Did anything happen like coitus?"*

Flavia laughed, *"No Henrici. Nothing happened. I felt sorry for you. In your drunken condition, I did not want you to sleep outside."*

———◆———

The war room was large and new. It was located in a military complex well outside of the walls of Rome. It was made of reinforced stone and concrete. In the middle was a large table-sized crude colorful map of Italy, and its capitol, the city of Rome. There were mannequins about, dressed in Roman armor holding the latest technology of swords, armor, spears, and archery. There were displays of small models of battering rams, military carriages, and catapults. The room always had a feeling of victory. Today that feeling would be one-hundred times more intense.

The Roman Military made Flavia wait in a lobby far from the war room. The culture of these men would never allow a woman to enter this domain. Henry felt intimidated and alone when he entered the room. There were six men staring at him. Each strong stare was telling him, "What the hell is this?"

He approached the map, clumsily holding his Model 1873 along with dozens of sheets of papyrus, each sheet displaying a specification of his rifle. Henry was relieved when he saw a more familiar face enter from the other side.

*"Look at who is here. The life of the party, last night. The little man child, Henrici,"* Mark Antony laughed.

General Ramies said to Antony, *"What is the meaning of this? A little man with an eye patch and a fancy stick? Does Caesar know of this waste of time?"*

General Ramies was an old and battle-tested veteran of many wars. He was called to the meeting with two more top ranking generals and three of Rome's best weapon designing engineers.

Antony told him, *"Caesar is the one that ordered this meeting."*

Ramies coughed at him, *"Caesar? Uhm, then where is he?"*

Julius Caesar entered from the back also. He was greeted by loud pounds on the chest, along with chants of "Hail Caesar" from his men.

When he saw Henry, he laughed also, *"The great Henrici. I am surprised you are still alive. I thought that big woman was going to smash and smother you."*

An embarrassed Henry apologized, *"I am very sorry if I misbehaved last night. I had too much wine. I do not remember anything. I passed out."*

Ramies broke in, *"Sir great Caesar, I am trying to raise and train three new legions to assist you in the assault on Parthia. That is over thirty thousand men. What does this little man have that can interrupt my work?"*

Caesar said, *"Change of plans General. We will only need one legion. Show him Antony."*

Antony picked up the rifle. He asked Henry, *"Is it loaded?"*

Henry nodded but warned, *"I would not advise firing in these close quarters. There is a good chance of a ricochet."*

Antony started firing the gun as fast as he could. The echoing blast of the weapon in the small room made all the men cover their ears. He hit the amour on the manikins and with each and every bullet shot, there was a new hole. He shattered the iron swords and spears. He shot and destroyed the small models of Roman military might.

When the gun was empty, he asked Henry, *"What is a ricochet?"*

*"That is when a bullet hits a hard object at an angle that makes it go astray in a different direction."* He pointed at the General, *"Like that."*

Ramies was holding his left arm, trying to keep the blood inside him. His face was grimacing in pain.

*"Don't shoot up my Generals, Antony,"* Caesar said.

Antony examined the wound on his arm. *"You had better go see a medic, Ramies. It looks like the bullet went right through your arm."*

The old war veteran said through the pain, *"No, bring the medic in here. I have to see this."*

Henry showed them the specs on the rifle. He explained to them how the trigger and hammer ignite the bullet, how the bullet explodes, and how the molten lead spins through the rifling of the barrel at a speed so fast, it is unseen. He emphasized how important training would be, a fact that the Romans already knew. He told them that making the weapon in small blacksmith shops would be inefficient, and they would risk this secret escaping to the enemies of Rome.

*"I suggest you train archers to be riflemen. They are already well trained at aiming a weapon,"* Henry said.

*"Yes Henrici."* Caesar already had a plan. *"We will build a large blacksmith shop, with room enough for hundreds of workers to construct the rifle. My best weapon designers will assist you Henrici. I want all our best commanders here to create a legion that will be invincible—a legion armed with five hundred riflemen."*

Henry told them, *"We have to check the quality of every rifle. They must be made to the precise specification. I do not want the soldiers to look like me."*

Antony asked, *"Yes Henrici, what happened? Why the eye patch?"*

*"There was a malfunction with the first test of the rifle. Burning gunpowder scorched my eye out. We already have a remedy for the problem."*

Antony told Caesar, *"You know, I kind of like the eye patch. It makes him look a little mysterious. What do you think, Julius?"*

*"I do not like it. It makes him look like a pirate."*

———◆———

Flavia and Henry sat in the mess hall at the barracks enjoying a lunch of fried pork, dates, and grapes. He told her about the successful meeting and how Mark Antony shot up the place, including Ramies' left arm.

*"General Ramies is a very strong man. The bullet went right through. He grimaced a little, but he did not want to leave the meeting."*

*"And how is your headache, Henrici?"* Flavia asked.

*"Still very bad. I will never drink wine again."*

The still-hungover Henry held his head. There was a calendar on the wall near their bench. He looked at it as he dealt with the pain.

*"No! No!"* he said. He lined up six grapes for months, then eighteen dates representing days, across the table. He knew the date today was September thirtieth. He did the calculations again, then again. He ran outside to a

111

sundial in the yard. He studied it. He studied the time. Flavia followed the panicked Henry.

*"What is the matter, Henrici? You look like you just saw a God."*

*"It seems I have made a horrendous miscalculation. No doubt because of my most serious accident. I underestimated by one day. We need to get back to your father's villa at once."*

*"Henrici, you can't leave. They are going to give you your own apartment. You will have your own office when the new blacksmith factory is complete."*

Henry had to lie fast. *"Yes, it is about the rifle. I left some important data in the barn, important data on the mass production of the rifle. We have to get back right away. Where is Achilles and the carriage?"*

She guided him to where she parked the carriage. They hooked up Achilles and Henry took the reins. He swung a whip wildly to get the horse moving.

*"We are not going to bring Cornelius, Henrici?"*

*"No, Caesar ordered the team to keep making rifles until the new facility is complete."*

Flavia reached below the bench of the carriage. She felt to make sure it was there. Now, she was glad she took it.

When they got past the Servian wall of Rome, Henry used the whip to get Achilles to a full gallop.

*"Henrici, you have to slow down. You are going to push the horse to his death. What is the big hurry? This unexplained haste is more than information about the rifle."*

Ahead they could see the start of the five miles of forest. Both Flavia and Henry wished they had Cornelius in the back.

Two more brothers Marcellus were hiding in the thick layers of trees. The two highwaymen were both muscular like their late brother Titus. Cicero was delighted when he saw the carriage in the distance.

*"This is our lucky day, Rufus,"* he told his brother. *"These are the two that killed our brothers. I saw it from afar. They had a big slave in the back, he threw Lucius to his death then he stabbed Titus brutally."*

*"This is so great. No big slave this time. Let me stop their horse. I just might have my way with the girl before I kill her. Sweet revenge and we get all the wealth that they have,"* Rufus laughed with glee.

When the carriage got close, Rufus ran out from the forest and stopped Achilles by grabbing the browband. When the horse stopped, he went to Henry's side of the carriage.

*"Please do not resist. Give me all your belongings, and we will kill you quickly. Resist, and your deaths will be slow and long. And lady, I will have my way with you before you die. Do not resist."*

Flavia was already standing up in the carriage. She had the second ever Model 1873 braced against her left shoulder. She had it pointed confidently at the bandit.

*"What is that?"* the robber asked.

Flavia simply said, *"Goodbye."*

She fired twice sending two projectiles of hot lead into his chest. He died so fast he didn't get a chance to see the blood spurting out of him.

His brother heard the loud blasts. Instead of riding away with fear, the stupid Cicero drew his sword and charged his horse towards the carriage. Flavia reloaded the gun with the lever. She fired three times until the highwayman fell off his horse to his early death right before he got to Henry. There was blood pouring out of his left eye.

Henry looked at the sight. *"You planted the bullet into his left eye, easily sending the mass of lead through his frontal lobe, then the temporal lobe of his brain. He died in an instant."*

*"Again, I do not know what you are talking about. He still has his right eye, maybe we should give that to you. You need one."*

*"No, that would not be possible. That would require a team of expert doctors and hours of extensive surgery."*

*"Shut up Henrici. This horse looks young and strong. I wonder who they stole him from. Help me hook him up. Achilles needs a rest."*

They tied Achilles to the back of the carriage to give him a break from pulling the heavy cart. Henry started pushing the new horse just as hard.

Flavia said, *"I am going to keep this rifle right here on my lap until we get to the villa."*

Henry looked at the pretty young woman holding the lethal weapon. He said in his nerdy Latin, *"You are the first person in history to ever ride shotgun. You should be wearing a cowboy hat."*

*"Henrici, I am not going to ask you what that means."*

Throughout the trip, Henry kept looking at the sun as if he was trying to figure out what time it was. As they got closer the villa, Henry got even more agitated.

Flavia told him, "*Stop Henrici, we need to switch horses. Achilles is tired again.*"

"*We do not have time to stop. I have to get to the villa.*" He looked at the sun, "*I do not have much time.*"

"*You had better tell me what is going on or I will use this rifle to shoot your other eye out.*"

"*Please do not do that Flavia. If you do, I will be blind and dead.*"

They switched horses and Henry got the fresher horse to a full gallop quickly.

"*What should we name this new horse, Henrici? How about Felix, after the late Felix the pig.*"

"*Yes, Felix the pig is a very nice name for a horse.*"

The sun was about to set on this warm September day. Large thunderclouds were moving in from the west. Henry and Flavia quickly rode past the small orchard of grey-leaved olive trees then Henry stopped the carriage in front of the villa and jumped out. He ran past the large rock to the oversized umbrella pine tree. Flavia followed him.

"*Where are you going, Henrici?*" she yelled.

When she caught up to him, he was using both hands to frantically dig in the rich brown dirt near the trunk of the tree.

"*Henrici, this is where I found you for the first time. You were naked right here.*"

"*Yes, I was. It is time for me to go. I found them!*"

Henry dug up the two small black spheres. He quickly took off the plastic wrap that surrounded them when a flash of lightning and then a roar of thunder yelled at them from above.

He pleaded with Flavia, "*Please, please go away. I will be leaving very soon.*"

"*Henrici, you cannot tell me what to do. You are leaving where? There is no horse. There is no cart. Are you going to fly away like a bird?*"

"*Kind of like that. Say goodbye to Cornelius and all of the rifle team for me and mostly, goodbye to you, Flavia.*"

"*You cannot go. Caesar will not let you go. I do not want you to go. You cannot! What are those black balls for?*"

Henry stood up and faced her as he held the two spheres tightly, one in each hand. Another flash of light then a roar of thunder came from the sky as he said, "*They are electromagnetic shockers. They will take me into the future.*"

*"The future? What are you talking about? The future? Wait a minute, you are going to see that Sherrie girl, the beautiful Sherrie."*

*"Yes, I do hope to see her most shortly."*

A dotting rain started to hit the tree above them.

Flavia got slightly anxious, *"Henrici, why are those balls flashing that strange red light?"*

*"Yes!"* Henry's hands started to shake in anticipation. *"I made it in time. The shockers are now activated. Flavia, I think I do sort of love you a little bit, but mostly a lot."*

*"If you love me, then you cannot leave. I will not let you."* She got more alarmed, *"Henrici, why are they flashing green now!"*

*"Goodbye, Flavia."*

The loud sound that filled the air was like a million hissing snakes ready to strike. Soon, there was a bright yellow light surrounding Henry filling the darkening evening with light that looked like the morning sun. When the yellow light turned to a brilliant blue, Flavia was not frightened. She threw her arms around him and yelled over the noise, *"No! Henrici! You cannot go!"*

The light got brighter around them and Henry yelled even louder, *"Flavia! No! Let go!"*

There was a huge flash of brilliant light and a gust of powerful wind.

When the light and wind subsided, all that was left by the tree were two electromagnetic shockers and two pairs of Roman clothing.

# XII

# The Assault on Parthia

INVICTA IS A LATIN WORD MEANING UNDEFEATED OR UNCONQUERED.
This one word was the motto of the entire Ancient Roman military.
Every Roman General had the virtues of Roman pride, Roman honor,
and Roman courage. If a Roman army was defeated, there was only one
solution and that was vengeance. Every Roman General knew this, and no
General knew this more that Julius Caesar. Invicta always reigned supreme.

The Parthian Empire had been around for over two-hundred years, and
for two hundred years this empire had been a thorn in the side of Rome. In
53 BC, they soundly defeated the Roman General Marcus Crassus, a great
general in his own right. Humiliated, he was executed by the Parthians. To
make matters worse for Caesar, the Parthians also sided with Pompey the
Great during Caesar's civil war against his rival Roman General.

The new Emperor had planned an assault deep into the east, past the Ara-
bian tribes to Parthia, to finally destroy them and make Parthia a province
of his new Roman Empire. The date to begin this crusade was set at March
18, 44 BC, three days after the failed assassination attempt against him on
the Ides of March. Caesar postponed this date. He needed another week to
make sure the Roman Senate was dangling under his puppet strings. Once
he was sure the Roman Senate would not challenge his authority, Caesar
would have total power. He was the true Emperor of Rome and now the
time was right for his revenge. The Roman culture did not accept the kind
of defeat and humiliation meted out by the Parthians. Caesar had to avenge
the great General Marcus Crassus. He would command eight legions to
move east, some from Greece and some from Italy. As was Caesar's way,
the legions moved quickly, some by land and some by sea.

This first assault into Parthia did not go well. His rivals were skilled at
maneuvering their armies. They were experts at the counterattack. They

used heavily armed cavalry using spears and javelins to attack enemy lines. Their most effective weapon was their first wave, light cavalry made up of mounted archers wearing only tunics. They would quickly advance towards their enemy, shooting arrows at their victims, then quickly retreating.

Caesar's legions could not advance. He was forced to retreat with his exhausted men to friendlier ground and set up camp near the eastern shore of the Mediterranean Sea to the west of the city of Jerusalem. He was to return to Rome to raise three more legions of reinforcements. Caesar needed to meet with Mark Antony in Rome to plan their next battle strategy.

When Caesar arrived back in Rome, six months after his departure, the fifty-seven-year-old Emperor was exhausted. He met with Antony briefly on his return. It was late at night and Caesar needed rest. He was not happy to hear about a welcoming banquet Antony had planned for the following evening, but he knew he had to attend.

Antony reminded him about the demonstration of a new weapon at the banquet. He told him that his most trusted Centurion, Maximus, had seen the weapon and was amazed. Caesar was too tired to comprehend. His once sporadic dizzy spells had now increased both in frequency and in intensity. Antony told him that the Centurion called it the weapon most foul. Caesar feel asleep out of sheer exhaustion.

Caesar and Antony met a week after the Demonstration of the rifle. Henry Garfield and Flavia Antonius were gone. They just vanished. It was of the upmost importance that they be found.

They were grilling their head mole, Aries the Spy.

Caesar was not happy. *"Did you find them? It has been four days since I gave you this assignment."*

*"We pay you and your people top compensation, but for what? Where are they?"* Antony was even angrier.

The little spy started to sweat from his forehead. He wiped it off with a handkerchief. *"I have top men working on this. We have three leads so far. The first two are based on the theory that the two young ones fell in love."*

Antony looked at Caesar, he said, *"That seems unlikely. The beautiful Lady Flavia and the little man child Henrici? Very unlikely."*

Aries the mole responded, *"We have witnesses that say the two fell in love. They feared restitution from the lady's suitor, Victor Rallis, and her Father Valens*

XII • The Assault on Parthia

*Antonius. One lead says they escaped to India, the other into Hispania. I have top men traveling to both locations."*

Caesar said, *"I know both these men. It would not be wise to be on the bad side of either man. What about the third lead?"*

*"This one is less likely. We found an old woman that was worshipping at The Temple of Jupiter six nights ago. At around the hour of six, she swears she saw a couple matching the description of our missing two, standing near the statue of Jupiter. Soon they were surrounded by fire. They held each other in their arms, then vanished. She passionately claims that they were ascended into the heavens by Jupiter himself."*

*"Get out of here you little mole and find them!"* Caesar ordered.

As the little man ran out of the room he said, *"Yes, Your Majesty. Do not worry, we have top men searching for them."*

*"Soldiers have already searched every residence and business in the city,"* Antony said, he sat down in front of Caesar's desk. *"We need to find them, but we do not really need them. The small shop has already made eight weapons. Construction has already started on the giant weapons factory. We know how to make the weapon."*

*"I understand that, Antony, but it would be nice to know where they are."*

———◆———

Valens Antonius sat at his desk in his office at the villa and waited for a report from his lead servant. Soon the head servant Nefeli entered the room and she brought along the young attractive African servant Naima. The both greeted the Aristocrat with a bow.

Nefeli spoke first, *"Naima, tell Sir Antonius what you saw that night. Just like you told me."*

Naima was scared and nervous. Her voice was shaking. *"Sir Antonius, I saw Lady Flavia and little Henrici arrive in the carriage, returning from Rome. Henrici ran out of the carriage and Lady Flavia followed him. I got jealous because I am in love with Henrici. I thought they were going to do some love making. I followed them from a safe distance to spy. I am so sorry."*

Nefeli encouraged her. *"Go on Naima."*

*"Yes, what did you see? They have been missing for weeks."* Antonius was getting anxious.

*"They went behind the big pine tree in front of the villa. There was thunder and lightning all around. It sounded like they were arguing. Soon Henrici was*

119

*surrounded by lightning and Flavia put her arms around him. A horrible loud hissing sound filled the air, and they vanished in a huge flash of light."*

"*Show him,*" Nefeli ordered.

Naima had a cloth sack. She pulled out of it two sets of clothes and two black shiny spheres. "*This is all that was left after they vanished.*"

"*What are those black balls?*" Antonius was more agitated.

"*I do not know. They were very hot when I first found them.*"

Valens Antonius was now very angry. "*Why did you wait so long to tell me. It has been weeks. Burn those clothes. Burn it all. Now, get out and close the door!*"

Now alone Valens Antonius had a desperate look on his face. The daughter he loved so much was now gone. He remembered her as a baby and as a little girl. The memories made him more despondent. He said to himself, "*It seems like Henrici was from Hades. Maybe he was Hades himself. Either way I am a total failure as a father.*"

He went to his closet and took out a large animal cage and put in on his desk. Inside were some tree branches and a twenty-inch asp. The snake was two shades of black and was not happy about being locked in a cage. Valens opened a small door on the cage and put his arm inside. The angry snake stuck him five times filling his blood with venom. He closed the cage door and sat down at his desk. The brave Roman did not scream as the deadly venom tore apart his inner blood vessels. It wasn't long before he was dead. Suicide by snake.

———◆———

Caesar stopped most of the construction in Rome. He focused all Rome's resources on the construction of the new weapons factory. It would have over two -hundred thousand square feet of manufacturing space. His lead engineers recommended fifty charcoal forges to heat and melt all the carbon steel, brass, and lead that they needed. There would be room for twenty-five wood workers to carve the stocks of each rifle. In the back of the facility, they would have over a hundred men working on the ammunition. The Romans realized immediately that the weapon was useless without an ample supply of bullets.

The plant would be constructed adjacent to the military facility just outside of Rome. Caesar brought in an entire legion to guard the compound and assist with any task needed. No one unauthorized would be allowed anywhere near the munition's factory.

A little over a mile away was a mill used to grind barley grain. The Romans confiscated the mill and planned to convert it to a gunpowder manufacturing plant. Here they would grind the sulphur, charcoal, and saltpeter, and blend it using Henry's formula exactly to his specifications. Henry told them to be extra careful and to always have plenty of water ready. He told them one spark could blow up the entire mill.

Training had already begun at a facility outside of Rome. The military leaders used Henry's advice and started training the most qualified and decorated archers. With the eight rifles they had, these men adapted quickly to the new weapon. And they had the time of their lives firing the new rifles.

Caesar wanted the first training to be as real as possible for the new riflemen. Many of the men that were scheduled for crucifixion were brought to the training yard. Fifty yards away from the future marksman, they gave the condemned man a five second head start to try to run away. None of them lived more than five seconds before their bodies were blown apart by fifteen projectiles of molten lead. At least their deaths were quick. This was a much more humane way to die than the hours-long, excruciating death of a crucifixion.

They had cleaned up the war room after Antony's rampage with the rifle. Caesar wanted the hole-filled armor and the hole-filled walls left alone as a reminder as to what they had. The crude table map of Italy was replaced with a crude map of a battlefield in Parthia.

Caesar, Antony, Octavian, and six of Rome's top Generals met to plan the Assault on Parthia. The plan was to use one Legion to do most of the work. Caesar had renamed this Legion the Thirteenth after his most powerful Legion that crossed the Rubicon River five years before.

The eighteen-year-old Octavian was not afraid to speak up, *"With the power this weapon possesses, we must lure the Parthian army towards the Thirteenth. Five hundred rifles can defeat the poor fools."*

His adopted father told them, *"Let us not be too confident, Octavian. This weapon has not been tested in battle. The Thirteenth will still need support."*

*"I agree,"* Antony said. *"But any support needs to be far away. They must seem like no threat to the Parthians. The Thirteenth should charge rapidly, then halt and wait for the Parthian cavalry."*

*"Yes, and once the carnage begins, the eight other Legions slowly close in and clean up any remaining mess,"* Caesar said with a smile.

Octavian said, *"With this weapon, I do not think there will be much to clean up."*

Using small models placed on the map, they came up with the basic battle as illustrated below.

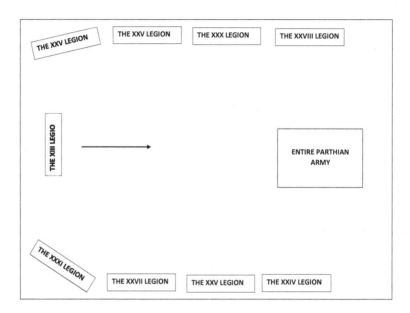

With hundreds of workers and slaves going twenty-four/seven, they estimated completion of the rifle factory at less than a month. Then another two months to create the five hundred rifles and to train the men. Caesar wanted the riflemen in groups of four—two riflemen, with one always firing while the other would reload. There would be one superior legionnaire and one of the best cavalrymen assigned to guard the riflemen with their lives. Each horse would carry additional ammunition and if a rifleman did go down in battle, the legionnaire and cavalryman would also be trained to pick up a discarded rifle and use it.

The Romans would use two of their existing tactics to assault the Parthians. The first was the triple line. Usually, the front line or the *velites* would be the least-experienced solders. Armed with spears, they would hurl the pointed sticks at the opponent, then retreat behind the more experienced soldiers. Next would come the *principles*, followed by the most experienced third line, the *triarii*. Caesar changed this tactic. He did not want any inexperienced men involved with the new Thirteenth Legion. He replaced the *velites* with the more skilled *principles* in the front rank, the most experienced veterans, the *triarii* in the middle, and the new riflemen in the back rank.

The second tactic they would use was called the tortoise (*testudo*). Taking after the shielded animal, the Roman legionaries would line up in three rows of eight men. They would use their five-foot-high and curved three-foot-wide wooden shields to completely surround them, creating an effective barrier against catapulted fire and an archer's arrows. Caesar had them make a new shield for the Thirteenth that was a little wider and higher, giving more room to hide what was inside the turtle shell. Each tortoise would be hiding eight riflemen.

The new Thirteenth Legion was like royalty in Caesar's mind. He recruited some of the former heroes of the elder Thirteenth and gave them the best of everything. He knew he could build an amazing loyalty with the new Thirteenth, like the loyalty he had with the original Legion that crossed the Rubicon River years ago. When it was time to sail to the eastern shore of the Mediterranean Sea, they would use only the best ships filled with the best food and supplies. Nothing was too good for this new Legion, this new super Legion.

Mark Antony was upset. *"I should go with you Caesar. I need to see how the weapon performs in actual battle."*

*"I need you in Rome. You are my Master of the Horse. Your main responsibility is to rule in my absence. There is still a feeling of possible revolt and riot in Rome; that is why I need you here."*

*"You are going to take Octavian to Parthia instead of me."*

*"Yes Antony. Octavian is still too young to rule. He will learn a lifetime of lessons on this voyage."*

*"Very well. Please keep me informed on the performance of the weapon. I will be there with you in heart."* A disappointed Antony left Caesar's office.

———◈———

Six months after Caesar left his eight Legions on the eastern shore of the Mediterranean Sea, he returned. His generals were surprised that he returned with only one Legion. They were expecting three Legions of reinforcements.

General Tullius was an old veteran of Caesar's civil was against General Pompey. The over sixty-year-old was grey haired but still in the shape of a fifty-year-old. Caesar had left him in command of the eight Legions in his absence.

They greeted each other with a chest pound. Tullius told Caesar, *"You made it back not a minute too soon. There have been many minor skirmishes around the outskirts of the camp. The Parthians are up to something soon. We have captured eight Parthian spies in recent days."*

The two men sat in Caesar's main tent. They were joined by Octavian.

*"It is good you have these spies,"* Caesar said. *"Let us take them to the yard. I want to give you a demonstration, General."*

He had his ten best rifle men meet them in the yard. They wore long black tunics with a silver steel helmet and breast plate. Around both their shoulders and crisscrossing in the center of their chests were belts lined with sixty .40-.44 brass and lead bullets.

The eight bound Parthians were made to stand fifty yards away from the gunmen. Caesar ordered his men to take aim.

Octavian interrupted, *"Father, we should spare two of them to go to the Parthian King Orodes. To tell him and his armies what to fear."*

*"Do you really want to tip our hand to the enemy, Octavian?"*

*"Yes. First, they will never believe them. Second, when they do hear and see this, they will be in even more than the worst fear."*

Caesar agreed. They pulled two of the spies aside, then Julius Caesar gave the order, *"Ready, aim, fire!"*

The first firing squad in history got everyone's attention. The riflemen did not know when to stop. Once an initial shot ripped through the spy's flesh, more and more shots tore through them, leaving gobs of blood and guts escaping from the condemned men's bodies. The barrage did not stop until each man had fired all fifteen of his rounds.

A huge crowd of hundreds of legionnaires and officers developed around the dead men. An astonished General Tullius led a large round of applause accompanied by hysterical chants of "Hail Caesar!"

Caesar told his General, *"Did I mention that we have five-hundred of these weapons?"*

The two Parthian spies were given strong, fast horses with hope that they would alert the villages and cities of the barrage of Roman might that was coming. Caesar gave them a two-day head start before starting his campaign. The armies left their camp to the east of Jerusalem in one giant group of over 45,000 men. They traveled north to the city of Palmyra in Syria, then south towards his main objective, the capital of the Parthian Empire, the city of Ctesiphon. After crossing the Euphrates River, Caesar sent four Legions towards the north of Ctesiphon and four towards the south of the city. Only the Thirteenth Legion would head directly towards his target.

Ctesiphon was located just to the east of the Tigris River. Caesar and his generals knew that the battle would take place between these two rivers. When they approached the Tigris, they could see the huge Parthian army waiting to protect their capitol city and to protect their leader, King Orodes II, from the Romans. The eight Roman Legions to the north and south could not be seen. This is exactly as Caesar had planned it. He ordered the mighty Thirteenth to move forward at top Legion speed.

General Tullis estimated the size of the Parthian force to be at about 80,000 strong. That made him a little nervous. The Thirteenth Legion had only 5,654 men, but five hundred of those men were already well-trained riflemen. Julius Caesar was not nervous at all.

Caesar ordered the distant Legions to start their approach towards the battle. Then, he ordered the Thirteenth to fall into the three ranks, forming a "U" shape. All the generals along with Caesar and Octavian waited two hundred yards behind the gauntlet.

Soon, they saw a dusting of earth and the sound of horses coming from the distant enemy, the rumble of thousands of horses charging at them. Caesar gave the order for a complete halt. The Thirteenth stopped and waited for the first round of Parthian light cavalry, the archers.

When the archers got closer, the first rank of Roman principles needlessly threw their spears at the far-away enemy, not coming close to a strike. They then got on their stomachs and used their shields to protect the riflemen's lower body. The next rank, the triarii, got on one knee and used their shields to protect the mid-section of the men behind them. Two hundred and fifty riflemen aimed their weapons at the incoming onslaught while two hundred and fifty more waited on one knee for their turn. When the horses were two-hundred yards away, the order rang out so all the Thirteenth could hear it. *Fire!* was shouted again and again.

The charging archers wore only tunics with no armor at all. Their strategy was to get close enough to the enemy and shoot a few arrows then quickly retreat. With the sound of over two thousand horses pounding the earth, these men could not hear the thunderous roar of the rifles, the roar of two hundred and fifty bullets coming straight at them. Soon some of the

Parthian riders noticed their compadres falling off of their horses. Some horses were tumbling to the ground while others threw their legs high into the air, whinnying loudly and throwing the rider down hard into the dust.

After the first fifteen shots, in a matter of minutes, half of the charging force was down. The barrage did not stop. As the first round of riflemen got on one knee to reload, the second group got up to fire. Their job was much easier. The archers were now much closer.

A few archers stopped to draw their bows. Before they could pull back the string, their bodies were blown apart by unseen molten lead. Some retreated in fear of the blood around them while some fled at the deafening sound of an unknown weapon that was killing their fellow soldiers in seconds.

Some archers tried to reach the flank at the right of the line. They were quickly blown apart by the marksmen on that side. After a period of less than ten minutes, there was no more charge. Most of the over two thousand archers lay dead on the ground. Only a handful were smart enough to retreat, and only a few arrows made it to the Thirteenth . They were all easily stopped by Roman shields.

Caesar said to his generals, *"I think Octavian was right. He said the other Legions would have little work to do to clean up."*

*"Father, have you ever seen such victory? Such victory so quickly?"*

*"No Octavian, but there is more victory to come."*

Now, the Thirteenth waited for the next round of attacks.

More cavalry was on the way, thousands of men on horseback riding past their dead colleagues and refusing to retreat. They wore amour of brass and leather and each man carried a nine-foot razor sharp javelin. The Roman generals knew the Parthian strategy. They would ride up close to the legionnaire and try to stab them repeatedly with their javelins. This time the officers waited until the enemy was only fifty yards away.

They again gave the order to fire. Some of the riflemen had become accomplished marksmen. They aimed at the enemy's unarmored faces. The bullets smashed Parthian noses and the brains behind them in a mass of blood.

Still some Parthians tried to get close. Very few retreated and the closer the enemy got, the easier was the rifle's job. The bullets tore through the brass and leather armor with ease leaving piles of dead cavalrymen stacked up in front of the Thirteenth Legion. The sharpshooters were told to try to spare the horses. A horse was a valuable commodity to a Roman Legion.

After just over forty-five minutes of battle, the Thirteenth Legion had more horses then they would ever need.

The riflemen reloaded and replaced their belts with belts full of fresh bullets. Caesar ordered full Legion speed towards the Parthian army.

The Parthian military did the same and when they got closer, the Parthian officers saw their men falling down and dying. There were no arrows, no spears, no swords, just hundreds of men dying along with the merciless sound of fiery death. They ordered their catapult men to try to land tons of fire-filled stones into the oncoming Legion. The Roman generals expected this. Soon, all the men that were manning the catapults were dead before even one was fired.

The Parthians hastily ordered a full retreat, but as they retreated their men continued to fall. Thousands died during the retreat, but some made it to the Tigris River. They quickly loaded their small ferries with as many men as would fit. The Romans did not even need to use their own catapults. They used the already loaded Parthian catapults to hurl stones of fire at the escaping boats, hitting several and burning and drowning hundreds of men. The Parthians on the west side of the river were totally trapped. Some tried to swim across. Others tried to hold their ground. As the riflemen got close, thousands of brave Parthian soldiers were soon no more.

Caesar order his five hundred riflemen to line up on the western bank of the Tigris. The Parthians in the water were sitting ducks. With no opposition, the rifle men had a field day, picking off boats of soldiers and picking off stray swimmers. When this massacre was over, out of over 80,000 Parthian men, only about 700 made it to the other side of the river. The Romans lost only five men.

Caesar made camp on the other side of the Tigris River. He would march into the Capital city of Ctesiphon in the morning. A large campfire was burning fresh ox for their supper. Caesar, Octavian, and his Generals sat around the large flame. Each man had a goblet of wine. Octavian was right. The eight other Legions joined them now. None of them had seen even a minute of battle.

After the toasts of victory were complete, Caesar got back to business. He said to General Tullius, "*General Tullius, you will be the new governor of The Roman province of Parthia. We will keep four Legions here under your command.*"

Octavian wanted to sound important, *"Caesar has decreed that the other four legions march west across Arabia and make camp just east of the Ptolemaic Empire. They will enter on Caesar's command."*

*"Yes, Octavian. I will take the Thirteenth back to the Mediterranean. From there we will sail to the outskirts of Alexandria. We will march unopposed into Egypt and make her another new province of the Roman Empire. I must retire now. Rest well, gentlemen. Tomorrow will be a glorious day."*

Octavian waited a few minutes, then he made the short walk to Caesar's tent. He entered and knelt on one knee next to his resting father. *"Is everything okay? You do not look well."*

*"Never tell the men this, but the dizzy spells are becoming more frequent and more intense. That is why I put this task off until tomorrow, when it could have easily been done today. I will be fine by then."*

Octavian was still concerned. *"They have good doctors in Egypt. You must see them."*

*"I will get their opinions as you wish."*

*"I have to ask you this. You will see her. You will see the Queen?"*

*"Yes, I will."*

*"Well, the rumor is rampant. Is her son Caesarian, your son?"*

Caesar sat up in his bed and looked Octavian in the eye. *"I only have one son and that is you."*

*"But the queen insists he is your son. With mad vigor she insists."*

*"Do not listen to this raving woman. She is just being who she is. She is just being Cleopatra."*

———◆———

The walled city of Ctesiphon had eight crows' nests set up high above the twenty-foot wall. Each nest had an archer waiting. When they brought back the string of their bows to fire an arrow, they were immediately shot dead by Caesar's best marksmen, sending their dead bodies falling to the ground. With all the Parthian archers down, the Romans did not need to use the tortoise tactic to get close to the walls. They got close with no resistance. They used a battering ram to easily break down the front gate. Once inside, to the Romans surprise, all the remaining soldiers and Parthian officials were kneeling in surrender. There weapons were piled in a huge stack in front of them. When the Romans identified the top General of the Parthian military, they brought him to Caesar.

Caesar said to him, *"These are the terms of your unconditional surrender. Bring me your King and his court, and I will spare your men."*

The general led Caesar and his rifle heavy entourage to the center of the city. There was a grand castle of beautiful gray and built five stories high. Caesar sent ten riflemen along with twenty legionnaires inside with the Parthian general.

Once inside there would be sporadic gunshots, followed by silence. Soon out of the front gate of the castle came the great King, Orodes II. He wore a long purple robe with a golden crown on his head. Behind him were ten of his family, his wife, three children, and members of his royal court. Each one had a rifle pointed at them.

Caesar made the family kneel down in front of him, with ten rifles pointing at the group.

He said to all in a loud voice, *"Today we avenge the death of the great Roman General and statesman Marcus Crassus. He was a man that possessed all Roman virtues and man of complete Roman dignity."*

The Parthian King broke in, *"Great Caesar, please repent and spare us. This weapon you have that destroys armies in just mere hours must be the work of Satan. Repent from your sins and spare us."*

Caesar gave the thumbs down sign. With the three young children crying, the rifles made sure their deaths were quick. The reign of King Orodes was now over.

Caesar kept his promise. He spared all the remaining Parthian soldiers. He only had the officers shot. Now, he would head back the Mediterranean Sea with only his Thirteenth Legion. They would sail to Alexandria to annex all the riches and luxuries of the Ptolemaic Empire. They would own all the extravagances of Egypt.

Egypt would soon belong to Caesar, along with their magnificent Queen.

# XIII

# The Queen of Egypt

S HE SAT IN HER GOLDEN THRONE HIGH ABOVE ALL THE MEMBERS OF her court. Below her were her military generals, her most trusted advisers, and her much needed bodyguards. On each side of her were two young Egyptian beauticians. The main task of the two young girls was to make sure she looked perfect, which she always did. Wearing hundreds of golden rings around her long black hair and a lengthy gown of silver and golden silk, she looked down on her subjects. She knew what she had to do. The Queen of the Ptolemaic Kingdom, Cleopatra VII heard the rumors of a Roman massacre in a raid on Parthia. She knew this wasn't a rumor. She knew what Caesar had.

She ordered her Generals in Greek, *"When Caesar arrives, and he will arrive, we are to surrender…. we are to surrender unconditionally to Rome."*

Her head General Masudi was a proud Egyptian man with military heritage going back over two hundred years. In his full military uniform, he questioned the Queen in the Egyptian language, *"My Glorious Queen, why do we surrender so easily? These rumors of a Roman weapon that can destroy armies in just hours are pure Roman propaganda. Let us fight and defeat the Romans and save the riches of Egypt from their foul hands. We have spotted only one Legion approaching from the east by sea. We can surly defeat one Legion."*

Cleopatra got angry. She stood up from her throne and scolded her general in the Egyptian language, *"Do not question me. The rumors of this weapon are true for I have seen it. The Parthians are now part of his Empire and we will be part of the Roman Empire also. If we fight, we will be destroyed. I will keep my throne; I will answer to Caesar. But believe me, I can handle Caesar."*

General Masudi left the meeting in a mood, and it was not a happy one. He did not believe his Queen. He was a very, very proud Egyptian.

---

Caesar docked his ships just to the east of the city limits of Alexandria. He would unload his Legion onto the shores of Egypt and march into the city to a hopefully triumphant return. Alexandria was a new, modern city filled with riches and wonders. To Caesar, Alexandria's greatest treasure was their Queen. He longed to see Cleopatra. She had a way with him that he could not resist. Apparently, no man could repel her desires.

Caesar, Octavian, and the Generals and Officers rode on horseback behind the over five- thousand legionaries. They marched slowly. Caesar had no reason to fear an attack from the Egyptians.

When they got to the outskirts of the city, they saw an Egyptian army of over ten thousand strong. At first, Caesar thought it was a welcoming committee.

Octavian said, *"Father, I don't believe this is a welcome. They are in battle formation."*

He responded, *"I cannot believe this. These men do not have to die."* Caesar ordered his Legion into the three-rank formation with the riflemen in the back.

---

General Masudi was an Egyptian nationalist. He believed the civilization that lasted for almost thirty centuries should never surrender to these barbaric Romans. He defied his Queen and formed his army against her wishes. He didn't care. After he defeated this one Roman Legion, the General would turn his army against Queen Cleopatra. He would launch a coup against her and have her executed. Then, he would crown himself King of a new period in Egypt, the Masudi age.

From well behind the combat line he got his first report on the battle. A young sweating soldier on horseback rode up quickly, he informed the General, *"Our men are dying. They are dropping like flies before we even get close enough to fire an arrow or throw a spear. There are no arrows or spears coming at us, just a thunderous sound of smoke and death."*

The General and some of his advisers got on horses to see the battle close up. As they approached, they saw men falling off their horses. Foot soldiers falling while screaming in anguish. Horses were dropping to the ground, struck by some unseen force. Soon the man to the General's right fell off his horse. It was his brother Hakor. Masudi got off his horse to see what happened. There was a hole in the middle of his tin and brass chest plate. He knew now that the Armageddon weapon was true. His brother was dead.

Caesar stopped the barrage after over eight thousand of the Egyptian soldiers were dead. His cavalry was able to surround the Egyptian army and stop their retreat. It did not take his men long to find General Masudi. They made him kneel as Caesar and Octavian got down off their horses to face him.

*"What is the meaning of this fruitless attack on Rome? I told your Queen that I would expect a complete surrender,"* Caesar held his face and slapped it hard.

The General tried to save his skin. *"Yes, spare me great Caesar. It was Queen Cleopatra that ordered the attack. She did not believe the stories coming out of Parthia. She thought the weapon was not real, only the work of magicians and wizards."*

Caesar almost wept, when he realized what he would have to do to her. He would have to make an example of the beautiful Queen Cleopatra.

The Romans bound his hands and gagged the General and used a rope to tie him behind a horse. They then rode the three miles to the gates of Alexandria. When the general could not keep up with the horse, they simply let the horse drag him over the rough terrain.

⸻

Caesar entered the Queen's throne room with Octavian, his generals and ten riflemen. They threw the almost dead General in front of her. Cleopatra sat above a few of her advisers. Her two beauticians stood on each side of her.

Caesar tried to act furious at the Queen of Egypt, he spoke in Latin, *"Cleopatra! I told you what to do. Those men did not need to die. They would have been trained to be a great Roman Legion. I am going to put you in a cage and parade you through the streets of Rome until you starve to death."*

Cleopatra stood up from her throne. She slowly walked down four golden steps with her violet eyes staring at Caesar. When she was two feet away, she waved her arm and said also in Latin, *"Leave us! Everyone leave us!"*

Caesar nodded his approval and soon the two leaders were alone. Caesar could not resist. He tried to put his arms around her.

She pushed him away and yelled in his face, *"You are going to put me in a cage and parade me through Rome? The mother of your only heir? The mother of your only son, you are going to cage me like an animal?"*

Caesar tried to respond, *"I told you to surrender. You did not. You must pay."*

*"Are you stupid, Caesar? Do you forget I have seen the weapon? I know what it can do. I have an insubordinate General. My order was for him to surrender. This was a coup against me. I am not stupid Caesar, and I knew the reports from Parthia were true."*

Caesar was a little embarrassed, *"I guess I should have spoken to you first."*

*"Yes, you should have. Stay with me tonight. I have a proposal for you in the morning. You may never agree to it, but I can only try."*

Julius Caesar put his arms around her. This time she did not resist. As he kissed her, he wished the wonderful night ahead would never end.

Everything in her palace was astonishing. The best marble furniture. The best upholstery made of silk in beautiful shades of yellow and red. The sculptured artwork was almost as magnificent as the hand-crafted mosaics adorning the walls in shapes of dozens of Egyptian gods and Egyptian hieroglyphics. Her bedroom was no different. Her bed was the size of three king size beds and shaped in a perfect circle. There was a silver and blue silk canopy above and bedsheets of golden cashmere and lamé covered with plush pillows of every color.

After an exhausting night with his lover, Caesar was awoken by a boyish voice that was speaking perfect Latin, *"Good morning Father, I hope you slept well."*

The five-year-old Ptolemy XV Caesar, better known as Caesarion, was the splitting image of Caesar from his musty brown hair to his bright blue eyes. He seemed unusually confident for a five-year-old.

Caesar looked to the right of the bed and saw that Cleopatra was gone. He looked at the young boy and before he could answer he heard another voice, *"Your son asked you a question, Caesar. Are you not going to answer him?"*

Cleopatra's long straight hair was now dyed a perfect white and was adorned with jewels of gold and gems of purple amethyst. The dark makeup around her eyes made them resemble the violet eyes of a cat. The long white and purple gown she wore had a long silky white shawl that was hanging down behind her. Her two young beauticians were holding the ends of the cape off the ground as she walked toward Caesar.

The Queen said to the young girls, *"Take Caesarion away and leave us alone. We have much to discuss."*

After they left, Caesar got out of bed and put a purple robe on to cover his naked body. Cleopatra told him, *"I know you know he is your son. After seeing him again, you must know this be true."*

*"What I know of this does not matter. All that matters to me are the people of Rome."*

Cleopatra got a little upset, *"To Hades with the people of Rome! You should care just a little about us, about your family."*

*"I have an image to uphold. When I return to Rome shortly, the people will welcome me back with the biggest triumphal in the history of the world. You and Caesarion will be very comfortable here in Alexandria."*

She got a little more upset. *"Comfortable? You think I need to be comfortable? I need you to listen to my proposal. The first thing you have to do is divorce this Calpurnia woman."*

*"That cannot be done. She has a long line of high-ranking Roman heritage. She has been my wife for many years"*

Cleopatra was now almost yelling, *"Wife? What kind of wife is she? She is old and barren. She cannot give you a son. I have, and I can give you four, maybe five more. Answer me this great Julius, can Calpurnia give you a night like you had last night? Can she?"*

Caesar smiled, *"No she cannot. Only the Queen of Egypt can do that. I'm not sure I could take many more nights like that."*

*"So, listen to me. You do not need Rome. You do not need Octavian. Divorce her and marry me. We can rule the world as husband and wife from right here in Alexandria. Rome is old and tired. The modern and beautiful city of Alexandria could be the capital of the world."*

Caesar started to get a little impatient, *"Octavian is brilliant. He has learned so much in the three years since you saw him last. He will be my successor."*

Cleopatra walked five steps away from him. She abruptly turned around and pointed her right finger at him, *"You do not need Octavian! While we rule together, you can mold your real son Caesarian into the leader that you are. He already looks just like you."*

Caesar suddenly got down on one knee. He held his head with both hands and let off a soft moan as he fainted to the floor.

*"Caesar!"* Cleopatra ran to his side. *"Caesar what is wrong? Servants enter at once!"*

Two male servants managed to get the unconscious Caesar back into Cleopatra's bed. She ordered her beautician to summon the best doctors in Egypt. Now, all she could do is wait by his side and hope the great Julius Caesar would wake up.

Cleopatra had ordered the servants and doctors to tell no one of this incident. When his eyes opened four hours later, she sighed with relief. He looked at her. She took his hand and said softly, *"I am so glad you are awake. Was I a little too much last night?"*

He tried to smile and whispered, *"You were so beautiful last night, like you are every minute of the day. Get the doctors and servants out of here."*

When everyone left, Cleopatra returned to his side. He told her, *"These spells of dizziness are becoming more frequent and more intense. I am afraid that I have little time left in this world."*

*"Do not be a child great Emperor. You will have many more sons."*

*"I wish I could agree with you great Queen. I have always loved you, now more than ever. But now, I wish to speak to Octavian."*

Cleopatra tried to keep her cool, *"Octavian again? I will summon him, but I will tell you once more that you do not need him any longer."*

She walked to the door and Caesar said to himself, *"No my Queen. I need him more than ever now."*

Cleopatra waited outside her bedroom door for the Emperor's adopted son. When he approached, she confronted him. *"How long have these dizzy spells been happening?"*

The young curly haired Octavian said sarcastically, *"For years, former Queen. You didn't poison him, did you?"*

*"You know nothing of our love, little boy."*

*"There is no love. All he desires is your beauty and speaking of little boys, this little Caesarian cannot be his son, can he?"*

Cleopatra looked him in the eye and sternly said, *"All you have to do is look at him and that will answer your question."*

*"Yes, and he lets you call him Caesar, like myself and my father. You know, I asked one of my advisers what I should do about this Caesarian issue. Do you want to know what he told me?"*

*"I do not care, but what did he tell you?"*

Octavian entered the bedroom. He turned around and said to her, *"Too many Caesars is not a good thing."*

———◆———

Caesar recovered in less than a week. Now, it would soon be time to return to Rome. He would have half of the Thirteenth Legion stay in Egypt to keep the peace. The rest would travel back to Rome with Octavian and himself to enjoy their elaborate victory celebration. He was still a little shaky. He sat on a throne with four handles so four slaves could walk him to the ship.

He saw Cleopatra approaching the dock with the usual entourage of people following her. He noticed there were three women dressed in black with long black head scarfs covering most of their faces. He quickly ordered Octavian to board the ship.

The Queen got close to the sitting Emperor. *"I bring you gifts great Caesar. Gifts that will give you eternal life."*

*"What is this gift Cleopatra? I have all I need from the Egyptian people."* Caesar's voice was soft and shaky.

She pointed to the three women dressed in black. *"These three women have over three thousand years of learned knowledge. Take them to Rome with you."*

*"What? What knowledge do they possess?"*

Cleopatra started to get emotional. *"I know you will never grant my first proposal about your son Caesarian, but you must grant this second one. When your time comes, do not burn yourself like a savage. Cremation is the work of barbarians. These three women have learned thousands of years' experience in embalming and mummification. They will preserve your body so when the Gods feel it is time, you will rule the world again."*

Caesar noticed a tear falling from her eye. He told her, *"So, I will accept your gifts and consider this proposal."* Caesar took her hand and kissed it. *"Goodbye Great Queen. We will meet again."*

*"We will meet again. But not here. We will meet again in the afterlife."*

As the slaves carried him to the ship, the tears were now rolling out of Caesar's eyes.

—◆—

His twenty-three-day trip back to Rome gave Caesar a chance to rest. Still the dizzy spells would come and go. When he got to Rome, he was taken to his palace outside of Rome. Mark Antony was the first one he met on his return. They met by his bedside. Caesar was too dizzy to stand.

Antony took his hand. *"You will beat this illness great Caesar. What do the doctors say?"*

*"I have seen Egyptian doctors. I have seen Roman doctors; it is all the same. They give me herbs and potions that do not work."*

Antony tried to be sympathetic. *"You will be fine tomorrow. This is the day of your triumph. It will be the biggest and most magnificent in the history of Rome. We have developed fireworks. There will be gunpowder explosions. Legionaries and riflemen marching through the forum. Chariot races galore and even more gladiators will battle than ever before."*

*"Sounds amazing, Antony. You planned it well."*

Antony got closer to Caesar's ear, *"I have an unusual request to ask. Since I did not get to attend the assault on Parthia, I would like to request five well stocked ships, and one Legion with maybe fifty riflemen."*

*"Make it a hundred, Antony. The factory is making more than we need. Where do you want to go? Conquer India? Maybe China?"*

*"No great Caesar, I want to go the other way. I want to sail across the Sea of Atlas. I want to find the land of America."*

*"Now wait a minute Antony, we do not even know if this place exists. It might be just a tale from the imagination of that little man child."*

*"He knows how to make the rifle. He had to learn that somewhere. Imagine the riches they must have if it exists. It is worth the risks of a few ships."*

Caesar thought for a moment. If something was to happen to him. If the dizziness never stopped, it would be good to have Antony and Octavian as far apart as possible.

He told him, *"Yes Antony, this will be granted. After the celebration tomorrow start making plans. I wish I could go with you to find this land of America. Have you heard anything about the two young ones?"*

*"I am so sorry Caesar. You do not need this burden now."*

*"Tell me,"* Caesar ordered.

*"The spies are out of leads. They think they are dead."*

*"You know this makes my heart bleed with tears."*

Antony cried also, *"I understand great Caesar. My heart bleeds also."*

The triumph was a grand as Antony had described. On almost every street corner fireworks were flying into the air. Gunpowder explosions were exploding as riflemen shot their weapons into the air. The Roman Forum was packed with thousands of people dancing and praising their great leader, Julius Caesar. Antony and Octavian were in a perch far above the revelry below, soaking in all the glorious victory. Each one ignited the crowd with fiery speeches praising the Emperor. As the day became night, the free wine made the celebration even grander. There was only one thing wrong with the triumph. There was no Caesar present. He was still too sick in the bed in his palace.

———◆———

Cleopatra kept hearing Octavian's voice over and over again in her head. *"Too many Caesars is not a good thing. Too many Caesars is not a good thing."* She was already planning her escape. She had heard that Caesar was gravely ill. When the Emperor passed away, Cleopatra knew that one of Octavian's first orders of business would be to have her five-year-old son Caesarian killed.

Her plan was to take a large entourage to India and live with her allies in exile there. It was not the perfect plan. She knew Rome's riflemen would soon be knocking on India's door.

Over two months had passed since Caesar had departed from Alexandria. On this day she received two messages from Rome. The first one she already knew. It informed her that Caesar was gravely ill and near death. The second message was different. It was an invitation of sorts. Cleopatra read it twice.

She quickly got her aides together. *"Listen everyone, there has been a change of plans. We are not going to India."*

Murmurs of *"Where are we going?"* came from the group.

Cleopatra looked at the note again. *"We are going to a faraway place, to a mysterious place. With Mark Antony, we are going to a place called America."*

———◆———

The room was dark and filled with the smell of Damascus Rose, Queen of Heaven, Frankincense, and Sweet Myrrh. The incense was burning in every corner of the room. The soft sound of a lute was accompanying the clear alto voice of a woman singing in Latin, some of the poems of Virgil. His wife Calpurnia sat at the right side of his deathbed and wept softly with her sisters and aides. To his right sat Octavian.

It was now September the third, 41 BC (713 AUC). Henry Garfield's warning of an assassination attempt gave Julius Caesar over three years of very productive life. Octavian Caesar was still only twenty-two years old. When his adopted father would pass into the afterlife, he would now own this enormous burden. He would become the second Emperor of Rome and he would now rule the world. It seemed convenient that Mark Antony was not around. He was sent by Caesar on a mysterious journey to a mysterious place. Octavian looked into Caesar's eyes. They were foggy and seemed to have no life. Octavian took his hand and quietly wept also.

The three Egyptian women dressed in black were in the back of the room out of Caesar's sight. Against the advice of Octavian, Mark Antony, the Senate, and all his aides and generals, Caesar put in his will that there would be no cremation. His body would be embalmed and mummified by the Egyptian women the Queen of Egypt had given him, a process that could take over a month. Then he would rest in the new magnificent Temple of Julius Caesar. This was the only gift he could give his real love. This was his gift to Queen Cleopatra.

The dying man started to shake violently, then he suddenly stopped. His eyes cleared up as he motioned Octavian to come closer. He whispered into his ear, *"They are not dead. The little man child and the young girl did not run away. They are here in Rome."* Before he took his last breath, he whispered. *"Not in this Rome but a very different Rome."*

Gaius Julius Caesar was now resting in the afterlife.

---

# XIV

# The Homecoming

S HERRIE MELBOURNE HEARD A HIDEOUSLY LOUD HISSING SOUND COMING through the darkness. Then there was a large flash of light like she had never seen before. Sherrie reached up and pulled the string on a single lightbulb that hung above her bed. The dim light revealed a little man and a slightly taller young woman. The two young people were holding each other, and they were both buck naked.

Sherrie's eyes were wide open as she looked at them in amazement. She tried to keep her voice as quiet as possible. She spoke in Latin, *"Who in the name off Hades are you two? Where did you come from?"*

Flavia told Henry, *"Yes Henrici, what just happened? This is the beautiful Sherrie, I presume. She does not look that beautiful to me, and why are we naked?"*

Flavia noticed a small open closet. Inside were six tunic-like brown dresses with green trim, each one was exactly the same as the next. There were no other clothes. Flavia quickly put one on and threw one at Henry.

She looked at him. *"You had better start telling me what is going on. This is your suitor, Henrici? She does not even know who you are."*

Henry spit his eyepatch out of his mouth then quickly put it on. He then tried to put on the dress. *"Sherrie seems to be suffering some kind of acute memory loss. Maybe she does not recognize me because of my eye. This is not where I left her."*

Sherrie begged them as quietly as she could, *"Please, please be quiet. I just made it to level four. If they find you, I will be demoted back down to level two."*

Henry tried to speak to her in English, "Sherrie, maybe if we speak English it will jog your memory. Flavia cannot speak English."

Sherrie looked puzzled, she kept speaking in Latin, *"What is this gibberish you are speaking? I only speak Latin and why do you wear that patch?"*

He switched back to Latin, *"I had a most unfortunate accident in Ancient Rome. That 'gibberish' was English. You speak English, Sherrie."*

*"English? Nobody speaks English. That is a dead language. Wait a minute, you are Henrici, and you must be Flavia."* Sherrie looked at her small clock, then turned off the light. *"It is time for bed check. Please hide under the bed and be quiet. Do not let her see you."*

Sherrie waited patiently until the door to her room opened. A large gray-haired woman with a clipboard was shining a flashlight into the tiny room. She asked, *"Is everything alright in here 45712MS? I thought I heard some noise."*

Sherrie answered her, *"I am so sorry ma'am. I worked so hard today, and I was so tired. I fell out of bed."*

*"That's fine. Your master wants you to work a double shift tomorrow."*

*"Of course, I will. And ma'am, do you think he would let me have my second day off after the double? I have only had one so far this month."*

*"I will inquire."* The big woman closed the door.

Sherrie kept the light off. She whispered to them, *"About nine months ago, I got transferred from southern North America to Rome by my master, Doctor Pillar. Ever since I got here, I have been hearing voices. I thought I was going crazy, but they seemed so real. There were voices of a little man named Henrici, a woman named Flavia, and even a slave named Cornelius. Voices of Julius Caesar and Mark Antony. I even heard the voice of Queen Cleopatra. I don't understand any of this, but now, here you are."*

Henry said, almost crying, *"This is very strange. That is precisely the same amount of time I spent in Ancient Rome. Sherrie and I must be slightly connected by an electromagnetic field that has formed a vortex that is penetrating both paralleled time lines from here and into my time in Ancient Rome."*

Henry was now crying as softly as he could. Flavia whispered at him sternly, *"Stop crying Henrici. You have a lot of explaining to do. You said you were going into the future. How far in the future did you take me?"*

*"I did not take you. You piggybacked a ride by grabbing ahold of me."*

Flavia demanded an answer, *"How far, Henrici?"*

*"We are over two-thousand years into the future now."*

Flavia screamed in a whisper, *"Two-thousand years! Why did you do this?"*

He whispered, *"I should not have. But don't you see Flavia? It is not supposed to be like this. This is all wrong."* He turned to Sherrie, *"I told you Sherrie. I predicted this would cause a cataclysmic catastrophe and I was right. I told you we should not have done this. You talked me into doing this and now you are the biggest victim of this most unfortunate experiment."*

Sherrie said, *"I did not ask you to do anything. I do not even know you."*

*"In my world you knew me, and you knew I could travel through time. You convinced me to go back over two-thousand years, to warn Julius Caesar about his imminent assassination. You convinced me to show them how to make a powerful weapon, and now, Rome never fell."*

Flavia asked him, *"What are you taking about, Rome never fell?"*

He told them, *"Yes Rome never fell. Can't you see, Flavia? Sherrie is a slave."*

◆

The room looked like a tiny jail cell. Sherrie's single bed barely fit inside. There was a bathroom with a toilet, a sink, and a small shower. It was clean but looked old and broken down. The bathroom, like the small closet, had no door.

The only light fixture was the bulb that hung down over Sherrie's bed. She turned it on, so she could see her guests. Henry took a hard look at his hoped-to-be girlfriend. The twenty-year-old looked tired and worn-out. Sherrie's blond hair had a few streaks of gray and was cut to just below her ears. Her long white nightgown showed Henry that she was even thinner than before. She almost looked malnourished. Henry thought she didn't look twenty. She looked like she was pushing forty.

Sherrie whispered to them, *"If this is true Henrici, what was the world like before we supposedly did this?"*

Henry told her that she was a successful college student. He told her about the United States, the land she lived in, a land that was a democracy, a land that had abolished slavery over one-hundred and fifty years prior. Then he told her about her family.

*"I had a family, Henrici? I barely remember my parents. I was sold when I was just five years old."* Sherrie cried silently.

Flavia said to him, *"Henrici, if you can travel through time, and if we are over two-thousand years in the future. Then we can go back. I do not belong here."*

*"Yes Henrici. You can go back and make things the way they were in your world. I would not be a slave anymore,"* Sherrie said quickly.

Henry thought for a moment, *"I am not sure that is possible. This is a different society. I do not have my research, my computers, or my workshop. In the movies, once time is changed, it is impossible to change it back."*

Flavia said, *"I know I will be asking millions of questions, but what is a computer, and what is 'the movies'?"*

*"I saw a movie once. It is like moving pictures. On slave appreciation day, they let us watch one once when I was twelve years old. A computer is a machine that watches us. Slaves are not allowed to have them or use them."*

*"A machine that watches? How is that possible?"*

Sherrie showed Flavia her left wrist. There was a small scar, *"See this? There is a computer chip inside of me. They know where I am at any time but here is the good news. Since I made it to level four, they will no longer monitor me. If I make it to level five, I can reproduce. If I get to level six, I am almost assured my freedom."*

Henry told them, *"I need to find out as much about this new Rome as possible before we can make a decision on what to do. Can you tell us, Sherrie? Tell us about this place."*

She looked at the two of them scrunched down on the floor in their brown and green tunics. *"I will, but I do not have much time. I have to work a double shift tomorrow. I need to get a little sleep."* She turned off the light and began to talk.

Sherrie never went to school. She learned to read and write on the job. Any history she knew she had to learn from other slaves.

She told them of the last Emperor of Rome, Tiberius XXVI. Over two-hundred years ago, he had finally defeated the alliance of the Chinese and the Japanese, and at this point in time, Rome ruled the entire world. Tiberius truly believed he was a God and he murdered millions of his rivals who did not believe that. Anyone that didn't praise him as a God would be publicly crucified in the worst way. He killed hundreds of politicians from all the provinces of the world and he also killed millions of slaves. Anyone that refused to believe that Tiberius was divine found themselves hanging from a tree.

This eventually caused massive revolt around the world. Rome soon lost its grip on China and Japan, and India and Russia soon followed the revolution. The Senate of Rome reacted by forcing a coup on Tiberius and destroying his government. They hung Tiberius from a tree in front of hundreds of thousands of Romans in the Great Colosseum in Rome. He was the last Emperor of modern Rome.

The Senate set up a new government elected by the people. They called it the New Roman Republic. "This Republic is what rules Rome today," she told them.

Now Sherrie talked about something she knew very much about. From the years 2708 AUC (1954 AD) to 2922 AUC (1968 AD) there was a disastrous slave revolt that spread throughout the world. Slaves had no rights and were being murdered by civilians, sometimes just for the fun of sadists. The revolution turned into a war. Over five million slaves were killed along with close to a million military and civilians.

*"This was before I was born, Henrici. But every slave knows the story. We were massacred by the thousands. Many brave slaves fought back with their bare hands against guns and bombs. Our great leader, Justus, arranged a truce with the Romans. Before the treaty could be signed, he was brutally murdered with knives by pro-slavery factions."*

Flavia interrupted, *"I have learned that slavery was an abomination. Now I firmly believe, this slavery has to stop. My slave Cornelius taught me this. I can't really believe I'm saying this, but it looks like slavery has been a disaster for over two-thousand years."*

Sherrie continued, *"The treaty was eventually signed in 2922 stopping the violence. The document that made the peace goes by two names, The Bill of Rights for the Bounded and The Constitution of the Slaves.*

Sherrie knew them all from memory.

1. No military, civilian, or owner shall abuse the Bonded physically or sexually.
2. An owner must provide humane room and board for every slave owned.
3. A slave can improve their status by using hard work and loyalty to rise from level one to level six, with a chance to win their freedom at level six.
4. If a slave reaches level four, they will no longer be monitored, unless an infraction occurs.
5. If a slave reaches level five, with owner's blessing, they will be allowed to reproduce.
6. An unruly slave will get a speedy trial. If found guilty, humane execution will be the sentence.
7. All slaves will work one shift (ten hours) a day. They are required to work two double shifts (twenty hours) per month.

8. A slave will receive two days off per month.
9. A slave will receive ten credits per month (adjusted for inflation every five years).
10. The slave must wear their work uniform as their lone identification when on the job or in public.

Henry had to sleep in the fetal position on the floor while Flavia joined Sherrie in the small bed. He was woken up by the sound of water running. The light was on and Flavia was blocking Henry's view to the shower.

"*Do not look in here, Henrici. Sherrie is taking a shower. Turn around.*"

Henry did that. It was five in the morning and Flavia turned around and looked at the slender blond drying off after her shower. It seemed like Sherrie had showered in the fountain of youth. Maybe it was her long, serious talk with her new time-traveling friends, but she looked twenty years younger.

Flavia said to her, "*I take back what I said when I first saw you, Sherrie. You are very beautiful.*"

"*Thank you, Flavia. I had little sleep, but I feel great today. I think you two are going to help me.*"

"*We will,*" Henry whispered with his back turned. "*I am the best computer hacker. I know if I had a computer, I could hack into this Roman system and change you to level six right away.*"

"*As usual, I have no idea what you are talking about,*" Flavia said.

Sherrie said, "*Me neither. Slaves cannot use computers, but I think I know where to find one. For now, you two have to stay here. Remember, whisper, whisper, and only whisper. Do not go outside. There are cameras in the halls. I will sneak you back some food during my break, then when my twenty hours is complete, I should have a day off. We can make a plan then.*"

"*I am not going to ask, what is a camera? What is it you do Sherrie? What is your work?*" Flavia asked.

Sherrie looked cute in her little brown and green dress. "*Oh, I am just a barista. I work for my master. He has a few shops called Kactbruss.*"

Flavia looked at Henry with a question mark look on her face.

"*She makes various flavors of coffee drinks for customers,*" Henry told her.

Flavia said, "*I am not going to ask. What in the name of Hades is coffee?*"

———◆———

The coffee house was packed that Monday morning and after ten straight hours of work serving ungrateful and rude customers, Sherrie got a half an hour break. She managed to take two ham and egg sandwiches, and she was also allowed one large drink. She put them in a paper bag and then hurried back to her room, which was two blocks away.

The brown crumbling complex had two hundred and fifty single rooms, all exactly the same. There was only one entrance and exit in the front. The two security guards at the front gate let Sherrie through, then she took an elevator up to the third floor. When she entered her room, she saw Flavia sitting on her bed and Henry sitting on her pillow on the floor.

She said to them still in a whisper, "*I got us two egg-o-eats with ham. I could only get one drink, so we have to share.*"

Sherrie used a butter knife to cut each sandwich into threes. They each got two pieces.

"*This is good nourishment. I am very hungry,*" Henry said as he gobbled down the meal.

Flavia told them, "*Me too. I am starving. Yum, this is an unusual egg, bread, and meat mix,*" Flavia finished her meal, then said, "*I have just spent ten hours in this little room with Henrici. I do not think I can go ten more. I want to get out and see this new Rome of yours, Sherrie.*"

"*Do not do that,*" Sherrie warned. "*Just wait for me to finish my shift. I have tomorrow off and I have some ideas on what we can do.*"

Sherrie took a sip on the straw sticking out of the beverage.

"*What is that in the papyrus goblet?*" Flavia asked.

"*It is called a paper cup that has my favorite drink in it. Try it.*" Sherrie handed Flavia the cup.

"*How do I drink from it? It is closed on top.*"

Henry explained, "*Suck on the red straw just a little, and the beverage will enter your mouth.*"

Flavia did that, and the warm pick-me-up entered her mouth. Her eyes got big and round, "*In the name of Mars and Venus what is this? I have never tasted anything so good.*"

Sherrie told her, "*It is my favorite. It is called Cherry Café Mocha with Whipped Cream. It is a coffee drink.*"

Flavia took the top off the top of the cup, so she could see what was inside. She took another sip, this time without the straw. With whipped cream on her upper lip she said, "*I am not sharing this with anybody.*"

"*That is alright with me. Caffeine makes me restless,*" Henry said.

Flavia looked at Sherrie and thought about her dismal life of slavery, *"I am so sorry, Sherrie. You can have the coffee drink."*

*"No, you enjoy it Flavia. I will get another cup when my second shift is over. Please you two, just wait here for me. I have to get back to work or I will be late. Oh, I almost forgot."* Sherrie opened the top drawer of her small two drawer dresser. Under her underwear she found a purple bound hardcover book.

She handed it to Flavia, *"Read this. It is the only book they let us slaves have."*

As Sherrie rushed out the door, Flavia opened the book. *"What is this Henrici? It is like many scrolls all bound together."*

*"It is called a book. They do not need scrolls anymore, Flavia."*

They spent the first part of Sherrie's second shift quietly taking turns reading to each other. The book was simply titled *The Life and Times of the Great Julius Caesar.*

When their eyes got tired, Flavia laid down on Sherrie's bed. She listened to Henry talk as he sat on the floor. He did not know what to expect in this new Rome, so he told her about his world. He explained what electricity was and how that single lightbulb worked. He told her about cars and showed her the old brown truck they could see through the small window in the room. Then he talked about trains and airplanes. He tried to tell her about computers and the internet. The intelligent Ancient Roman girl seemed to start to understand everything.

Flavia sat up and said, *"It is very unfortunate what happened to Sherrie's life, and we will help her Henrici."*

*"Yes, we will come up with an ingenious master plan."*

*"All these things you are telling me are fascinating. I want you to teach me everything about this New Rome. Teach me about these carriages with no horses. Teach me about these lamps with no fire. Teach me how these machines can fly high in the air. Teach me everything Henrici."*

*"Everything is too many things. Remember I am from a different world."*

Flavia looked down at her little friend. *"You must know me by now and you must know you have no choice in this matter."* She whispered as loud as she could, *"Teach me Henrici, Teach me!"*

<hr />

Sherrie was closing down the now locked-up coffee shop. She had to put all the coffees away and clean the espresso machines. She had to sanitize all the equipment then sweep the floors and complete many more minor tasks before she could leave. She was surprised when someone entered the door she had just locked.

She knew who he was even though she seldom ever saw him. Doctor Pillar was a middle-aged man with greying hair and a nicely trimmed beard. His glasses were thin-rimmed and almost looked dark.

Sherrie did not look him in the eyes. She looked at the floor and said, *"Sir Master, it is so nice you are here. What can I do for you? Thank you so much for helping me get to level four so quickly."*

The man said to her, *"You have to do something for me. You cannot refuse."*

Sherrie noticed the man smelled of wine. *"Whatever you wish."*

*"I am having a party at my villa outside of Rome on the western coast. After your day off tomorrow, I want to take you there to entertain us. It is just two of my friends. Surely you can handle three men. We want it all at the same time. A little foursome."*

Sherrie was shocked. She continued to look at the floor. *"Master sir, you cannot do this. Article one in our Constitution forbids you from sexually abusing any of your slaves."*

*"You know 45712MS, your name is Sherrie, right? A lot of us masters are getting tired of that god-damn constitution of yours. We are starting to take matters into our own hands. First, if you refuse, I will make sure you are knocked down to level one in no time. And second? Well, have you noticed how some of your colleagues have been disappearing? I have heard a rumor that there is a place where owners enjoy watching disobedient slaves suffer, and then they just disappear. Will you obey me Sherrie?"*

Sherrie tried to think fast. She knew she only had one answer for now. She looked him in the eye, *"Yes master sir. I will oblige you. I will give you anything you wish."*

*"I thought so. I have given the guards at your slave house permission to let you come and go whenever you please. You will not try to escape because if you do, we will activate your chip and find you instantly. I will see you in a few days. Make sure you arrive at your prettiest."*

Sherrie was rushing home as fast as she could. She carried a big bag. Since she agreed to his proposal, she convinced him to give her three beef sandwiches and three garden salads. She also had two Café Mochas and a hot chocolate for Henry.

They would feast on this meal and try to figure out a plan. She prayed to the Gods that her time-traveling friends could help her with a plan for her escape from this monster, her master Pillar. She had one day. Her mind raced, and she realized that she needed that one day to get the little Henrici in front of a computer.

# XV

# The Day Off

"*IF WE WERE BACK IN MY ROME, I WOULD TAKE ONE OF THOSE RIFLES AND blow that guy to bits.*" Flavia was very angry.

Henry said, "*I do not think that is an option in our current situation.*"

Sherrie wasn't that tired. She was mad. "*I like the rifle idea. Did you ever see one of the first rifles invented in Ancient Rome, Flavia?*"

Henry quickly said, "*That is not important right now. We have to come up with an ingenious and effective plan or Sherrie will be raped by three men.*"

Flavia told them, "*When I saw our slave Cornelius with fresh scars all over his arms and back, applied by the whip of a wicked farm foreman, I knew slavery was the most inhumane injustice. The bastard masters of years ago are no different from the bastard masters of today.*"

Sherrie said, "*I can't argue with that, Flavia. Look, I just need to sleep for two hours. I just worked a twenty-hour shift with little sleep. You two think of a plan but I already know what we have to do. When I wake up, it will still be dark out.*"

When Sherrie arrived back, after working her double shift, she had told them about her encounter with Doctor Pillar. It was now past hour two in the morning. With Sherrie's day off tomorrow, that gave them twenty-eight hours until Sherrie's next shift. The Doctor told her he would pick her up at hour seven in the morning.

At hour four, Henry woke up. The light was on and this time Sherrie was blocking his view to the bathroom. "*Turn around Henrici. Flavia is taking a shower. Do not look.*"

He said back, "*Okay, but who is going to block the view for me? I need a shower also.*"

"*Do not worry, Henrici. We won't look.*"

When Henry's time to shower came, he told them, *"Do not look now, I am getting in."*

Both girls were sitting on the bed with their backs to Henry. When he said this, they both turned around to peek.

Henry covered his privates, and whispered as loud as he could, *"No fair. No peeping at me."*

They both turned around giggling. Sherrie said to Flavia, *"His voice drives you crazy, but sometimes he is so cute."*

*"I have been under that spell many times. One minute you want to kill him, the next you want to love him. In Ancient Rome they called him a man child."*

*"That is exactly what he is. Did he ever talk about me in Ancient Rome?"*

Flavia said, *"Yes, all the time. It was beautiful Sherrie this, then beautiful Sherrie that. He told me you promised him something if he was successful in his mission and apparently, he was."*

*"What could that be that I promised?"*

*"I will tell you later, now let's concentrate on the plan."*

Sherrie got a little nervous, *"Do you think the plan will work, Flavia? The Doctor told me that some of the owners have a place where they torture unruly slaves and then the slaves disappear. There was this boy named Florence. I thought he might become my mate. One day he was just gone, and I believe the same will happen to me if we fail."*

*"I think we will all die if we fail. I have seen Henrici do some amazing things. If he does what he says he can do, we will succeed."*

---

Sherrie started the plan. At hour five in the morning, she left the room and elevatored to the ground floor. The guards let her through the front gate. Both had a smirky smile like they knew who she was going to see. She started walking towards the coffee house carrying the big bag she used for the food the previous night.

She always passed a laundromat and at this hour, and many of the washers and dryers were filled with clothes but unattended. She entered and saw that there was only one impoverished older woman inside.

The elder Roman citizen said to her, *"Hey young one, slaves are not allowed in here."*

Sherrie already had a response, she said in a sexy voice, *"Oh, this thing? I am going to see my boyfriend now. He loves to do roleplay. He loves it when I dress up like a slave."*

The woman smiled and continued folding her clothes. Sherrie opened one of the dryers. She was in luck. It was filled with women's clothes. She found a short blue and green flowered dress that would be perfect for Flavia. There were also some light brown women's pants. Sherrie had always wanted to wear pants. These might be a little short for her, but she didn't care. She also took a nice yellow blouse. She opened the next dryer. This one was filled with men and women's clothes. She found a short sleeved green buttoned-down shirt. For some reason, she knew it would look great on Henry. There were also some blue denim jeans that were probably too big for him. She didn't have time to be picky. She folded the clothes, put them in the bag and got out of there fast.

She walked back to the housing complex and sneaked around to the back of the building. She soon found her third story window and saw Flavia was waving to her. Henry had used the butter knife to easily pick the cheap lock on the small window. It opened just enough for Flavia to fit through. They tied the bedsheet to the bed and threw it out the window. Flavia jimmied down the sheet until she was at story two then she let go. Sherrie broke her fall as the two girls fell to the floor.

Now it was Henry's turn. He pulled the bedsheet back inside and untied it from the bed. He squeezed through the window and hung on to the window sill, leaving his body dangling. He was still wearing the brown and green dress.

Flavia whispered loudly, *"Let go, Henrici. Now, let go."*

*"I cannot. I am too scared."*

Both girls whispered in unison, *"Do it, Henrici, now."*

Henry used all his strength to reach up and shut the window. Then he fell to his fate, into the arms of the two beautiful young girls. When he reached their waiting arms, all three fell to the ground. They sat there for one second staring at each other. Then, they all got up and ran to the old brown truck. Behind the old wreck they changed clothes.

Flavia put on her short dress. *"This is pretty, Sherrie. It is a very short tunic. What is this strange fabric?"*

*"I think it is polyester. Look at this Flavia, I finally get to wear pants."*

Flavia looked amazed. *"I have never seen clothes like that. Henrici has some too."*

*"Yes, but mine are too big. Did you get me a belt, Sherrie?"*

*"No Henrici, I did not have time to accessorize. Just hold them up."*

Sherrie put all her slave clothes into the bag. The three pairs of brown sneakers that were issued to Sherrie for work were a little big for Flavia. They fit Henry perfectly.

The truck was left open and the three got into the front seat. Henry was behind the wheel with Flavia to his right. He jimmied the ignition keyhole with the butter knife until it came off then he pulled out the wires and he knew exactly which ones to cut. This took a while.

*"Hurry up, Henrici. I just saw a light go on the fourth floor,"* Sherrie said.

*"This is not easy with a butter knife."*

When Henry finally got the wires cut and exposed, he touched the two power lines together. There was a clacking rumble but no start. He tried again. Another clack and rumble and then, nothing.

Sherrie was getting anxious, *"Come on Henrici. If that slave up there reports us, we will be dead before we start."*

He tried it again, and this time the rumble continued.

*"Yes!"* Sherrie said, *"Let's go, Henrici."*

*"We have one big problem here. I do not know how to drive."*

Sherrie got a little more nervous, *"What? Shouldn't you have told us that before?"*

*"I thought you could drive, Sherrie. You sort of drive in my world. Just not very well. You hit a stop sign. Anyway, it might look suspicious, a guy driving with an eye patch."*

*"Henrici, they do not let slaves drive unless that is their job, and I am a barista."*

Flavia calmly said, *"Let me drive. It cannot be that different than driving a horse and carriage."*

*"I think that is a very good idea,"* Henry said. *"Let us switch places. You go below me. These wires are still hot."*

Flavia passed below him as Henry held the wires carefully, she put both her hands on the steering wheel. *"Teach me Henrici."*

Sherrie said, *"Let me get this straight. We are going to let a girl from Ancient Rome that just saw a car for the first time today, drive us?"*

*"It is the best choice. Flavia is not afraid to do anything."* Henry looked at the pedals below. *"This is not good."*

Their luck just got worse. There were three pedals. The truck was a manual shift. Henry told her about the gas, the brake, and the clutch. He told her that he would shift the gears at first. Flavia pushed down the clutch and Henry put it in first gear. Flavia tried to press the gas and ease off the clutch. There were two violent jerks and the truck abruptly stalled.

"*This is never going to work,*" a very nervous Sherrie said.

Flavia said, "*Give me a chance, Sherrie. I can do this.*"

She tried it again. This time she got it going. When Henry said "*shift*" Flavia used her left foot to press down the clutch. Henry put it in second gear. Soon the truck started veering to right. There was a loud screeching crash. Flavia had just sideswiped a parked car to the right.

"*You have to steer also, Flavia.*" Henry grabbed the wheel and tried to straighten her out. He again said "*shift*," as he put it in third gear.

Henry said, "*Maybe we should go back and leave a note on that car. That is what we do when there is a minor accident in my world.*"

"*Are you crazy, Henrici?*" Sherrie said. "*I am an escaping slave, in a stolen car. You think we should go back and leave a note!*"

"*I guess that was not a good idea.*" Henry saw something that looked like an abandoned supermarket to the right. "*Turn in there, Flavia.*"

The breaks screeched as Flavia over maneuvered her right turn and the truck stalled again just as it entered the lot. Henry got it going right away and told Flavia to drive to the back. There Flavia practiced starting and stopping, shifting gears, and steering. After just forty-five minutes she had almost mastered the art of the drive. The three quickly decided that Flavia would drive, Henry would assist, and Sherrie would interpret the Roman rules of the road.

Flava said, "*I am ready. Let us do this. Are you sure you know where this bank place is, Sherrie?*"

"*I've only been there once, but I know where it is. We are going to do this!*"

Henry tried to sound enthusiastic, "*It is showtime!*"

Even literate slaves were not allowed paper or pens. The Roman government had created the Consul of Bondslave to regulate this always-suffering group. These cronies felt tht writing between slaves could promote alliances amongst them that could lead to riots and revolution. So far, the Slavery rights group, TSWD (Treat Slaves with Dignity), although they tried, could not change this policy.

So, a slave had to memorize everything. Directions, addresses, numbers, names, anything a citizen could write down, a slave had to memorize. Sherrie had an amazing memory and this constant exercise only enhanced it. She knew how to get to the next part of their plan—to The Bank of the Bonded. It was about a thirty-mile drive and they had to cross through the middle of Rome. This was the most magnificent city the world had ever seen.

Sherrie told Flavia to turn right onto the expressway. It went right through the center of Rome, but Flavia wasn't fazed. Once she figured out how to drive, she was totally present in the moment, and was game for anything.

Sherrie told her, "*Speed up Flavia, look in your mirrors and merge into traffic. Henrici, help her.*"

She got thru traffic fine and Sherrie told her, "*The sign says sixty miles per hour. Match that on the speedometer.*"

"*I do not know what these symbols mean,*" Flavia said.

Henry explained, "*That is because those are digital numbers. You can only read Roman numerals.*"

Henry pointed to the sixty on the speedometer, and Flavia matched that speed.

"*This is such an adventure. The different buildings that are so big, these cars that can go so fast, even the mirrors are so clear. We have mirrors in my Rome, but they are wavy and hazy. I would not know what I look like without the pond behind our villa where I could see my reflection.*"

Henry nerdily said, "*I will tell you, Flavia, that you look the prettiest.*"

Sherrie said with a little jealously in her voice, "*Are you sure about that, Henrici?*" Henry thought he better not say anything else.

Flavia stayed in the right lane. She got a little nervous when they went down a slight decline but as it leveled off, she relaxed. She thought she saw something to her left. Henry kept telling her to keep her eyes on the road.

Sherrie said, "*Flavia, look at that.*"

She briefly looked to left and again Henry told her not to. She said to him, "*Henrici, you take the wheel for a minute. I have to see this.*"

The view of downtown Rome was more than spectacular. Rome was home to the ten largest buildings in the world. Each one looked like shiny glass, some shooting up and angles more reclined than the Leaning Tower of Pisa. The glass-colored light of the structures shone even brighter in the morning sun. Colors of blue, red, yellow, and more, filled Flavia's eyes with wonder as each skyscraper seemed to outshine the next.

Then she saw Rome's jewel, a perfectly round cylinder of a building of gold that shot up one-hundred and fifty stories. It had a mushroom top that extended out from the cylinder over one hundred yards. There were sixteen huge white Roman columns planted in the ground around the cylinder building, each one shooting up one hundred and fifty stories until it attached to the mushroom keeping it from tumbling to the ground. Near the middle were four arms coming out at an angle from the building, each one holding a smaller cylinder building in the sky. All four had smaller mushroom tops with the same white roman columns for support.

Flavia looked back at the road for a second, then she looked at it again. She had tears in her eyes. *"Look at those things! They are flying. They are flying!"*

The building had a number of elevators visible from the outside, but the government mostly used shiny drones of gold and silver buzzing up and down in rhythmic motion carrying passengers to their requested floor. This was the building of the Roman Government called The Headquarters, the building that housed the New Roman Consuls and the New Roman Senate.

*"This is not a very good idea to have me drive from here because I only have one eye,"* Henry said.

Flavia took back the wheel. She went back to driving as carefully as she could.

Sherrie said, *"Soon we will be coming to the New Roman Colosseum Complex. It will be on your left."*

*"What is a Colosseum?"* Flavia asked

Henry answered, *"It was built after your time in Ancient Rome. Construction was complete in the year 80 AD; I mean 833 after the founding of the city. It was built to house sporting events and almost 80,000 spectators could attend. There were gladiator fights and chariot races, and they would feed people to lions and tigers. In my world it is now a ruin and a very popular tourist destination."*

*"A ruin, Henrici?* Sherrie pointed her finger to the left. *"Look at that."*

The main amphitheater was restored to its original splendor. It looked as grand as the day it opened in 80 AD. Lined with gold and silver, the broken-down walls that Henry knew were fully restored with modern windows of blue and green. But the original building was dwarfed by a much larger super stadium. Built in the same architectural style as the original, this was three times as large. The new complex could hold over 200,000 patrons. Henry gasped.

Gone were the games of Gladiators and chariot races. The Romans liked a game where they kicked a ball into a goal. But their real love was a game where two teams of twelve would compete on an open field to try to advance a ball, shaped like a prolate spheroid, into the defending team's goal, either by running or throwing the ball.

The violent game left the New Romans filled with excitement. The biggest problem they had was the amount of deaths to the young athletes. Last season alone they had a record twenty-five deaths. There was a push to give the players some padding, and against the will of the game's traditionalist, actual helmets to protect the young men. The New Romans simply called this game 'Kill the Guy with the Ball.'

Sherrie said, *"If you make it to level five and you have the denarius, a slave can go to one game a year."*

*"You are going to be a level six very soon,"* Henry said.

*"Yes, if we pull this off, and we* are *going to pull this off."* Flavia stepped on the gas.

Sherrie guided Flavia off the expressway and down three different streets to get to their destination. They pulled into a small parking lot at the Bank of the Bonded. Not many slaves had cars. She went to the back of the small red-bricked building and parked next to a dumpster. Sherrie rolled up her brown pants and put her slave dress on over her clothes.

*"I have been saving my credits since I was a little girl. Now, I am glad I did. Wish me luck. This should not take me too much time."*

Henry said, *"Good luck. Why is there no sign on this building?"*

*"That is because Romans do not want anything that has to do with slaves in their neighborhoods. Everyone knows what it is though."*

Sherrie went into the bank and came out ten minutes later. She went behind the truck and took off her slave dress. She put it in the bag with the other two and threw the bag into the dumpster. She went to the window of the truck and said, *"I just took out half of what I had. I thought any more would look suspicious. It is more than enough to get us through the next part of the plan. Let's go."*

Flavia and Henry got out of the truck and the three walked directly towards the main street, abandoning the old brown truck.

*"I am going to miss this thing called a truck,"* Flavia said. *"That was so much fun learning to drive her through this New Rome."*

With that, the three abandoned their stolen truck and walked. First, there was the tall eloquent blond with short hair wearing a yellow blouse and tight brown pants that only covered half of her shins. She walked nearest the street. Next to her was the sandy brunette from Ancient Rome with sparkling blue eyes in a darling blue and green flowered mini dress. Finally, hobbling on the end was the eye-patched nerd wearing his green button-down shirt and holding up his cuffed blue jeans so his pants would not fall down. Sherrie saw a small clothing store on their way. She went in and bought Henry a belt. He felt better but hoped they didn't look too out-of-place.

They walked down the busy street towards the Roman Metro, and in a short while, they made their way into the underground subway of this New City of Rome.

# XVI

# The Cult

THE UNDERGROUND SUBWAY, WITH ITS CARS OF RED AND WHITE, seemed modern, clean, and new. The trio was traveling east on the underground red line. The subway seemed safe with Metro Police Officers seen walking diligently through their rounds to make sure it was secure.

Flavia was fascinated, *"You mean they have these trains going all about the underground of Rome? I cannot believe this."*

Sherrie bought them three passes from a vending machine, and they went through the turnstiles towards their train. *"They do, and there are six different lines. This one runs through the safest part of Rome. Soon, we will transfer to the yellow line going north. That one will be a little different."*

They got on and found seats. Henry was sitting between the two girls as their train whizzed thru the dark tunnel. He asked, *"Are you sure you know where we are going, Sherrie?"*

Sherrie explained to them that her potential mate, Florence, had made a trek to this mysterious place a few times. He told her they had a computer and access to the internet. She was sure that Henry could use the computer to hack her up to a level-six slave and then declare her freedom. Florence had given her precise directions on how to get there and detailed instructions on what to do when they arrived. Sherrie thought she would never need to use this data for anything. She memorized it anyway and now, she was glad she did.

They got off the red line and took a walk through the underground station towards the yellow line. Sherrie warned them, *"Be on your best guard. There will be no more Metro Police here. We have to enter a very different Rome, the most dangerous part."*

When they got to the yellow line everything seemed dark, dirty, and unkept. Colorful graffiti covered every wall and billboard ad. Then they saw the first yellow-line train; it too, was covered with large words and pictures of graffiti in bright yellow, red, and blue. Some of the words were poetic Latin. Some of the pictures were almost pornographic. Each sentence and painting came from the souls of desperate Romans trying to express their lives in vibrant color.

They got on the dirty northbound train and Sherrie knew their exit was a place called Vinvichi. It was the second-to-last stop. On the interior of the train there was as much graffiti as the paint-decorated outside. There were quotes from actual Ancient Roman graffiti wondrously scratched onto every available space.

Henry read a few to the girls, "*This one says, Celadus the Thracier makes the girls moan!*"

"*I imagine he was quite a Thracier. Whatever that is,*" Sherrie said.

Flavia told them, "*It is a tribe of barbarians east of Rome.*"

Henry read again, "*Weep, you girls. My penis has given you up. Now it penetrates men's.*" Henry was too embarrassed to read the rest. Instead, he said to them, "*That is not a very nice quote.*"

The two girls laughed as Henry read another one, "*If anyone does not believe in Venus, they should gaze at my girlfriend.*" Henry briefly looked at the two girls sitting around him. He truly did believe in Venus.

Sherrie and Flavia took a nap, both girls had their heads sleeping on Henry's two shoulders. A small impoverished Roman man covered with shaggy black hair and a disheveled black beard approached them. He pointed a six-inch knife at Henry. He woke the girls up when he said, "*Give me all your money, or I will cut you all good.*"

Flavia woke up and quickly said, "*That is not going to happen.*"

She took what she learned from Cornelius the slave. She quickly grabbed his wrist with both hands and twisted it until they heard a snap. The knife fell to the floor as Sherrie jumped on the back of the much smaller man, tackling him to the ground. Henry picked up the knife and with his hands shaking, he pointed it at the man and said, "*Be gone highwayman.*"

The little man got up and ran to the back of the car, thru the doors and disappeared into the cars beyond.

Sherrie said, "*We still have two more stops, but we had better get off at the next one. He may come back with some of his friends. Henrici, hide the knife in your pants.*"

The three got off the train and went up the stairs to the street level. The sun was starting to set in this dark and eerie part of Rome. There was one bright spot, a brightly lit restaurant with a red sign that read, *Imperium Americae.*

*"Let's go in here and eat. I have never been to one of these. Us slaves, we do not get out much, but I hear it is pretty good. They have American food."*

The three sat in a booth near a window. A slave-dressed waitress soon came up to them and asked for their order.

Sherrie felt bad for the young slave. She knew what the woman had to go through every day. Sherrie politely ordered three number twos with large drinks.

While they waited for the food, Flavia said, *"It looks a little scary out there. Not like the brilliant Rome I saw when we were driving. How far do we have to walk to get to this place?"*

*"Since we got off the train too soon, it will be twenty-one blocks. I can still get us there."*

Henry said, *"It is getting darker and scarier. Don't you wish we had Cornelius with us, Flavia?"*

*"I sure do Henrici. I also wish I had one of those rifles."*

Sherrie explained, *"Rome has very strict gun laws. Not even citizens are allowed to have them. The government is always afraid of uprising and revolution. Even that knife in Henry's pants is illegal."*

Soon the waitress brought them their three plates.

*"What is this?"* Flavia said as she stared at the plate in front of her.

*"This is just like the food from my world,"* Henry said with excitement. *"It is a hamburger."*

*"A hamber-what?"* Flavia took the top bun off. She separated each ingredient and laid them out on her plate. *"I know this is lettuce, this is tomato, this is onion, what kind of meat is this, ox?"*

*"No, it is beef,"* Henry said.

*"What is a beef? Is it like an ox?"* Flavia asked.

*"Most people think beef tastes better than ox,"* Henry told her. *"I do know that is true because I have eaten ox in Ancient Rome."*

Flavia picked up the little slice of brine-soaked cucumber. *"And what is this?"*

*"It is a pickle,"* Henry said.

Flavia took a little taste. *"Yuk! That is awful. Too sour."*

Sherrie said, *"You do not take it apart, Flavia. You eat it all at once. I cannot wait for any more questions and answers, I am starving."*

Flavia put her meal back together, minus the pickle, and the three quickly ate.

*"One more question,"* Flavia said. *"What are these?"*

Sherrie told her, *"They are fried potatoes. We call them Gaulic Fries."*

*"Where I am from, we call them French fries,"* Henry said.

The two girls said in unison, *"What is a French?"*

Sherrie knew the later it got in this part of Rome, the more dangerous it got. The sooner they started their walk, the better. It was against the law to leave a tip for any slave worker, but Sherrie managed to slip the waitress a few denarii.

They quickly walked through the unlit streets of northern Rome. The sidewalks were filled with homeless Romans, most of them asking for a handout as they passed. Most of the businesses that lined the street were abandoned and closed, the windows broken and covered with cracking and rotting boards. Crumbling flats and grimy small apartments seemed to be the norm in this forgotten land.

When the government ran low on slaves, the Roman policy was to pick up these homeless by the truckload. Each person was charged with vagrancy. There would be a quick trial and a sure conviction, and the sentence was always a condemnation to level-one slavery, which meant the most back-breaking work known to the world. Most of these new slaves did not live long. They would just die. To many it was better to die than live a horrible life of bondage.

Sherrie led them briskly through the streets when they saw three young men approaching them. One of them yelled, *"Look at those girls! It is going to be a fun night!"*

Sherrie just said, *"Run!"*

As they were running as fast as they could, Henry said, *"We must run faster. They are gaining. If they catch us, they will rape you two."*

Sherrie said while puffing hard, *"Henrici, if they catch us, they will rape you also."*

*"Give me the knife, Henrici,"* while running as fast as they could Henry handed Flavia the knife. When they made a left turn, Flavia stopped and hid against the wall of a building. The first poor boy that passed the wall got a knife stuck in his belly. Flavia twisted it hard. The thug screamed as

XVI • The Cult

Flavia pulled it out of his dying body. As he fell to the ground, she pointed the blood- drenched blade at the other two assailants.

She said with fire almost coming out of her eyes, *"Leave us or die. My father rode with the great Julius Caesar himself. I know how to kill, and I am not afraid to kill."*

The two boys quickly ran in the opposite direction. Flavia caught up with her friends and Sherrie said, *"We had better hurry. They might come back with more. We are almost there."*

They came to a small dark and dingy alley near their destination. Spider webs and the smell of urine accompanied them on the walk to the end of the alleyway. An urban racoon stuck his head out of a trashcan and snarled at them loudly, sending Henry jumping off the ground. They walked slower until they reached what looked like a black door. There was no knob, no hinges, just a large black rectangle.

*"This is it,"* Sherrie whispered.

*"Should we knock?"* Henry asked.

*"No, No!"* Sherrie explained. *"I have to knock in a code. We will only get one chance. If I mess up, they will not let us in."*

Sherrie searched her memory. When she was sure she had it right, she knocked in a strange Morris like code: (dot-dot-dot-dot-dot-dash-dash) (dot-dot-dot-dot-dot-dash) (dot-dot-dot-dot-dot-dash-dash-dot-dot).

The door slowly opened with an eerie sound of cracking and creaking.

The doorman was totally dressed in black. He wore a black robe with a black sash around his neck. His head was shaved totally bald. In his hand was a kerosene lamp giving the dark night just a touch of light. He smiled and said, *"How can we help you, my children?"*

Sherrie, speaking too quickly, explained to him her dilemma, how she was being forced into sex, how Henry could help her win her freedom with access to a computer, and how there were street thugs chasing them right now.

*"Do not worry about those boys. No one will harm you here. We wish to help everyone, believers and non-believers alike. Before you can enter, we have a new question. I need you to answer one question and one question only."* The man in the black robe asked, *"What year is this?"*

Flavia answered first, *"The year is 715 after the founding of the city."*

The man showed a slight frown.

*"No Flavia, you forgot that this is the future for you."* Sherrie then said, *"The year is 2773 AUC."*

This time he frowned even more.

Henry noticed a small brown wooden cross hanging from a chain around the soft-spoken man's neck. He said, *"No, you are both wrong. The year is 2020. Two thousand and twenty years after the birth of Jesus Christ."*

Their doorman smiled widely, *"Yes, my children. You may enter and become true believers."*

They walked into a small dark corridor. The huge black door shut with a crash so loud it startled all three of them.

*"I am so sorry my children. The big door needs maintenance, just some routine maintenance."*

They walked down a cobweb-filled hall, with the only light coming from the man's lantern. They came to what looked like an old worn elevator door. He pushed the call button and the door opened. He motioned for them to enter. The four people barely fit in the small lift. He pushed a button on the inside and the door closed, the elevator started to descend.

*"What is this? Please explain Henrici,"* Flavia said.

*"We are in an elevator, we are going down."*

The elevator swung slightly left to right as it descended creaking and banging all the way. Suddenly it stopped with a crash, the small light above them went off, leaving the lantern as the only light.

Their escort started hitting the button panel with his fist. The light came back on and their journey down continued. *"My children, I am so sorry. The elevator needs maintenance, just some routine maintenance."*

Sherrie asked him, *"Good sir, what is your name? What should we call you?"*

*"I am Father Peter. I am a Priest and disciple of the truth, the word of Jesus Christ, and I know you are Sherrie, Flavia, and Henrici."*

*"That is right sir and how do you know that?"* Flavia asked.

*"The Holy Father just knows things sometimes."*

Then Sherrie asked, *"Where are we going?"*

Henry interrupted, *"I believe we are going to a church."*

The Father smiled. *"Yes my son, you are correct."*

Flavia and Sherrie both asked at the same time, *"What is a church?"*

The elevator hit the bottom with such a crash, it hurt their necks. The door opened, and the priest said, *"Enter, my children."*

They walked to an arched, wooden double door. Father Peter opened it for them. *"Please be as silent as possible. There are worshipers praying here."*

The chapel was dark, the only light coming from small votive candles of yellow and red spread around an altar. The altar contained a large marble table with goblets of gold and a golden thurible, a type of canister, that was filling the room with the smell of burning incense. Facing the altar were ten rows of wooden pews and in those pews were a dozen men and women kneeling on the floor in a deep, dense trance of prayer.

Flavia walked to the right of the altar. There was something that got her attention. *"Who is this?"* she asked.

*"This is the beloved Virgin Mother Mary and her son Jesus Christ,"* The Father told her.

The statue was life-sized and sculptured of white marble. With a veil covering her hair the woman had a very slight smile as she gazed at her baby in her arms.

Flavia whispered, *"Mary? She looks so serene, so happy and content."*

*"She should be, my child. She is holding the son of God."* Father Peter took them to the last pew in the back and sat with them. *"Please be silent about what you saw today. If the Roman suppressors found out about us, they would not hesitate to kill us all. We must worship in total secrecy, like we have done for over two-thousand years. Wait here and pray. I will return shortly with permission for Henrici to use the computer."*

He left, and Flavia and Sherrie tried to contemplate their surroundings. Flavia asked, *"If she is a virgin, how can she have a baby?"*

Henry said softly, *"They believe the baby was conceived by God."*

*"You mean like the father Jupiter and his son Apollo?"*

Sherrie told her, *"No, Flavia. I have heard of these people. They are called Christians. They believe in only one god, The Father, the Son, and the Holy Spirit."*

*"But that is three, not one,"* Flavia said.

*"I can tell you this, Flavia. If you had stayed in Ancient Rome, you could have been alive at the same time as Jesus. You would be sixty-six years old when he was born,"* Henrici said.

Soon, Father Peter returned. He whispered to them, *"He wants to see you three."*

*"Who wants to see us?"* Sherrie asked.

*"This is very unusual. He never asks for this, but he senses something. The Holy Father wants to see you."*

He took them through a door to the right of the altar and they walked down hundreds of steps down a circular staircase which led to another dark hallway. A wooden, arched door was again opened by Father Peter. Inside was a dark, mini version of the chapel they saw before. The only light was coming from the same yellow and red small candles. There were only three wooden pews filled with eight kneeling bald men dressed in the same black as Father Peter. Also kneeling were eight women dressed in long black gowns with white trim and a white veil covering their hair. They were all staring at a large wooden cross. Hanging on the cross was a statue of what looked like a dead, crucified man. In the back of all this was what looked like a silver throne. In front of the throne was a man, also kneeling. When the four entered the small chapel, he stood up and two of the kneeling women also got up and went to both sides of the man. They guided him to the right side of the altar through a small door. Father Peter then escorted Sherrie, Henrici, and Flavia through that same door.

The two women helped the man to his chair behind a black wooden desk. The room was almost totally dark. As he sat down, he said in a voice even more calm and serine than Father Peter's, *"Thank you, sisters. You may leave us now. I am sorry it is so dark in here and as you will see, I have little use for light. Turn on the lamp, Father Peter."*

When he did that, it revealed a man short in stature and almost glowing in presence. He was dressed in a puffy white gown with a white zucchetto, a small skullcap, on his head. His eyes had no iris and no pupils. They were almost totally grey throughout.

Father Peter said, *"This is The Holy Father, Pope John Gregory. He is the six hundred and seventieth Pope of our Holy Catholic Church."*

The Pontiff said, *"I am sorry it is so somber today. Usually we are a little more fun, but you come on The Day of the Sun. This is our day of worship."*

*"Sunday is also the day of worship for Christians where I come from. Thank you for seeing us, Your Highness,"* Henry said.

Father Peter told him, *"He is not a king, Henrici. You address him as Holy Father."*

Pope John Gregory said, *"Let me feel your hands."*

Sherrie held her hand above the desk. The Pope used both his hands to hold it. He said, *"I feel enormous stress inside you. Stress from a life of bondage. You are here to seek relief from this stress."*

*"Yes, Holy Father you are correct."*

Next, Henry held out his hand, *"You are a very intelligent young man from far away. I believe you are from the land of America."*

"Yes, Your Highness, I mean Holy Father. You are correct."

Flavia was next. He took her hand and his blank eyes grew to almost twice their size. Sweat started beading off his forehead and he dropped her hand. He took a handkerchief and wiped his face. *"You are the one I sensed when you entered our church. You are very different, very special. You are from a place very close and also, so very far away."*

The three remained silent.

He went on, *"Take the girls to a comfortable room, then take Henrici to the computer. Give him all the time he needs."*

Henry awkwardly bowed as they left the room. He was ready to start the next phase of their escape plan.

——◆——

The room had two bunk beds, a chair, and a sofa. As the two girls waited, another Father came in and took their picture with a small phone. Flavia and Sherrie only had to wait four and a half hours until Henry returned.

He said, *"Sorry it took me so long. The computer was all in Latin, so it took me a little longer, but I was 100 percent successful."*

He handed them each an identification card. *"Some of the Fathers were very good at helping to make these."*

Flavia looked at her card. *"That is me on this card. Who painted that tiny little picture of me on this card?"*

*"It is not a painting, Flavia. It is a photograph,"* Sherrie said.

Henry told them, *"I also have train tickets to the Port of Brindisi. That will take us five hours. Then I have tickets on an overnight ferry across the Adriatic Sea to the Province of Greece. We will plan our next phase there."*

*"What about that other thing Henrici?"* Sherrie asked.

*"Oh yes, I was able to hack into the system of the Consul of Bondslaves. It was pretty easy going. I found you by using your slave number 45712SM. I was able to change your status to level six and declare you a freed slave."*

Sherrie jumped up and gave Henry a hug and a kiss. Flavia joined in, making it a three-way hug.

Sherrie said with glee, *"You did it Henrici. You did it!"*

A knock on the door interrupted their celebration. Father Peter entered the room. He said to them, *"We have briefed the Holy Father on your plan of escape. He says it is flawed. Temporarily it will fool the Romans, but soon they will discover the hack and find her. The only solution is that it has to be removed."*

"*What needs to be removed?*" Flavia asked.

Sherrie pointed to her left wrist. "*This needs to be removed. The computer chip inside of me.*"

Father Peter took Sherrie and Flavia to a small room that was well-lit and clean with tables made of stainless steel. There was one hospital bed and the smell of antiseptic lingered through the small space. Soon, three of the Sisters came in. Gone were the white veils and black gowns. The Sisters wore green scrubs with blue hairnets covering their hair. Each one washed their hands thoroughly and put on blue surgical gloves.

The Father said, "*Sister Teresa is a skilled surgeon. She has performed this procedure many times. The problem is we have no anesthesia here. The only thing we can give you for the pain is wine.*"

"*Do not give Henrici any of that,*" Flavia laughed.

Father Peter poured her a glass of a red wine.

"*I have never tasted wine before. Slaves are not allowed to drink alcohol.*" Sherrie took a sip. "*It tastes wonderful, like sweet fruity syrup.*"

"*Drink it down quickly, Sherrie. You will need two more glasses before we start.*"

Sherrie did that. After a few minutes the Father asked, "*How do you feel, Sherrie?*"

"*I feel wonderful, a little numb, and so, so happy.*" Sherrie started to slur her speech, "*I think I want to dance.*"

"*Just like Henrici,*" Flavia said.

They laid Sherrie down on the bed and the two sisters cleaned her wrist with antiseptic then held her left arm steady. Sister Teresa skillfully cut a half inch round incision into Sherry's wrist with a sharp scalpel. Blood began to flow from the surgical wound and the nurses used a vacuum suction to suck up the blood and keep the path clean for Sister Teresa to dig deeper inside of the wrist. Sherry winced in pain as the surgery progressed, but she did not yell or cry.

Flavia held Sherry's right hand tightly. She whispered into her ear and told her the story of the drunk Henry and the heavyset Roman woman dancing the night away in ancient Rome.

The Romans did not make this easy. The Sister spent twenty minutes digging deeper and deeper. Sherries body was tight and stiff as she dealt with the mind-boggling pain and soon, Doctor Teresa said, "*I got it.*" She used scissors like forceps to grab the one-half inch disk and pull it out of the young girl. She showed it to them, and then put it in a small plastic case. Then the surgeon began to sew the wound closed with a needle and thread, while the other sisters used more antiseptic to clean the lesion. They used gauze and bandages to finish the job. The surgery was now complete.

After an hour of recovery time, Father Peter and the two sisters escorted Sherrie back to the room. He told the three of them, *"Sleep well tonight. You can start the next part of your plan tomorrow afternoon. Good night my children."* He shut off the light, and the three laid down to bed.

Flavia was too anxious to sleep. She said, *"I know I have only been here a few days, but I miss my Rome. Did you know we met both Julius Caesar and Mark Antony, Sherrie?"*

*"The voices in my head told me you did. Was Mark Antony handsome?"*

Flavia said with a bubbly voice, *"He was so, so handsome and we saw Queen Cleopatra."*

This talk was making Sherrie's pain subside. She said, *"You did? Was she beautiful?"*

Henry broke in, *"Yes, she was very pretty. It is so sad that the two of them had to commit suicide."*

Sherrie was still a little drunk when she said, *"Are you stupid, Henrici? They did not commit suicide. I know Flavia left Ancient Rome too soon, but everyone else knows the story."*

Sherrie felt like talking. As they lay in the darkness, she told them a story that every Roman and almost every foreigner and slave knew.

# XVII

# The Voyage of Antony and Cleopatra

HENRY INTERRUPTED HER.
    *"Wait a minute Sherrie, I know my history about this. They did commit suicide."*

The slightly drunk Sherie quickly recanted, *"You are full of ox crap Henrici. Even the lowest level one slave knows this story."*

*"Then this must be another part of history we changed Sherrie. I told you we should not have done this."*

Flavia intervened, *"Let Sherrie talk Henrici. I want to hear this. This happened after I left Ancient Rome."*

Even as a slave, it seemed like Sherrie was a natural historian. Flavia and Henry could not wait for the story to come off her tongue.

---

Cleopatra VII Philopator started the journey from Alexandria, Egypt to the Port of Gades in Southern Hispania on June 26, 714 AUC (40 BC). She traveled by sea in her great barge that she called The Serenity. Her ship had one giant sail of gold and used one hundred oarsmen to push the craft west through the Mediterranean Sea. She ordered her captain to use the northern landscape of Africa to guide the ship to her rendezvous. She wanted to stay as far away from Rome as possible.

She had her entourage with her of course; one hundred and fifty advisors, servants, body guards, and slaves traveled along with her. The Queen of Egypt needed this support for her lavish lifestyle, even when she was running from the most feared Second Emperor, Octavian of Rome.

Cleopatra always had a flair for an entrance. After the thirty-three-day trip, she wanted to make sure Mark Antony remembered her every move as her ship entered the port. She laid down on a stage at the front bow of the ship on a bed of blue and white silk sheets glistening in the morning sun. A gold and purple canopy protected her from the drizzling sky that filled the air with mist from the sea. She had lutes and harps accompany and the voices of a soft Egyptian choir fill the air with music as the barge slowly entered the port. Cleopatra lay in splendor as she waited for Antony to observe her skilled seduction.

Her little bald-headed advisor, Kamuzu, was dressed in a maroon toga covered with beads and trinkets. Cleopatra called him over to her bed. She spoke in Egyptian with anger, *"What is this Kamuzu? Where is Mark Antony? I do not see any welcoming committee at all."*

The little man told her, *"You cannot trust a Roman. Warmongers and savages, they are. We should return to Egypt at once."*

Cleopatra knew she could not do that. Any return to Egypt would mean sure death for her now seven-year-old son, Caesarian, and most probably death for her also. She got up and ordered Kamuzu and three of her body-guards to accompany her as she disembarked from the ship. When they reached the port, they were greeted by four Roman soldiers and the tall Centurion Maximus. He said to her, *"Please my lady, I have orders to embark you on to Mark Antony's ship."*

Cleopatra was furious, *"You will address me only as Queen. Now take me to Mark Antony at once."*

The Centurion scoffed at her but nonetheless led her small group to the General. They found him on a dock in front of his five ships. These were the ships that would take him to this unknown land called America.

The grand vessels were Roman warships called Trireme. These wooded masterpieces of the sea had two masts. The mast in front supported a smaller square sail of white striped in red. The mast in middle had a square sail that was three times larger of white and blue. The wooden ships were all painted with identical red and green stripes around the entire vessel. At the bow, on both the port and starboard sides, were painted colorful eyes of red, white and green, one on each side, the keen eyes of the Gods guiding the ship safely through its journey. At over thirty-five yards long, they had room for three levels of rowers with seventy-five on each side. Most of these rowers were not slaves. They were free foreigners looking for Roman citizenship or young Roman citizens looking for adventure and status.

When Cleopatra saw Mark Antony, she walked up to him and yelled in his face in Latin, *"What is wrong with you, Antony? This not the way to welcome the Queen of both Egypt and Macedonia."*

The thirty-two-year-old Monarch had her hair still bleached to a perfect white. Her violet eyes were lined with dark eye makeup with small flakes of gold making her look very cat- like. She smelled of exotic frankincense and amber, the finest perfume money could buy, and she wore an elaborate nightgown of woven gold with silver lace.

Antony smiled as he answered the aggressive woman, *"Welcome Cleopatra. You are right on time, and I am afraid with Caesar gone now, Emperor Octavian has already stripped you of your titles in Egypt and Macedonia. You are queen no more, Cleopatra."*

She pushed the much bigger man with both of her hands. *"You Romans are scoundrels, warmongers, and heathens. I wonder why I would travel with you."*

The handsome forty-six-year-old Antony still looked young and in great shape. He still had a full head of greying, curly hair and a muscular body that looked like he could ride into battle at any time. *"You travel with me because you know Octavian will search the world to find you and your son. Before he died, Caesar made him Emperor and Caesar decreed, no more civil wars. By taking you on this voyage, I get just a little taste of spite on the young Emperor. Is this all you brought with you, these four people? I have room for them."*

*"Of course not, Antony. My entourage has one hundred and fifty, and I expect the best accommodations for each and every one."*

Mark Antony laughed loudly, *"I have no room for them. That is way too many."*

*"What do you mean it is too many? That is exactly the amount of people I require, not one more or one less."*

*"Cleopatra, we have hundreds of men traveling. We need food and water for all on a long unknown journey. You can bring six and only six."*

Cleopatra's angry eyes stared right at him. *"This is what I will do. My ship will travel to this America place also. It was constructed by the finest Egyptian craftsmen. It will make the journey much easier than those Roman garbage scows you sail."*

Antony agreed, *"As you wish, former Queen. But if you cannot keep up with my magnificent fleet, we will leave you in the dust."*

Cleopatra's voice suddenly changed from anger to an almost soft singing, *"In that case, Kamuzu, a few of my servants and I will travel on your garbage scow. I need to teach you some things."*

*"What are you going to teach me woman? I am now forty-six years old."*

*"You know so little for a man that old."* She whispered to him, *"I will teach you the Egyptian way. The only way to love."*

———◆———

The morning sun glistened the Mediterranean Sea as it rose over the eastern horizon. A night of too much wine and too much woman made the swaying of his still- docked lead ship, intensify by tenfold. When the early sun awoke Mark Antony, the first thing he did was to lean over and vomit on the deck of his cabin. He was relieved to see there was no woman in his bed to see this embarrassment. Cleopatra was already gone.

Antony groggily made his way to the main bridge of his ship. His Captain, or Trierarch, was already there. He was a wealthy Roman that actually owned the ship and he was also a battle- tested man of the same years as Antony. The Trierarch wore proud Roman armor that showed his rank and status. His name was Trierarch Severus, a well-kept dark-haired and bearded man that loved his vessel as much as life itself, the vessel that he called The Conqueror.

With the help of a small twenty-oared tugboat, Trierarch Severus guided the Conqueror out of the Port with his wooden ship's wheel. Behind him were four more Roman Triremes all fully stocked with sixty days' worth of food and water for over six-hundred men. Behind this small fleet was the Egyptian barge, The Serenity. Her one-hundred oarsmen would need all their will and might to keep up with the swift Roman Trireme warships.

When Antony joined his Captain on the bridge, he told him, *"All is well on this glorious day for a voyage. The sky is clear, and the gods have given us this wonderful summer day to set sail to this land of America."*

His Trierarch said as he slowly turned the wheel, *"Yes Antony, a glorious day it is. My navigators can use the sun to guide us west but pray for clear and warm nights. The Northern Star will be a much better escort to help us to find the land you seek."*

They had already passed the thin Strait of Gibraltar in western Europe and now trekked out into the seemingly endless Sea of Atlas. The plan was to sail west into uncharted waters. They had no knowledge of where this destination was, only the word of a young man child. They knew it was a place where a devastating weapon called the rifle was invented and Mark Antony hoped to find many more riches in this mysterious realm.

The ship crashed the waves with its one-hundred and fifty rowers plowing into the sea with the oars of many Roman naval victories, propelling them forward at a speed of over five knots. To Antony this was so different than defeating and massacring the many rivals of Rome on land. He felt the open sea fill his face with wonder and anticipation. As the shores of Europe disappeared, the sea ahead grew larger and more satisfying. Mark Antony felt this might be his greatest victory yet.

His thoughts of this new world were interrupted by a voice from behind, a voice he already knew so well.

*"Antony! The accommodations on this garbage scow are inadequate. I demand more water, better food, and better service. My four servants cannot do every-thing for me."*

Cleopatra's servants were all dressed in long white tunics, and she had two of them holding up her long blue silk shawl off the floor. Her white hair was now full of curls hanging down to her shoulders. She wore a necklace of large red rubies and a long matching red-shimmering tunic that hung down to her bare feet. Two more of her servants were cooling her face with red and yellow flowered fans as her adviser Kamuzu waited patiently behind her.

When Trierarch Severus heard this, he was beside himself, *"What did this has-been Queen say? Get her off my bridge, or I will have her thrown overboard. This is the finest ship in all of Rome."*

Mark Antony smiled as he led Cleopatra and her people off the bridge towards the starboard side of the ship. When they got there, she told her small entourage, *"Leave us!"*

She looked up at Mark Antony, *"Do you side with that captain of this scow over me? After what I gave to you last night?"*

*"I do not side with anybody. Cleopatra, you cannot insult a proud Trierarch like that. He is the best sailor in Rome. I need him to make this journey."*

*"Put a sock in it, Antony! I will say whatever I want. You invited me, so I want all of my demands met."*

Antony tried to argue with the Queen, *"You complain so much and we are only on our first day. This trip will be long and hard. You need to grow up, Cleopatra."*

Cleopatra did not back down. *"Why do you speak to me with such a forked tongue? If this keeps up there will be no more nights like what you experienced last night."*

Now Antony did back down, *"Okay, let's not fight on our first day to find this land of the rifle."*

*"That is fine Antony. Did you bring that little man child that built it?"*

*"No, it seems that he just disappeared, along with Flavia Antonius."*

Cleopatra wanted to insult him one more time, *"I know you are half-stupid, Antony, but don't you realize that if we find this land of America, they will have many of these rifles, and they will destroy you?"*

*"I am not that stupid Cleopatra. I actually brought you along for two reasons. Reason one was to spit on the face of Emperor Octavian. Reason two is that you are the best diplomat in the world. Is it true that you speak five languages?"*

*"You know I do. I speak Latin, Greek, Egyptian, Persian, and Syrian. I do not speak the language of this America."*

*"You will learn Cleopatra. That is what you do."*

Day one through ten at sea all seemed the same to Antony. He would begin his day with a briefing by Trierarch Severus and his navigators. He would make his inspection of the ship and crew, making sure to spend enough time with the always sweating oarsmen below. Then after lunch he would have to spend time arguing with Cleopatra about whatever she felt like arguing about. Then a night filled with wine and hours of lovemaking. It was purely erotic for him because no two nights were ever alike.

This day she was in top arguing form. She dismissed her servants and said to him, *"Antony, I need to go aboard my barge. This is of the upmost importance, and it has to be now."*

*"We cannot stop, Cleopatra. We have already had to stop twice, to wait for that so-called ship of yours. Now you want us to stop again so you can get in a boat and transfer over?"*

*"Yes, and then you will have to wait for me to return."*

*"What is so important to cause me this grief?"*

Cleopatra wore a necklace of large red rubies and a long, matching red-shimmering tunic, the same outfit she wore on the first day of the journey. *"I have had to wear this dreadful outfit twice now. You cannot expect me to dress the same every day."*

*"Get out of here, Cleopatra. We are not going to stop for a wardrobe change."*

*"You will. I know every man on this ship desires me. I see that Trierarch Severus turning his eye towards me all the time. Maybe I will dump you and teach the Trierarch my Egyptian ways."*

The frustrated Antony said, *"Okay you win. But what am I supposed to tell the Trierarch we are stopping for? Your vanity is no reason. We are running through our supplies at a rate quicker than expected."*

*"Just tell him that I need to check on my son Caesarian and my crew. They need to see their Queen happy and heathy; you know all of this is true."*

Antony went to the helm of the ship to order the Trierarch to stop.

They used a small transfer boat to get Cleopatra, Kamuzu, and her servants over the rough wavy sea to her waiting ship. Mark Antony sent two of his best sailors along with Centurion Maximus to escort Cleopatra safely to her ship. Her crew threw a roped ladder overboard to transfer them aboard. Cleopatra had no problem climbing up to the deck of her ship. The Serenity crew threw ropes at the small boat to bring aboard Cleopatra's huge wardrobe trunk.

When she got on deck, she pulled Kamuzu aside and said quietly, *"Did you get what I asked for?"*

*"Yes, my queen. I think we did quite well. It is safely hidden in your wardrobe trunk."*

*"Good work Kamuzu, and what about the other things that go with it?"*

Kamuzu opened a knapsack he had over his shoulder and showed her. It was filled with brass and lead trinkets.

*"You are the best adviser I have ever had, Kamuzu."*

When Cleopatra got to her cabin, she had her servants change out her clothes to all new extravagant outfits. Kamuzu hid the stolen items in the most secure locker on the ship. Now, she called for Caesarian.

When she saw him, she smiled. Every day he looked more and more like his father, Julius Caesar. The seven-year-old had dark brown hair and his father's famous blue eyes. He seemed to also inherit his demeanor, drive, and intelligence.

His Mother hugged him as he entered the cabin. She spoke to him in Egyptian, *"This journey has been long and hard, my son. How are you holding up?"*

He told her sturdily, *"This is so exciting, mother. Going off into the abyss with the hope of finding a brave new world. Why do you not travel with us?"*

*"I wish I could, but I have to handle this big-headed Roman, Mark Antony. He is stubborn and needs so much Egyptian training. You know I do this for you and only for you."*

*"I understand mother. Emperor Octavian wants to have me killed. Will I ever get to meet the great Mark Antony someday, mother?"*

*"I promise you will. Once we get to the new land. I think we have at least fifty days until then. Just study hard with your teachers and advisers. Learn to be a great leader like your father."*

*"I will mother. I learn so much every day and I will help you lead the people of this new land."*

*"I know you will my son."* Cleopatra hugged him again. *"I must return to Antony now. I may not see you again until we get there. Do you know where we are going, Caesarian?"*

Caesarian answered quickly, *"Of course mother. I will see you again in the land called America."*

---

*"This trip is taking way too long. Are you sure you know what you are doing Antony?"* Cleopatra scolded.

It had now been sixty-five days since they left the coast of Hispania. The Romans had the best-sighted men standing in crow's nests on the ship's masts, each one searching the western horizon for something, for some sight of land. So far, like the days before, nothing but endless sea.

Mark Antony answered her, *"You are right on both counts, Cleopatra. We are running low on supplies. The oarsmen are exhausted. Some of the men believe we are going to fall off the edge of the earth soon. There are also rumors of mutiny. I think it is time to turn back."*

She scolded him some more, *"You are a coward, and you are stupid. We do not have enough supplies to get back. Stand up to these savage Roman sailors. Are you a General or a mouse?"*

Antony did not hear a word. He was drinking wine out of a cracked goblet and looked stressed and in agony. He had the ultimate decision to make: To have his six hundred men starve at sea by turning back, or to go forward to an unknown destination for an unknown amount of time? These questions plagued him.

Cleopatra knew what she had to do tonight with the stressed-out Antony. She now walked alone to the port side of the ship. She looked to the southeast. She saw some clouds. Her stomach tightened up and her head almost burst.

That night Cleopatra was laying on top of Antony. As she pushed him deeper inside of her, she massaged him in a place he had never felt before. She massaged him until he yelled and exploded so loud that it alarmed the ship's crew. She got off of him and let him recover for a few minutes.

She said in her singing voice, *"Antony, I have some good news and some bad news. Which to you want to hear first?"*

He was still breathing hard, when he said, *"More bad news? What can be worse than starvation, mutiny, and this failure? Tell me the good news."*

*"Alright, I am carrying a child. It is your child. I think there are two."*

He hugged her and kissed her on the cheek, *"I guess that is very good news. More heirs for my legacy. They may be the first Americans, or we die at sea before they are born. What can be any worse that what we have now? What is this bad news?"*

*"It is hundreds of time worse than what you say. I will show you in the morning."*

The next morning, Cleopatra, still in her silver silk nightgown, dragged the hung-over Antony up onto the ship's deck on the port side. The sun was rising in the east and still visible over the eastern horizon. The wind was warm and humid and seemed to be blowing harder by the minute. The dark clouds that Cleopatra saw the previous day had grown by fifty.

She pointed to the southeast and said, *"That is a hundred time worse than your other problems."*

*"It looks like a summer storm. Our Romans ships are built to handle any summer storm."* Antony's head was aching. *"I have too much to worry about now, Cleopatra. We will survive this summer storm."*

*"You are wrong, Antony. Look at it with clear undrunk eyes. It stretches almost as far as the eye can see to the east and the west. It is coming right at us. Order your ships to turn away to the northwest, as fast as your rowers can row. It is our only chance."*

A sudden huge gust of wind blew past them knocking them both onto the wooded deck of the ship. Mark Antony quickly got up to order his ships to go northwest as fast as possible.

The tropical storm that Cleopatra saw a day earlier was now a full-blown hurricane. The storm developed in the northern hemisphere in the middle of the ocean and was traveling at twenty knots to the northwest. The best Mark Antony's small fleet could do was six.

The storm reached them in a matter of hours. The sustained winds of ninety miles per hour tossed the great Roman ship, The Conqueror, like it was a small toy, and the pounding thick drops of rain started to fill her with gallons of liquid hell. Cleopatra waited below in her cabin with Kamuzu and her four servants as Mark Antony, Trierarch Severus, and the ship's crew were on the deck desperately trying to guide their ship out of the storm as the angry tempest threw its entire wind and rain-driven wrath on Antony's small fleet.

A young officer yelled at Antony and Severus on the bridge, *"We are taking on too much water! The oarsmen on the lower deck are up to their waists in water."*

Servius ordered over the sound of wind and rain, *"Take all the men you can spare. Use every bucket we have and form a line. Bail every drop of water out of my ship!"*

Cleopatra was being bounced around in her dark cabin. She had put on a practical brown tunic with a brown turban to cover her hair. She wore good deck-gripping Roman sandals. All five of them were on the floor as the violent waves rocked them across the floor. Two of her servants had already vomited on to the wooden ground.

*"I am going up to the top deck,"* Cleopatra said in the darkness. *"I would rather drown in the open sea, than drown in this hole in a garbage scow."*

As her servants waited below, Cleopatra made their way through the dark halls and up the stairs to the rain-soaked deck of the ship. With the wind rocking the helpless vessel back and forth, the two slowly made their way to the bridge, holding on to anything they could find, or risk being thrown to the deck, or even worse, to be blown off the ship and into the deadly sea.

When Antony saw her, he yelled, *"Cleopatra! Get back down into your cabin! It is much too dangerous up here!"*

*"No, Antony! If we are going to die, I want to die with you!"* She yelled back as she went into his arms.

Trierarch Severus yelled as loud as he could, *"Have the oarsmen move us to the starboard side. I see a dot of sun to the right!"*

After over two hours of storm, the ship's navigators had no idea what direction they were going. They were going in the direction the storm wanted them to go. With the ship still taking on water, the wind and the sea suddenly calmed. They were heading towards a large patch of sunlight.

Antony completed his hug of Cleopatra, then gave his Trierarch a mighty chest salute, *"You are the greatest sailor in the world and a great Roman and friend Severus. We made it."*

The sails of the ship were long gone, but one mast still remained. The Trierarch sent a sailor up to the crow's nest. The sailor yelled at them from above, *"I see one of our Trireme and look ahead there is the Egyptian barge."*

Cleopatra smiled widely. She knew her son and crew were safe. Now she had to explain to the Romans what she felt, what she knew was right. She made a circle on the deck with a small piece of rope and tried to explain to them, *"Order all the repairs you can Antony at once. This is not over."* She pointed to the rope circle. *"The storm is a gigantic vortex swirling like a backwards circle. It pushed us deep to the north. This calm we are in now is the middle of this whirlpool. Soon, we will come to the other side, pushing us south with rain and wind just as strong as it was before."*

The sun started to fade away in the clouds and the wind started to pick up again. Antony knew Cleopatra was right.

For the second time, a huge gust of wind almost capsized The Conqueror to the starboard side, filling the ship with tons of unneeded water. The brave young oarsmen that stayed at their post on the lowest deck were now drowned. The remaining mast of the ship had been cracked like a twig by a force of wind so strong, it threw many of the deck crewmen into the waves of death.

Antony and Cleopatra hung on the stump of the mast with all their might. For two more hours the ship swung back and forth, out of control. There were no deck crew, no navigators, and no Trierarch Servius. Antony saw a gigantic surge of water wash him away like a goliath spitting off a fly.

Still below two decks of rowers smashed their oars into the violent sea. Pushing the ship forward to an unknown direction and an unknown place. Every one of the remaining lives left on the ship felt the rocking begin to slow. On the top deck the rain began to subside and after over six hours of hell, the mighty Conqueror made it through the storm. The clouds above the ship began to scatter, Mark Antony could tell it was around hour four in the day. The rowers from below started to convene on the top deck. Antony knew why. The ship was slowly sinking.

Still in his arms, Cleopatra said, *"I think we are through it, Antony."* She thought she saw something. She ran to the starboard side of the ship. She pointed and yelled, *"Look!"*

The Egyptian barge, The Serenity was still afloat and still looked very seaworthy. Her sails were gone but Cleopatra could see her oarsmen turning The Serenity towards them.

Cleopatra said to him, "*I told you Antony. Your garbage scows are built for speed and killing. My ship was built by the best shipbuilders in the world. It was built for safety and comfort, and that is why it survives.*"

Mark Antony ordered his remaining crew to release the four small transfer boats. He, Cleopatra, Kamuzu, her servants, Centurion Maximus and a few officers got in the first boat. The other three were loaded with men according to rank. Mark Antony promised the remaining men that the life boats would keep returning until every man was safely aboard the Egyptian barge.

As the sailors rowed the small boat towards the Egyptian ship, Cleopatra could see her son Caesarian waiting for her on the starboard stern of the ship. She waved to him with a big smile.

Once aboard, Antony and Cleopatra went to the top deck and looked towards The Conqueror. They could hear faint screams from afar as the rear bottom of the ship filled with water lifting the front stern high into the air. They could see men yelling and jumping into the turbulent water as the ship's stern pointed straight up with its two painted eyes looking at the cloudy sky above, as if the ship was pleading to the Gods for help.

As the ship slowly entered the sea, Antony was distraught and broken. He felt the pain of his men's lungs filling with sea water and their brains exploding as they yearned for air. He looked on in horror and said to Cleopatra, "*Six-hundred men dead and for what? I killed six-hundred of my men because I wanted the glory of finding new riches.*"

Cleopatra tried to console him. She held his right arm with both of her hands, "*It is not your fault, Antony. No one could ever predict a storm like that.*"

He watched the life boats return with only seven saved sailors aboard. "*I cannot take this anymore. We are taking this barge back to Rome.*"

"*You will not. This is my ship and you have no authority here. We will continue on our quest to find this new land.*"

Mark Antony turned to her and stared with angry red eyes, "*It is you that did this to me.*" He put his hands on her arms and started shaking her violently. "*You will do as I say! All you do is disagree with me! You will do as I say!*"

Soon, Antony was surrounded by six Egyptian guards, all with long swords drawn. Before Cleopatra could say stand down, they were interrupted by the gleeful Egyptian shouts of, *"Land! Land!"*

More shouts, this time in Latin, *"Land! Land! Land!"*

Cleopatra and Antony rushed to the starboard side of the ship. There, just as the sun was setting in the east, to their west, was a very long shoreline stretching for miles and growing darker by the minute.

Cleopatra took his arm again. *"We found it, Antony. This must be it."*

*"Yes, it must be. We will go ashore in the morning."*

Cleopatra agreed, *"Yes, the morning it will be. I have so much to prepare."*

*"Good, Cleopatra, and can I ask you one thing? Do you have any wine aboard this barge?"*

————◆————

The small transfer boat hit the shore at about hour eight in the morning. Inside were Cleopatra, Mark Antony, Centurion Maximus, two Roman guards and two Egyptian guards. The guards were armed with only Egyptian swords, knives and arrows. All the rifles that Antony had brought on the voyage were now sitting at the bottom of the ocean.

Cleopatra wanted to impress these new people with all the Egyptian flair she could. She wore a long blue and yellow silk gown with lace of gold and red rubies. Her white hair was tied in braids with ribbons of blue. Her neck and arms were surrounded by large rubies, sapphires, and amethysts. Her painted face made her eyes seem so large that they shouted out her royalty.

Mark Antony did the best he could to look Roman with the Egyptian uniforms found on the Serenity.

Antony and Maximus jumped out first. They both took an arm of Cleopatra and gently lifted her off the boat then softly set her down on the shore. Cleopatra looked ahead. There was about fifty yards of sand, then what looked like thick jungle. She sensed something.

Antony fell to his knees and filled his hands with the white sand. He kissed the sand and prayed to the Gods.

On the sixty-seventh day of their journey, something amazing happened. On October 2, 714 AUC (40 BC), Queen Cleopatra VII of Egypt and General Mark Antony of Rome discovered America.

# XVIII

# The Queen of America

SOON THE THREE OTHER TRANSFER BOATS ARRIVED CARRYING EQUAL amounts of Roman and Egyptian soldiers. The summer sun was warm, and the sea was blowing the air towards the jungle ahead giving some relief from the wet sweltering humidity that came with this land. The storm had blown down some of the trees and brush near the coast. The jungle beyond seemed unscathed.

Mark Antony scanned the coast both to his left and to his right. *"I do not see anything. We must have landed in the wrong place. There is nothing but jungle and sand."*

Cleopatra disagreed, *"No Antony. This is the place. There are people here."*

*"You are so wrong Cleopatra. Where are the cities? Where are the docks and ships? Where are the farms and people? We should return to The Serenity and explore the coast some more."*

Cleopatra felt she was right. *"We need supplies before we starve. No time to explore Antony, I know there are people watching us right now. They are hiding in the jungle."*

Antony ordered the soldiers to be alert, *"If you are right, Cleopatra, why do they not wipe us out with their rifles?"*

*"I do not know. All I know is that they are very scared. They have never seen anything like us,"* she replied.

Centurion Maximus noticed something. There was a young girl to his left sleeping in the wet sand letting the waves of the ocean cool her off. He ran towards her. The young girl woke up and sprinted towards the safety of the jungle as the strange large man ran after her. He barely caught her just before she entered the thick brush.

She screamed and kicked wildly as Maximus brought her to Antony and Cleopatra. Her tongue spit out panicky words that often sounded like clacks and pops from her mouth.

*"Be easy on her Centurion,"* Cleopatra ordered. *"She cannot be more than fifteen."*

Her young skin was dark brown, giving her more than adequate protection from the hot sun above. Her hair was long, dark and straight, and her brown eyes stared at the woman in the strange outfit. All the young one wore was a small fur skirt around her waist.

When her eyes met Cleopatra's, she screamed and kicked even harder.

*"She is scared to death of me,"* Cleopatra said. *"Gently put her down and hold her Centurion."*

Cleopatra stepped away and moved out of the sight of the girl behind some rocks. She removed her silk gown that left her in a light brown loin cloth loosely covering her. She took off the jewelry and tried her best to remove her makeup with her silk gown. She returned to the frightened girl, got down on one knee and gently smiled at her.

The girl calmed down slightly and smiled back at her.

Cleopatra tried Latin first. She patted her chest and said, *"I am Egyptian."* She repeated, *"I am Egyptian."*

Then she took the girl's hand and patted her on her own chest. She gently said, *"You are?"* She repeated, *"You are?"*

The girl had a puzzled look on her face, so Cleopatra patiently went through the routine again and again. Finally, the girl said in her clicking and clacking own language, *"I am Wayohakbee."*

Antony heard a ruffling coming from the jungle. Soon, a bare-chested barefoot man appeared from the bushes. He was followed by many more. They kept coming out on to the sandy beach until there were over one-hundred. Each one held a sturdy wooden spear with a sharp pointed rock fastened to the tip.

Mark Antony ordered his men, *"Prepare for battle!"* His men drew their swords and his archers pointed their arrows at the native men.

Cleopatra yelled at him, *"Stand down, Antony. Do not kill them. They mean us no harm."*

She pointed to The Serenity as to show off the big ship. There were a few u's and ah's coming from the men. Cleopatra slowly approached a man she thought might be their leader. All the men were very short and had beautiful shining dark skin and long unkept black hair with the short grass skirts covering their waists. This man was different. He looked much older and wore a necklace of turquoise stones all polished to a soft shine.

The former Queen of Egypt said to him softly in Latin as she put her hand on her chest, *"I am Egyptian, I am Egyptian.* She gestured towards the older man. *"You are Wayohakbee."*

He smiled along with most of the men. He nodded yes, then said in the Wayohakbee tongue, *"Yes we are the Wayohakbee."*

Cleopatra spent the next hour trying to communicate better with the Wayohakbee men. She wanted to find out if this old man was their leader. She went to Mark Antony and repeated to them as she pointed at him, *"Leader, leader, leader, big leader."* Over and over again to try to get her point across.

She went back to the man in the turquoise and pointed at him. She asked, making sure her voice went way up to show a sure question, *"You leader? You leader?"*

The old man seemed to understand. He nodded his head left to right and said something that sounded like, *"Nak."*

Cleopatra held her hands out and said, *"Then, where is your leader?"*

The man gestured as if he wanted her to follow him.

*"He wants us to follow him Antony. He wants to show us something."*

Antony told her, *"I would not do that Cleopatra. I have heard that primitive tribes like this will eat the people they meet."*

Cleopatra scolded, *"Be quiet Antony. They are not going to eat us. Let me go with Centurion Maximus and a few solders. I need to see this."*

They did not have to walk far. The thick brush soon turned into a clearing that still surrounded them with jungle and trees. The cool shadows from the dense trees and bushes gave the clearing a magic-filled, enchanted feeling.

There were women in the tall trees picking some strange fruits and tossing them to more women below who filled bags made of grass with the colorful plums, mangos, and tiny yellow apples. A man seemed to be returning after a hunt with a dead wild pig slung over his shoulders. The animal was an obvious victim of the stone tipped spear he carried.

The native man in turquoise led Cleopatra to a woman sitting near a burning campfire. This woman was constantly barking out orders to the people around her in a language that Cleopatra could not understand. The man pointed at her.

Cleopatra slowly approached her. The woman looked very young for a leader. She wore a dress of fur around her waist and her shoulder bore a cape of the same animal pelt. Her skin was the same beautiful dark brown as the men. She was also barefoot and bare-breasted with necklaces and bracelets made of the same turquoise that the man wore. When she stood up, Cleopatra could see her long hair hanging down below her fur-covered waist.

She looked at Cleopatra in wonderment as Cleopatra looked at her the same way. The Egyptian held out her hands. She said, *"I am Cleopatra. You are?"*

She touched Cleopatra's amber skin and stared into her violet eyes. She firmly said, *"Masuva."*

She turned to the elder man and started not quite an argument but what sounded like a heated discussion. Cleopatra noticed immediately that the signs and gestures they made with their hands were almost as important to the communication as the click-clackety sounds they made.

Masuva turned to the hunter with the pig and barked out some orders. He took the pig to a bed of banana leaves and set it down. Soon five women surrounded it and started scraping off the fur with large sharp stones as to clean it for a feast.

The two women spent the next two hours sitting down face to face trying to communicate. With the progress going well, Cleopatra could not help noticing the bountiful harvest growing larger by the minute. She rubbed her stomach to indicate hunger, then she had the soldiers gather two hundred and six rocks. Masuva understood right away that that meant there were two-hundred and six of them. She pointed to the sky and made a circle with her fingers. She put the circle on the ground and made a large arch over her head till her circled fingers hit the ground on the other side.

Cleopatra stood up with her and took her hand, *"Thank you."* she said with a smile.

As they left Centurion Maximus said to her, *"What was that all about?"*
*"She wants us to come back tomorrow for a feast,"* Cleopatra responded.
*"Well, who is she?"*
*"She is Masuva. She is the Queen of America."*

—◆—

Mark Antony had all the able-bodied men and a few recruits from the Wayohakbee tribe surround the grounded Serenity. They lifted her out of the water and slowly dragged her through the sand until they were sure they were far enough away so high tide could not drag her back out to sea. The men then placed large rocks around her to make sure she was stable and not about to tip over.

When Cleopatra arrived, she was told Mark Antony was already on board. She climbed the roped ladder, got on deck and headed to their quarters.

She opened the door and saw Antony sitting at a table with a glass of Egyptian wine. *"They have so much food Antony. They have invited us all to a feast tomorrow."* Cleopatra told him as she sat down.

*"Are we the main course? If they have all this food, we should take it from them."*

*"No, Antony. This is the perfect place for us. We can raise your two children here, so far away from all the corruption of Rome. We can teach them all the good of Rome and Egypt without all the sleaze and evil that our world possesses."*

Antony said to her, *"You know Cleopatra, you call us heathens and scoundrels and that is exactly what we Romans are. We are conquerors. I am going to conquer these primitives, take their food. Then I am going back to Rome, once the repairs are done on the barge."*

Cleopatra said with anger, *"You will never do that. The Serenity is my ship and we are staying here. You can make a canoe out of a tree and sail back to Rome if you wish."*

Antony took a large gulp of wine. *"Do not argue with me, Cleopatra. My mind is made up. I do not belong here."*

*"Come with me to the feast tomorrow. I am sure I can convince you to change your mind. Drink more wine, Antony. I have some new things to teach you tonight."*

———◆———

Cleopatra did not want any of the men to carry weapons to the feast. They compromised that Centurion Maximus, two Roman and Egyptian guards, and of course Mark Antony would carry swords. They entered the jungle at about hour two in the day. With Mark Antony and Cleopatra leading the over two-hundred of their people, they approached the clearing in the jungle. They heard people laughing and singing in a loud unknown tongue. When they broke through the brush, there was a sudden silence. Hundreds of Wayohakbee were staring at them. Cleopatra quickly took Antony by the hand and took him to the tribe's leader.

When they approached her, she said, *"Greetings Masuva."*

Masuva did her best and said, *"Clepata."*

*"Yes, yes, and this is the great Roman, Mark Antony."*

Masuva took his hand in both of hers. She nodded in approval. Mark Antony nodded back and had trouble keeping his eyes away from her sizable bosom.

They all sat down around the camp with Cleopatra and Antony sitting next to Masuva around one of the ten campfires. Masuva shouted out a few words and the party started up again.

Men were tapping sticks together in a violent fast rhythm while women started filling large banana leaves with fresh tropical fruit and vegetables. There were men with sharp stones cutting off the meat of pigs and gouging a sharp stick inside the piece. The women would then hold the meat over the fire and roast it to perfection. Then there was the fish. Hundreds of fresh tuna, grouper, and flounder just waiting for a man to clean and bone them and put them on a stick for a flawless roast. They served Antony and Cleopatra first, but it wasn't long before the entire entourage had a banana leaf full of fresh ecstasy.

Soon some of the young Wayohakbee men and women started dancing in a line around the camp to the rhythm of the clacking sticks. As they passed them, a young man took Cleopatra by the hand and made her join the line.

Dressed in only a short brown tunic and bare feet, Cleopatra did well to keep up with her young hosts. Mark Antony watched the Queen dance. Gone were the fancy silk gowns. Gone was the elaborate makeup, the priceless gems and jewels, the expensive perfumes. To Mark Antony, Cleopatra never looked more beautiful. Her small baby-bumped stomach made her essence sparkle even more. Mark Antony's heart softened.

When she returned to her seat, Masuva touched Cleopatras stomach, then she pointed at Mark Antony. Cleopatra smiled wildly and nodded yes, then she held up two fingers. The two women hugged each other.

Centurion Maximus was enjoying his meal, and soon some of the young boys stood near him staring. He gestured the boys to sit down. He started telling them stories in a language the boys did not understand. He used all the drama in his voice and used wide gestures with his hands to try to describe many of the great battles and victories of the great Roman legions. Occasionally he would pull out his knife and pretend to stab an imaginary enemy and make an exaggerated gasping sound of a dying foe. The boys looked on in wonderment with wide eyes and smiles.

Caesarian approached his mother while she was improving her communication with Masuva. He said to her, *"Mother, look at all the boys listening to the Centurion. It seems like they understand him."*

*"Yes, my son. Maximus seems to have a flair for the dramatic just like I do. Go join them. Make some friends."*

As he got near to the group, the Wayohakbee male children all looked at the strange white boy. They had never seen such pale skin and such bright blue eyes. Some of the younger ones giggled at the sight of him, only to be hushed by the older boys. Centurion Maximus quickly got their attention back by pulling out his long sword to violently kill an imaginary enemy.

Cleopatra was fascinated by the huge catch of fresh fish on display. She picked up a white flounder and gestured, where did it come from?

Masuva stood up and said in words Cleopatra was already starting to understand, *"Come with me. I will show you."*

Cleopatra took Antony's hand and yelled to Caesarian to join them. They walked about a half mile through a cut-out path in the jungle. Soon, they could hear the sound of joy and laughter. The jungle opened to a cool-shaded lagoon surround by bushes filled with large wildflowers of blue, yellow and red. Young men and women were swimming in the still water while a line formed near the trees. They had made long sturdy vines and attached them to a tree. Then using the ropes, they would swing wildly towards the water, letting go high in the air and then splashing with a crash into the cool lagoon.

Along the shores of the lagoon, young men were talking politely to young women hoping to find a way to make her his mate.

Caesarian asked, *"Mother, that swinging looks like so much fun. Can I try it?"*
*"Yes, just be careful and don't cut in line."*

Caesarian had no trouble removing his tunic and sandals. Wearing only a light brown loin cloth he ran to the rear of the line of Wayohakbee. His hosts were too polite to their pale white guest. They let him go to the head of the line. He climbed to the top of a large rock and took the durable vine with both hands then he pushed away from the stone and swung out over the lagoon. He let go of the vine too late forcing himself to do a flip, then landing headfirst into the water producing an almost perfect dive. When he came up from the water, he was greeted by standing Wayohakbee all giving him a yelling applause in their clackety popping language.

Cleopatra said to her man, *"Do you see how happy these people are? This is a true paradise, the best place in the world to raise your children."*

Mark Antony's heart softened some more, *"Yes, Cleopatra, these people are very happy. Primitive, but very happy."*

When the sun started to leave them, Cleopatra thanked Masuva for all the wonderful hospitality. She made sure she understood that they would return the next day to show them some of their own.

As they took the short walk back to The Serenity, Cleopatra took Mark Antony's hand, she said to him, *"This is the perfect place. This is our place Mark Antony."*

Mark Antony did not reply.

That night Antony drank more wine than usual. He fell asleep in a drunken stupor long before Cleopatra came to his bedside. It was after hour one in the morning when he woke up violently screaming that his end was near, *"Ahh! Aug! I am drowning! My life is going as the sea takes me to Hades!"*

Cleopatra tried to bring him back. *"Antony, wake up!"* She shook him. *"Wake up! You are having a nightmare."*

Mark Antony lit an oil lamp. *"I know Cleopatra for I have had this dream before. Six hundred of my best men dead because of me. Please forgive me, but I am returning to Rome. There I will take my life and die as a Roman."*

*"You will not! You are drunk again. This is my ship and you are not going anywhere with it."*

Mark Antony violently pushed Cleopatra out of the bed and on to the floor. *"Be gone woman! Go sleep with your son. The repairs on the barge are almost complete. I have many of your Egyptians that are willing to join me. Tomorrow we will attack the Wayohakbee and ransack their village. Anything we need we will take for our journey back to Rome. If they resist me, they will all be killed."*

*"You cannot do that!"* Cleopatra threw her body at him and started swinging her fists, hitting him all over. *"You cannot hurt these beautiful people, and you cannot steal my ship!"*

Antony easily picked up the much smaller woman. He carried her to the door, opened it, and threw her on to the floor outside. He closed the door and slowly walked back to his bed. He noticed he still had half a bottle of wine left.

Cleopatra spent the rest of the night with Caesarian. She kept him awake. *"Why do you cry so, mother? We had such a great day."*

194

*"I cry because I love. I love so much I did not know which way to turn. But finally, I do know."*

———◆———

As the sun rose in the east, Mark Antony was sleeping with the empty bottle of wine still in his hand. He was awakened by a crying voice.

*"Get up Antony,"* a teary Cleopatra said.

The groggy man dropped the bottle on the floor. He sat up and tried to focus his eyes on the voice, then he heard the soft click. When his eyes were finally ready to focus, he yelled, *"Cleopatra! Where did you get that! Put it down. That is very dangerous."*

Cleopatra stood about six yards from him. She had a Model 1873 Winchester rifle with the butt end against her waist and the barrel pointing at Mark Antony.

With tears pouring down her eyes, she said, *"I love you so much, but I cannot let you alert Octavian as to where we are. He will send his assassins here to kill us."*

*"Put it down, Cleopatra. I will not tell him."*

With her eyes red from the tears she said, *"I cannot let you harm these people."*

Mark Antony tried to rush Cleopatra and disarm her. She quickly pulled the trigger sending the sharp sound of death throughout The Serenity. Antony felt the burning lead enter his stomach. He dropped to his knees and used both hands to try to stop his life blood from leaving his body.

Cleopatra threw the rifle on the floor. She rushed to him and also used her hands to try to stop the bleeding.

With Antony in total agony, she said to him crying, *"I am so sorry. I love you so much, but I love my son more."* She held him in her arms as the life slowly left him. As he closed his eyes for the last time, she thought she heard a soft, *"Thank you."*

Cleopatra's advisor, Kamuzu, picked up the rifle off the floor. He pulled the lever down and then back up and held it clumsily as he pointed it at the door, ready to fire on any Roman that entered. He almost fired on the young boy.

Caesarian entered the cabin and walked past the advisor. He had heard the loud exploding sound echoing through the ship and rushed to be with his mother. Then he saw her holding the dead Mark Antony, shaking him as if she was trying to wake him up.

She seemed incoherent and not in this world, she said over and over again, *"Wake up Antony, wake up. You cannot be dead. Wake up. Please my gods, wake him up."*

Caesarian said to his crying mother, *"What happened mother? What did you do?"*

*"Can you not see?"* Cleopatra held up both of her bloody hands and cried loudly, *"I did it for you. I did it for you, Caesarian."*

———

A tear fell from Flavia's left eye as she said to Sherrie, *"She loved him so much, but she had to decide who should live. She chose her son."*

*"Yes Flavia, even to us slaves Cleopatra is considered the God of Motherhood,"* Sherrie answered.

Henry asked, *"So what happened after that? What happened after Mark Antony died?"*

Sherrie continued, *"Nobody really knows as this was over two thousand years ago. Archeologist found ancient scrolls at a site on the panhandle of south-eastern North America. They even found the rifle that they believe was used to kill him. There were many scrolls found before he died. The Romans kept very keen records. After the death there was basically nothing. The Wayohakbee had no written language."*

*"So, what happened to the Wayohakbee tribe?"* Flavia asked.

*"Wiped out by the Romans hundreds of years later with their advanced weapons. One thing I heard was that of the four civilizations of Ancient America, The Wayohakbee are the only one that did not practice human sacrifice. They found evidence of Egyptian influence throughout the panhandle, in their art, diet, and culture. Cleopatra did try to help them."*

Henry said, *"We must sleep now. We need to be very alert when we continue our well- thought-out master plan tomorrow, to get Sherrie as far away from Rome as possible."*

*"One more question for Sherrie before we sleep,"* Flavia asked, *"Who gets the credit for inventing the rifle?"*

*"Remember Flavia, us slaves do not get to go to school, but from what I have heard, the credit goes to Julius Caesar, Mark Antony, and some unnamed philosopher."*

Flavia laughed, *"I did not know you were a philosopher, Henrici."*

*"I am a scientist working on top-secret experiments. Right now, I wish I was a philosopher, then none of this would have ever happened."*

# XIX

# The Posse

FATHER PETER WOKE THE THREE FUGITIVES UP EARLY JUST BEFORE dawn. They took cool showers then got dressed and ready for the next phase of their master plan. They enjoyed a nice breakfast courtesy of the Church, but before they could leave, Father Peter asked them to attend a somber ritual that they called a mass. After the mass, they had to sit with a group of worshippers all discussing the writings of this black book they all held. They called this discussion a Bible study.

Sherrie was anxious to get going, but all three felt the least they could do was to attend to thank their hosts for all their help and hospitality.

When it was time to go, Father Peter escorted them up the cranky elevator and across the dark hall to the big black door.

*"I feel your upcoming adventure will have very positive results,"* the Father told them.

*"Thank you so much for everything."* Sherrie kissed him on the cheek. *"I learned so much here in such a short time. I will return some day."*

*"That is all we ask of you."*

They said their goodbyes then the Father pushed a black button by the door. It opened with such a crash that it shook the hall.

*"I am so sorry my children. The door just needs some maintenance. Just some routine maintenance,"* Father Peter explained.

It was after hour twelve in the day when they left the safety of the church and entered the dark world of Northern Rome.

They made it to the underground as fast as they could, then took a train east to the over ground train station in Tivoli. From there, it was a five-hour ride to the Port of Brindisi.

It was already hour six at night when they arrived at the port town. Their ferry ride across the Adriatic Sea left at hour seven the following morning and with money running low, their best choice for a hotel was a sleezy little place near the train station. It was called '*Motel Cheap but Good.*'

As they approached the front entrance, Sherrie said, "*This place stinks but we need to save all the money we can. We definitely do not want to sleep outside with the homeless.*"

On the short walk from the train station to the motel, there were dozens of homeless people lining the road. Some were lying on the ground drinking out of bottles covered with paper bags. Some of the men and woman had their faces and teeth destroyed by a street drug that Sherrie had heard about called crevice. It was snorted through the nose, and it was so addictive, it would quickly turn the victim into a monstrous zombie in a matter of weeks.

Sherrie paid a few denarii for the room in advance. It was a small chamber with two double beds, and that was it. There was only one community bath in the building that was shared by all the motel's guests. When they opened their room's door Flavia asked, "*What is that awful smell?*"

Henry said, "*I am totally sure it is human urine.*"

"*I know this place is bad, but it is only for one night,*" Sherrie said.

Henry added, "*Yes, we can handle one night here. I see there are only two beds. I would be glad to offer my services as your male protector and sleep with one of you two girls.*"

Flavia and Sherrie looked at each other, then Flavia said, "*I do not think we need any services like that Henrici.*"

"*Yes Henrici,*" Sherrie said. "*And for that lame attempt, you can sleep on the floor tonight.*"

There was one window in the room, covered by a torn red curtain. Flavia opened it by two inches and looked outside. "*There is something going on out there.*"

Outside on the dark street was parked a large white bus with no windows. It had the white and black symbol of the Consul of Bondslave on each side. There were men and women dressed in green uniforms armed with pistols. They would approach a homeless person, pick them up, handcuff them, and without asking one question, escort them inside the bus.

Sherrie took a look. "*You see, that is why we do not want to sleep outside. They would take us too. It looks like Rome is short on slaves.*"

"*At least they won't have to sleep outside anymore,*" Flavia said.

Sherrie replied, "*Yes, for some it will be better, but for most it will mean certain death. Close the shade Flavia. Wait until they go away.*"

*"Who are they?"*

Sherrie answered, *"They are the Consul of Bondslave, the evil government organization that regulates us slaves. What they really do is abuse us and I am sure they have one by now. I have been gone for more than twenty-four hours."*

*"Have one what, Sherrie?"* Henry asked.

*"A picture. A picture of me."*

---

*"I got a hot one boss. The hottest we have had in years."*

He was a bald man with no legs. He sat in a swivel type wheelchair and rolled it from computer to computer, typing briefly into each one before he moved on to the next. He went to a printer and took a freshly printed document. He handed it to his boss.

*"Pretty girl for a slavey,"* his boss said.

The picture was a full-length photo of a blond woman. She wore a green jumpsuit with a white patch over her right lapel that read 45712MS.

*"How much?"* she asked him.

*"Just a cool seventy thousand."*

*"Seventy thousand!"*

*"Yes, the owner is some doctor guy named Pillar. He's got the dough. He owns over one hundred of those Kactbruss coffee houses. He claims he asked the slavey to help clean up after a party he was having at his home, then he says she spit in his face and called him a scummy douchebag, then she ran out. She has been gone for over two days. I think this guy wants her executed."*

She took a long look at the photograph. From the numbers and lines behind the girl it showed her to be about five foot eleven inches.

*"She is a tall one. She's an inch taller than me."*

Her dark brown skin was a contrast to the white girl in the photo. Makala Melius was raised in the province of North America. Her parents were Roman citizens from the Southern African province of Zambia, and wealthy citizens they were. Makala got the best education money could buy in America. Her major was business, a field that she soon started to hate. It was too boring and mundane for the overly active young woman. She knew what she wanted to do when she captured her first escaped slave at the age of twenty-one. As her business grew with one capture after another, she soon got the attention of the Consul of Bondslave. If any case proved too difficult for these government cronies to handle, they would call these specialized bounty hunters and soon Makala's business was at the top of Bondslave's list of government -certified bounty hunters. This bounty business was her life. She named her thriving business 'The Posse.' She soon had enough money in the bank to move The Posse to Rome—because that is where the real denarii lived.

Even though the company brought in top denarii, the team had only three employees. Makala, her legless computer man named Breeso, and a guy that was still asleep on this early Tuesday morning, Valcamus.

Makala said to her bald old employee, *"Do you have anything on her yet?"*

Breeso used both hands to push his wheelchair away from one computer towards another. *"Makala, those stupid goons at Bondslave could not find a lit match if it was stuck up their asses. They checked the slave house cameras the morning she escaped and found nothing, so they gave us the case. I simply hacked into the security systems of the building across the street from the slave's room. Check out the big screen."*

A clear colored video appeared on a sixty-four-inch screen above all the computers. It showed a blond girl walking outside behind the slave's quarters. She was carrying a large paper bag.

*"That is the slavey,"* Breeso said. *"Now look at the third floor."*

They saw somebody waving and soon a white sheet came out of the window. A young woman in a slave dress came down the sheet and let go at the second floor, falling on to the suspect.

*"Who is that?"* Makala asked.

*"I have no idea."*

Next, the sheet disappeared back through the window. Then, another girl in a slave dress was hanging from the ledge. She let go falling into the other two as all three were knocked to the floor.

Makala laughed, *"That looked like a bit from a Three Stupoids short."*

The three in the video started running towards the camera, when Makala said, *"Stop it Breeso and zoom in."*

The stopped video showed a clear picture of all three of them.

Makala said, *"Look at that third girl with the eye patch. That is not a girl at all, it is a guy. Why is he wearing a slave dress?"*

*"Don't know boss, one more thing. The owner says the slavey is a level four. I looked her up and she is actually a level six and a freed slave. Not only that, but her monitoring chip has been turned off."*

*"Isn't that normal for a freed slave? Can you turn it back on?"*

Breeso looked up at his boss, *"It would be almost impossible. I am a great hacker, but to do that you would need a super genius hacker, like the best hacker in the world."*

———◆———

Henry let the two girls wait in the line in front of him. Before they embarked on the ferry, Sherrie had bought them each new back packs where they could store some extra clothes and supplies. Now, money was really tight for them. Once on board, they went up to the top deck of the five- layered ferry to watch the ship depart from the port.

Sherrie felt the soft mist of the sea and saw the beautiful Mediterranean Sea both for the first time. Sherrie raised her arms towards the water. *"This is so wonderful. I have only tasted this short abundance of freedom for two days now. I will never be a slave again. Even if they catch me, I will never be a slave again."*

*"They will not catch us,"* Flavia said. *"With Henrici's master plan we will all be safe shortly."*

*"That is right, Sherrie. Once we get to Greece, we will have to take a long bus ride to Athens International Airport. There, we will put Sherrie on a flight to America."*

*"So, a machine is going to fly up in the air and carry her to America?"*

*"Yes,"* Henry said. *"Like that."*

A large passenger plane with Latin Airlines written on the side was taking off from Brindisi Airport flying east towards Greece.

With wide eyes, Flavia said, *"That is amazing. I cannot wait till I get to fly in one of those."*

Henry said, *"You will, I promise, now remember the plan, Sherrie."*

*"I know, Henrici,"* Sherrie said. *"I will get a job there in America, and you two will get jobs in Greece until you have enough money to join me."*

*"Yes, in a place called New York. Some big city or something,"* Flavia said.

Sherrie told them, *"It is the biggest city in the world. I cannot wait to see Manhattan Island."*

*"I think it is time, Sherrie,"* Henry said.

Father Peter had had his staff embed Sherrie's monitoring chip into a hand- sized rock. Sherrie threw the rock out into the Adriatic Sea.

*"Goodbye slavery. Goodbye slavery forever,"* Sherrie said with a sparkle in her eye.

They spent the rest of the day looking at the sea and talking about their future. The tickets that Henry hacked came with three meals and only one small cabin. They enjoyed a lunch of fresh gyros, then a Greek feast of Moussaka and Falafel Fritters with hummus. When it started to get late, they went to their cabin on the lowest level. Sherrie opened the door and the three entered. There was barely enough room for them to stand. Inside was one small single bed a dresser and one door.

Henry said, *"This bed is very small. It looks like one of you girls will have to sleep on the floor with me."*

Sherrie looked over the situation. She grabbed the mattress and pulled it off onto the floor, *"I will take the box spring. Flavia, you can have the mattress."*

Henry protested, *"This way there is no room for me to sleep. Where should I sleep?"*

Flavia opened the small door. Inside was a toilet, a small shower, and a sink. She said, *"Henrici, if you curl up in the fetal position you will have plenty of space to sleep in this bathroom."*

---

*"Look who finally joined the party,"* Makala Melius said.

Her second employee entered the computer room looking a little red eyed. Valcamus went by only one name, Valcamus. He was a six-foot two-inch-tall man that had his arms blessed with huge biceps. The dark handsome Greek man had worked for Makala for over four years now. She hired him because he had the brawn and just enough brains to keep him out of trouble.

*"I am so sorry I am late boss,"* the Greek told her. *"A couple of young ladies kept me up late last night. You should have joined us boss. It was a good time for all."*

Makala sparked back at him, *"Are you crazy Valcamus? Do you think I would join one of your disease-infested orgies?"*

*"No Makala. These girls were clean."*

Breeso interrupted them. *"I got something else here boss. Seems that an old truck was reported stolen a couple of hours after the escape. Must have been hotwired."*

*"What was the slavey's job, Breeso?"* Makala asked.

*"She worked as a barista in one of Pillar's coffee houses."*

*"A hot-wiring slavey barista? That seems unlikely. She must have been aided and abetted by the other two,"* Makala said.

Valcamus asked, *"What other two?"*

Makala handed him a printed-out photo of the three people from the video, *"The slavey is the tall blond."*

Valcamus took a look. *"Wow, a hot blond slavey, a wild looking brunette, and a nerdy looking transvestite with an eye patch. This is crazy. How much is this job worth?"*

*"Just a cool seventy thousand,"* Makala said.

*"Seventy thousand? I am working overtime on this job. I cannot wait to capture and then meet these fine two specimens of the female species."*

Makala scolded him, *"You know Valcamus, you signed a contract when I hired you. We honor the Bill of Rights of the Bonded, especially article number one, no sexual abuse of any kind on any slavey."*

*"Who's talking abuse? I just want these young ladies to meet the grand stallion called Valcamus."*

*"I hate to interrupt you two,"* Breeso said as he stared into a computer. *"I have something. They just found the stolen truck. Guess where?"*

*"Tell us,"* Makala ordered.

*"On the other side of Rome, at the Bank of the Bonded."*

*"No shit,"* Valcamus said. *"Let's get over there right away, Makala. See what we can dig up."*

Breeso interrupted again, *"You might want to delay that."*

*"Why?"* Makala asked.

*"Boss, remember when I told you that only the greatest hacker in the world could turn on the slavey's monitoring chip?"*

Makala said, *"Yes."*

Breeso said proudly, *"Well, you are looking at him. I think I just turned it on. I am just waiting for the signal to come back."*

---

Sherrie got up from their short night's sleep and looked out the small round window. She sighed at the sight of the sun sparkling off the Adriatic Sea. She gently woke up the sleeping Flavia on the mattress next to her box spring.

*"Wake up Flavia, it is morning. In about eight hours we will be at the Port in Igoumenitsa, Greece."*

Flavia woke up a little startled, *"What dreams I had Sherrie. I dreamt I was near Rome at my Father's villa. It seemed so real. Why am I here, Sherrie?"*

"*I do not know. But I do know one thing Flavia. Henry brought you here for a reason.*"

"*No Sherrie. I was the one that came here. It was my choice. I made a mistake and grabbed him at the wrong time.*"

"*Either way, Flavia you are here for a reason.*"

Henry opened the bathroom door. "*I am so glad that night is over. My back is causing me too much unwanted pain from sleeping in a most uncomfortable position.*"

They all took showers and got ready for the next phase of Henry's master plan. They would debark from the ferry in Greece. Using the fake ID's, the church made for them, they would easily get through the Greek security because the flawless fake ID's showed them as being Roman citizens. They would then proceed to the bus station at the port and get comfortable on the first bus to Athens. Again, Henry was the last to shower.

"*Hurry up Henrici,*" Sherrie yelled through the small door. "*I want to go up on deck and sunbathe for a while.*"

"*What is sunbathing? I want to try it,*" Flavia asked.

"*I do not really know. I think it is when free Romans lay in the sun to get their skin darker. I have never tried it, though suddenly, I feel like I have done it hundreds of times.*"

———◆———

"*Boss, you'd better get over here, I got some bad news,*" Breeso said.

Makala and Valcamus rushed towards the legless man in the swivel wheel chair.

"*I need good news Breeso, not bad news,*" Makala said as she looked at the computer screen.

There was a blinking red light on a map of the Adriatic Sea, near the coast of Italy.

The computer man said to them, "*It looks like her chip is at the bottom of the sea. That means she committed suicide. And that means no seventy thousand.*"

Makala thought for a couple of minutes. "*That does not make sense. That must be at least fifty miles from the coast. Why would the slavey escape from her quarters, somehow get fifty miles across the sea, then jump in?*"

"*Maybe she tried to swim across,*" Valcamus said.

"*No, as far as I know they do not give slaveys swimming lessons and besides, that is fifty miles. Breeso, can you chart any passenger vessels that went through that coordinate?*" Makala asked.

"*I think so.*" Breeso typed for a minute, then stared at the screen. "*Yes, there are a bunch. But when I zoom in, only one went almost directly over the coordinate, a ferry, its number is 40359.*"

"*Where is it headed, Breeso?*" Valcamus asked.

"*Igoumenitsa, Greece. These morons at the ferry company have to tighten their internet security. I just hacked into the ferry's passenger manifest. There are over five hundred. I got pictures of each one.*"

Breeso started to quickly flip through the pictures.

"*Stop Breeso, go back one,*" Makala ordered. "*That looks like the other girl. Her name is Flavia Antonius. Save it and print it Breeso.*"

After the next picture, Makala stopped him again, "*That looks like the transvestite. He is Henrici Garfield? Print it.*"

The next picture came, and Makala said, "*That is the slavey. Her name is Marylin Monroe. That has to be fake. Sounds like that mass killer from Western America, Marylin Monroe Manson. He killed twenty-six.*"

"*I didn't tell you I have her real name. 45712MS is named Sherrie Melbourne. How do you know all three of them didn't jump into the sea, Makala?*"

"*They did not. I just know it, and I know they are on that ferry.*"

Valcamus said, "*That means they somehow got the chip out of her wrist.*"

"*They did. When do to they get to Greece, Breeso?*"

"*About eight hours.*"

Valcumus's eyes lit up. "*That is great, boss. We can take the Valca-wing. It can get us there with plenty of time to spare. We can nab them and bring them back to Rome for a big payday.*"

"*You mean that piece of shit jet of yours?*" Makala looked worried. "*Not only is it a piece of shit, but you are the worst pilot in the world.*"

"*Don't worry boss, it is all auto pilot now. Let's go!*"

Makala looked at him sternly, "*If you say, 'to the Valca-mobile' I am going to hit you in the face.*"

Valcamus sat in the pilot's seat with Makala sitting as the co-pilot. The old corporate jet had room to seat six in the back. The Greek got it for free for not reporting the abuses of a rich slave owner to the authorities. Valcamus didn't seem to be doing much because he had installed all the latest autopilot technology. He was playing video games as the Valka-wing climbed to an altitude of thirty-thousand feet at an air speed of close to five-hundred miles per hour, flying southeast to the Greek port city of Igoumenitsa.

Valcamus noticed Makala looking at all the printed photos of the three suspects. She flipped through them over and over again.

*"Why do you look at those pictures over and over? You should have them memorized by now,"* he said to Makala.

*"Look at this young girl."* She showed him a picture of Sherrie. *"She might be executed, and for what? Just because she was born a slave. She never did anything wrong."*

Valcamus responded, *"She should not have spit on her owner's face and then try to escape."*

*"Do we really know she spit in his face? Even if she did, does that constitute death? And what about the other two? We are condemning them to a life of class one slavery, and we don't even know who they are."*

*"You are breaking your own rule, Makala. Never get personally involved with a slavey. Just capture the slaves and collect the dough. That is what you have always said."*

*"Well this one just smells bad. Maybe it is time to start breaking rules. The rumor of another slave revolt is growing louder and louder."*

Valcamus didn't hear her. He was scoring big on his video game.

---

Flavia went first. She showed the security officer her fake ID. He nodded then sent her through a metal detector. She walked into the province of Greece with no problems. Henry went through next with the same good results.

When the guard looked at Sherrie's ID he said, *"Marylin Monroe? Are you related to that killer from America?"*

*"No sir,"* Sherrie said.

*"You must have had some sick parents."*

*"Yes, sir."*

He let her through. When she they got far enough away, she whispered to Henry, *"Are you stupid, Henrici? Why did you have them put Marylin Monroe as my name?"*

*"Because in my world, Marylin Monroe was a beautiful female movie star. I did not know that in your world, he was a notorious serial killer."*

Flavia looked at the signage. *"The bus station is this way."*

They started walking down a wide crowded hallway towards the next phase of Henry's master plan.

———◆———

*"I have a visual. Looks like they are headed to the bus station,"* Valcamus said.

*"I think I see them,"* Makala replied back.

The two bounty hunters were communicating through small mikes and earphones connected to their cell phones.

*"Remember, Valcamus, I want this to go down as discreetly as possible. Too many people here. I will give the signal when the time is right. And like I said, you take the slavey, and I will take the other girl. I do not think we need to worry about the transvestite."*

*"You can't see that? It looks like the transvestite is no longer a transvestite. He is wearing pants."*

The long hall made a left turn and it got much thinner and less crowded.

When it looked like the hall was bending to another left Flavia said, *"This does not feel right. Is there another way to get to the station?"*

*"The sign says the bus station is this way, Flavia,"* Henry said.

*"I know that Henrici, it just does not feel right. Let's be on our guard."*

Valcamus and Makala walked towards the three. With Valcamus walking towards Sherrie and Makala walking towards Flavia, they were not too concerned with Henry walking between the two girls.

Once they passed them, Makala said, *"Now!"*

Valcamus quickly grabbed Sherrie by her arms and pulled her close to him. He pulled his silver pistol out from under his coat and held it to her head. When Flavia saw a woman with a gun coming towards her, she used the same trick she had done on the homeless thug, the one she learned watching Cornelius. She grabbed the woman's wrist with both of her hands and twisted it until she heard a snap. The gun fell to the floor as Makala grabbed her broken right wrist. Flavia slid across the floor and picked up the gun. She looked at the tall man holding a gun to Sherrie's head. She then pointed Makala's blue pistol at Makala's head.

Henry reacted the best he could. He lunged towards Valcamus. The tall Greek simply raised his right foot and kicked Henry hard right below his jaw. Henry fell flat on his back, his head hitting the tiled floor with a huge thump.

Valcamus saw the tense situation. He said to Flavia, *"Give her that gun little lady, or I am going to blow this slavey's head off. She is wanted dead or alive."*

Flavia held the pistol with both hands pointing it closer to Makala's temple, *"I am the daughter of Valens Antonius. He is a great warrior that rode into battle with Julius Caesar himself. I know how to kill, and I am not afraid to kill."*

Valcamus said back, *"I do not know what you are talking about, but I do know this. If you do not give her that gun, I will blow your friend to Hades, and then I will kill the eye-patch kid next."*

Sherrie started to struggle in a vain attempt to get away from the large man's hold. She said as loud as she could, *"Don't give it to her, Flavia! Let him kill me. Please let him kill me. I will never be a slave again. Please Flavia, let him kill me!"*

Flavia thought it though for a minute and she immediately knew what she had to do. She turned the gun around and handed it to Makala.

Sherrie screamed, *"Why did you do that, Flavia! I want to die! I need to die. I can never be a slave again."*

Makala took the gun with her unbroken left hand and pointed it at Flavia, *"Get on your knees girl."*

*"Are you okay?"* Valcamus asked.

*"I am fine,"* Makala said. *"She broke my wrist Valcamus. How did she do that?"*

A large train-station crowd started to form around them as the bounty hunters handcuffed their prisoners.

As Makala and Valcamus escorted them out of the station, a crying Sherrie said softly this time, *"Flavia why didn't you let them kill me?"*

She answered, *"Because Sherrie, if we are dead, we have no chance. If we are alive, at least we have a slight chance."*

Henry said, *"I agree with Flavia. Although I calculate the odds of us escaping at 8,987, 543 to 1, we still have a chance, a very small chance, but a chance."*

# XX

# The Stuffing

"*At least I get to fly in one of these things,*" Flavia said as she looked out the small window of the Valka-wing. "*It is amazing how tiny everything looks from up here.*"

The three prisoners were in the back of the time-worn corporate jet. They had two shoulder belts around them, each crisscrossing around their chests, along with locked lap belts holding them tightly in their seats. They were all still handcuffed.

Up in the cockpit, Makala Melius was deep in thought as she continued to look at pictures of their three captured runaways. Valcamus was trying to pilot the plane when a gust of turbulence shook the Valca-wing for a few seconds.

"*I wish you would put it on auto-pilot, Valcamus. I do not want to die in a crash into the Adriatic Sea.*"

"*Fine, I will if you stop looking at those pictures.*"

Earlier, Valcamus did his best to set the bone in Makala's right wrist, then he wrapped it tightly with a long gauze bandage to hold it in place. The pain was unbearable, but Makala did not make a sound.

"*This still stinks to high Elysium, Valcamus. I am not sure this is right.*"

"*Come on, Boss. This is the biggest payday we have had in a long time. Don't get soft-hearted now. That girl broke your wrist and for that alone they deserve whatever punishment the Romans give them.*"

"*Maybe I deserved a broken wrist. I am going back there to talk to them.*"

Makala went into the back and knelt in the aisle seat in front of the bound prisoners so she could see all three of them.

Henry spoke first. He said in his nerdy voice, "*I would be very grateful for a drink of water. This most unfortunate ordeal has left me very parched.*"

Makala got up to retrieve a bottle of water. She opened it, put it up to his mouth and let Henry take a few gulps, then she gave some to Flavia. When she held the bottle in front of Sherrie, she angrily said, *"Get that bottle away from me. I would rather die of thirst than take one drop of your filthy water."*

Makala said, *"Listen 45712MS, I am just doing my job. We cannot have slaves escaping all over the place."*

Now Flavia got angry, *"You are most probably sentencing her to death. At least show her some dignity and call her by her name."*

Makala looked at the young slave girl. She felt a dent in her heart as she said, *"Okay. I am sorry, Sherrie. Maybe if you had not spit in your owners' face, then run away, you would not be in such a bad place. All he asked is for you to clean up after a party."*

Flavia yelled, *"That is a lie! She never did that. Sherrie's owner told her she had to have sex with three men, all at the same time. He did not ask her to clean up after the party. He wanted her to be the party."*

Makala said, *"I know that is wrong, but all slave owners probably do this, don't you think?"*

Flavia got angrier, *"Then that makes it okay? And if they do, then that Constitution is full of ox crap. I knew slavery was an abomination in my Rome, Cornelius the slave taught me that. Now I am positive that slavery is even worse here in this Rome. Slaves are human beings, and they deserve the same rights as any other Roman citizen."*

*"Slave owners do not care about the Constitution, Flavia. That is why there is going to be another slave revolution, even bigger than the last one,"* Sherrie said.

Makala felt another dent in her heart. She looked at Flavia and said, *"You seem to be so passionate about this. What was that all about, when you said your father rode into battle with Julius Caesar?"*

Henry answered for Flavia, *"That is very true. I know because I met her father and Julius Caesar."*

*"I suppose you met Mark Antony and Cleopatra also,"* Makala said.

Henry and Flavia said in unison, *"We did."*

Makala went back to the cockpit, she sat down and said to Valcamus, *"They are kind of nutty, but I still do not know what to do here. That Flavia girl is different. I do not know what it is, but there is something totally bizarre about her."*

Valcamus said, *"To me those girls back there are a couple of hot-looking slaveys."*

*"Shut up Valcamus and try to help me here. What should we do?"*

212

*"Here is what we do. I heard that ruckus back there, Makala. You are getting too involved with this case. That is not our job. We just turn over the slave, get the check, and move on to the next case."*

———◆———

When the bounty hunters arrived at the main office of Bondslave in Rome, Makala was given the reward check as Valcamus turned over the prisoners to three guards. As the three convicts were led away, Sherrie turned around and gave Makala a long repulsive stare. *"Goodbye bounty hunter. I would get my revenge with you in the afterlife, but it looks like you will be spending your afterlife in Hades."*

Makala walked to the exit with the check still in her hand.

Valcamus said, *"Let me see it boss. Let's celebrate, first we go get Breeso, then over to Rico's for food and booze. It is all on me."*

Makala saw a trash can near the exit. She took the check and ripped it up into small scraps of paper, then threw the confetti into the can.

*"What are you doing?"* Valcamus protested. *"That is seventy thousand."*

Makala said sternly, *"Do not worry, Valcamus. You and Breeso will get your share of the money. But I do hereby decree that The Posse is officially dissolved. I quit."*

———◆———

The guards took them to a long row of small jail cells. Some of the cells had inmates inside that looked like newly recruited homeless bound for a future life of slavery. The guards opened three cells with iron keys and the doors opened. They escorted each one into their own tiny cell and removed their handcuffs. There was hardly any room to stand. Each cell had a worn-out cot, a toilet, and a dirty hand sink. All three of them sat down on the cots as the guards locked the doors.

With Sherrie in the middle cell, she said to the other two convicts, *"I do not care if we failed, Henrici. I got to sense the sweet taste of freedom for a few days. I will die soon and never have to be a slave again."*

Henry said sadly, *"I am so sorry my master plan was not successful. It is all my fault."*

Flavia could hear Henry crying softly. *"Henrici, we all failed, but it is not over yet. We are still alive, and we still have a chance."*

Soon, the guards returned and this time each one was with a woman. The three women all looked sort of the same, each wearing white lab coats and big round geeky glasses. The only difference in the three ladies was one had blond hair, one had black hair, and one was a brunette. They each carried a small clear plastic bag. The guards opened the doors and the women entered each cell. With a gloved hand, the three pulled out a large cotton swab out of the clean clear bag with their gloved hands. They said almost all at the same time, *"Open wide."*

Henry did this and the blond woman stuck the swab into his mouth and moved it around to get as much saliva as possible. With a little resistance, the other two ladies repeated the procedure on Flavia and Sherrie. Then all three white-coated ladies replaced the swabs in the plastic bag and sealed it tightly shut. They swiftly left the cell and the guard relocked the doors.

*"What was that all about?"* Flavia asked.

Henry said, *"That is to check our DNA. They use it to positively identify us."*

*"Yes Flavia,"* Sherrie said. *"They can use your spit to find out who you are. They have my DNA on file. Now they will know for sure that they are killing the right person."*

*"Maybe there is another Henrici Garfield in this timeline that has my DNA."* Henry said.

*"Sherrie, they are not going to kill you. Do they have my DNA on file, Henrici?"* Flavia asked.

*"No way, Flavia. They have no DNA from an over two-thousand-year-old girl."*

They spent night one, and then day two in the same cramped cell. The prisoners had all the water they needed from the sink. Their meals consisted of dry bread with some kind of vegetable shortening on the side that smelled a little rancid. There was always a piece of gooey loose tofu and a piece of fruit that was close to being fermented. They had little to do during the day but to lay on their cots, talk softly, and stare at the ceiling.

Later that afternoon the three lab-coated ladies returned with the guards. This time they looked a little more tense. They repeated the swab routine on all three of them, but this time the black-haired lady had a scissors. She used it to clip off a small lock of Flavia's hair and place it in a separate plastic bag. The guards locked the door, and they were all gone.

*"I do not know why they did that again,"* Henry said.

*"Why did they take some of my hair, Henrici?"* Flavia asked.

Sherrie said, *"Maybe they liked the color. I always liked that sandy brunette hair you have."*

The only people they saw for the next two days were guards walking back and forth in front of the cells. They got the same meals of tofu mush and bread but today was suddenly different. This time a guard brought them each a grilled piece of halibut with lemon, broccoli, and a baked potato covered in butter.

*"I do not like this,"* Sherrie said. *"This is too good for us."*

*"I do not care. I am eating it. I am starving,"* Flavia said.

After their meal, the guards returned. They opened the cells and one of them said, *"You have to come with us. But you must wear these."* He held up a two-patch blindfold and put it around Sherrie's head to cover her eyes.

Henry said, *"I only need one patch. I already have one over my right eye."*

Sherrie then said, *"I think this is it my friends. At least I know that I am done for. That was our last meal. It was nice knowing you two."*

Handcuffed to their escorts, the guards guided the blinded convicts slowly for a rather long walk. Soon, they could all sense that they were being placed in a vehicle of some sorts.

They were sitting in rows with a guard by each one's side. Flavia was in the front, with Sherrie in the middle row, and Henry in the back.

Sherrie said to her guard, *"Why don't you just kill me right now. Why let the slave owners have all the fun? You can say that I fought you so hard, that you had no choice but to kill me."*

Her guard didn't say a word.

The engine of the vehicle stopped, and the guards got them outside into the open air. They were then escorted into a building. Flavia recognized the sensation they now felt. It was the motion she felt at the church elevator, only this one was much smoother and much, much faster. They left the elevator and after a short walk, they heard a door being unlocked. Once inside the guards took off their blindfolds and released the handcuffs.

Standing in front of Flavia was the dark-haired woman. She still had on her white lab coat. She said to her, *"Flavia, I have been assigned to help you three with whatever you need."* She took Flavia's hands and held them tightly while she gazed into her eyes. Then she handed her a beeper. *"My name is Laura. If you need any of the slightest thing, just push this button, and I will be here in a flash."*

Laura and the guards left them in what looked like a luxurious living room. There were plush sofas and chairs in red and blue with clean polished tables of dark and light wood skillfully placed. The walls were adorned with modern Roman paintings depicting some of the most beautiful landscapes of the Roman countryside.

Flavia and Henry went off to explore the rest of the apartment as Sherrie sat on the couch with a disgusted look on her face.

Henry yelled from afar, *"There are three bedrooms, each one with a huge king-sized bed, and there are four full bathrooms. The big one has a bubbly heated hot tub and an enclosed sauna."*

Flavia yelled from another room, *"I think this is the kitchen. There is a big silver box that is cold inside. It is filled with fresh fruit, vegetables, raw meat and big tubs of milk. There are stoves and something that looks like an oven."*

A knock on the door sent Flavia running towards it. She opened it and noticed the three guards standing at attention around the entrance, each one holding a large well-equipped rifle.

Laura greeted her at in the doorway, *"I am so sorry to bother you Flavia. May I come in?"*

Flavia motioned her into the room and closed the door.

*"I just stopped by to see if the accommodations suit you, Flavia. If you wish, we have a chef on duty that will prepare you any food you want exactly to your tastes."*

*"A chef!"* Sherrie said with anger.

Laura continued, *"I do have to take a blood sample from each of you."*

Laura sat Flavia down, wiped her wrist with an alcohol wipe, then gently stuck a needle into a vein on her wrist. *"Did that hurt Flavia? If it did, I am so sorry."*

*"I am fine, Laura."*

Laura preformed the same procedure on Sherrie and Henry but without much concern for their well-being.

When finished she put the blood samples in a small black bag, then said to Flavia while gazing into her eyes, *"Remember Flavia, if you need any slight thing, just push that button."* Laura suddenly dropped the little black bag. She threw both her arms around Flavia and hugged her as tight as she could. Flavia pushed her away.

With tears in her eyes Laura said, *"I am so sorry. I don't know what came over me. Please forgive me, Flavia."*

With embarrassment written all over her face, Laura picked up the bag and quickly left the room.

The disgusted look on Sherrie's face turned into a smirky smile. She said in a singing voice, *"Looks like Flavia has a girlfriend."*

*"Flavia cannot have a girlfriend because she is not a lesbian. Did they even have lesbians in Ancient Rome, Flavia?"* Henry asked.

*"Of course, Henrici and you are right, I am not a lesbian."*

*"That is very good for me. That means I have a chance with you."*

*"What!"* Sherrie said. *"I thought I was your most beautiful!"*

Henry's voice got shaky. *"Yes, that is true Sherrie. You are my most beautiful."*

*"What?"* Flavia said. *"You told me you loved me once."*

Henry tried to change the subject. *"I am very hungry. Should we call for the chef or cook for ourselves? I learned how to make some very good gourmet meals on the hotplate back in my workshop."*

Sherrie tried to warn them, *"Don't you two even wonder why we are getting this first-class treatment? I am sure this is all paid for by the slave owners and it is not because they love us. Here is what we should do. I know what is happening here, we should not eat anything."*

Flavia asked, *"What is happening Sherrie? I am starving, there is so much great food in that kitchen."*

*"We should not eat anything. That is exactly what the slave owners want us to do. Not all slaves know this, but I do. This is what the owners call The Stuffing."*

---

The Roman government was in near shambles. The New Republic had been near collapse for years. The economy had been in negative GNP for over a decade, unemployment was putting millions of Romans and non-Roman citizens on the streets where their only hope to get out of homelessness, was to become a slave.

The threat of another slave revolt was also very real. Once the rumors of this rebellion solidified, the Roman stock market crashed again, forcing the Republic into an unpresented depression.

The forty-two-year-old war with China was going worse than the Government would let the people know. The province of Korea was now almost under total Chinese control. That left the Romans' most bitter enemy a stones-throw away from their Province of Japan.

Most of the hierarchy of the Roman government knew they were near doom. They called this hierarchy a democracy and each province had two elected Consuls. They held most of the power within their specific province, but the two consuls of Rome had fifty-one percent of the power of the Roman Republic. A province could not make a law or a change in policy without the yea vote of both Roman Consuls.

Twenty-four percent of the rule went to the Consuls of the other Roman provinces and the rest was in the hands of the Roman Senate. The Senate was an unelected branch of the government that was appointed by the Consuls and a group of judges. They were the most corrupt group in the Roman Government, with wealthy members using their affluence to bribe judges and Consuls to earn their appointments. Most Senators did not use their power to benefit the people of Rome. Rather, they used it to benefit their cronies and criminal associates, making these corrupt Senators some of the richest citizens of Rome. The constant corruption was like throwing dozens of stones at the crumbling economy of the Roman Republic.

Gratis Simony was one of the elected Consuls of Rome. He was an old military man who during his generalship, had scored many great Roman victories over the Chinese and many others. A proud member of the more liberal Julian Party, he did try to avoid corruption every day he served on his three-year term. When a session with the other Consuls was convened, or a joint session with both the Consuls and the Senate, the elder states-man wore a grey wig to cover his balding hair and a pitch-white toga to help cover his ever-expanding belly. The people of Rome loved his dagger the most. He wore it outside of his toga in a holder around his waist. The dagger's sharp blade had his family's crest done up with golden sculptures of swords and eagles made of sapphires and diamonds. The twisted blade had a fake appearance of solid gold. The gold leaf simply hid the stronger-than-steel, titanium blade.

His office near the top of the one hundred and fifty story Headquarters of the Roman Government was large and magnificent. Gratis sat behind his desk in his common business suit of jet black with tight black calf -high boots and a long red tie holding his white shirt closed.

A young girl intern brought him a piece of paper. He looked at it for a few minutes, as if to study every word, examining them with all his wisdom. He said to her, *"Have them check it again."*

She said back, *"Yes sir. That will be four times now."*

*"Have them check it again."*
*"Yes sir. Our forces have a victory against the Chinese in the province of Korea."*
*"I have heard, that is very good news. Have them check this again."*

———◆———

Flavia asked Sherrie, *"Okay Sherrie, what is a stuffing, and why should we not eat?"*

*"Do you not see? The slave owners want to stuff us with food. Not to get us fat, but to get us strong. They want us to survive their hideous torture for as long as possible. That is how they get their thrills."*

Henry said, *"I do not believe that here in this Modern Rome they would torture people for fun."*

*"Yes Henrici, they do."* Sherrie got more serious. *"They make wagers on these sick games. They bet on which slave will die first; they bet on which slave will scream the most. I have heard they even give an award for the slave that begs for mercy the best. Then they kill the winner, very slowly."*

*"I cannot believe that these slave owners could do that to another human being,"* Henry said.

Flavia said, *"I have heard about some hideous tortures used in my Ancient Rome. There is one where they kill a donkey and cut out its guts. Then they stuff the victim inside the dead animal and sew him in tight, leaving only his head exposed. They put the victim out in the sun and slowly maggots and ants will eat away at the animal's and eventually the victim's flesh. It's a slow painful death that might take days."*

Sherrie said with sarcasm, *"Thanks, Flavia. Now I have to worry about being sewed up inside a dead donkey."*

*"That was a long time ago Sherrie. I think we should eat and keep up our strength. We cannot win this battle if we are weak in mind and body,"* Flavia said.

*"I agree with Flavia,"* Henry said. *"I am going to use that modern kitchen to cook us all some of my very tasty hot-plate specialties."*

———◆———

He entered the Simony office without a warning or a knock. The young man had won the nickname of Mark A. because his brown curly hair and muscular build resembled the Ancient bust of the great Roman General Mark Antony. He had just won his first election to the Consul of Rome in a landslide and the young Sivus Tulius was a politician on fire. His party was the conservative Pompus Party and he campaigned on the slogan "Bringing Rome back to the Greatness of its Historic Past." He was wearing the same black business suit as Gratis. He took off his dark glasses and said, *"My esteemed Co-Consul, I have heard that the victory over the Chinese in Korea is false. Just some more of your fake news."*

Gratis Simony did not say anything. He just handed him the paper he had been studying.

The young Sivus read the note. As the letter slowly fell to the floor, he mumbled, *"Fake news. It has to be more fake news."*

# XXI

# *Pugio Conflictu*
# (The Dagger Conflict)

T HE DAGGER WAS A SYMBOL TO THE ELITE ROMAN LAWMAKERS. Although not required by law, the tradition to wear daggers in plain sight grew after the failed assassination attempt of Julius Caesar. Past Senators, Consuls, and Emperors alike followed the custom. It would be an insult to conceal them as the dead Senator traitors did over two thousand years ago. What had been a show of respect and gratitude to Caesar had turned into gross symbols to show political status, and family pride. To some, it also symbolized a belief that the great Caesar was divine.

Since the failed assassination attempt, and in the history of two Roman Empires and three Roman Republics, there were many *Confligit Pugione* (Dagger Conflicts). Only legal in joint sessions of both the Consuls and the Senate, they were permitted when a dispute of a law, policy, or decision was so far out of reach between political factions, that the only way to resolve it was the Roman way. This was to pull their daggers and fight until a resolution was reached. Many legislators died in these conflicts, and the dead were buried with the highest Roman honors and their killers would never be revealed. This was the Roman way to resolve an impossible debate. The public would never be told the details of the fight, but any half intelligent Roman would figure out who won by who returned from the chamber and by the decision that was reached.

---

Flavia had never seen a television before. After a brief explanation of the technology from Henry, Flavia began to enjoy the continuing dramas called *Operas de Saponem* that were shown throughout the day. She also enjoyed the sporting events and the music that was always showing on the 110-inch screen. But most of all, she was riveted by the news reports. Flavia was fascinated that everything the was happening in the world could be seen live right before her eyes. What she could not know was how much was kept from the people by the Roman Republic's very stringent government censorship.

It was dinner time, and Henry brought Flavia another hot-plate specialty. It was a fried tortilla folded and filled with melty white cheese, shredded beef, lettuce, and some diced jalapeno peppers.

He told her, *"Please Flavia, try again to get Sherrie to eat. We have been here two days now, and she has not eaten anything."*

*"I will try again, Henrici. All she wants to do is stare at the ceiling."*

Flavia entered Sherrie's room with a full plate of food. The closet in each room had a large wardrobe of clothes for each prisoner that fit them near perfectly. Today, Sherrie laid on her bed dressed in fairly tight dark blue denim jeans with a plain white T-shirt and no shoes. She continued her practice of laying on her back and blankly staring at the ceiling.

Flavia said, *"I wish you would please eat something. It has been two days now and you have not eaten. Henrici made this dish he called Mexican food. He said it is a quesadilla, and it is really good. At first it was a little too spicy for me, but now I love it so much."*

*"Oh yes, Mexico is in the province of North America. They are a class of half-Hispanian and half of the American Aztec tribe. I have never tried their food. I do hear it is spicy."*

*"Good then have some."*

*"Why Flavia? We are just going to die. Maybe I will starve before those wicked slave owners can kill me."*

Flavia sat on her bed. *"I have only known you for a few days Sherrie, but you already feel like a sister to me. I never had a sister, and I really need you right now. Think how I feel in this strange Roman world, a Rome so magnificent and so equally evil. Please stay alive with me. Do not give up."*

Sherrie took the plate and picked up the quesadilla. She took a small bite, "Oh my gosh, it is spicy but so good."

There was a loud knock on the front door. Flavia got up to see who it was.

——◆——

The chamber of the Roman Republic was easily large enough to comfortably seat the three-hundred and sixty-six Consuls and the two-hundred Senators of the Roman Government. There were six arched rows of high-backed marble chairs, each one surrounded by live vines of living green ivy. Each chair had a thick marble pillar in front of it, and the pillars were cut to the exact height as the lawmaker requested. Imbedded in the pillar was a computer. There the legislator could see the proceeding, make comments, and most importantly, vote. In the front row there were only four seats, one each for the two Consuls of Rome and the other two for the Speakers of the Senate. No outsider ever saw this spectacle of a hall. The room was reserved for the eyes of the elite Roman lawmakers only.

Due to public pressure, and only six years prior, the wealthy Roman cronies let women into the Senate. Now six years later there were already seventy-five women out of two hundred Senators. There were many more elected women Consuls. The women now occupied one-hundred and two out of the over three-hundred posts.

The joint session that convened today brought with it the foul stench of dissent and debauchery. There were many issues to discuss. Every member always wished for fair compromise and a logical conclusion to their differences. There were many debates scheduled on this particular day, but the goal of resolution was not very likely.

Then there was the war. The Chinese kept pushing forward against the Romans in the war in the province of Korea. Many Roman legions fought bravely, but the Chinese seemed to have endless troops. When a Chinese army was defeated, a new one almost immediately appeared to continue fighting against the increasingly weary Romans.

Most of the conservative Pompus Party and many of the liberal Julian-Party politicians felt that the only path to victory was to use nuclear weapons on the Chinese. An agreement had been signed during the early years of the long running Roman Chinese war. Both sides knew that nuclear weapons could destroy the world but now, many of the lawmakers felt this was the crumbling Roman Republic's only chance at victory.

When in the chambers, the lawmakers were required to wear long white togas with minimal flash or flare. The only decorated item allowed was each Politician's precious dagger.

This Chinese war was the first debate on the day's agenda. It was going to be a long day and night for these Roman men and women.

---◆---

When Flavia opened the door, Laura and two of the armed guards entered the apartment. Laura was in tears as she said to Flavia, *"You have to come with us. You have to wear this blindfold."*

*"Why does Flavia have to go?"* Henry asked.

Laura cried even louder, *"I cannot tell you! I cannot tell you."*

When Sherrie heard this, she ran towards them screaming, *"No! you cannot take Flavia. Take me! I am the escaped slave."*

She ran hard towards them until a guard grabbed her and pulled her away. Sherrie cried again loudly, *"Please take me! I deserve to die."*

Flavia walked to Sherrie; she took her hand. *"I will be fine Sherrie. I will see you, my sister, in the afterlife."*

*"Be strong, Flavia. Always keep your dignity,"* Sherrie told her.

When the door closed, Sherrie ran back to her room and threw herself on the bed. Henry sat down on the couch, wiping his one crying eye.

---◆---

Order was lost. The joint session was getting more vicious with every passing second. Senators and Consuls were yelling at each other's faces just inches apart. Some were using their chests to shove against their rivals as they yelled obscenities at close range. The boisterous mess got louder and rowdier with every scream, and with every scream, more men and some women joined the fracas.

The two Consuls of Rome were supposed to be in charge. The older Julian Party member Gratis Simony was banging his gavel in a vain attempt to restore order. His much younger counterpart Sivus Tulius was taking a different approach. He was shouting every swear word he knew at all the Julians he could see, including Gratis.

Soon, two young rival Senators became more violent, and their argument made its way to the floor in front of the assembly. As the pushing got harder and more intense, the Julian Senator was pushed so hard he slipped and went down, his head thumping hard on the marble floor. His Pompeian enemy saw the best opportunity for victory. He pulled his dagger and jumped into the air to throw his body towards his grounded nemesis. With little time to think, the lawmaker on the ground drew his dagger and held

224

it tightly against his stomach with the point waiting for the arrival of the diving man. When the young man landed on his foe, a loud scream echoed through the large hall. The arguing halted suddenly as a dead silence filled the chambers. All they could hear was a gagging death as the sound of squirting blood covered the young Senators.

The first *Confligit Pugione* in over fifty years had begun, a fight to the death by many of these proud Roman lawmakers.

When the agonizing death was the only possible outcome of the scene on the floor, the young Pompeian Consul of Rome, Sivus Tulius broke the silence. He yelled loudly so his voice filled the hall with rage, *"What foul evil has this man produced? Such deceit must be stopped. This death we witness today before us is the result of my rivals trying to create and preserve fake news. The death before us is proof that the evil disgusting Julians prefer fake news above life itself. I Sivus Tulius, the only true Consul of Rome, will fight this fake news."* He pulled his dagger and held it high above his head. *"I will fight this fake news to the death!"*

The young man turned and pointed his knife at his much older Co-Consul. He swung it wildly at Gratis Simony almost swiping his chest and ripping a diagonal tear across the front of his toga. Simony dropped his gavel on the floor and replaced it with his own gem-filled dagger.

———◆———

*"Breeso, I thought I told you to pack up all these computers?"* Makala Melius ordered.

She was trying to salvage every denarius she could get out of her debunked business. She could get decent money for the computers then lease out the secluded lair to the highest bidder.

Breeso said back, *"I don't know if you noticed boss, but I do not have any legs. Get Valcamus to do it."*

*"Yes, where is that lazy bum? I told him to meet us here."*

*"Before you shut us down boss, the world's greatest hacker has done it again. I went from the system of Bondslave, then got into the system of DNA identification. It was child's play. Take a look at this."*

Makala read the screen. Her eyes got bigger and she read the screen again. Then she pushed Breeso so hard she almost knocked him out of his wheelchair. *"Son of a canus femina! I told you there was something going on here. Can you put that on social media, Breeso?"*

Suddenly, Valcamus entered the room and said, *"Sorry I'm late boss but…."*

*"I know, two ladies kept you up late,"* Makala said back.

Valcamus explained, *"Actually, it was three this time."*

*"Come over here and look at this, Valcamus. I love it when I am so right,"* Makala said.

The handsome young Greek came to the computer screen. He read its contents several times then he said to them, *"That cannot be true. That is just some more of that Julian fake news."*

Makala scolded, *"Shut up, Valcamus. Did you get this on social media Breeso?"*

Breeso answered, *"Yes Boss, All I have to do is hit the enter key and within hours, everyone will know about this."*

Makala reached down and hit the enter button.

———◆———

Gratis Simony's rather large belly was getting the best of him. His wind was long gone along with almost any chance of beating his much younger rival in this knife fight. Each stab that Tulius threw at him was getting closer and closer to his flesh. Around him he could hear men fighting in mortal combat. Senators and Consuls, yelling and struggling in hand-to-hand knife fights that sent men screaming to their deaths.

The younger man Tulius was in his prime and was obviously in superior physical condition. His fourth swipe at his almost defenseless foe caught blood. There was now a bleeding contusion across Simony's chest.

Sivus licked the blood off of his dagger and laughed, *"You are through old man. You and all of your fake news will die today."*

Gratis was gasping for breath and struggling to stand straight. He saw his rival drop his guard for a second. This was his last and final chance. He used his age-old experience as a lineman on the Roman Army's "Kill the Guy with the Ball" national team. He quickly threw all his weight with his right shoulder against his young opponent. It was the perfect tackle. Sivus Tulius fell on his back with all the weight of the old man on top of him, the powerful blow sending his dagger skirting across the marble floor.

Keeping his weight on him, Gratis Simony held his dagger high above the tackled man's chest. Both men fought for the knife with Sivus trying to pull it away as Gratis used all his will to press the dagger closer.

He yelled slowly and loudly as his battle was almost won, *"This! Is! Not! Fake! News!"* He plunged the knife into Tulius' chest, slowly twisting his family's blade deeper and deeper until it reached his heart. Gratis made sure that all that was left of the man's heart was a sloppy mess of guts and blood.

As Gratis got off his vanquished rival and stood up, he could hear men dropping their daggers to the floor. The screaming and fighting quickly turned into near silence. The Romans started to salute the victor with hard pounds on their chests and soft chants and cheers of approval.

Gratis said to his surviving fellow Roman citizens, *"As sole Consul of Rome, I hereby declare that this Confligit Pugione of 2773 AUC is now over. We will bury our esteemed comrades with all the gratitude, honor, and dignity that Rome can contrive. These brave Romans gave their lives for her. They gave their lives so Rome could prosper once again."*

At that moment, the geneticist, Laura Paige, entered the hall from the front of the assembly. Still wearing her white lab coat, she stopped in her tracks and witnessed the bloody carnage in front of her. She counted at least thirty-two dead lawmakers and more than fifty of them wounded. Guards started coming in the hall with stretchers to remove the bodies as a team of medics tried to patch the stab wounds on the survivors. She continued towards Gratis. With a medic trying to dress and patch his bloody chest she whispered into his ear, *"Sir Consul, there has been a breach in the DNA security system. Soon the whole world will know."*

*"How much time do we have?"* He asked her.

*"Three hours at the most."*

Gratis Simony again stood up to speak to his assembly, *"Mend yourselves quickly my friends. As the Confligit Pugione has dictated, the proceedings must go on. For the sake of the lives of our departed comrades we must conclude this. We have only three hours."*

———◆———

The Lady entered from the back of the hall. All she could see was a path of light in front of her as darkness shielded the room around her. To her left was a beautiful blond woman, her light makeup was skillfully applied to bring out the shade of her long pink and gold gown. Her mouth was silent as she escorted the lady down the path of light. To her right was an equally beautiful dark-skinned young man. He wore a black toga lined with lace of gold. He too remained silent as the two young Romans escorted the Lady, slowing waking down the path of light. Both escorts wore a wreath of fresh green leaves circling their young heads.

The Lady herself was dressed in an elaborate gown of shimmering silk. The white color of the gown was laced with thin strips of purple. She had a purple and golden sash around her left shoulder while her right shoulder was bare. A slash in the gown left her right leg bare to show her silver sandals with laces of gold crisscrossing her leg up to just below her knee. Her eyes were lined with purple makeup and glitter that matched the amethyst necklaces, rings, and bracelets she wore. She noticed boxes of metal that seemed to be following them. These boxes had what looked like one eye that seemed to be staring at her.

When they reached a mark on the floor the escorts stopped her. The light grew around the perimeter of the room. The escorted girl saw rows of marble chairs lined with green ivy, and they were all filled with tired-looking men and women staring at her.

The Lady was defiant. She said loudly to them all, *"Why do you dress me as such if you are only to kill me. Kill me quickly or slowly for I am not afraid. My father rode into battle with the great Caesar himself. I know how to kill, and I know how to die. I will die like a great and brave Roman."*

There were gasps from the crowd followed by a surprising soft applause. The Lady suddenly realized that this was not what she expected.

An older heavy-set man sitting in the front row stood up and clapped his hands once. An upbeat Latin hymn quietly filled the hall with the soothing sound of perfect human voices. Four female dancers appeared from the left, dancing a ballet high on their toes to the enchanting hymn, each one carrying a bouquet of roses of pink, yellow and, orange, dropping the flowers in front of the lady.

Her voice seemed to be amplified as she asked, *"What is happening?"*

She looked behind her to her left. There was a line of over a hundred young women behind her, each one dressed in gowns of alternating colors of pink, yellow, and orange. To her right she saw a line of over a hundred young men. The togas they wore alternated, one in black and then one in white. Everyone wore wreaths of green on their heads and moved slowly forward to the rhythmic sound of the choir.

The Lady asked again, *"What is going on?"*

Soon, the music got louder as the lines of women and men formed a heart shape with the Lady and her escorts at the inner point of the heart. In the back outward point of the heart, on the women's side, the girl on the end held a small black box. She passed the box to the next girl in rhythm to the music, then the next girl passed it on with each girl holding a still different pose as the box left her.

As the box made its way around the left circle of the heart, the Lady asked again, *"What is happening? What is going on?"*

The music reached a loud crescendo as the box made it to her young woman escort. The girl took it and knelt on one knee, holding the box high above her head.

The sole Consul of Rome, the wounded Gratis Simony, got up from his front row seat. He stumbled a little but managed to slowly walk towards the Lady in white and purple. When he reached the three, the loud music stopped, and the room went dark. A spotlight turned the darkness around the Lady and the sole Consul of Rome into a brightness that everyone could see.

Gratis Simony opened the black box. Inside was a wreath of solid gold and silver leaves, each leaf surrounded by tiny gems of purple amethyst.

He took the crown out of the box and gently placed it on the Lady's head. Then he got on one knee. He took her left hand in his and placed his right fist pounding his heart.

He said loud enough for everyone in the hall to hear. He said it loud enough for everyone in the Roman world to hear.

Flavia didn't quite know what to do, so she stood as proud as she could.

What happened next would have shocked anyone. But Flavia had been through too much and had learned to be prepared for anything. Gratis Simony looked the young woman in the eyes and proudly said, *"HAIL CAESAR!"*

The assembly hall lit up as the loud music returned. The Senators and Consuls stood up cheering as cries of Hail Caesar echoed through the room.

Flavia did not back off. She knew that she could not exhibit any weakness as she had suddenly realized what was happening. Without flinching, even the smallest bit, she stepped forward and said with all the precision and confidence she had, *"I guess I always knew. Even as a little girl I always knew. Now I know it for sure. My father did not ride into battle with Caesar. My father is Gaius Julius Caesar!"*

All the young women and men that formed the heart now crowded around Flavia, each one holding out their hands with the hope of touching their new royalty. The young people echoed the cries of "Empress!" and "Caesar!"

filling the hall with even more vigor and excitement, as this stunning scene was broadcast live throughout the entire Roman world.

Most of the world welcomed the first Empress of the New Roman Empire. Some felt she was a savior of sorts, some hated and scorned her, and some felt she was a gift from the divine Julius Caesar.

Little did they know that she was really a gift from an eye-patched little time -traveling nerd named Henry Garfield.

# XXII

# The Promise

A rhyme as told by Caesar's men:
    'Watch well your wives, ye cits, we bring a blade,
    A bald-pate master of the wenching trade.
    Thy gold was spent on many a Gallic whore;
    Exhausted now, thou com'st to borrow more.'
Modern translation:
    "Lock up your wives, our commander is bad news.
    He may be bald, but he fucks anything that moves."

Julius Caesar was quite a womanizer and he didn't seem to be too particular about who he slept with. He would sleep with Queens and royalty, common citizens, prostitutes, and even slaves. His sexual appetite was well known throughout the Ancient Roman world.

Back in 66 BC, while serving his term as Quaestor in Farther, Hispania, he met such a slave. Her name was Marilla. A slave by birth from the far north of Hispania, she had a smooth amber skin with a soft smile that Caesar noticed the first time he saw her. She tended to his household, and with every move she made, there was a rhythmic, dance-like grace as she accomplished her chores with near perfection. She never looked at him. She never spoke to him in public. She just went through her day with her soft smile always glowing.

Nine months later when Caesar saw the tiny new life, he openly cried. The baby's fare skin and big blue eyes brought love into Caesar's heart and from that first look, he called her Flavia.

One year prior to Flavia's birth, Caesar had married his first wife, Pompeia. It was a politically arranged marriage to help keep political peace between Caesar and some of his rivals. Caesar suddenly didn't care about this marriage. He wanted a divorce so he could be with Marilla and his daughter.

His advisors and friends were appalled by this idea. They quickly convinced him that a scandal as big has a slave marriage could ruin the up-and-coming politician and create many new enemies along with bringing back old ones.

A compromise was reached. The plan was to call on Caesar's friend and companion of many military campaigns to aid him. The dedicated General Valens Antonius never had time for a wife, and they decreed that he would wed Marilla and raise Caesar's daughter. Caesar would set him up with profitable businesses and give him a beautiful villa on the outskirts of Rome near the Mediterranean Sea. There Flavia could grow up away from the pompous city of Rome, away from the corruption and filth that filled the Roman Republic. She would be happy in a shielded world with little or no conflicts or stress.

Valens never spent much time with his foster daughter. He never understood how she felt so empty and unfulfilled. He never knew she was totally bored until she met a naked man child named Henrici.

—◆—

The art of DNA (deoxyribonucleic acid) is an exact science. No two people can ever have the same DNA. When it is found, this science can easily detect who did what in almost every crimes scene.

When the ailing elder Julius Caesar met Queen Cleopatra VII for the last time, he would not grant her request to make their son, Caesarian his successor and true Emperor of Rome. He did grant Cleopatra's second request, not to have his dead body cremated by a huge bonfire.

The three darkly clad women embalmers that Cleopatra gave to Caesar as a parting gift, did a magnificent job at mummifying his body. He laid in grace for over two thousand years and when the science was discovered and perfected, the Romans had a good solid sample of the DNA of the great one.

When the Romans recently captured the escaped slave and her associates, the impossible happened. The DNA data was checked and rechecked. The method was checked and rechecked, and not just by the top geneticist and biologist. They used experts from every field. Physicists, astronomers, chemists, it didn't matter who studied the data, the result was always the same.

The great *Confligit Pugione* of 2773 had little to do with the war against China, and it had little to do with the crumbling Roman economy. Thirty-two Roman lawmakers died for a different reason, and they did not die in vain, they died to save the people of Rome. Scientific fact is not fake news. Flavia Antonius was the daughter of Julius Caesar and most Roman's believed that Flavia Antonius was also their savior.

———◆———

Flavia's new desk was almost twenty feet long. The desk was really a long rectangular grey and white slab and on it was stacks of papers, books, phones, and computers. It might have looked like a mess to most, but Flavia knew what exactly everything was and where.

She had kept the geneticist Laura Paige on as her top assistant. Laura would follow her around her office doing whatever she was asked.

Today was the first day of the second month of her Emperorship. Her office was full of aides and advisors as Flavia moved from paper to phone, from computer to pen, from phone to computer. The Empress had no problem keeping her energy level high throughout her fourteen-hour days. Her cabinet and staff were more and more amazed every day as "Teach Me," became a catch phrase of the new Empress whenever she did not understand a policy, technology or conflict. Her staff would do that and once she understood, they were again amazed at her wise decisions.

Laura told her, *"Madam, your eleven o'clock is here, that former slave girl."*

*"Okay Laura, I want everybody out of here, and no microphones and no cameras."*

*"I will make sure that happens, Madam."*

Her staff left through one door as Sherrie Melbourne entered through another. She looked fashionable in her tight yellow denim pants with a navy-blue long-sleeved button-down blouse. Her blond hair was done up in a bun, and she had on some small round glasses to aid her sight. She was quite a contrast to Flavia's purple and gold business suit.

Flavia ran towards her and gave her a hug, *"Hello sister. How have you been? They better be taking good care of you."*

*"They have."*

Flavia had her sit down, then she made her way behind her long desk and sat down in front of her.

Flavia asked, *"Now, what can I do for you 45712MS?"*

*"First of all, I thought I was free, and second, you called me here."*

Flavia laughed, *"I am just kidding you. With this job sometimes you need to laugh."*

Sherrie asked, *"I'm not sure what I am supposed to call you."*

*"Come on girl, you know my name is Flavia."*

*"Okay, Flavia. They let us watch the whole thing, the crowning, on that big television in the apartment. You looked so beautiful and so strong."*

*"Thank you. They make me wear purple all the time. It is some kind of sign of royalty. I am so tired of purple."*

*"So why did you look so surprised at first? Did they not tell you what was going on?"*

*"They did not."* Flavia got a little angry. *"And I tore that Gratis Simony a new asshole at first. He explained that there was no time and that he was too wounded, but most of all he said he knew exactly how I would react. Then he said I performed perfectly."*

*"I think he is right about that Flavia. It was the most beautiful thing I had ever seen."*

Flavia asked, *"So how is he, Sherrie? How is our little man child?"*

Sherrie answered, *"Henrici is fine. He was getting a little antsy stuck in the apartment for so long so now he is taking apart some of the kitchen appliances. I have no idea what he is doing, but he seems happy."*

<hr />

Henry Garfield had indeed made himself busy in the kitchen of the luxury apartment he shared with Sherry. He had taken apart the blender, the toaster, and the microwave oven. All the inner parts of the appliances were on the kitchen table, now all connected with red wires to the recently removed motor of the large refrigerator. He had this sparking contraption connected to a small laptop computer with a USB port.

Henry typed frantically into the computer and as he did, his invention threw even more yellow sparks. He said to himself in English, "The earth's electromagnetic field seems to be much stronger in this timeline."

A fizzing sound filled the kitchen. The outer portion of the gut-free toaster started glowing with a soft yellow flare that surrounded it. Soon, the glowing changed from a bright yellow hot to an even brighter blue hot then suddenly, the toaster vanished as a pulse of warm air blew through the room.

Henry stood up and said in his nerdy English, "This is a great scientific breakthrough of the upmost importance. My top-secret experiment was 100 percent successful." He adjusted his glasses and said in Latin, *"Now I am 100 percent positive that I can transfer my clothes through time."*

———◆———

Sherry then asked, *"What about you Flavia, don't they know that you are only twenty-one years old?"*

*"I am not twenty-one. I was born in 688 after the founding of the city. It is now 2773. That makes me 2,085 years old. Plenty old enough to run this Roman scrap heap."*

Sherrie inquired, *"Don't they ever ask you how you got here?"*

*"They have. I just say, 'one minute I was in Ancient Rome, the next I was here.' That seems to satisfy them, and it is true. Did you hear Sherrie? I am going to China in two weeks. We are going to start negotiations to end this long and worthless war."*

*"China! How fun that sounds. Can I go?"*

*"No Sherrie. I need you here. Word has leaked about my other plan to abolish slavery in just six months. And just like that, I suddenly have thousands of enemies. Thousands of Romans want to kill me."*

Sherrie stood up. *"That is wonderful Flavia. I mean about the abolishing slavery, not the killing you part. What can I do to help? I want to help you with this."*

*"I am going to appoint you to a new position. The title is the Ambassador to the Bonded. You are perfect for this job, not just because you are a former slave. You speak well, you are so smart, and you present yourself with extreme confidence."*

*"Where do I sign up? I would do anything to get back at those scummy slave owners."*

Flavia said, *"That reminds me, I have someone here I think you would like to see."*

Flavia hit a red button on one of her phones, she said, *"Bring him in."*

Two armed guards entered Flavia's office. In-between them was a middle-aged man with a sloppy grey beard and hair. Flavia had them uncuff him and they sat him down next to Sherrie. Flavia asked the guards to leave.

*"Doctor Pillar I presume?"* Flavia said.

Sherrie looked at him with scorn in her eyes, *"Flavia, can you get this disgusting thing away from me. He smells bad, even worse than a stinking slave owner, and he is one of those."*

Pillar protested, *"You cannot do this to me. You arrest me for no reason. I am a respected member of the Roman community. I want my lawyer."*

Flavia stood up and said with anger, *"Haven't you heard? I am the Empress of Rome and I can do pretty much whatever I want. Now, you claim that Ms. Melbourne spit in your face and escaped from your bondage."*

*"Yes, I gave her a very minimal task to perform. She refused my orders and spit in my face. Then she escaped the next morning,"* Pillar explained.

Now Sherrie stood up. *"That is a lie! You wanted me to have sex with you and two of your friends. You threated to demote my status if I refused. That is why I escaped."*

Pillar said smugly, *"When this gets to trial, we will see who the judge believes, me or a low- life slave?"*

Flavia told him, *"You do not understand, Pillar. This is a trial, and I am the judge. I think I believe Ms. Melbourne."*

*"You cannot do this. If you do, you will make many enemies."*

Flavia said, *"Pillar, I already have thousands of those. A few more will not matter. This is a violation of article one of The Bill of Rights for the Bonded. I think a fair sentence would be life as a stage-one slave. What do you think Ms. Melbourne?"*

*"That is too good for him. Have them kill a donkey, then tear out its guts. Then they can stuff Pillar inside and sew it up with only his head showing. He can die in the sun as maggots and ants slowly eat him alive,"* Sherrie said.

*"Do you know how to sew, Sherrie?"* Flavia asked. *"You can do the honors and sew him in."*

*"I do not know how to sew. But for this, I will learn."*

Pillar got scared. *"No! do not do that. I will do anything. Anything to make this right."*

*"There is one thing you might do,"* Flavia said. *"Release all your slaves. If they want to work, you pay them a fair wage."*

*"Yes, and you have to give them two days off a week, and two weeks of paid vacation a year,"* Sherrie said.

Pillar cried, *"No! I cannot do that. I will go broke. I will be ruined."*

Flavia said to Sherrie, *"I am going to call the guards, have them kill a donkey, strip out its guts and bring it in here."*

"*Okay, Okay. I will do it. I will go broke and be a homeless soon, but I will do it,*" Pillar said with his hands over his crying eyes.

"*It will not be bad at all,*" Sherrie said. "*Make a sign and put it out in front of every one of your coffee houses. It should say 'All our drinks and food are made with 100 percent slave-free labor.' People will love that and be willing to pay more.*"

Flavia said, "*Yes, do that also. Now, get out of here.*"

As he timidly left, Sherrie said to Flavia, "*Madam Caesar, can you have someone spray some air freshener in here. Your office still stinks like a rotten slave owner.*"

"*I know this is going to be hard for you, but if you take this job you are going to have to be more diplomatic than that.*"

"*You want me to be nice to filth-laden slave owners?*"

"*Yes Sherrie. One of the first things I learned on this job is that to get anything done, you have to have a civil communication with your rivals. Come to my side of the desk, Sherrie.*"

As Sherrie joined her, Flavia hit a button on the wall. A gold and silver curtain slowly started to open both left and right from the middle, revealing a window that was the entire back wall of her office. From her penthouse office and residence, one hundred and fifty stories high atop the Roman government building, The Headquarters, the two girls stood side by side and gazed at the magnificent view below. The view of downtown Rome made Sherrie gasp. Hundreds of skyscrapers were growing from the ground below them and the city seemed to never end. Each building below shouted at them in colors of blue, red and yellow shiny glass, some pointing at them at angles more reclined than the Leaning Tower of Pisa. The sun glistened off the glass-colored light of the structures, filling their eyes with sparkling wonder.

Sherrie said with watered eyes, "*This is all your responsibility. Millions and millions of people are depending on you. How do you handle such a burden?*"

"*Sometimes it is not easy Sherrie, but I know I can do it. It is in my genes; it is in my DNA. I also know you can be diplomatic with slave owners.*"

"*Okay Flavia, I will try. I am not sure I can do it, but I will try.*"

"*Great, now I need you to start your new job soon. When I get back from China, you can begin. You will lead a team to make this Emancipation Proclamation that I wrote really work. You will have to travel around the Roman world and speak to the people. Show them how this will work for the benefit of all of Rome. You will need many armed guards twenty-four hours a day. It is a very dangerous job; thousands will want to kill you. Are you still in?"*

Sherrie quickly responded, *"Of course, Flavia. Anything to help. After being chased by gang members and being caught by ruthless bounty hunters, I can handle it."*

*"That reminds me, my office has been contacted by one of those bounty hunters, that girl that caught us, Makala Melius. It seems she has a lot of guilt about the life she has led. She wants to help."*

*"Flavia, you want me to use that scummy girl to help us slaves, after what she has done for years, capturing us and abusing us?"*

*"That is what I am talking about. This will be a good test for you. All I ask is that you talk to her. She seems to be devoted to this cause. You can do what you want after that."*

*"I will try. I will talk to this Makala, and Flavia; I promise I won't try to kill her."*

Phones across Flavia's desk started going off with loud rings and pings. Flavia quickly silenced them all. *"That is my staff. They are like a bunch of babies. If I am out of touch with them for ten minutes, they start going crazy."*

*"I should go now,"* Sherrie said.

*"No, let them wait. I have one more thing. I want to get you and Henrici out of that apartment. We found a villa just south of Rome on the coast of the Mediterranean. If I remember right, it is not far from the villa I grew up in two thousand or so years ago. Spend a few days there and relax. There will be many armed guards to watch over you and a few servants to serve you."*

*"Sounds too nice. You know, you told me once that I promised Henrici something. It was in his world. You told me you would tell me later. Now is a good time. What did I tell him?"*

Flavia whispered in her ear.

Sherrie's eyes got big. She stood up and said with an embarrassed smile, *"Oh my gosh. I said that?"*

*"He mentioned it several times Sherrie. Go now and start thinking about your new job, but most of all relax. I really liked what you said earlier, sister."*

*"What did I say?"*

*"I really liked it,"* Flavia took both her hands. *"You called me Madam Caesar."*

The eye-patched Henry Garfield walked along the beach in his big blue shorts and his green button-down short -sleeved shirt. He had managed to find a pencil pack that fit his right lapel pocket and he filled it with pencils and pens. The soft soothing sea let white sudsy small waves cover his bare feet with water, then he saw a shiny rock and picked it up. He tried to throw it into the sea. Somehow the rock left his hand and flew backwards behind him towards the setting sun to the east.

"I cannot even throw a rock." He looked behind him. There was another stone in the sand sitting next to his mis-lunged rock. He picked it up and discovered it wasn't a rock. It was a misshapen piece of metal, about two inches in diameter. Polished shiny by the sea, it reminded Henry of something. He picked up the glossy nugget.

*"Henrici! Come here! Hurry up!"* Sherrie yelled at him.

She was laying on a lounge chair under a large orange and red canopy that was protecting her from the evening sun. The villa behind her was a full three -stories high with perfectly trimmed umbrella pine trees coming out of the lush green grass. The wooden structure had huge windows in the front for a breathtaking view of the Mediterranean Sea.

Sherrie wore a very short backless red dress. She had the front zipper down low, so it showed plenty of cleavage.

When Henry got close, she said to him, *"Lay down Henrici, I ordered us some drinks."*

Henry laid down on a lounge chair next to her. He said, *"We have been here over a day now, and you finally want to talk to me?"*

*"Yes, I have a lot on my mind, and I needed some time to work up some courage."*

Ignoring what Sherry said, Henry showed her the misshapen sphere. *"This reminds me of something I invented in my top-secret workshop in my world. This is tip top-secret so you cannot tell anyone."*

*"What are you talking about Henrici?"*

*"I invented an electromagnetic shocker so I could travel through time. It looks like this black sphere. Flavia gave you a job, but nothing for me."*

*"So, what do you want?"* Sherrie asked.

Henry explained, *"I have already made some major top-secret scientific breakthroughs in the apartment, and I thought that since Flavia is The Empress of Rome, she could loan me some money so I could build another workshop. Then I could make more shockers and go back in time and change everything back to the way it was before."*

"*Bad idea, Henrici. You said yourself that that would only make things worse. I don't know what I did in your world, but here I have a chance to help free millions of slaves. I am going to be saving countless lives, and besides Henrici, look around here. This place does not suck. I do not want anything to change.*"

A tall older butler dressed in a white suit broke up their conversation. He set down on the small table between them two double shot glasses filled with an amber liquid and two brown bottles of beer.

"*Anything else Madam?*" he asked Sherrie.

"*That will be all. We will have dinner at nine,*" Sherrie answered. "*Try this Henrici. It is from the province of Mexico. It is called tequila.*"

Sherrie took the glass and drank it down in two gulps. She slammed the shot glass down hard against the table. She took a beer and washed the alcohol down with three big swallows.

She said wide-eyed to Henry, "*Oh my gosh Henrici, that was so good. Now it is your turn.*"

"*I cannot drink tequila. It makes me do crazy and embarrassing things.*"

"*Do it Henrici, or else.*"

Henry took the glass and tried to down it like Sherrie did. He spit up the tequila with a string of loud coughs as the booze squirted all over him.

Sherrie laughed, "*You can try again. I will have the butler bring us some more.*"

"*Please no Sherrie, that is too strong for me,*" Henry said while still coughing.

"*Okay, I think you have had enough.*"

Sherrie sat up from the lounge chair and put on her flip flops. She stood up and took Henry's hand. She led him through the tall wooded double doors of the Villa, then though the parlor and up a white marble, spiral staircase. On the third floor she led him down a hall until they got to her room. She let him inside and shut and locked the door.

Her room had a large oval bed covered in red bedspreads with dozens of plush colored pillows around it. There was a large picture window showing off her view of the sea.

Sherrie looked him in the eye and got closer to him. "*Flavia told me I swore something to you, something I said in your world, if you completed your mission. What was your mission, Henrici?*"

Henry started to stutter. "*It, it, it, does not matter what you said in my world. Ev, Ev, everything is different now.*"

"*What was your mission, Henrici?*"

*"I, I, I was to stop the assassination of Caesar and build him an 1873 Winchester repeating rifle."*

Sherrie smiled and kicked off her flip flops sending them high into the air. Then she let the red dress slowly fall off of her to the floor. The white thong around her waist was then pulled down her long legs until it rested softly on the red dress.

Henry tried to talk. *"I, I, ah, ah, oh."*

The beautiful buck-naked girl stood in front of the much shorter Henry. She kissed him on the forehead and said, *"I guess it is time I kept my promise."*

# About the Author

**C. R. FABIS** has spent the last thirty-five years creating desserts for restaurant chains across the country. His creations have been enjoyed by millions of people. The dessert chef also has a keen passion for history and science fiction. He has combined those passions in his first novel *Rome Never Fell*. Mr. Fabis lives with his wife in beautiful Colorado. They have brought four wonderful children into our world.

Excerpt from Cal Fabis's upcoming novel

*My Name is Maggie Love*

If you want to be notified of the release date,
please email info@HugoHousePublishers.com.

## CHAPTER 6

# In Her Teens

MAGGIE ARRIVED AT THE GAS STATION A LITTLE EARLY. SHE DIDN'T worry that he would stand her up. He was a guy and she offered him sex and sure enough, at seven fifty-five a yellow brown Ford Pinto pulled into the station. Josh Wilson was driving. When he stopped, Maggie got in the passenger seat.

Maggie tried to keep her voice soft and sexy, "Hello Josh. I am so happy you came."

"Okay, it's Debbie, right? Where do you want to go?"

"I have a secret place where I take all my boyfriends. Get on Topanga Canyon and go south. It is in the hills about twelve miles away. This is such a cool car."

"Yeah, my old man got it for me brand new, when we took league. I caught a touchdown pass in the last minute that won the game."

"You're so good Josh," Maggie tried to sound sexier. "You don't even have to wear seat belts."

"Hell no, if I don't make the NFL, I'm going to join NASCAR because I'm a great driver. You know you are kind of pretty when you take off those glasses."

"Thanks Josh. Maybe we can do this every time your girlfriend goes away."

They got off the highway and headed towards Topanga State Park. Soon they were going up a dark winding road. They passed a few swanky houses, then the paved road turned into dirt.

"When are we going to get there?" Josh asked.

"It's just a little further. The road ends soon, and we will come to a dirt roundabout. That's where we park."

When they got to the roundabout Josh said, "There's a car here. I thought you said this was a secret place?"

"Oh, that car is always here. I think it's a wreck. Don't park to close to it there might be a homeless living in there."

When they parked, Maggie put her arms around Josh and gave him a long passionate kiss. She smacked her lips softly and said, "Take your pants down Josh. My mouth is watering for it."

Josh did exactly that, then Maggie said, "It will be much better if you're strapped in."

She reached across him and grabbed the lap belt. She buckled him in then did the same thing with the shoulder harness. Maggie quickly took the keys out of the ignition. She opened her door and walked over towards her waiting Volkswagen.

"Where are you going?" Josh asked.

"I'll be back in a sec."

She opened the door of her car then turned on her cassette player full blast. It was playing the song 'If You Really Love Me'. Maggie headed back to the Pinto, walking in rhythm to the music, and carrying a plastic two-gallon jug filled with a clear liquid. In the other hand she had a large plastic glass.

With the passenger door still open, she crouched down and said, "Do like this song Josh? I think I remember hearing it the other night. The night you raped me."

Josh tried to undo the seat belt. He struggled and said, "There's something wrong with these things. It won't open."

"You know Josh, you shouldn't leave your car unlocked at night. It makes it much easier if someone wants to tinker with it. I like to tinker."

With Stevie Wonder singing in the background Josh said, "When I get out of here, I'm going to kill you."

Maggie replied, "You got it all wrong Josh. I am going to kill you."

Maggie took the jug and filled the glass with liquid. "Look at this glass, Josh. It looks just like the one you gave me the other night. The night you raped me."

She threw the liquid at Josh's face.

He yelled in a panic, "Ow! That stings! What is this gasoline? Are you crazy?"

"Yes Josh. I get very crazy when a guy rapes me. You're a big boy. You need more glasses."

She threw two more glasses of gas at him. As he fought to try to get off the seat belts, Maggie reached into her back pocket and took out a box of stick matches.

She took one out of the box and showed it to Josh, "I'm going to make sure you never rape a girl again." She struck the match against the box and it lit with a small flare.

Josh was crying, "Debbie don't do this. I'm sorry. Debbie, please don't do this."

"Here's the thing, Josh. My name's not Debbie."

She flicked the match at Josh and as he ignited, she firmly said, "My name is Maggie Love!"

Josh started screaming and patting his body to try to put out the fire. Maggie went around to the front of the car and opened the hood. She poured the rest of the gas over the engine, making sure to get plenty near the fuel line. She put the jug and glass on the side of the engine and lit another match. She dropped it on the gas. The engine erupted in flame then she closed the hood until it almost locked.

Another thing Josh," Maggie said over his screaming. "These Pintos have a bad reputation of blowing up. Too bad yours is going to blow up also."

The screams got louder has the fire stated to burn deeper into Josh's skin. The panic got so loud that Maggie wanted to cover her ears. Then the squealing screams suddenly stopped.

Maggie walked briskly to her car, "One more thing Josh. With your pants down, the cops are going to think you were out here jerking off."

She got into her car and started to drive away. Through the rear-view mirror, she saw the violent fiery explosion. When the fire reached the fuel tank, it blew the trunk hood ten feet into the air.

———◆———

Maggie and Sally got back to the apartment after ten PM.

"Let's pack tomorrow and leave about nine in the morning. I'm going to call Cilvia and tell her what's going on."

Maggie dialed the phone. "Is Cilvia there?"

She listened for a while then dropped the phone receiver. The long-curled cord made it bounce back up a few times after it hit the floor. Maggie stood there wide eyed with a blank stare.

"Maggie, are you alright?" Sally asked.

Her voice was choked up, "Cilvia's dead."

"No, Maggie, it can't be." She hugged her daughter.

Maggie didn't hug back. "They found her in the bathroom at a park tonight. The cops say it was a drug overdose or a suicide. It wasn't, I know she would never do that."

"Think of all the wonderful things you two did together. Remember her Love."

Maggie finally hugged her Mom back. "She loved the sky mom. Cilvia loved the sky."

Maggie retreated to her room and closed the door. She laid down on her bed and looked at the ceiling then she felt something present.

"Not now Inspector, I just lost my best friend," she said.

Inspector Lawrence sat down at the bottom of her bed. "I'm sorry Maggie, but this is not about that. Do you repent for the killing of Josh Wilson?"

Maggie got up and sat next to the Inspector. "No, the fucking bastard raped me. I don't think this is about repenting at all. This is to show me what a failure I am. I supposedly have this amazing mind and I couldn't save Cilvia." Maggie's eyes were red and teary.

The Inspector took a puff off his cigarette. "You had nothing to do with her death. Do you repent for killing Josh?"

"No, I don't. I could have put off the Colorado trip for a few days and been here when she needed me and I can tell you one thing, those porno guys are going to get their's."

"Knowing you I'm positive that will happen. Please, Maggie repent."

"I think I remember telling you this before, "Cram it up your ass. What are going to do now? Throw me out of a flying airplane? Are you going to cut my head off?"

"There's no need for that anymore. He reached up and touched Maggie's forehead.

Maggie's mind exploded.

CPSIA information can be obtained
at www.ICGtesting.com
Printed in the USA
BVHW081331220720
584347BV00004B/274

9 781948 261364